ANNALS

OF

THE FRENCH STAGE.

VOL. I.

P. CORNEILLE.

ANNALS

OF

THE FRENCH STAGE

FROM ITS ORIGIN TO THE DEATH OF RACINE.

BY

FREDERICK HAWKINS.

IN TWO VOLUMES.

VOL. I.
789—1667.

GREENWOOD PRESS, PUBLISHERS
NEW YORK

Originally published in 1884
by Chapman and Hall

First Greenwood Reprinting 1969

Library of Congress Catalogue Card Number 68-57607

SBN 8371-2172-8

PRINTED IN UNITED STATES OF AMERICA

PREFACE.

FROM one point of view these volumes may be said to go over new ground. Notwithstanding the light recently thrown in France upon the development of her old literature, especially that of the Middle Ages, no English writer has thought fit to illustrate, at least upon anything like a comprehensive scale, the rise and progress of the theatre in Paris. In the present work an attempt is made to partly redeem that deficiency, and a want of all the leisure needed for the task has not prevented the author from carefully verifying his statements, from inquiring into opinions of questionable soundness, and from studying for himself the important plays which he has ventured to criticize. Being obliged to pass by a good deal without remark, and anxious to render the history as complete as possible, he has added a chronology of the stage for the period reviewed. It has been compiled from various sources, and, though of necessity imperfect, is the longest and most accurate hitherto produced. Pieces not of the usual kind are here distinguished by being described. It may be observed that these Annals, unlike most books relating to the theatre, give quite as much prominence to dramatists and dramatic literature as to players and their achievements.

THE FRENCH STAGE.

CHAPTER I.

789—1548.

THE French appear to have conceived a taste for spectacle at a very early period. In the eighth century, as the long night which came over Europe at the fall of the Roman Empire was yielding to the dawn of modern civilization, a band of Histrions, consisting of actors, dancers, and jugglers, gave performances in the streets of Paris for the diversion of the volatile populace. By this time, except in the monasteries, where the lamp of secular learning was kept alive for its own sake, tragedy and comedy had passed out of remembrance; but there is reason to believe that the tradition of the drama in its humbler and less inviting aspects still lingered among the laity. Probably in order to escape the pains and penalties imposed by the Church upon players of any kind, the

Histrions, wearing a sort of ecclesiastical dress, sang or recited dialogues relating to the acts of the saints (*urbanae cantilenae*). It may be thought that entertainments of such a nature were conducted with the utmost gravity throughout; in point of fact, as the materials of which the troupe was composed would suggest, they abounded in horse-play, dancing, magic tricks, and even unclean jest. Favoured by the clergy as a means of disseminating religious knowledge, they yet found a resolute opponent in Charles the Great, and a decree against their continuance was issued under his authority in 789. No further trace of the Histrions can be discovered, although they may have existed in the provinces long enough to make use of some *urbanae cantilenae* written by a canon of Rouen, Thiébaut de Vernon, at a much later time.

Evidently alive to the fact that the rude and unlettered people might be more easily taught through the eye than the ear, the clergy, who sought to dominate the human mind by limiting its range and satisfying its permitted aspirations, did something to fill the void thus created. They occasionally converted the churches into theatres. In the first place, the dramatic elements in the ritual were elaborated into action. Each of the great religious festivals came to include a figurative representation before the altar of what the service was designed to commemorate. Now the wise men from the East prostrated themselves around the cradle to which they had been guided by the miraculous star; now the Virgin was impersonated by a young girl bearing a child in her arms; now a priest burst from a mimic sepulchre to enforce the lesson of the Resurrection. Naturally enough, these *tableaux vivants*, which seem to have been conceived and executed in a reverent spirit, gave rise to a combination of action with dialogue. Dramas in Latin prose upon events recorded in Holy Writ were played by priests in the sanctuary, generally after the sermon. Inartistic in form, they were characterized by austere devoutness and simplicity of style, and the words of the original narrative were followed with scrupulous fidelity. How far the liturgical play answered its purpose we are not told, but that it proved of essential service to religion there can be no doubt. Next, strange as such inconsistency may be, the authors of these impressive pictures of early Christianity got up in the House of God itself a series of amusements in which all decency was set at defiance. Between the 26th December and the Jour des Rois, for example, an orgie to be known as the Fête des Fous was held in old Notre Dame and other cathedrals. Preceded by a priest bearing the mitre and the cross, the Bishop of Fools for the time being, usually a deacon or sub-deacon, repaired in procession from his house to the sacred edifice, seated himself in the episcopal chair amidst a merry peal of the bells overhead, and bestowed a mock benediction upon the crowd assembled around him. The aisles were then abandoned to the wildest revelry, if not actual licence. Bacchanalian songs, lascivious dances, coarse buffoonery, dice-playing at the altar,—these and other diversions were freely resorted to. Disguised as *baladins* or women, with their faces blackened or masked, many of the priests took an active part in the saturnalia, and, unless old chronicles have done them grievous injustice, gave themselves up to revolting debauchery. Finally, moving out of doors, a few roysterers, clerical and non-clerical, would mount a scaffold in the street, there to represent in expressive dumb show an indelicate contest between monks and nuns. "O Paris," exclaimed an Abbé de Chelles in after years, perhaps struck with remorse on looking back to his past, "que tu es séduisant et corrupteur! Que de pièges tes propres vices tendent à la jeunesse imprudente! Que de crimes tu fais commettre!"

Hardly less noteworthy than these strange alternations of reverence and obscenity on the part of the clergy is a rival institution of somewhat later origin. The minstrel, one of the most distinctive and picturesque figures of mediæval life, began to widen the sphere of his labours. In some respects, it will be seen, he

resembled the histrion-bateleur, in others the Gallic
bard of yore. Every summer, arraying himself in
parti-coloured costume, slinging a harp or a sort of
violin with three strings across his shoulders, and not
forgetting to attach a purse to his belt, the jongleur,
as he was called, ambled on a gaily-caparisoned mule
from town to town, from castle to castle. Introduced
and followed by feats of agility and legerdemain, his
song, which had but slight pretensions to literary merit,
and in which he accompanied himself with crude though
not inexpressive music, was in praise of latter day
heroes, historical and legendary, or of the simple piety
of the saints. His hopes, perhaps, were more than
realized. In the market-place he was surrounded by
an appreciative crowd ; at the grim feudal fortresses,
where the monotony of existence was broken only by
tournaments and romance, he proved one of the most
welcome of guests. High and low, old and young,
rich and poor,—all glowed with enthusiasm as he sang
of the prowess shown by the Christian warriors in the
valley of Roncevaux. He was also loaded with substantial gifts, some of his noble hosts placing on his
shoulders the costly cloaks they had worn during the
entertainment.

> Cils jongleors eurent bonne soldée ;
> Plus de cent marcs leur valut la journée ;
> Qui fut gentil de cœur sa robe dépouilla,
> Et, pour faire s'honneur à un d'els, la donna—

as the author of *Les Vœux du Paon* puts it. Nor did
his art cease to please when it lost the charm of
novelty. Jongleurs became attached to the permanent
retinues of kings and princes, barons and knights,
bishops and abbesses. Nay, a few of them were even
permitted to wear the golden spurs, in most cases,
perhaps, at the instance of influential and soft-hearted
châtelaines. It is not improbable that this distinction
fell to the lot of the jongleur Taillefer, who rode in
the van of the Norman host at Hastings with a song
of valour on his lips, and in advancing to battle, we
are told, played so many strange tricks with a lance
and sword that the Saxons regarded him as an emissary
of the Evil One, gave way to terror before a bow was
drawn, and accordingly enabled Duke William to become
a Conqueror with greater ease than he could have
anticipated.

Minstrelsy may be deemed the mother of a literature
which did much to pave the way for a revival of the
drama. The accents of these versatile gleemen aroused
the Muses from their protracted sleep. In nearly all
parts of what is now known as France the Gay Science
found more or less gifted votaries among the well-born
and cultured. The Trouvères and the Troubadours successively took up the lyre, the former to the north of
the Loire, where the masculine Langue d'Oil had struck
root, and the latter under the softer skies of the south,

where the Langue d'Oc, a tongue resembling Italian
rather than French, was spoken. Uninfluenced by
ancient models, but not free, especially after the first
Crusade, from a tinge of oriental imagery and refinement, the consequent efflorescence of poetry, viewed as
a whole, presents a striking picture of the thought and
sentiment of the age which produced it, the age when
chivalry was gilding the darker features of feudalism
and the misery they wrought. It is hardly necessary to
say that the older race of poets was more warlike and
less voluptuous than the younger, but each of them was
animated by a spirit of stern independence, a fierce
thirst for martial fame, ever-deepening devotion to
women, enthusiasm for Christianity, a tendency to
satirize the foibles of every class in society, and last, but
not least, an honour keen enough to "feel stain like a
wound." In other respects, however, the analogy
between them is at best slight. The verse of the
Trouvères extends over a wide field of thought, sentiment, and action. They sublimated the minstrel's
secular pæan into the sometimes Homeric *chanson de
geste*, heightened the force and beauty of the Arthurian
legends, raised the standard of the religious play by
inventing the *Mystère*, discussed points of gallantry in
dialogues termed *tensons* or *jeux-partis*, and relieved a
profusion of serious *romans* with *fabliaux* relating to
merry incidents of every-day life. No such variety of

power is apparent in the effusions of the more ardent
and unreflecting genius of the south. The Troubadours
relied almost exclusively upon the lyric, to which, aided
by the harmonious language of Provence, they imparted
a tenderness and grace peculiar to themselves. If, notwithstanding the fact that Latin literature was attracting
attention outside the cloister, the Inventors produced
nothing in the shape of tragedy or comedy, as was
probably the case, they are certainly entitled to the
credit of having assisted to prepare the ground for a
successful cultivation of both. By most of the northern
poets the value of dramatic effect was practically recognized. Evolved from the liturgical ¦play, the Mystery,
as may be seen from the earliest examples of it extant,
Adam and *Le Jeu de St. Nicholas,* which were played
in the open air ,was in advance of its prototype, not
only as being written in the vernacular, but in strength
of dialogue and action ; many of the romances and
fabliaux, notably *Aucassin et Nicolette,* perhaps the best
of all, might by a few strokes of the pen be converted
into acting pieces ; while *Robin et Marion* and *Le Jeu
de la Feuillée,* the chief works of the hunchback of
Arras, crabbed Adam de la Halle, have been shown to
contain respectively the germs of farce and comic opera.
Migrating again to the country of the Troubadours, we
find that, non-dramatic as their intellectual sympathies
may have been, at least one Mystery, *Les Vierges Folles*

et les Vierges Sages, was written in Latin and the
Langue d'Oc, together with *tensons* likely to foster a
taste for dialogue. Neither of these forms, it may
be presumed, was of Provencal origin; they are sug-
gestive of northern rather than of southern ideas,
and more than one poem might be cited to prove that,
as a result of the intercourse maintained between the
principalities by the nature of feudal tenure and the
customs of chivalry, the Troubadours were not ignorant
of what their brother Inventors accomplished.

The means by which this rich and varied literature
became known to the people at large was for some
time in its favour, but eventually the reverse. Jongleurs and jongleresses—for the minstrels were now
of both sexes—sang or recited from it wherever French
or Provençal was spoken. That its merits obtained
a wide acknowledgment there can be no doubt.
Once heard, a passage of noble poetry, with or without
the aid of music, could not be forgotten. " Many of
your love verses to me," writes Héloïse to Abelard,
" were so beautiful in their language and melody that
your name was incessantly in the mouths of all, and
even the most illiterate were charmed. You caused
women to envy me. Every tongue spoke of your
Héloïse ; every street and every house resounded with
my name." In other words, the minstrels were more
sought after and recompensed than ever, and their

social status rapidly went up. Making Paris their
head-quarters, those of the north formed themselves
into a corporation, acquired exclusive privileges, received permission to style their chief Roi, and became
so opulent that two members of the fraternity alone
could afford to build a church and an hospital in
the street they inhabited, the Rue des Jongleurs,
afterwards named the Rue St. Julien des Ménétriers.
At times, it would appear, they had formidable rivalry
to contend with. Some of the Trouvères and the
Troubadours were impelled by poverty to sing or
declaim their own verse for money, not only in courts,
with the smiles or tears of the fair to stimulate
their energies, but in the haunts of the down-trodden
yet always blithesome populace. Two poets immortalized by Petrarch—Arnaud Daniel, one of the most ill-
starred of lovers, and Ancelme Faidit, the friend of
Richard Cœur de Lion, himself a gentle Troubadour
when the battle-axe was out of his hands—were among
these "poëtes-comiques." Unfortunately, the wisdom
and self-respect of the jongleurs diminished as their
success increased. They donned grotesque dresses,
stationed themselves in market-place or village green,
and, describing themselves with the utmost composure as
genuine Inventors, supplemented some delightful verses,
perhaps even a religious dialogue, with rough buffoonery,
feats of legerdemain, tricks with monkeys, and doggerel

appealing to a vitiated taste. Nor did their change
of policy fail to bring more grist to the mill. It was
to no purpose that Philip Augustus and Saint Louis
banished them from the country, or that the poets,
particularly annoyed to find the honoured names of
Trouvère and Troubadour trailed through the dirt,
angrily denounced them as *bâtards,* repudiated any
sympathy with them in their new character, and ceased
to provide them with verse. The disesteem in which
they came to be held is clearly shown by the fact that
jonglerie was employed as a term for anything base,
coarse, or stupid. In the end, degraded by its association with persons of such a stamp, poetry gradually went out of fashion, its decline being hastened
in the south by the crusade against the Albigenses,
whose tenets had been accepted by most of the Troubadours, and in the north by the outbreak of the
Hundred Years' War. As for the minstrels, the last
we hear of them is in an *ordonnance* issued shortly
afterwards, to the effect that if they dealt in matter
of a scandalous nature they should be imprisoned and
kept on bread and water for two months.

One of the forms taken by this alliance between the
arts of poetry and music, however, was to receive
fresh vitality as time passed away. The clergy, who
had long since divested the Fête des Fous of its offensive peculiarities, continued to regard the drama as an

indispensable handmaid to religion, and the place of
the Latin prose play in the festivals of the Church was
now occupied by the Mystery in French verse. No
pains seem to have been spared to heighten the attractiveness of the latter in its new home. Characterized
in itself by a simple dignity befitting the treatment
of such themes, it was acted with much of the pride
and circumstance associated with Roman Catholic
worship. In vain does the eye look for a grander
or more impressive spectacle in its way than the
representation of a Mystery of the Passion in one of
those august Gothic piles, with its nameless something
between earth and heaven. Banners hung above the
fretted arches; the odour of incense filled the air;
tapers shone brightly in the dim light from the storied
and diversely-coloured windows; elaborate processions
wound their way through the aisles to the strains of
solemn music; the figures of the priest-players stood
out in clear relief against the splendour of the altar
as, facing thousands of rapt spectators, they gravely
declaimed, probably with appropriate gestures, the
dialogue intended to set forth the events which led
up to the Crucifixion. But it was something more than
a passion for sight-seeing that drew the people to the
church on such occasions. The Mysteries illustrated
what to nine out of every ten men and women were
the subjects of their most frequent and pressing

thoughts. It was an age of ardent, profound, un-
questioning faith, mingled with debasing superstition.
In all departments of thought the theological spirit
reigned supreme. The satire levelled at the clergy
on account of their laxity of morals stopped short
with the clergy ; it seldom or never touched Revelation
itself. Instead of being merely a house for prayer, as
it is with us, the church was the centre of intellectual
and social life, the true home of rich and poor alike,
the one great resort of the desolate and oppressed. In
these circumstances, it is needless to add, the Mystery
of the Passion soon won the heart of society at large.
No incident of a play relating to the life of the
Redeemer could have become wearisome by repetition ;
and the scene on Calvary, intensely realistic in treatment, was witnessed with an emotion which, softened
as it may have been by the knowledge of His ultimate
triumph, must have exceeded that aroused by any
masterpiece of Greek tragedy among the frequenters
of the marble theatre at Athens. Some parts of the
Mystery may now seem irreverent and perilously droll,
but the sacredness of its subject and surroundings
probably sufficed to check any tendency to mirth.
Even when the representative of Christ passed before
the altar on a mule, as he usually did in the entry into
Jerusalem, the audience, though always ready to look
at the ludicrous side of things, would make the sign

of the cross in their devoutest mood. Nourished by this religious fervour, the drama assumed a wide scope —wide enough, indeed, to include nearly every event of interest in the history of Christianity. It resolved itself into two distinct groups—the Mysteries, the groundwork of which was taken from Holy Writ, and the Miracles, which turned upon the supernatural acts ascribed to the Virgin and the saints.

So potent a means of charming the masses could not long be kept within the pale of the sanctuary, where, to use a simile from Goethe, it was like an oak in a vase of porcelain. It disengaged itself from direct ecclesiastical influence, ·returned to the market-place, and became an independent institution. Mysteries and Miracles were played by guilds and companies expressly organized for the purpose. No popular festivity was deemed complete without one of these instructive entertainments. For example, in the autumn of 1385, when Isabel of Bavaria arrived in Paris, " de jeunes gens y représentaient diverses histoires de l'Ancien Testament " in her honour. These plays were given on scaffolds in the streets, with the actors in more or less archaic costume, with an organ at the back to accompany a chorus of angels, and also with some attempt at scenery. " That is the finest Paradise you have ever seen or ever will see," an artist once remarked, proudly pointing to a canvas he had coloured for a Mystery. Distressing

accidents occasionally happened ; an actor who had the
courage to impersonate the Saviour nearly died on the
cross, and a Judas was found to have hanged himself
only too effectually. For persons of high degree there
were seat in a sort of pavilion, the remainder of the
spectators being left to stand or squat in the fore-
ground. In this new atmosphere, as may be supposed,
the religious drama underwent an appreciable change.
Broad farce was introduced into the most serious scenes.
Especially comic was the figure of the Devil, who,
appearing on the stage as he was popularly supposed
to be—as a deformed and hairy sprite, with horns,
dragon's wings, long tail, and cloven feet—was subjected
to the cruellest indignities. No indignity, however,
was then deemed too cruel for the presumed author
of all the ills and annoyances experienced by mankind.
Roars of laughter filled the air when holy men spat
in his face, when liberties were taken with his tail,
when a stalwart anchorite brought him to the dust
with a well-directed blow, and, above all, when St.
Dunstan seized him by the nose with the traditional
red-hot pincers. Notwithstanding such concessions to
uncultivated tastes, the Mystery, I think, was strengthened by its emancipation from the Church. It gained
in dramatic force, in pictorial effect, in variety of
character, in extent of thought and action, in everything that could rivet the attention of the spectators.

One of the companies formed to represent these
plays was destined to eclipse all others. In 1398 a
number of young artisans devised and appeared in a
new *Mystère de la Passion de N. S. J. C.* Soon afterwards, at the instance of wealthy and pious citizens,
they erected a hall at Saint Maur des Fossés, a village
near Paris, in order to continue their performances
without fear of being interrupted by bad weather;
but the authorities, manifestly alarmed by so great an
innovation as a permanent theatre, put their veto upon
the project. Four years later, the Confrères de la
Passion, as the artisans were called, appealed against
this decree to Charles VI., who, having seen their
Mystery performed, issued *Lettres* permitting them to
do as they liked. I extract one or two passages from
the edict: "Charles par la grace de Dieu Roy de
France, scavoir faisons à tous présens et avenir, Nous
avoir receu l'umble supplicacion de noz bien amez et
Confrères les Maistres et Gouverneurs de la Confrarie
de la Passion et Résurreccion Nostre Seigneur . . . .
donnons et octroyons de grace espécial, plaine puissance
et auctorité Royal, ceste foiz pour toutes et à tousjours
perpétuelment, par la teneur de ces présentes Lettres,
auctorité, congié, et licence de faire et jouer quelque
Misterre que ce soit . . . . soit devant Nous ou ai'leurs,
tant en recors comme autrement, ainsi et par la manière
que dit est, puissent aler, venir, passer et repasser

paisiblement, vestuz, abilliez et ordonnez un chascun
d'eulx, en tel estat que le cas le désire, et comme il
appartendra, selon l'ordenance du dict Misterre, sans
destourbier ou empeschement . . . . Et pour ce que
ce soit ferme chose et estable à tousjours, Nous avons
fait mettre nostre séel à ces Lettres : Sauf en autres
choses nostre droit, et l'autruy en toutes. Ce fu fait et
donne à Paris, en nostre Hostel lès Saint Pol, au moys
de Décembre "—to be precise, on the 2nd—" l'an de
grace mil IIII° et deux, et de nostre regne le XXIII°."
The Confrères, it is needless to say, did not allow the
grass to grow under their feet.   North of the Seine,
hard by the Porte St. Denis, an Hôpital de la Trinité
had been built by two foster-brothers for the benefit of
travellers arriving after the time for admission to the
city proper.   It was now in the hands of a few monks
of Hermières, who piously spent the funds at their
disposal upon themselves.   Here the Confrères had
taken up their quarters; and here, in a large *salle*
duly fitted up, they appeared in the *Mystery of the
Passion* and other sacred dramas on Sundays and
during some festivals of the Church.

Both the theatre and the work of the Confrères
demand our best attention, the former as being the
first constructed in Paris, and the latter as forming
the model on which similar entertainments throughout
the country were thenceforward given.   About mid-day,

having paid two sous for admission, the spectator passed into a hall sixty-three feet by eighteen in size, on the level of the street, and "soutenue par des arcades." Nothing like a tier was to be seen; the audience, which consisted in the main of sober citizens and their children, with a sprinkling of the clergy, had only the "pit" to stand in. The stage was divided by floors into three sections, each with a painting at the back. The highest represented Paradise, the next a spot in the Holy Land, and the third the infernal regions (*a*). In the first, which reached the roof, a man of severe and venerable aspect, enthroned in a *chaire parée*, impersonated the Creator, the Virtues standing by in picturesque attitudes. Most of the action, of course, passed in the second *étage*, whither angels and devils respectively descended and mounted as their presence on earth was required. It was through the mouth of a dragon emitting fire from its eyes and nostrils that the devil and his myrmidons came on and vanished. Some of the scenes were chanted to music, usually from an organ. It is clear that the Confrères overlooked the importance of dramatic illusion; no curtain was employed, and the players not at work sat in a semicircle behind those who were. In regard to decoration and costume, the *mise-en-scene*, if historically inaccurate, was in advance of anything previously accomplished in this way — so much so,

indeed, as to suggest that some one in the troupe was
no stranger to the spectacular displays patronized in
the East by the Greek Church. Judged by isolated
passages, the play might be deemed grotesque, indecent,
and even irreverent. Satan, in common with all the
denizens of hell, became more of a buffoon than ever.
Saint Joseph is sorely troubled in his mind on finding
that his wife is with child :—

> Elle est enceinte ; et d'où viendrait
> Le fruit ? Il faut dire, par droit,
> Qu'il y ait vice d'adultère,
> Puisque je n'en suis pas le père.

The Most High is thus apostrophized by an angel
immediately after the Crucifixion :—

> Père éternel, vous avez tort
> Et devriez avoir vergogne ;
> Votre Fils bien aimé est mort,
> Et vous dormez comme un ivrogne.

No such coarseness, on the other hand, is to be found
in the speeches of the chief personages—a proof that
if the Confrères played down to the vulgar it was not
from a want of knowing better. Viewed as a whole,
indeed, the Mystery is characterized in a high degree by
grandeur and tragic power, and it is easy to believe that
the merriment intentionally excited in some of its scenes
was drowned towards the close in very different feelings.
In its new aspect it was still supported by the clergy,
who advanced the hour of vespers to allow the faithful

to visit the Hôpital de la Trinité without having to
leave before the performance came to an end.

Naturally enough, the success of the Mystery, now
more pronounced than it had been, speedily led to the
introduction of a lighter and purely secular drama.
The seed sown by the Trouvères and the Troubadours
was to bear good fruit. Foremost among the guilds
in Paris at this time was that of the *procureurs* in
embryo at the Palais de Justice, the Clercs de la Basoche
(Basilica). Established in the previous century by
Philippe le Bel, it took an important part in the
administration of the law, attained to the dignity of a
royaume, had a Chancelier and Maître des Requêtes, and
was reviewed once a year by the reigning monarch. By
special favour, its leader, the Roi de la Basoche, was
permitted to appear at all public ceremonies in a velvet
cap similar to that which graced the anointed head.
Foiled by the terms of the Lettres Patentes of 1402 in
an attempt to deprive the Confrères of the exclusive
privilege of playing Mysteries, and burning with a
desire to add to their renown by means of dramatic
performances on their *fête* days, the Basochiens now
invented two kinds of plays—the *Moralité*, the figures
in which are chiefly personifications of sentiments and
abstract ideas, and the *Farce*, which may be roughly
described as a resuscitation of the homely fabliau
in a dramatic form. Nearly every vice and virtue is

represented in the former group. In one morality, for example, Gluttony and other Excesses, after revelling to their hearts' content at the invitation of Banquet, are carried off by various Diseases, while the host is condemned to death for leading them astray. Dull as these pieces may appear to us, they enjoyed considerable popularity in their day, as a taste for allegory had been diffused far and wide by the *Roman de la Rose* and other poems of the Trouvères. As for the farces, they gave practical effect to the suggestion thrown out by Adam de la Halle, and were the first French writings in which the mirror of the drama was held up to everyday life and character. Henpecked husbands, imperious wives, exasperating mothers-in-law, good-for-nothing monks, lip-valourous soldiers (one of whom, by the way, is seized with abject terror on beholding a scarecrow, which he takes to be an enemy),—these and other personages were connected with more or less whimsical adventures, the dialogue being often lighted up by a flash of wit, a hit at common foibles, or some pleasantry at the expense of the younger *procureurs.* Except at times of public rejoicing, when they played on a scaffold in the street, the theatre of the Basochians was the hall of the Palais de Justice, their stage the great marble table on which the banquets formerly given there by kings of France were served. As may be supposed, the Clercs were not long permitted to monopolize what they had invented. The

Enfants sans Souci, a band of educated and rackety youths, all of whom figured in the revels of the Court, and who, wearing on their heads a sort of hood, garnished on each side with an ass's ear, annually made a formal entry into Paris, of course with all gravity, under the leadership of their chief, the Prince of Fools, began to represent in the Halles what they termed a *Sotie,* in substance a copy of the farce, but differing from its model in being weak in story, political in purpose, and keenly satirical in character. That it hit the taste of its hearers there can be no doubt. The Basochians, in imitation of their imitators, added Soties to their repertory; while the Confrères de la Passion, uniting worldly wisdom to their piety, induced the Enfants sans Souci, doubtless in return for a share of receipts, to play such a piece at the Hôpital de la Trinité after each representation of the Mystery.

It was not long before the power of the drama as a means of influencing public opinion became manifest. Paris, in common with other parts of northern France, fell a prey to some of the worst ills that can befall mankind—foreign 'invasion and civil strife, pestilence and famine, anarchy and outrage. It was in vain that the Parlement strove to make its voice heard; the whole fabric of society seemed to be tottering to its fall. Intimidated by the aspect of affairs, the Enfants sans Souci, though continuing to fulfil their engagement with the Confrères, prudently drew in their satirical horns; but the Basochians, who from the nature of their calling might have been expected to uphold the authority of the law, audaciously subjected every person of note in the kingdom to a measure of ridicule which could not fail to increase the prevailing ferment. Happily for France, this ferment soon subsided. Jeanne Darc appeared; the tide of English invasion was rolled back; Charles VII. secured himself on the throne; order and tranquillity were gradually restored. The Basochians may well have feared that their ill-timed waggery would now expose them to a heavy punishment, but the Parlement contented itself with requiring them to free their Soties and farces in future from offensive and defamatory matter. In 1442, this leniency having been abused, it was further decreed that none of their pieces should be played until it had been examined by a censor appointed for the purpose. The Basochians respected this order as little as the first; and the Parlement, losing all patience, had them imprisoned and kept upon bread and water for several days. Under Louis XI., whose high qualities as a statesman are too often forgotten in the abhorrence excited by his treachery and superstition, and who, like Richard III. of England, had a corner in his heart for plays and players, the Clercs again found themselves in favour—nay, were forbidden to discontinue their *jeux* without leave.   More than repaying the obligation conferrèd upon them by the bourgeois-king, they enriched the literature of his reign with one of the most famous productions of the Middle Ages, the farce of *Maistre\ Pierre Pathelin,* from which " Revenez à vos moutons ". is taken.   Directly afterwards, however, their satiric zeal again outran their discretion, though in what way we are not told.   In 1476, by *arrêt* in due form, they were prohibited by Parlement, not only from playing, but from asking permission to play, under pain of banishment and the confiscation of their property. It was to no purpose that the then Roi de la Basoche, Jean l'Eveillé, set the second of these orders at defiance ; the Parlement, confirming their previous decision, added to the list of penalties already pre-scribed a sound whipping in the cross-ways of Paris. The next we hear of the Clercs is in 1486, when, no longer to be kept down, they treated the people to a satire upon the reigning monarch, Charles VIII., and were clapped in the Conciergerie for their pains.   In the opinion of the authorities, it is clear, anything like freedom of speech was to be put down at all hazards.

Soon afterwards, however, the political and social power which the drama had acquired was favoured and utilized by the Court.   During the reign of Louis XII., the Father of the People, the Basochians and the Enfants sans Souci were permitted to say what they liked. No restriction was placed upon legitimate and wholesome satire. "For," said the king, "my courtiers never tell me the unvarnished truth, and as long as the truth is withheld from me I cannot know how the kingdom is governed. The troupes of the Roi de la Basoche and the Prince des Sots have my authority to expose any abuse they may discover, whether at Court or in the town, and to ridicule whom they please. I do not wish to be exempt from their attacks; but if they say a word against the Queen· I will hang them all." The players, it need hardly be said, made full use of their new privilege, even to the extent of raising a laugh at the expense of their royal protector on account of his notorious avarice. His majesty seemed to have regarded the Enfants sans Souci with particular favour, as in the course of his contest with Julius II. they were prompted to set that Pontiff in a by no means flattering light before the public. For this purpose, a member of the troupe, Pierre Gringoire, well known as a getter-up of Mysteries in the country, wrote the *Jeu du Prince des Sots et Mère-Sotte;* and on Shrove Tuesday, 1511, his comrades, temporarily forsaking the Hôpital de la Trinité, played it on the scene of their early exploits, the Halles, to an audience composed of the highest and the lowest. The author, dressed in the petticoats of Holy Church, disported himself for an hour or two as the warlike

Pontiff, who was represented as disguising unbounded hypocrisy and libertinism under the cloak of religion, as seeking to increase his temporal power at the expense of the French, and as obtaining support among bishops and abbés by offering them rich benefices and other bribes. In the end, King Louis begins to suspect that his Holiness is not the Church—a suspicion not limited to Paris at this time—and in point of fact is only a sort of *Mère-Sotte.* The *Jeu* was followed by a *Moralité* and a *Sottise à Huit Personnages,* in the former of which the Pope reappears as an obstinate and confessedly immoral person. One of the characters in the farce was filled by a clever hunchback, Jean du Pontalais, now chiefly remembered in connexion with a piece of amusing boldness. It was the custom of this person to sally forth into a public place, execute a short but noisy fantasia on a drum, and, having brought around him a large crowd, give forth the name and expatiate upon the good qualities of the next pieces to be played by his brother Devil-may-cares. One Sunday morning, in the middle of sermon time, the congregation at St. Eustache, hearing the sound of his drum in the adjoining square, rushed out to hear what he had to say. The officiating priest followed, naturally in no very amiable mood. "It is like your impudence," he hotly told the farceur, "to make your announcements while I am preaching." "And it is

like your impudence," was the reply, " to preach while
I am making my announcements." The priest having
reported the incident to the magistrates, Pontalais
was kept in durance vile for six long months to learn
better manners. His disgrace, however, had no effect
upon the position of his comrades and their rivals.
Mère-Sotte did so much to weaken the cause of the
Papacy in France that the king's faith in the virtues
of satire was appreciably deepened ; and the Parlement,
smothering their prejudices against what it deemed his
mistaken policy, graciously insisted upon contributing
to the expenses of the entertainments it witnessed.

The breath was scarcely out of the king's body when
the Parlement again sought to fetter the drama,
probably foreseeing that under his successor, François I.,
the Court would present only too inviting a target for
the shafts of satire. Both the troupes in Paris received
orders to abstain from any reference to princes, princesses, and other eminent persons. The Enfants sans
Souci immediately returned to their innocent pursuits
at the Hôtel de la Trinité, where they became more popular than ever. For this gain, perhaps, they were mainly
indebted to the acting of a new comrade, Jean Serre,
the best living representative of *badins* and drunkards.
" When," writes Marot, himself a member of the troupe:

" Quand il entroit en salle
Avec sa chemise sale,

Le front, la joue et la narine
Toute couverte de farine
Et coiffé d'un béguin d'enfant
Et d'un haut bonnet triomphant,
Garni de plumes de chappons :
Avec tout cela je répons
Qu'en voyant sa grâce niaise
On n'estoit pas moins gay ni aise
Qu'on est aux Champs Elysées "—

certainly a graphic little sketch. Unlike the wiser
Devil-may-cares, the Basochians, as is shown by the
enormous number of decrees issued against them in the
course of a few years, continued to give a world of
trouble to the Parlement. In 1526 they appear to have
been in the sun, as their old enemies voted them 60
livres " pour leurs jeux et Sotises en faveur du retour
de François I." from his enforced detention in Spain
after the disaster of Pavia. Nevertheless, the censure
was still maintained in all its rigour. Suddenly the
Clercs hit upon an ingenious expedient for at once
evading the law and convulsing their audience. They
appeared in masks bearing an ugly resemblance to
persons obnoxious to the public. The Parlement,
hardly able to realize the fact that such effrontery
was possible, forbade the troupe " de faire monstrations
de spectacle, ne écriteaux taxans, ou notans quelque
personnes que ce soit, sur peine de prison et de
bannissement." Two years afterwards, in 1538, this
prohibition was withdrawn, though only to be renewed
in a more decisive form—the Clercs being threatened

with nothing less than the halter—in 1540. Yet again
did the offenders obtain forgiveness ; indeed, the Parlement made a concession to them which could hardly
have been hoped for. " Et quant à la farce et sermon,"
runs the *arrêt*, "attendu la grande difficulté par eux
alleguée de les monstrer à ladite cour, ayant égard à
leurs remontrances, pour cette fois, et sans tirer à conséquence, ladite cour leur a permis et permet de jouer
ladite farce et sermon sans les monstrer à ladite cour ;
cependant avec défense de taxer ou scandaliser parti-
culièrement aucune personne, soit par noms ou sur-
noms, ou circonstance d'estoc, ou lieu particulier de
demourance et autres notables circonstances par les-
quelles on peut désigner ou connaître les personnes, &c."
Perhaps this concession was due to the influence of
Marguérite de Valois, who, as we learn from Brantôme,
" often wrote comedies and moralities (in those days
they were called pastorals) and had them performed
by the ladies of her Court."

Notwithstanding the intermittent hostility of the
Parlement, farce was to outlive the graver drama
from which it sprang. For some time past the popularity of the Mysteries and Miracles had been steadily
declining. Evidently in the belief that too much of
a good thing could not be had, they were spun out
until the representation of the shortest occupied several
days, and the most pious spectator must have found

them as wearisome as a heavy sermon on a well-worn
text. Moreover, they had ceased to be in harmony
with the temper of the age. The dawn of latter-day
civilisation had broadened into what an optimist may
have deemed perfect day. The intellectual agitation induced by the cardinal events of the last hundred years
—the revival of ancient literature, the overthrow of
the Ptolemaic system, the downfall of the Moors
in Spain, the discoveries of the Iberian navigators,
the political changes witnessed in France, and last,
but above all, the partial liberation of the Church
from the thraldom of Rome—had lifted the human
mind out of the narrow ruts in which it had so long
been content to move. New ideas began to hold sway;
an ardent and restless spirit of inquiry went out over
the land ; opinions which seemed to be bound up with
life itself were rejected or profoundly changed. Unlike
other mediæval institutions, chivalry not excepted,
religion emerged with added strength from the ordeal
of this tendency to break away from the past. It is
true that a vague scepticism found expression in the
pages of Rabelais and Montaigne, but among the nation
at large the old child-like simplicity of faith gave way
to a higher sense of the dignity and grandeur of
Christianity. The Renascence, too, served to raise
the standard of literary taste, inasmuch as, aided by
the invention of printing, it was bringing imperishable

monuments of ancient poetry and prose within the
reach of all who could read.   In these circumstances,
of course, the sacred drama, with its odd intermixture
of the sublime and the grotesque, its crudeness of form
and substance, rapidly lost the charm it had hitherto
possessed.   Protestants and Romanists united in de-
nouncing it as likely to bring religion into contempt,
and its defects in the way of style were glaring enough
to evoke a shower of ridicule.   If a few Mysteries had
been conceived and executed in the spirit of *Paradise
Lost* they might have turned the tide, but the pieces
given at the Hôtel de la Trinité continued to have as
little of Milton's reverence and beauty of workmanship
as of his genius.   Indeed, the Confrères of the Passion,
so far from appreciating the necessity of reforming
their entertainments, sought to compensate themselves
for the coldness of the lettered playgoers towards them
by appealing more directly than ever to the unlettered
—in other words, by giving increased prominence to
what lettered playgoers deplored as a grave public
scandal.   The fact that Francis I. had voluntarily
renewed the privileges of the company may have led
them to regard their position as unassailable.   By this
change of policy, as events showed, they simply
accelerated their inevitable doom.   In 1539, the
Hôtel de la Trinité having been re-applied to the
charitable purpose for which it was established, they

migrated to an Hôtel de Flandres, near the Rue des
Vieux Augustins.   Four years later this house was
pulled down by order of the King, and the Confrères,
after passing some time without a fixed home, purchased
a portion of the Hôtel de Bourgogne, Rue Mauconseil,
from one Jean Rouvet.   Forthwith an application for
leave to play there was laid before the Parlement,
who, by an *arrêt* bearing date 17 November 1548,
expressly prohibited them from appearing in other
than secular pieces.   It was in vain that the distressed
troupe prevailed upon the Court to interpose in their
favour ; the Parlement, less compliant than that which
gave effect to the wishes of Louis XII., firmly refused
to alter its decision.   The Confrères, unwilling to perform in farces, let a theatre they had built in the Hôtel
de Bourgogne to the Enfants sans Souci; and the
French religious drama, the oldest institution of the
kind in western Europe, passed away, at least as far as
Paris was concerned, with the state of society which
permitted such things to exist.

It was not merely by putting an end to Mysteries
and Miracles in the gayest of cities that the decree
of the Parlement marked an epoch in stage history.
From the Carlovingian era, as we have seen, the clergy
had regarded the drama as an important ally of the
Church.   Alive to the widespread predilection for
spectacle, they had founded a new species of play

upon the liturgy, availed themselves of the improvements effected in it by the Trouvères, represented it
with all the splendid accessories at their command,
and gave it their support after it finally escaped from
the sanctuary. If they did not unreservedly approve
the features it then assumed—and some of them were
austere enough to denounce it root and branch—their
general attitude towards it remained unchanged. Except
at a comparatively recent period, when the stories
of Helen and Griselda and Jeanne Darc were retold in
Mystery-form(*b*), the play-writer drew his inspiration
exclusively from sacred records, and the value of his
work as a means of extending the influence of religion
can hardly be overrated. But the great majority of
the priesthood could not reconcile themselves to the
purely secular drama, especially after they saw that a
great revolution was in progress about them. Might
not the theatre be employed to disseminate ideas
more or less inimical to their doctrines and pretensions ? Were they not really warming a viper in
their bosom ? Had the holiness of Pope Julius saved
him from being held up to public derision by a
buffoon in the fish-market ? The decree of 1548 did
away with the only reason they had for dissembling
their hostility to the farce — namely, a reluctance
to throw discredit upon an institution which partly
devoted itself to the service of Christianity. Hence-

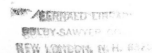

forward they were uncompromising opponents of theatrical amusement in any shape. They suddenly discovered that the drama was bad in principle, if not an old device of the Evil One for ensnaring the souls of the unwary. They reprehended play-going as incompatible with true devotion, purity of life, and sobriety of thought. They condemned the actor to a sort of social outlawry, declaring that unless he solemnly forswore his profession he could not receive the Holy Communion or be entitled to Christian burial. In other words, partly from an ascetic desire to minimize the pleasures of existence, but chiefly from a mistaken dread of the extension of popular intelligence and knowledge beyond very narrow limits, the anathemas launched by the primitive Church against the abominations of the Roman circus were virtually applied to an art which in point of morality was distinctly above the accepted standards of the time, and the records of which, I am constrained to add, were much cleaner than those of the antagonist it now had to face. In this case, however, the clergy found themselves as powerless as they had been in their opposition to the Copernican theory of the universe. Farce continued to flourish in the hands of the Enfants sans Souci, and a few years after the suppression of the Mysteries and Miracles the gap made by that measure was more than filled.

CHAPTER II.

1552—1629.

THE Renascence, that great unsealing of the waters, had an immediate and decisive effect upon every form of creative thought, and upon the drama more than any other. In Italy, where the movement took its rise, tragedy and comedy of the ancient pattern, but often instinct with the spirit of religion and chivalry, were flourishing side by side with a farce as indigenous to the soil as the Sotie was to that of France. The most typical of these plays, perhaps, were Trissino's *Sofonisba* and Rucellai's *Rosmunda*, in which true poetic feeling is much less conspicuous than accurate scholarship and arid pedantry. Now, it was inevitable that before long the example thus set should be followed in other countries. Italy enjoyed all the authority which a nearly unequalled success in the arts of peace can confer. In painting and sculpture, poetry and prose, commerce and industry, she gave the law to the world. France quickly fell under her influence ; the classical drama came to be enthusiastically imitated in Paris, and the boast of the

Cardinal d'Amboise, "we shall be more Italian than
Italy itself," was justified at least as far as this intensely artificial growth was concerned. England and
Spain were also disposed for a time to walk in the
steps of the Italian dramatists ; but in each of these
countries, thanks to great original genius, the regular
drama threw off the yoke of the old system, assumed
a much wider scope, and became distinctively national
in conception and substance.

In France, as elsewhere, this revival sprang from
the study of ancient literature in the colleges. The
speech-day programmes here had long included the
performance of some new sotie—a custom not free
from danger, as the scholars, not to be outdone in
temerity by the incorrigible Basochians, indulged in
satire at the expense of the Court itself. More than
one *défense* was launched against them by the Parlement ; and François I., finding that his blameless
sister, Marguérite de Valois, had been represented at
the Collége de Navarre as a "furie," clapped in prison
as many of the authors and actors as he could lay
hands upon. If the authorities apprehended a renewal
of the annoyance they were soon reassured. Formerly
shrunk from, though not omitted from the curriculum,
Greek and Latin learning was now in fashion with
mere striplings, and translations of classical plays took
the place of farces in the collegiate entertainments.

Hecuba and *Electra*, for instance, were rendered into French verse by Lazare de Baïf, his majesty's ambassador at Venice, for the Collége de Coquerel, whither his natural son, Jean Antoine de Baïf, was sent a few years afterwards. Among the friends of the latter were Pierre de Ronsard (who in his boyhood had accompanied James Stuart and Marie de Lorraine to Scotland as page), Etienne Jodelle, Dubellay, Rémi-Belleau, and Pontús de Tiard. Each of these youths had a genuine enthusiasm for classical lore; and eventually, in conjunction with their tutor, Dorat, they formed the project of enriching their native language by means of poetry in which ancient words, the Greek compound not excluded, should be introduced wherever practicable. The enterprise was essentially quixotic, but it is difficult to doubt that the Pléiade, as the seven poets were collectively termed, exercised in many respects a salutary influence upon the literature of their time. Not the least characteristic product of the new school was a version by Ronsard of *Plutus*, executed for the Collége de Coquerel in 1549. Each of these translations met with marked success; and Jodelle, who was intended for the profession of arms, but whose time appears to have been evenly divided between pleasure and the study of poetry and art, resolved to try the effect of some new plays upon the old lines.

In 1552, before the daring poet had completed his
twenty-first year, this idea was realized under conditions as favourable as the want of trained actors
and a good stage would permit. First came the
tragedy of *Cléopatre Captive*, the name of which is
sufficient to indicate its subject. It was represented
in the quadrangle of the Hôtel de Rheims, the audience
including Henri II. and the flower of his Court. Jodelle
himself impersonated the Egyptian Queen, and among
those who supported him were Jean de la Péruse, a
dabbler in verse, and Rémi-Belleau. Formed upon
the Greek model, even to the extent of introducing
a chorus, *Cléopatre* is written in the five-foot Iambic
couplet and alexandrines, depends upon narration to
the all but complete exclusion of action, and in point
of style may be described as an echo of that of
Seneca. Its comparative novelty, however, blinded the
spectators to its defects. Pasquier, who was present,
tells us that the king presented the author with five
hundred crowns from the royal purse, " et luy fit
tout plein d'autres graces, d'autant que d'estoit chose
nouvelle, et très-belle, et très-rare." Before long, too,
the performance was repeated in the presence of his
majesty at the Collége de Boncourt, all the windows
of which, like the court itself, were choked with
persons eager to witness the spectacle. Not content with the laurels he had won as a tragic poet,

Jodelle next produced a comedy under the title of
Eugéne, ou La Rencontre. It is a story of modern
French life, with a libertine abbé for the chief personage, and was acted with good success at the Hôtel de
Rheims and the Collége de Boncourt. Jodelle now
found himself in a most enviable position. He was
regarded on nearly all hands as a modern Sophocles.
The King, in common with the Dúchesse de Savoie and
other leaders of fashion, "le favorisait grandement."
His fellow Pleiades, in a spirit which speaks for itself,
made the welkin ring with praises of his "happy
courage" and its results. It is to be feared that on
one occasion his friends did him more harm than good;
they organized a Bacchic procession at Arcueil in his
honour, and the ceremony was sternly denounced by
Protestants and Roman Catholics alike as an insult
to Revelation. Industriously repeated by jealous
poetasters, this charge, to which some colour was lent
by the fact that he had painted an abbé in unflattering colours, went far to undermine the popularity
he had achieved. His next play, *Didon se Sacrifiant*,
written entirely in alexandrines, was received with
studied coldness by most of the audience, although
it is of higher value than *Cléopatre*, and has at least
one passage (the invocation to Venus) which deserves
to live in the memory. Mortified by the rebuff, he
ceased to write for the stage, and even under the

pressure of poverty could not be induced to return to
it.   He died at an early age, his last poem being one
in which he pathetically likened himself to neglected
Anaxagoras.

But his work survived him.   The accents of the
dramatic muses continued to be heard in the court-
yards of the colleges and at royal *fêtes*.   Seneca's
Medea and *Agamemnon* were successively reproduced
in French, the first by Jean de la Péruse, the poet
already referred to, and the other by Charles Toutain,
Lieutenant-Général of a vicomté in the north.   In
order to forget a love-disappointment, Jacques Grévin,
afterwards physician to the Duchesse de Savoie, but
at present not out of his teens, wrote for his Alma
Mater, the Collége de Beauvais, a couple of comedies,
La Trésorière and *Les Esbahis*, and one tragedy, *La
Mort de César*.   For the serious drama he had no
vocation; but his lighter pieces, the scene of which
is laid in the old Place Maubert, a well-known rendezvous, describe contemporary manners with some
gaiety and purity of style.   Marot's erstwhile rival, the
sprightly Mellin de St. Gelais, from whose raillery
Ronsard prayed to be saved, gave the world a *Sophonisbe* in prose; and in 1559, a year after his death,
it was played before Henri II. at Blois.   Gabriel
Bounyn, Maître des Requêtes to the Duc d'Alençon,
had the hardihood to compose a regular tragedy, *La

Sultane, on a modern story; Jean de la Taille, abandoning law at Orleans for poetry in Paris, made amends for two execrable tragedies by a pleasant comedy in prose, *Les Corrivaux;* Nicholas Filleul, hailing from Rouen, acquired sufficient influence at Court to cause a few pastoral plays after the fashion of the Italians to be acted for the diversion of the King. Belleau and Baïf, alarmed by these new departures, then recalled attention to the example of the ancients : the former made a five-act comedy in verse, *La Reconnue,* out of an incident of the time; the other, who often drew the rank and fashion of Paris to his house in the Faubourg Saint Marceau by giving a concert there, and who was authorized by the Court to establish an "Académie" de Musique, translated the *Miles Gloriosus* under the title of *Le Brave, ou Taillebras,* and in 1567 had the satisfaction of seeing it performed at the Hôtel de Guise in the presence of Charles IX. and Catherine de Médicis.

The new drama had not as yet exhibited much inventive or literary power, but two writers of widely dissimilar gifts now succeeded in relieving it from this reproach. Robert Garnier, Lieutenant-Général and Siége Présidial at Mans, had carried off a prize at the Jeux Floraux by an ode, and the applause bestowed upon this and other of his effusions encouraged him to take a loftier flight. Beginning in 1568, at the age of thirty-four, he wrote eight tragedies—*Porcie, Hippolyte, Cornélie, Marc Antoine, La Troade, Antigone, Bradamanthe,* and *Les Juives.* In speaking of his theatre I find it necessary to guard against a temptation to overpraise. To far-reaching scholarship, the fruit of a liberal education at Toulouse, he united a fervid imagination, rare delicacy of thought and feeling, and a fine sense of moral dignity. His style, though originally formed upon that of Seneca and the Pléiade, is often characterized by a majestic simplicity, notably in the choruses. Nor did he fall upon an unappreciative age. In the words of Pasquier, he " was allowed on all hands to have eclipsed his predecessors " in France. His success only stimulated him to expend increased care upon his work; the *Juives,* which relates to the capture of Jerusalem by Nebuchadnezzar, marks the culminating point in a course of progressive improvement, and prouder laurels would probably have fallen to his lot if death had not carried him off in his fifty-sixth year. His faith in the antique model did not prevent him from making a few important innovations. He regularly alternated masculine and feminine rhymes; *Bradamanthe,* in addition to containing the first confidant, was virtually the first tragi-comedy written in French. Each of these innovations was adopted by other dramatists, who, indeed, appear to have generally profited by his example. And one of his contempor-

aries, Pierre de Larivey, a native of Champagne, but
of Italian parentage (his real name, it is said, was
Giunti, of which Larivey is an approximate translation), exercised an equally inspiring influence in comedy.
In 1577, a band of Venetian players, the Gelosi,
appeared before Henri III. and his Court at Blois and
the Hôtel de Bourbon, the opposition of the Parlement
notwithstanding.   On their way to Paris they had
been taken prisoners by the Huguenots ; but the King,
at whose invitation they had crossed the Alps, ransomed
them with commendable promptitude.   According to
L'Etoile, their audiences were " larger than the congre-
gations of the four best preachers in the capital put
together," greatly to the disgust of that eccentric
annalist.   The repertory of the Gelosi seems to have
included examples of Italian comedy in its more popular
forms, such as the *commedia dell' arte*, a meagre outline of
intrigue and character, on which the actor extemporized
dialogue and by-play, and the masked comedy, which
introduced the spectator to Pantaleone, Dottore, Spavi-
ento, Pullicinella, Giangurgulo, Coviello, Gelfomino,
Brighella, and Arlecchino.   Larivey, who had some
connexion with the Court, was stimulated by these
performances to apply himself to dramatic work.   Six
pieces *facétieuses* from his pen, all more or less founded.
upon ancient or Italian plays, as he was the first
to avow, appeared between this time and 1579, and

were marked by a *rerve* peculiar to himself.   If one
of them surpassed the others it was *Le Laquais,* a version
of the equivocal *Ragazzi* (*c*).

Before long, as a consequence of the interest and
importance given to it by Garnier and Larivey, the
regular drama found a more permanent home than
châteaux and colleges could afford.   Notwithstanding
the War of the League, companies of actors were formed
in many parts of the country to play tragedy and
comedy, which instantly dealt a mortal blow at the
lingering Mystery and Miracle.   Incredible as it may
appear, the populace of Paris were not allowed at first
to have a share in the new amusements.   The Confrères
de la Passion, apprehensive that the establishment of
a second theatre would diminish the receipts of their
tenants at the Hôtel de Bourgogne, the Enfants sans
Souci, claimed the full benefit of the monopoly conferred
upon them in the Lettres Patentes of 1402 ; and the
Parlement, though proof against more than one attempt
to revive the sacred drama within the boundaries of
the city, sternly set their faces against any infringement
of that privilege.   For instance, hearing that arrangements were being made by some players from Bordeaux
to give classical pieces at the Hôtel de Cluny, in the
Rue des Mathurins, they required the *concierge*, under
pain of fine and imprisonment, to pull down the stage
within twenty-four hours.   But this protection did not

assure continued success to the Hôtel de Bourgogne. The old farce, satirical or otherwise, temporarily went out of vogue.   The Basochians disappear from theatrical history in 1582, and soon after that time the Enfants sans Souci ceased to act.   It may be presumed that the decline and fall of this peculiar dramatic growth afforded considerable satisfaction to some zealous Protestants and Roman Catholics, as one of the number, in the course of a Remonstrance to the King respecting the state of the kingdom, qualified the theatre in the Rue Mauconseil as the " cloaque et maison de Sathan," as a place for " mille assignations scandaleuses," and many other dreadful things.   The glee of the anti-theatrical party was of but short duration.   In 1588, having failed to induce the Parlement to rescind the decree against the Mysteries, the Confrères de la Passion,. more alive to the value of money than to the supposed dangers of the drama, let the Hôtel de Bourgogne and their privilege to one of the provincial companies just referred to.

Distracted as they may have been by the civil war, now at its height, the populace of Paris did not entirely overlook the novelty introduced by the new players, and as order and prosperity were restored by Henri IV. it took vigorous root in that city.   No entertainment had a tithe of the popularity then acquired by the drama.   Nailed to posts in the streets,

the announcements of the Hôtel de Bourgogne were
quickly surrounded by little knots of citizens, and the
theatre was not unfrequently crowded to its utmost
capacity. The curtain usually rose at two o'clock, an
hour after the opening of the doors. In winter, perhaps,
the performance began a little sooner, so as to enable
the spectators who remained until the end to reach
their homes before the footpads took advantage of the
darkness of the streets after nightfall to ply their
calling. Sixty feet by eighteen in size, the *salle*
was unprovided with either tiers or seats, and the
ground was covered with a thin layer of rushes. Here
the bourgeoisie stood or reclined, cavaliers and dames
of high degree being accommodated in tiers close to
the stage. It is pleasant to be able to add that
the audience occasionally included the genial and
chivalrous King, who liked to see and to be seen by
his liege subjects, and who, with his comically-arched
eyebrows and merry eyes, his gaunt figure and pleasant
laugh, was not to be mistaken for anybody else. The
theatre was dimly lighted with oil-lamps, but the play
of the actors' countenances might be clearly seen as,
arrayed in costume not wholly dissimilar from that
of their own time, even in pieces founded upon ancient
history or legend, and moving in front of tapestry
curtains, they declaimed the sonorous alexandrines of
Garnier and the lively dialogue of Larivey. The leader

of the troupe, Valeran Lecomte, "le faisait admirer de tout le monde," the Abbé Marolles tells us. It might have been supposed that so volatile a people as the French would have preferred the gay to the grave, the lively to the severe. In point of fact, their very volatility, giving rise as it necessarily did to a passion for extremes, caused them to welcome tragedy and comedy with equal warmth. Both these exotics were now acclimatized to Paris—a circumstance which may be held to confer additional lustre on the too-short reign of Henri the Great.

Indeed, the success of the players was substantial enough to deprive them of the monopoly they had purchased. In the interests of commerce, it should be understood, the Parlement had long since decreed that the privileges accorded to *corps* and *communautés* should not have effect at the fairs periodically held on the outskirts of Paris. Availing themselves of this licence, a few provincial comedians set up a theatre in the Foire St. Germain, the most popular institution of its kind in the country. The players of the Hôtel de Bourgogne, supported by the Confrères de la Passion, appealed against this proceeding to the Lieutenant-Civil, who illegally suppressed the new spectacle. The irritation engendered by so arbitrary a step was not to be repressed. The next time the established actors appeared on the stage they were assailed with a

volley of missiles and objurgations. In order to calm
the populace, the authorities, after threatening with
corporal punishment any persons who might take
part in a disturbance at the theatre, allowed the
comédiens forains to continue their performances, under
condition that they should pay to the Maîtres of the
Hôtel de Bourgogne two *écus* a year. It is characteristic of the government of Henri IV. that while firmly
repressing disorder he should have done away with
its cause. The Confrères, on the pretence that this
concession to the itinerant players would diminish
the value of their property in the Rue Mauconseil,
petitioned the king to make their privilege absolute in Paris, as well as to sanction a revival of
the Mystery. His majesty, as might have been expected of him, good-naturedly assented; but the Parlement, still determined to assert its independence,
declined to register the royal *Lettres* on the subject
except in regard to secular pieces of an inoffensive
nature. By way of giving effect to this decision,
perhaps, it was ordered that no citizen should
let a place or building in the city for the representation of *la comédie*. Nevertheless, the Confrères and
their tenants were not to be saved from competition.
In the same year (1599) another successful country
troupe, headed by Mathieu Lefevre, known to his
audience as Laporte, and Marie Vernier, his wife,

the first actress of whom any record is preserved (it
is unnecessary to take the *jongleresses* of old into
account), appeared at the Foire Saint Germain.   Mde.
was in herself a host; and in a few months, on the
understanding that they should pay an *écu tournois*
to the Confrères for each performance, her husband
received permission to establish in the Hôtel d'Argent,
at the corner of the Rue de la Poterie, near the
Place de Grève, what was soon to be known as the
Théâtre du Marais.

The rival troupes were compelled to rely a good
deal upon old plays, for of the many dramatists who
sought to outvie the achievements of Garnier and
Larivey only one can be said to have justified his
ambition.   I refer to Antoine Montchrétien, a name
associated with a rather curious history.   The son of a
Huguenot apothecary at Falaise, he became an orphan
at an early age, was educated by wealthy friends,
and, though intended for the profession of arms, became
a man of letters in Paris.   For the Hôtel de Bourgogne
he wrote a *Sophonisbe*, *Les Lacènes*, and *David*, all of
which appeared there before 1600.   It is probable that
in keeping out of the army he was not actuated
by a want of courage.   On one occasion, far from
believing that discretion is the better part of valour,
he withstood a dangerous attack made upon him by
the Baron de Gourville and two bravos,—an attack

for which they were required to pay him 12,000 livres damages.   About this time he composed an *Aman, ou la Vanité,* and a *Hector.*   Encouraged by the applause bestowed upon him, he laid siege to and won a widow of good birth, who turned out to be so wealthy that he assumed the sounding name of Montchrétien de Vasteville.   Next, finding himself under suspicion of having killed a gentleman of Bayeux *en trahison,* he fled north of the Channel, but was soon afterwards permitted by Henri IV. to return.   In the interim, let us hope, it had been found that the accusation against him could not be sustained.   By a strange freak of fancy, the moneyed poet, while at work upon another tragedy, *L'Ecossaise,* would amuse himself at a forge in the depths of Orleans forest by making cutlery in steel, the whole of which was sold, or at least exposed for sale, at a shop in the Rue de la Harpe, Paris.   He subsequently identified himself with the Huguenots at La Rochelle, and was on the high road to other than literary fame when a party of royalist soldiers, surprising him in a hostelry at Tourvilles, near Falaise, incontinently shot him dead. His contributions to the stage are of no ordinary merit.   Following in the track of Garnier, he not unfrequently surpassed his model, especially in the management of choruses.   His *Ecossaise,* which turns upon the fate of Mary Queen of Scots, is dedicated, seemingly by permission, to the son of its star-crossed heroine—an incident quite unique in the history of literature.

The dearth of good tragedies and comedies induced the theatres to turn their attention to a dramatic plant of native growth, the farce. The Hôtel de Bourgogne soon found that by doing so it had struck upon a mine of wealth. The company there was to comprise a trio of versatile comedians—Henri Legrand, Robert Guérin, and Hugues Guéru. Brought up as bakers in the Faubourg Saint Laurent, they had deserted their master's shop to play in a tennis-court near the Estrapade (a machine invented in the days of François I. to prolong the tortures of Protestants at the stake), and were employed in the Rue Mauconseil to play serious characters. In this walk, which they respectively filled under the names of Belleville, Lafleur, and Fléchelles, their acting is said to have been deficient in neither earnestness nor weight. But it was not until they appeared in farce that their cleverness became fully manifest. Here they again changed their names, Legrand being known as Turlupin, Guérin as Gros-Guillaume, and Guéru as Gaultier-Garguille. The first usually played a roguish valet, the second a pedant, the third a supremely stupid old man. Turlupin, in addition to being of good presence, had *élan* in a very high degree, and

E 2

in the domain of broad comedy was held to be
unapproachable. Gros-Guillaume, as may be inferred
from his cognomen, was enormously fat, probably in
consequence of too pronounced a taste for the good
things of this life. He had a fund of rich humour,
with large black eyes and strangely mobile features.
He kept the audience in a continuous ripple of
laughter, even when, as was not unusually the case,
he suffered so acutely from an internal malady that
tears ran down his face. Gaultier-Garguille was
hardly less popular, though in a different way. Norman by birth, he could yet imitate the Gascon to
perfection, and was drily funny in all his farcical
characters. His success may have been favoured by
peculiarly thin and bandy legs, but few things gave
him greater pleasure than to hide this defect under the
robe—the stage robe—of a king. Most of the songs
and prologues attached to the farces were of his
composition. For the rest, he married a daughter of
Tabarin, the buffoon who disported himself on a
scaffold by the Pont Neuf to attract attention to the
remedies devised by the charlatan Mondor for all the
ills that flesh is heir to. It is impossible to think of
the Trois Farceurs without a kindly feeling; they
became staunch friends, were never so happy as in
appearing with each other, and opposed the introduction of an actress into the troupe upon the ground

that they all might fall in love with her.   Essentially
French, their farces, I conjecture, did not remain
wholly free from a foreign influence as time passed
on.   In or about 1601 a troupe of Italian players found
much favour in the eyes of the Court.   Henri IV., not
content with royally applauding them at Fontainebleau,
placed the Hôtel d'Argent at their disposal on particular days ; while Sully, as we learn from his own
Mémoires, constructed a theatre in his château at the
Arsénal in order that they might perform therein
before their majesties and himself.   It may not be
ungenerous to suppose that a satire of the day, in
which the following lines were addressed to the King—

> Sire, defaites vous de ces comédiens ;
> Vous aurez, malgré eux, assez de comédies.
> J'en sais qui feront mieux que ces Italiens
> Sans que vous coûte un sol leurs fâcheuses folies—

was at least prompted by native talent.   But native
talent did not disdain to take a leaf from the book
of the unwelcome visitors.   Except Gros-Guillaume,
who whitened his face with flour, the farceurs came
forward in masks, and Turlupin's costume bore a close
resemblance to that of Brighella.   It is significant in
the same way that three stock personages should have
been added to the theatrical repertory under the
names of Le Docteur Boniface, Périne, and Dame
Gigogne.   The second and third of these were the

exclusive property of the Théâtre du Marais, where,
in default of such players as Turlupin and his companions, farce proved less attractive than in the Rue
Mauconseil. In order to increase their advantage,
perhaps, the elder troupe introduced an author-comedian
from Toulouse, Jean Deslauriers, *alias* Bruscambille.
He was not allowed to return to the provinces, and at
least two collections of his " Fantaisies," comprising
" plusieurs Discours, Paradoxes, Harangues, and Prologues Facécieux," all drawn from " l'escarcelle de son
imagination," were printed during his lifetime. He
seems to have had more refinement than the Trois
Farceurs, but never attained so wide a popularity.

Inferior to their rivals in farce, the company at the
Théâtre du Marais drew ahead of them in tragedy and
comedy, thanks to the tact and industry of a writer
who had recently come to Paris, and who, if I do not
misinterpret his intentions, was seeking to effect nothing
less than a radical change in the character of the French
drama. Beginning with *Les Chastes et Loyales Amours
de Théagene et Chariclée*, brought out in 1601, Alexandre
Hardi threw off *currente calamo* a variety of pieces—
" tragedy, comedy, tragi - comedy, history, pastoral,
pastoral-comical, historical-pastoral, tragical-historical,
tragical-comical-historical-pastoral." Nothing is known
of the previous history of this remarkable man except
that he was born in Paris in 1560, received what in

those days was deemed a liberal education, and then went into the country as a strolling player. His movements are shrouded in profound obscurity, but there is good reason to believe that he spent months and even years at Madrid. Deriding the laws submitted to by French dramatists, Lope de Vega, aided by a facility of invention never equalled, had formed in that city a new school of dramatic art—a school to which the term "romantic" is rather loosely applied—in a succession of plays marked by ingenious complexity of intrigue, comparative truth of language, and almost every conceivable variety of striking incident. No translations of these works had yet been made in France, and it was not until 1604 that a troupe of Spanish players—two of whom, by the way, distinguished themselves by murdering a beautiful comrade for the sake of some jewels she wore—appeared in Paris. Now, Hardi was more or less a disciple of the non-classical drama from the moment he began to write. He put his trust in action rather than narration. He subordinated everything to dramatic effect. He imported comedy elements into the deepest tragedy. He liked to carry on his dialogue in speeches of only a few lines each. He disregarded the unities of place and time to a greater extent than his predecessors, now shifting the scene of a piece from Athens to western Europe, and anon causing a personage to pass from youth to

old age in the interval between two acts. His lovers
are made to embrace and kiss each other on the stage—
that is, to act precisely as lovers in real life might be
expected to act. Above all, as though to show that
such innovations were not of independent origin, the
majority of his plays, while founded upon ancient
history or legend, are studded with details borrowed
from Spain. If so audacious a plagiarist had chanced
to pay a visit to London at this time, when the gifts of
Shakspere were beginning to find their highest and
most lasting expression, the *Merchant of Venice* and
Hamlet, with other pieces known to the patrons of the
Blackfriars and Globe Theatres, might have been transferred to the Paris stage as original French work. In
his enthusiasm for the new system, however, Hardi
did not entirely abandon the old, and his *théâtre* was
less an imitation of the first than an attempt to blend
it with the second. That he exposed the stability of
the established drama to a crucial test there can be no
doubt. His writings brought fame and fortune to the
theatre in the Rue de la Poterie. He was saluted on
nearly all hands as a " Maître." Valeran Lecomte found
it convenient to transfer his services from the Hôtel de
Bourgogne to the other playhouse, where, in conjunction
with Marie Vernier, he increased his already high reputation. In truth, the new dramatist united a keen
sense of stage effect to grandiloquence of language, and

the audience was too much excited by his forcible " situations " to observe that he fell below Garnier and Montchrétien in imagination, dignity, and grace.   His masterpiece, perhaps, was *Mariamne*, the first of many adapt-
ations to theatrical purposes of the narrative in Josephus.
It appeared soon after the assassination of Henri IV., an
event which Billard de Courgenay, a poetaster of the
day, thought fit to commemorate in a tragedy having
that idolized monarch for its hero, and Louis XIII., at
present a mere child, as one of its speaking personages.
From this time Hardi exhibits a change for the worse.
Beset by poverty, aware that the public liked novelty
for its own sake, and finding that his name—for
the names of authors were now given in the bills—
ensured success to anything he wrote, however trivial
it might be, he took less and less pains with his work.
He deliberately merged the poet and the artist in the
playwright.   He took incidents from various sources,
huddled them together with no higher object than that
of carrying away his audience, and tricked them off in
verse written with truly fatal facility.   Most of his later
pieces are said to have been composed and represented
in a week.   " Heaven be praised," he would exclaim,
" I can subordinate all loftier aspirations to the demands
of my trade."   By doing so, it seems, he put money
into his purse ; but the liberal theory he had embraced was not unnaturally brought into disrepute,

at least with some of the more cultivated playgoers,
by its association with such dross as that which now
emanated from his pen.

Before long a deep reaction against this theory became
apparent. Four poets not unworthy of the name arose
almost simultaneously at the Hôtel de Bourgogne in
support of the pre-Hardian drama. First in order of
time was Théophile Viaud, the son of an advocate
practising at Bordeaux. In 1617, at the age of twenty-
six, he threw off, among various kinds of poetry, a
Pirame et Thisbé, which not undeservedly took the town
by storm. His connexion with the stage, however,
ended as soon as it began. He courted notoriety by
means of licentious verse, and for several months was an
exile from the country of his birth. Even this stroke of
authority had little or no effect upon his future conduct.
He was at least concerned in the authorship of the
Parnasse Satirique; and the Parliament, deeming him
guilty of *lèze majesté Divine*, sentenced him to be burnt
alive in the Place de Grève. The culprit discreetly
sought safety in flight, but was arrested in Picardy,
immured in Ravaillac's dungeon at the Conciergerie, and
told to prepare for the worst. The sentence upon him
had meanwhile been executed in effigy. Happily, he
was not to share the fate of the bundle of rags made up
to resemble him. Powerful influence being exerted in
his favour, the Parliament, after a cruelly protracted

deliberation, contented itself with sending him for a
season into exile. In the short time yet left to him—
for he died young—he amply justified this leniency; he
forswore his evil ways, made his peace with the Church,
and generally set a good example to his fellow-men.
He also ceased to write for the theatre, although an
unrepresented tragedy, by name *Pasiphae*, has been
placed to his credit. But the cause he had espoused
did not suffer from want of adherents. Ill-educated in
early life, yet no stranger to Tasso's *Aminta* and
Guarini's *Pastor Fido*, the Marquis de Racan, in *Les
Bergeries, ou Arthénice*, gave the world a pastoral in
which comparative regularity is allied to refinement,
elegance, and tenderness. Handsome Jean Gombaud,
who had gained a footing at the court of Marie de
Médicis by means of some verses on the death of
her husband, became a rival of Racan on his own
ground, and may well have succeeded in making him
uneasy for his laurels. Then a bard of the mature age
of sixteen, Jean Mairet, came foward with *Chriséide et
Armand*, a tragi-comedy, and *La Silvie*, a tragi-comedy-
pastoral. Born at Besançon, whither his grandfather,
a descendant of an old Roman Catholic family in
Westphalia, had found it convenient at the opening of
the Reformation to retire, he had lost his parents by the
plague, and was now a boarder at the Collége des
Grassins, Rue des Amandiers, Paris. It did not require

exceptional sagacity to perceive that the author of *La Silvie* would make a name for himself in the arena of letters.

Fortunately for the classicists, the school they warred against was soon to lose its principal support. In 1623, placed above want by the proceeds of his work, " old Hardi," as he had come to be called, bade an informal farewell to the theatre, his last production being a pastoral entitled *Le Triomphe d'Amour.* By this time, according to his own confession, he had put together no fewer than six hundred plays (tradition says eight hundred), forty-one of which have come down to us. Hitherto, perhaps, his literary importance has not been adequately recognized. He was persistently decried by those who rejected his theory ; and the world at large, reluctant to believe that one who wrote so much could have written well, has adopted their estimate without taking the trouble to ascertain how far it is borne out by facts. His work in general is supposed to be loosely ordered, to abound in vulgar claptrap to the absolute exclusion of poetry, and to bear about the same relation to the best examples of the modern European drama as a gaudily-coloured print of a bold buccaneer or evil-minded earl does to a picture by Raphael or Leonardo. This impression, I think, would be appreciably modified if he were studied at first-hand. Bombastic and slovenly he unquestionably was ; but in most of his pieces, especially those which

appeared before his necessities induced him to write
against time, there are many fine thoughts finely
expressed, many bursts of genuine passion, many firmly-
drawn characters, many signs of a practical tact which
any dramatist would give much to possess. At his best,
however, he was not the man to attain the end he
obviously proposed to himself. Nature had denied to
him the genius necessary to accomplish in France a
revolution in dramatic art such as England and Spain
had recently witnessed. His *théâtre*, though admirably
adapted to its purpose, was not of a kind to kindle
enthusiasm among the literati, to uproot settled prepos-
sessions in favour of a different sort of art, to become
a law to fellow-workers in the same field. In truth,
only one of his innovations can be said to have survived
him. Down to his time the honour of having a play
represented was deemed sufficient compensation to the
dramatist. Hardi received three *écus* for each of his
pieces; and but few of his successors failed to bear in
mind the precedent thus established.

Hardi's disappearance was followed by a sharp
contest for supremacy between the classical and the
romantic. Racan and Gombaud, like Théophile,
contented themselves with a single contribution to the
stage; but Mairet, whose success had opened to him
the doors of the most exclusive Parisian society, continued to labour with all the ardour of youth, and

was induced by the Cardinal de la Valette and the
Comte de Carmail to pay more attention to the unities
of place and time. On the other hand, three authors
of no inconsiderable merit threw the weight of their
influence into the opposite scale. Balthasar Baro,
formerly secretary to the Marquis d'Urfé, whose *Astrée*
he had recently completed, brought forth a *poëme-
heroïque* entitled *Celinde*, the personages of which
are made to play a little tragedy on the story of
Judith and Holofernes. Hardly less precocious than
the author of *La Silvie*, Jean Rotrou, the youngest
representative of one of the most ancient families at
Dreux, was the next to enter the lists. In 1628, at
the age of nineteen, he had the unquestionable pleasure
of seeing two pieces of his composition—*L'Hypocon-
driaque* and *La Bague de l'Oubli*—performed at the
Hôtel de Bourgogne with good success. Based more
or less on the practice of Hardi, they yet presented
evidence of original thought, if not of a natural talent
for the drama. Rotrou soon came to hold important
offices in his native town, but all the leisure they left
him was spent in Paris, where a rare nobility of
personal character endeared him to even his rivals.
Conspicuous among the latter was Georges de Scudéri,
a dashing officer of the French Guards. Descended
from a good old Provençal family, he was born at
Havre de Grâce in 1601, entered the army in his teens,

and had already acquired some notoriety in the capital
as a fine gentleman with a mania for collecting
paintings, coins, and tulips. Madeleine de Scudéri,
his sister, had meanwhile made their name famous by
writing short pieces of poetry; indeed, she was known
as the "modern Sappho" and the "tenth muse."
Pressed for money—for his patrimony and his pay
were not sufficient to gratify the expensive tastes he
had contracted—Georges turned his attention to the
stage. His first essay was *Ligdamon et Lidias*, a
tragi-comedy. In the preface thereto he poses before
his readers as one writing simply for his own diversion.
"The printers and the players," he says, "will bear
witness that I have not sold what I might have expected them to buy." In all probability he had given
away the piece on the understanding that it should be
acted and otherwise published. He certainly had no
intention to go on writing for nothing, as may be
inferred from the fact that, in order to keep his head
above-water, he prevented his sister, over whom he
had a strong influence, from accepting three advan-
tageous offers of marriage, compelled her to keep
her study for a prescribed number of hours every day,
and spent upon himself a considerable portion of the
fruits of her partly-enforced industry. Notwithstanding
many defects, *Ligdamon et Lidias*, in which the example
of Hardi is frequently followed, and to which, I suspect,

Madeleine contributed more than one graceful line, was sufficiently well received to make the players look for other pieces from the Sieur de Scudéri. On the same side was Jean de Schélandre, whose only surviving play, *Tyre et Sidon*, had been printed long previously. The classicists, alive to the formidable nature of the opposition arrayed against them, manifested increased vigour ; and Mairet, after distinguishing himself in the suite of the Duc de Montmorenci in the war against the Huguenots, brought out a *Sophonisbe* similar in structure and treatment to Trissino's very " regular " tragedy on that subject.

In now became evident that the elder of the two schools was crushing its rival. Nearly every writer of tragedy evinced an increasing tendency to construct it in conformity with the "Aristotelian" precepts, to give it the most perfect symmetry of form, and generally to infuse into it a serene and lofty dignity. Except as regards theatrical effect, the practical value of which had been too conclusively shown to be overlooked, the theory and practice of Hardi were gradually abandoned. In comedy the dramatist enjoyed a little more freedom, but even here it was thought necessary to observe a code of laws not always favourable to the display of humour and natural truth. Nor will this strange contraction of the scope and power of the drama be a matter of surprise if the

dominant spirit of the age is borne in mind. The
reaction towards culture which set in at the end of the
civil wars had not been productive of unmixed benefit.
It had given rise to extremely artificial tastes among
the leaders of Parisian society. The graceful triflings of
a Voiture were accepted as poetry, the unreal shepherds
and shepherdesses of *Astrée* as the quintessence of
literary beauty. Moreover, it was the fashion to affect
extreme delicacy of thought, sentiment, and expression. Introduced into France by Antonio Perez, the
fallen Secretary of State to Charles V. and Philip II.,
and afterwards by Marini, who had cultivated it in
Italy, the *estilo* invented at Cordova by Gongora—a
style akin to the euphuism ridiculed by Ben Jonson
in *Cynthia's Revels*—was finding a swarm of imitators.
Even the language of passion and the formulæ of
politeness became a tissue of hyperbole, of trope and
figure, of extravagant metaphor and emblem. In vain
did Malherbe and Balzac stand up for French pure
and simple; intelligible speech was regarded as a
distinctive mark of ill-breeding. .It was the age of
the *précieuses*—the age when elegant ladies, holding
their receptions in bed, with their guests grouped about
them, rapturously listened to conversation in which,
as La Bruyère puts it, "a flight of rhetoric not very
easy to understand was followed by something more
obscure, to be outdone in its turn by increasingly

incomprehensible enigma after enigma, each greeted
with prolonged applause." And in no quarter did
this transcendentalism flourish more than at the hôtel
(situated under the shadow of the Louvre) of the
self-respecting Marquise de Rambouillet, the heroine
of Racan's *Bergeries*. In the eyes of such over-refined
society, of course, the romanesque drama found little
or no favour. It was decried as bizarre, inartistic,
fit only for the common people. If, notwithstanding
her decadence as a nation, Spain had begun to exert
a moral and social influence in France—and an inclination in Paris to dress and swear in the. most
approved Castilian fashion leaves no doubt upon the
point—the name of Lope de Vega was treated as
synonymous with theatrical barbarism. The system
he derided, with its studied regularity of form and
elaborate declamation, was accounted a triumph of
good taste by the occupants of the *loges* at the Hôtel
de Bourgogne. In all probability they would have been
more impressed by a hand-made cascade than a moun-
tain-torrent, by a finely laid out garden than the rugged
grandeur of Swiss or Highland scenery. Moving
amongst the best company of the capital, Rotrou and
other poets were insensibly induced to modify or lay
aside the principles on which they had started, and
the school of Jodelle slowly overbore its once powerful
antagonist. Nevertheless, its supremacy was still far

from being assured. It presented but few examples of imperishable merit, and was emasculated by an inclination among the poets to adopt the style of the *précieuses*. Happily for its interests, though hardly so for those of dramatic art, there was now to arise a writer who brought himself to accept its precepts, who aimed at vigour rather than refinement in language, and who soon developed a genius rare enough to give him almost undisputed authority as a model for imitation.

CHAPTER III.

1629—1637.

Not the least meritorious public servant in France at the beginning of the seventeenth century was M. Corneille, Avocat du Roi à la Table de Marbre de Normandie, Maître Particulier des Eaux et Forêts in the Vicomté of Rouen, &c. In the second of these capacities, it appears, he often found himself exposed to considerable danger. In the event of famine visiting the northern province—a far from unusual occurrence—the people would set all authority at defiance, hang the guardians of the peace, and wreck any house from which they could obtain the means of alleviating their misery. M. Corneille acted in such emergencies with vigour and decision, especially when, in 1612, a swarm of breadless peasants laid waste the forest of Roumaire and the adjoining country. His home was in the Rue de la Pie at Rouen; and here, on the 6th June 1606, his wife, *née* Marthe Le Pesant de Boisguilbert, gave birth to one of the greatest of French poets, Pierre Corneille.

The future dramatist grew from infancy to manhood in the city which had witnessed the martyrdom of

Jeanne Darc—a little network of crooked and narrow streets, lined with wooden houses, but dignified by the venerable cathedral erected in their midst. He was educated with the Jesuits, who ardently wished him to become one of themselves. In this they were to be disappointed, although from the first he was of a devotional and even austere turn of mind. There is still preserved a prize which he gained in his thirteenth year—a folio volume stamped in gold with the arms of the Lieutenant-Général au Gouvernement de Normandie, who had to defray the cost of such presentations. His college days over, Pierre entered upon the study of the law, and at the end of 1627, four years before the regular time, was authorized by Lettres Patentes, obtained by the influence of his father, to act as an advocate.

But the bar was not to number him amongst its willing votaries, notwithstanding the fact that he soon became Avocat du Roi à la Table de Marbre and Premier-Avocat à l'Amirauté de Rouen. He was neither quick-witted nor ready of speech; and at length, obeying an imperious instinct, he turned his thoughts to poetry. His earliest verses, it is said, took the form of tributes to a pretty neighbour, Madame Dupont. Soon afterwards, by a mere accident, this taste came to be enlisted in the service of the theatre. Mdlle. Milet, residing with her parents in the Rue des Juifs, No. 15, was introduced by her accepted lover to the young advocate-poet, to whom she promptly transferred her affections, but who, it would appear, did not regard her with equal favour. Now, a troupe of strolling players, headed by one Mondori, were in the habit of entertaining the citizens of Rouen with a selection from Hardi's plays. For this troupe Corneille wrote a comedy entitled *Mélite, ou les Fausses Lettres,* and having for its heroine the fickle Mdlle. Milet herself.

The stroller chief was so well pleased with the piece that he took it to Paris, and in 1629 it was produced at the Théâtre du Marais. In more than one respect it must have been a surprise to the audience. By no means a great work, it yet showed a disposition to rely upon character instead of caricature, upon natural, spirited dialogue instead of stupid jest. Corneille afterwards said that in writing it he had only a little common sense and the example of Hardi to guide him; he might have surely said that he was indebted to the former far more than to the latter. In the result, the playgoers did not know whether they should applaud or be silent, and *Mélite* was at first deemed unsuccessful. But as time went on it gradually won favour. The first three performances, we are told, brought less money than the most unprofitable of those given later in the same winter.

Mondori did not go back to the country. He became

the principal actor at the Théâtre du Marais, now transferred from the Hôtel d'Argent to ·a tennis-court in
the Vieille Rue du Temple. The company there had
undergone many changes since its formation. Mathieu
Lefevre, Marie Vernier, Valeran Lecomte, Dame Gigogne,
and Docteur Boniface, with others, had disappeared.
Their places were occupied by Jodelet, d'Orgemont,
Belle Ombre, Beau Soleil, Beau Séjour, Belle Fleur,
L'Epi, Le Noir, La France (or Jacquemin) Judot, and
Mdlle. Le Noir. The majority of these names, it need
hardly be said, were assumed. Jodelet (Julian Goffrin),
who had been many years on the stage, possessed a
fund of rich, broad humour. His face was so comic that
he had only to show himself on the stage to evoke roars
of laughter, which were redoubled by the interrogative
look of helpless amazement he directed at the laughers.
In him, no doubt, the three farceurs at the Hôtel de
Bourgogne had a formidable rival. Of his comrades no
record is preserved, but the estimation in which they
were held as à body justifies us in concluding that their
talents were far above mediocrity.

Increased success fell to the lot of the company under
its new leadership. Mondori at once showed that as
a tragic actor he had no comparison to fear. "This
illustrious man," says Tristan, "owed no triumph to
accident' or a want of intelligence in his audience.
Merit such as his would have been rewarded in ancient

times with crowns and statues. No man ever appeared
on the stage with more honour. He there showed
himself to be penetrated with a sense of the grandeur
of the passions he represented. Endowed with the
faculty of self-abandonment, he imprinted upon the
mind the sentiments he expressed. His change of
countenance seemed to come from the movements of
his heart. His elocution and action, too, were excellent." And the gifts of attainments here spoken of
were allied to physical advantages—a symmetrical
figure, majestic bearing, and fine features. It is to
the credit of his good sense that in playing a hero
of antiquity he never wore a peruke, although other
actors still clung to such anachronisms. Clever at
impromptu speaking, he became the "orator" of the
troupe—the person whose duty it was to make announcements to the audience. In comedy he yielded
the palm to Gandolin, a youth whom he had taken from
his provincial troupe—now disbanded—to strengthen the
Marais company. There exists a portrait of the new-
comer, with the following lines subjoined :—

> Gandolin, par sa rhétorique
> Nous fait la rate épanouir,
> Et pour n'avoir plus la colique
> Il faut non seulement l'ouïr.
> Quelque fables qu'il nous raconte
> Elles ont un si bel effet,
> Que chacun y trouve son compte
> Et s'en retourne satisfait.

It would seem that to his talents for comedy in general Gandolin united a special aptitude as Harlequin.

The competition between the two theatres was evidently very keen. Eight plays by the chief dramatists of the day were given in rapid succession. Mairet wrote *Antoine et Cléopatre* and *Soliman :* Rotrou was responsible for *Cléagénor et Doristée, Les Occasions Perdues, L'Heureuse Constance, Les Menechmes* (a close imitation of the Roman comedy), and *Hercule Mourant.* Hastily written, these pieces, with the exception of the last (Rotrou's first essay in tragedy), will not repay perusal. In *Soliman,* by the way, Mairet softens the character of Roxelane by representing her as animated chiefly by the desire to save her son from the fate which must overtake him if Mustapha should gain the throne. Nor were the actors content to rely exclusively upon established writers. Manuscripts which had been treated with indifference were eagerly read. By procuring a letter of introduction from a person of consideration, a young and unknown dramatist might be sure that his hopes would soon be realized, at least as far as the production of his play was concerned. In the result, among others, two of the literary toilers of Paris gained a hearing. One, De Rayssiguier, a Languedocian, had attached himself to the Duc de Montmorenci, and, probably on account of that circumstance, had been imprisoned for some months by Cardinal

Richelieu. On obtaining his release he came to Paris, partly to try his fortunes with the pen, but chiefly in the hope of assuring his future by marriage with a well-to-do lady. Now he is pouring out his soul to a Caliste, now to a Silvie, now to an Olinde. Both as a dramatist and fortune-hunter, however, he completely failed, and his last days seem to have been passed in extreme poverty. Duryer, the other new dramatist, had but little less reason to exclaim against fate. He began life, it is true, under favourable auspices. He belonged to a noble family, and through their influence had obtained the honourable but far from lucrative post of *secrétaire du roi.* In an evil hour, as would-be-wise De Rayssiguier would have put it, he married a portionless girl, who presented him with seven children in about as many years. His noble family, disapproving of the match, entirely discarded him; and at length, reduced to want, he sold his office for a mere song, strove to earn a livelihood for himself and those dependent upon him by translating for booksellers, and turned his attention to the theatre. Ill-provided with money, he resided, not in Paris itself, but at a little village a mile or two away. Here, one bright summer afternoon, he was visited by Vigneul de Marville and one or two friends. "He received us," writes the annalist, "with delight, spoke to us of his plans for the future, and showed us his

works. It touched us to find that, unashamed of the
poverty he was in, he wished to give us a collation.
We sat down under a tree ; a cloth was spread out
on the grass, and while his wife brought us some
milk he procured some cherries, fresh water, and brown
bread. The repast seemed to us very good, but we
could not bid the excellent fellow adieu without being
moved to see him so ill-treated by fortune." Better
days, however, were in store for the struggling author,
at this time only in his twenty-seventh year. His
first play, a tragi-comedy called *Argénis et Poliarque,*
suggested by the *Argénis* of Barclay, was cordially
received, and the Duc de Vendôme made him his
secretary.

In the autumn of 1632, a company of provincial
actors, duly observant of the new life infused into the
drama, set up a third theatre in the Rue Michel-le-
Comte, in the Jeu de Paume de la Fontaine. For a
time it seemed that the enterprise would succeed ;
neither the Hôtel de Bourgogne nor the Théâtre du
Marais interfered with them, and the Lieutenant Civil
licensed them to play for at least two years. The
people in the neighbourhood, however, promptly drew
up a petition to the Parlement against the project.
They urged that as the Rue Michel-le-Comte, which
consisted of twenty-four *maisons à portes-cochères,* was
extremely narrow, the inhabitants—mostly persons of

quality or officers of the Cours Supérieures—would
be subjected to considerable inconvenience by the
assemblage of playgoers' coaches. The thoroughfare, in
fact, would be hopelessly blocked, and unless the people
living there wished to be plundered by lackeys and
footpads they would have to wait until the performance
finished before they could enter their houses. In the
following March, the Parlement, mindful of the social
importance of the petitioners, decreed that no piece
should be represented in the Jeu de Paume aforesaid
until further orders,—and the *arrêt* was not permitted
to become a dead letter. Not long afterwards, according
to the *Gazette*—a paper just started by Le Docteur
Renaudot in order to amuse his patients, and remarkable
as being the first periodical publication ever issued in
France—another troupe proposed to establish themselves
in the Faubourg St. Germain, but without effect.

Corneille, to whom this activity in the theatrical
world was in a great measure due, produced at this time
a tragi-comedy entitled *Clitandre*. Here, as in his first
piece, he seemed as anxious to astonish as to interest his
audience, though in a very different way. " During a
journey which I made to Paris," he writes, " I perceived
that *Mélite* was not in conformity with the time-rule—
the only rule then known." M. Corneille was evidently
unacquainted with more than one famous play. " I
heard, too, that my fellow-dramatists censured it as

possessing too little effect, and the style as too familiar. In order to justify myself, and to show that this sort of play might be distinguished by true dramatic beauty, I undertook, in a spirit of bravado, to write one which should be in accordance with the twenty-four hours' regulation, full of incident, in a style more elevated, but generally worthless." In other words, he "wished to censure rather than comply with the tastes of the public." In the case of a rising dramatist such self-stultification is hardly credible, but the sincerity of Corneille is placed beyond doubt by the fact that *Clitandre*, much unlike *Mélite*, is overcrowded with incidents and inflated in expression. By the force of contrast, it would seem, the audience were driven to the conclusion that the author of *Mélite* was taking a wrong course, and that the sooner he returned to the path opened up by that comedy the better. The object with which *Clitandre* had been written, he tells us, "was completely attained."

Jealous of the honours already gained by the young Rouen lawyer, a hanger-on at the Palais Cardinal, the Abbé François le Métel de Boisrobert, proceeded to measure his strength against his in dramatic writing. Lettered Paris may well have been on the tip-toe of expectation as to the result. The Abbé was not only the inseparable companion of the all-powerful Richelieu, but had the reputation of being the most amusing talker

in the capital.   In his early life, during a visit to Rome,
his prowess in this respect commended him to the
notice of Pope Urban VIII., who besought him to enter
the Church.   The young man's parents had intended
him for the law, and his tastes, to say the very least of
it, did not incline him to the ecclesiastical state.   But
the prospect opened up to him by the personal good-
will of the Pope was too alluring to be resisted; he
promptly qualified himself for holy orders, and was
made a canon at Rouen.   If his Holiness chanced to
hear of the doings of his *protégé* he must have felt
rather ill at ease.   Nearly the whole of Boisrobert's time
was spent in Paris, where, thanks to remarkable gaiety
and humour, he was admitted to the choicest society.   At
the Palais Cardinal he quickly established a firm footing.
No festive gathering there was deemed complete without
him.   No one could more effectually make Richelieu
throw off the cares of state than this unctuous Abbé.
" Monseigneur," said a physician to the Cardinal, " we
do all we can for you, but our drugs are useless unless
you mix them with a dram or two of Boisrobert."
Richelieu was not wanting in gratitude ; the Abbé
received at his hands the titles of King's Almoner and
Councillor of State, letters of nobility, and, strange to
add, the Abbey of Châtillon-sur-Seine and the Priory
of Ferté-sur-Aube.   Boisrobert was now forty years of
age, but neither the process of time nor the nature of

his calling appears to have had the slightest effect upon
his mode of living.   He was always to be found at the
Palais Cardinal, the theatre, or the gaming-table.   He
never permitted his sacerdotal obligations to interfere
with his pleasures.   He once found a man dying in the
street from wounds received in a duel, and therefore in
urgent need of the consolations of religion.   But the
lively Boisrobert was on the way to a fashionable
gathering ; so, briefly enjoining the victim to " think of
God and say his Bénédicité," he hurried on.   In a few
short intervals of solitude he composed a tragi-comedy
on the story of Pirandre and Lisimène ; and the result,
if not equal to his own expectations, was such as to
encourage him to take up the pen again.

Another novelty, the *Comédie des Comédiens*, by one
Gougenot, is of more interest to us than it may have
been to old Paris.   In the first two acts, which are
written in prose, the personages are some of the players
of the Hôtel de Bourgogne themselves—Bellerose, Le
Capitaine Matamore, Gaultier-Garguille, Gros-Guillaume, Turlupin, Boniface, Mdlle. Valliot, Mdlle.
Beaupré, Mdlle. Beauchâteau, Madame Bellerose,
Madame Gaultier, and Madame Lafleur. Bellerose,
whose real name was Pierre le Messier, had joined
the troupe in 1629, and was now recognized as its chief.
He excelled in both tragedy and comedy, though
reproached by more than one of his contemporaries

with an affected and colourless style. He displayed
ease, grace, and at times very considerable power.
Madame Beaupré's name is remembered in connexion
with a lament that the good old days when a piece
could be procured at short notice for three *écus* had come
to an end with the advent of Corneille; but of the
other players introduced in *La Comédie des Comédiens*,
the Trois Farceurs excepted, little or nothing is known.
It must be pointed out that two members of the troupe
as at present constituted, Alizon and Montfleuri, are
not mentioned in this piece. The former had closely associated his name with nurse characters, which
he invariably played under a mask. Montfleuri, by
birth a gentleman, had been educated for the army,
had served the Duc de Guise as page, and might have
had many opportunities of distinguishing himself in the
service of the State if a passion for the stage had not
led him to become a tragic actor. In parts made up of
" transports and bursts of rage " he seems to have been
extremely effective—nay, was declared on good authority to be inimitable. But to return for a moment to
Gougenot's piece. It represents the players preparing
themselves for the performance of a tragi-comedy,
which occupies the last three acts.

Three comedies by Corneille—*La Veuve, La Galérie
du Palais*, and *La Suivante* — here arrest our attention. The first, though somewhat weak, won high

praise, especially from Scudéri and Mairet. " Le soleil," exclaimed the former, " est levé ; retirez-vous
étoiles ! " It is worthy of note that the action of *La
Veuve* is spread over no less than four days. " I have
sought," the author writes in effect, " to find a mean
between the severity of the rules and the liberty which
is only too common on the French stage ; the first is
rarely capable of *beaux effets.*" By *La Galérie du Palais*
a much-needed reform was accomplished. Many young
and sprightly women now graced the boards, and
Corneille, having need of a servant in the piece, substi-
tuted for the unlovely nurse a sort of soubrette. The
change was hailed by all thinking persons as one for the
better, and before long the obnoxious character became
a thing of the past. How Alizon bore the loss of his
favourite part we are not told. The title of the piece
was hardly well chosen, as it referred to only the first
act. In that act, by the way, we find a graphic sketch
of the Galérie in question, one of the favourite resorts
of idlers, foreigners, and lovers. *La Suivante*, while
pleasantly written, is disfigured by more than one grave
defect. The whole of the plot is made to turn upon a
character in itself not very strong—that of a rather
commonplace soubrette. In his eagerness to reintroduce
this character, in fact, Corneille temporarily lost sight of
an important principle of dramatic effect. Moreover,
he permitted himself to fall into injurious affectation.

VOL. I.   G

The five acts into which the piece is divided are of
exactly the same length, and in one scene the characters
speak only one line at a time. *La Suivante*, if not
in accordance with all the unities, certainly manifested
an unfortunate regard for regularity of form.

The Hôtel de Bourgogne, the theatre in which these
pieces were produced, was now to lose the three farceurs
who had so long upheld its fortunes. Gros-Guillaume,
it would appear, had the hardihood to caricature on the
stage some exceedingly unpopular magistrates. The
player paid dearly for the hilarious applause drawn down
by the performance; he was arrested behind the scenes,
hurried into a coach, and conveyed to the Conciergerie.
This measure had a far more serious result than even the
offended magistrates could have wished. The loss of his
liberty, joined to painful misgivings as to the results of
his imprudence, preyed so much on the prisoner's mind
that he died. Gaultier-Garguille and Turlupin took their
loss to heart. It is hardly too much to say that they
never held up their heads again. Nor will their grief
seem unnatural or excessive when it is remembered that
since youth they had been associated with Gros-Guillaume
on the stage, and had all along been united to him by
the ties of the closest friendship. Far advanced in
years, they were unable to withstand so heavy a blow,
and in less than a week after Gros-Guillaume died it
was found that his old comrades had both joined him

in the grave. In death, as in life, the three farceurs were to be inseparable.

The void thus caused in the theatre was filled up in a most unexpected way. Louis XIII. ordered six members of the Marais company—Jodelet, La France, Judot, Le Noir, L'Epi, and Mdlle. Le Noir—to transfer their services to the Hôtel de Bourgogne, in the prosperity of which he appears to have taken some interest. The first was still popular; but Bellerose, evidently anxious to make his company as strong as possible in comedy, engaged a certain Bertrand Harduin de St. Jacques. The new-comer, curiously enough, had had no experience of the stage. Educated for the medical profession, he had in some wild mood run away from home, and had since gained a precarious livelihood with a band of peripatetic quack doctors by expatiating in public upon the marvellous qualities of their nostrums. It was necessary that a person holding this office should have some wit and power of repartee, and the erstwhile medical student, if tradition may be trusted, amply met the requirement. Suddenly, by favour of Bellerose, he was transformed into a comedian at the Hôtel de Bourgogne, where, probably out of deference to the feelings of his family, who were well connected, he took the name of Guillot-Gorju. The manager's faith in him was abundantly justified; the confidence to face an audience was already his, and in a short time he so

far mastered the technicalities of the stage as to bring
into effective play a fine sense of humour. He proved
especially popular as *médecins ridicules*, in which he
would recite with equal volubility and correctness the
names of an infinity of drugs. But for the mask he
wore on the stage he would have been pronounced ugly,
although blessed with a pair of roguish black eyes. The
reinforced company, it may be added, first employed
their full strength in a representation of Scudéri's
Trompeur Puni, and the forced union decreed by the
King was hailed with obvious delight. Mondori, at
whose expense his rivals had gained in strength, must
have keenly felt the injustice with which he had been
treated, but his spirits did not sink under even such a
reverse as this. In the words of the *Gazette*, " ne
désespérant point du salut de sa petite république, il tâche
à reparer son débris, et ne fait pas moins espérer que
par le passé de son industrie."

The wind must have been tempered to the shorn
lamb, for immediately afterwards a goodly number of
new plays were ready for representation, and some of
them could not but have fallen to the lot of a man so
esteemed as he was in the double capacity of actor
and manager. Perhaps the most important of all was
Corneille's *Place Royale*, in many respects a clever play,
but now remembered chiefly by reason of an idle charge
brought against the author. M. Clavaret, an advocate of

Orleans, had abandoned the law for the drama, and by some unexplained means had just had a piece bearing the same name played before the King at Forges. No sooner did the second *Place Royale* appear than he accused Corneille—with whom, it appears, he was slightly acquainted—of writing it for no other purpose than to expose a rival to damaging comparisons. "Had you," he writes, " been able to rise superior to a wish to overshadow me you would have given your *Place Royale* another name. From the time you knew I was treating this subject you resolved to appropriate it, either to gratify your jealousy of me or the actors you serve. This, however, has not deprived me of the satisfaction which I could fairly expect, has not prevented the estimable persons who have flocked to the representations of my play from honouring it with some praise. Besides, it has been fortunate enough to delight the King more than any of the pieces lately represented before him." The accusation made in this letter is obviously groundless. Corneille had no reason to be afraid of Clavaret, and it is a significant circumstance that the *Place Royale* of the latter, although " elle eut la gloire et le bonheur de plaire au Roi," was never printed.

But we have tarried too long with the Sieur Clavaret and his imaginary grievance, especially as the illustrious statesman who now shaped the destinies of the country is about to cross our path. The character of Richelieu presents an almost unique combination of strength and weakness, of large ideas and petty foibles. In all the great tasks he undertook—in the extinction of the Huguenots as a political element, in the conversion of the old feudal confederacy into an absolute monarchy, and in the elevation of France in the scale of nations at the expense of what had long been the preponderating power in Europe—he triumphed by the sheer force of a vigorous intellect, sustained by high moral courage and unfaltering determination. His mind once made up, he went straight to his object, now eking out the lion's skin with the fox's, anon striking with a hand of iron at those who barred his way, and finally, as he is himself reported to have said, " covering up all with his red cassock." Surrounded by avowed or secret enemies, the more numerous and hopeful on account of the vacillation of the King, he lived in a state of constant peril from their machinations, but generally succeeded in keeping them at bay. Nor was this all ; the armour of the warrior could at times be seen through the robe of the Cardinal, and his formation of the Académie Française was largely due to an enlightened faith in the importance of learning. But the international fame he won as a statesman was not enough for Richelieu. Yielding to the impulses of a morbid self-esteem, he wished to shine in other ways. He affected to be

versed in Hebrew and Arabic. He posed at the Hôtel
de Rambouillet as a metaphysician by discussing theses
of love. Covetous of literary distinction, he composed
" beaux livres de devotion," and would have given much
to be the author of a good play. He was not even
exempt from purely personal vanity ; occasionally, in
order to set off the shapeliness of his figure to the best
advantage, he would present himself to the ladies of
his acquaintance—the more readily if Marion Delorme
happened to be among them—in the guise of a young
and seductive cavalier.

The Cardinal's taste for dramatic work now assumed
unexpected prominence. He formed a brigade of five
poets to assist him in writing a comedy. In the first
instance he had recourse to the unctuous Boisrobert,
who, it need hardly be stated, accepted the invitation
with alacrity. Next came Guillaume Colletet, an Avocat
au Parlement, but with a greater predilection for verse-
making than law. He was thrice married, the bride in
each case being a domestic servant. The third author,
Claude de L'Etoile, son of the annalist, was blessed with
creative fancy and a little fortune, and might have
made a name for himself if he had not frittered away
his time and energy in pleasure. His judgment was
held in high respect at the Palais Cardinal, although
he often discomposed his eminence by ridiculing the
supposed necessity of rhyme. The other poets bidden

to the proposed collaboration were Corneille and Rotrou, the former of whom, I suspect, owed the honour less to an appreciation of his excellence as a dramatist than to the fact that he had written some graceful lines of welcome to Richelieu and Louis XIII. when, in the previous year, they paid a formal visit to Rouen. The disgust of Scudéri and other writers on its being found that his eminence had ignored their claims was probably beyond expression. The brigade completed, it was arranged that their works should be played at the Palais Cardinal, in a salon set apart and fitted up for that purpose.

In receipt of a pension from Richelieu, whom they termed their maître, the Cinq Auteurs, as the newly-formed body was called, produced a comedy known as *Les Tuileries*. The groundwork was supplied by the Cardinal, and each of his poets, by arrangement among themselves, wrote a particular act. Colletet, moreover, took charge of the monologue, in which, speaking of the Tuileries garden, he said :

> La canne s'humecter de la bourbe de l'eau,
> D'une voix enrouée et d'un battement d'aile
> Animer le canard qui languit auprès d'elle.

Richelieu was so well pleased with these lines that he presented the author with fifty pistoles. " Understand," he said in doing so, " that this is only for them ; the King is not rich enough to permit of my paying for the rest." It was in reference to this incident that Colletet wrote :—

> Armand, qui pour six vers m'as donné six cents livres,
> Que ne puis-je, à ce prix, te vendre tous mes livres.

The Cardinal himself wrote the prologue, but at the last moment, perhaps seeing that he was ill at such numbers, he induced Chapelain, in consideration of a liberal gift, to stand forward as its author. Eventually, on the 16th of April, *Les Tuileries* was represented before the King and his Court, the Cinq Auteurs, who were so pointedly eulogised in the prologue that for a moment every eye must have been directed to them, occupying a form in the best part of the *salle*. How the piece was received we are not told, but that it fell short of even reasonable expectation can hardly be questioned.

The next piece worked out by the Cinq Auteurs was *L'Aveugle de Smyrne*. It had scarcely been completed when Corneille seceded from the brigade. The pride and exultation with which he entered upon his task at the Palais Cardinal had given place to very different feelings. Richelieu, as may be supposed, did not prove a genial collaborateur. He regarded the five poets as mere tools, and was not too solicitous, perhaps, to keep them unaware of the fact. It is true that he permitted them to criticise the suggestions he thought fit to offer. The prologue of *Les Tuileries*

being read to him, he recommended the substitution
of "barbotter dans" for "s'humecter de." Colletet
objected to the proposed alteration, and the same night
set forth in writing his reasons for doing so. His
eminence, while reading this document, received intelligence of another triumph of the French arms, and
was obsequiously told that nobody could resist him.
"That is not so," he said; "I find successful opponents
in Paris itself." In the result, the prologue was recited as it originally stood. But the Cardinal was
in no wise disposed to consider suggestions as to his
part of the work—namely, the plot. He probably
never dreamt that any of the poets would venture
upon such effrontery. Evidently blind to the extent
of the Cardinal's *amour propre*, and anxious that all
parts of the comedy should hang well together, Corneille made a trifling change in the groundwork of
the act intrusted to him (the third). His eminence's
resentment knew no bounds. He angrily told the
presumptuous poet that if he wished to remain at the
Palais Cardinal he must have more *esprit de suite*—in
other words, must submit to the will of his superior.
The condition was one which Corneille could not fulfil;
and presently, after finishing his share of the work on
L'Aveugle de Smyrne, he suddenly discovered that urgent
business required his presence at Rouen.

His servitude at the Palais Cardinal had not taken up

so much time as to prevent him from advancing his
individual fame, and before leaving Paris, unless I am
wrong in my chronology, he saw two more plays from
his hand brought out at the Hôtel de Bourgogne.   The
first was *Medée*, avowedly an imitation of Seneca's
tragedy on that subject.   Fontenelle asserts that
Corneille here attained the sublime   If he did so it was
in only one line—

Que vous reste-t-il contre tant d'ennemis ?   Moi !

which, it has been well said, " announced " the Corneille
of the future.   Be this as it may, the Latin dramatist
was adequately represented by his successor, and in some
respects—especially, perhaps, by the addition of the
episodes of Ægée and Pollux, the former being derived
from Euripides—was unquestionably improved upon.
" Pour donner à ce monarque," Corneille writes, " un
peu plus d'intérêt dans l'action, je le fais amoureux de
Créüse, qui lui préfere Jason ; et je porte ses ressentiments
à l'enlever, afin qu'en cette entreprise, demeurant
prisonnier de ceux qui la sauvent de ses mains, il ait
obligation à Medée de sa délivrance, et que la reconnais-
sance qu'il lui en doit l'engage plus fortement à sa
protection, et même à l'épouser."   The unity of place
is violated in *Medée*, certainly to the advantage of
probability.   *L'Illusion*, the second piece, was not to
sustain the fame achieved by Corneille's other comedies.
In both plot and character it is singularly bizarre, with

but slight charm of style. "If," writes Corneille's biographer, "I dare to say what I think of it, its failure was great." It is probable that he would not have thought or said as much if the dramatist himself had not described the piece as a "galanterie extravagante, unworthy of consideration."

Back again at Rouen, Corneille continued to act as an advocate, but gave his best thoughts to the study of dramatic art. The affront put upon him by the Cardinal must have rankled in his mind, and it did not require extraordinary sagacity to perceive that by writing a fine play he would take a dire revenge upon his eminence. By rare good fortune, he became acquainted at this time with a M. de Chalon, formerly secretary to Marie de Médicis, and now residing in retirement at Rouen. The old man's opinions as to stage matters were not to be despised; he had been a constant playgoer in Paris, and was well read in Spanish dramatic literature. "Monsieur Corneille," he once said, "your comedies, it must be admitted, are full of *esprit*. But permit me to say that the track you are pursuing is unworthy of your talents. By adhering to it you will acquire only an ephemeral reputation. In the Spanish drama there are subjects which, treated in our taste and by a mind such as yours, would produce great effect. The language is not a difficult one ; set about learning it, and you shall have all the assistance I can render." Corneille eagerly accepted the offer; and M. de Chalons, whom we may picture to ourselves as a genial old courtier, dressed in the Henri Quatre style, did not fail to keep his word.

By dint of earnest application to his Spanish studies Corneille found himself in what he must have regarded as a new world. Invariably free from the influence of the classical model, Lope de Vega, now on the point of death, had created a drama singularly rich in incident, shot through with many golden threads of poetry, and in complete harmony with the spirit of the nation to which he belonged. In the first of these qualities, as everybody knows, his work is particularly effective. It abounds in surprises, imbroglios, duels, assassinations, disguises, wild adventures, hairbreadth escapes, lovers' stratagems, midnight assignations, and sharp conflicts between antagonistic passions and interests. The actors who represented it were obliged to lay in a large store of masks, dark lanterns, sliding-panels, trap-doors, and rope-ladders. Nevertheless, it never assumes an ordinarily melodramatic aspect. In the most prosaic examples I am acquainted with there are many fine bursts of passion, many gleams of pure tenderness, many animated expressions of chivalric sentiment. Last, but not least, it has a distinctively national character. It always breathes, whatever the subject may be, the spirit of a typical Spaniard—a man fully contained within himself, devout to superstition, quick to resent injury, unostentatiously enthusiastic, intensely proud of the past greatness of his country, ever disposed to lend an ear to the story of romantic adventure, morbidly keen upon all points of personal honour. It is permissible to suppose that Lope's end was hastened by overwork, for we are credibly assured that in addition to his *Autos Sacramentales* he produced no fewer than a thousand plays. His work was now continued by Calderon, who did not equal him in fertility of resource, but surpassed him as a poet and artist. In one respect, it must be said, the Spanish drama was conspicuously weak. It manifested little or no appreciation of the importance of character. Its personages are endowed with no striking individuality, no fascinating idiosyncracy. This defect apart, the work of Lope and Calderon is of the first order, and was held in due reverence by the young advocate at Rouen from the moment he brought himself to understand it. But that reverence did not cause him to follow their example in setting the so-called laws of the Stagyrite at defiance; indeed, unlike Hardi, he was almost entirely weaned by a knowledge of Spanish plays from the principles—or, as he would now have put it, the want of principle—on which they were based.

Las Mocedades del Cid, a tragi-comedy by Guillen de Castro, the friend and rival of Lope, fixed itself more firmly in Corneille's mind than anything else. Nor

is this a matter of surprise. The name of the chief
character is alone sufficient to give a special interest to
the piece. Both history and romance, the latter especially, describe Roderigo Diaz de Bovar, usually called
the Cid, as the most prominent Spaniard of the heroic
period, as a pattern of knightly virtue and grace. His
valour was equalled only by his wisdom, generosity, and
forbearance. More than five centuries had passed away
since his death, but even now, at a time when mediæval
ideas and institutions seemed to belong to a more or
less remote past, the fame of his prowess exerted an
inspiring influence, not only in Spain, but throughout
western Europe. *Las Mocedades del Cid*, if it exhibited
him only on the threshold of his career, had the merit
of effectively dramatizing a passage of his early life
—his attachment to and marriage with the daughter
of a man whom he had slain in an unavoidable duel.
It is hardly necessary to state that Guillen de Castro
was not allowed to have exclusive possession of
such a story; Diamante, another popular dramatist,
took it in hand, and the great Lope himself, in his
Estrella de Sevilla, availed himself of similar materials
under fictitious names. The mere perusal of *Las Mocedades del Cid*, it would seem, was enough to induce
Corneille to essay his powers on the same subject. He
had a keen sympathy with the chivalric spirit, and
a dramatist with far less experience than he had

might have seen that the conflict between love and duty in the minds of the hero and heroine would, if impressively treated, take an audience by storm.   Before long he sat down to write *Le Cid*, striving to adapt the incidents to the requirements of the classical stage without losing their essential significance, and drawing from the old romances concerning Roderigo any detail that might add to the force of the picture.

While Corneille was at work upon this play the dramatic world in Paris showed abnormal activity. Novelty followed novelty at very brief intervals, and the brains of the players must have been almost turned by the number of speeches they had to learn.   Mairet, Rotrou, Scudéri, and Duryer frequently presented themselves in effect to the audience, but to comparatively little purpose.   From among half-a-dozen pieces by Rotrou, one only, *Les Sosies*, a free and somewhat piquant version of the Roman *Amphitryon*, was in any sense worthy of himself.   In sheer desperation, per-haps, the leaders of the two companies allowed several untried authors—Charles Beys, Calprenède, Isaac de Benserade, Desmarets, and Vion d'Alibrai—to have a hearing.   The first is now remembered simply because Louis XIII. commissioned him to write an epic in refer-ence to recent glories of the French arms, and because he was incarcerated for a short time in the Bastille on suspicion of lampooning the Government.   For the drama, it is clear, he had no special talents. The same remark may be applied to Calprenède—a more than usually irascible Gascon, who had arrived in Paris four years previously, become a cadet in the Régiment des Gardes, and ingratiated himself with the Queen by reason of some cleverness as a story-teller. His literary reputation, such as it was, depended almost exclusively upon a few heroic romances, in his own time the admiration of Paris in general and the Hôtel dè Rambouillet in particular. Of his notorious irascibility one instance may be given. Richelieu, being asked by him to pronounce an opinion on some of his plays, said he thought the lines " lâches." " Cadédis," he hotly exclaimed, clapping his hand upon his sword, " comment lâches ? Il n'y a jamais eu rien de lâche dans la maison de la Calprenède." His eminence did not deign to notice the thoughtless movement ; at all events the Gascon was not sent to cool his temper within the walls of the Bastille. Benserade belonged to a good family in Normandy, had been educated for the Church, and was now sowing his wild oats in the capital. A passion for Madame Bellerose led him in the first instance to write for the theatre, where he found himself completely out of his element. In no very long time he gave up all thoughts of the ecclesiastical state, and Richelieu, to whom he was related, thereupon accorded him a pension. Desmarets owed something to Richelieu—to wit, the posts of Contrôleur-Général de l'Extraordinaire des Guerres and Secrétaire-Général de la Marine du Levant. He had little or no taste for poetry, but the Cardinal induced him to make a few essays in the drama. The name of Alibrai reminds one of an unpleasant history. Brother of Madame de Sainctot, he might have done well in life, but soon became a notorious sot. " I have at least made myself famous in the cabarets," he once wrote, evidently in answer to a hint that he had not turned his gifts and opportunities to the best account. He certainly did not make himself famous as a dramatist.

The *Cid* was finished ; and Corneille, doubtless rich in hope, brought the manuscript to Paris. He had no choice but to leave it at the Hôtel de Bourgogne or wait awhile, as Mondori was drawing what proved a veritable prize in the dramatic lottery. I mean a tragedy called *Mariamne*, in many respects a remarkable work. The interest usually excited by the announcement of a new play was deepened in this case by the name of the author. François Tristan, now thirty-five years of age, was descended, if we may believe his own statement, from Peter the Hermit, and numbered among his ancestors the terrible grand-prévôt of Louis XI. In early life he found an influential friend in the Marquis de Verneuil, but soon afterwards he had ·

the misfortune to kill a garde-du-corps in a duel, and as the edicts against duelling had not fallen into abeyance he deemed it prudent to take refuge in England. His resources failing him, he set out for Spain, there to place himself under the protection of a relative, Don Juan de Velasquez. He crossed the Channel in a fishing-boat, and then started south on foot. In Poitou, coming to his last coin, he had recourse to Scévole de Sainte Marthe, who, struck by the refined manners of the tramp, received him as a favoured guest, made him give up the idea of going to Spain, and procured for him the post of secretary to the Marquis de Villars-Montpézat. The cloud which had so long hung over his prospects now passed away. Having accompanied the Marquis to Bordeaux, where the Court then happened to be, he was recognized by the Premier Gentilhomme de la Chambre, introduced to the King, and informally absolved from his offence. I next find him in Paris, nominally as Gentilhomme Ordinaire to Gaston d'Orléans, but devoting the whole of his time to gambling, gallantry, and tragedy-writing. It would seem that while in London he had been prevented by poverty, or an at best imperfect acquaintance with the English language, from paying many visits to the theatres there ; for no trace of English inspiration can be detected in anything he wrote. His first play, *Mariamne* (imitated from Calderon's *Tetrarca de Jerusalem*), proved extraordinarily successful, though not so much by reason of its own merits, conspicuous as in some respects they were, as of the power which marked Mondori's impersonation of Herod. According to Père Rapin, the audience were so deeply affected that they " dispersed with a pre-occupied air, an effect similar to that produced by the great Greek tragedies on the Athenians of old."

Corneille—proudly anxious, perhaps, to match himself against the new luminary while *Mariamne* was in the full tide of its popularity—had the *Cid* brought out as the year drew to a close. His confidence in its attractiveness was more than justified by the result. In regard to the plot, no doubt, the piece laboured under a serious disadvantage. The marriage of a woman to one at whose hands her father had met his death, albeit in an honour-able and necessary duel, must have been deemed a repulsive incident ; and the dramatist, instead of soft-ening that repulsiveness by spreading the action over a number of years, by which the healing influence of time might have been exercised, had unfortunately thought fit to construct the piece in compliance with the twenty-four hours rule. In the space of one day, therefore, Chimène rises to the full consciousness of her attachment to Rodrigue, discovers that he has shed her father's blood, passionately exhorts the King to punish him with death, and then consents to accept his hand in marriage.

Quodcunque ostendis mihi sic incredulus odi.

Lope de Vega, in his *Estrella de Sevilla*, had sent the heroine to a nunnery instead of the altar, and the French tragedy would have gained in pathos and moral beauty, to say nothing of probability, if it had ended in a similar manner.   But the defects of the *Cid* were far outweighed by its merits.   The double strife between love and duty was depicted with matchless force and sympathy.   The haughty spirit of the great vassals of mediæval Spain shone forth in all its energy.   Imaginative power, vivid portraiture of character, glowing energy of thought and expression,—nothing seemed wanting.   The effect of such a play at a time when the romantic spirit had not died away may well be conceived.   The audience were worked up to something like a frenzy of admiration, and the curtain fell upon by far the greatest triumph yet achieved on the French stage.

Nor was that triumph ephemeral.   *Le Cid* had what was then thought a long "run."   From one end of Paris to the other it formed a subject of discussion. Men who cared nothing for the theatre and its works were induced to share in the sorrows of Rodrigue and Chimène.   Parents taught their children to recite the most striking passages.   "Beau comme le *Cid*" became a familiar proverb.   Richelieu's niece, Madame de Combalet, to whom the play was dedicated, probably in return for some kindness she had shown the author at the Palais Cardinal, became a sort of heroine in public estimation.

The Court, it would seem, was not behind the town in
ardour of approbation.   The tragedy was represented
at the Louvre no fewer than three times.   Louis XIII.
and his Queen personally complimented the poet upon
his work.   M. Corneille *père* was granted letters of
nobility, nominally in recognition of the energy and
decision he had displayed in the discharge of his
official duties, but really, perhaps, because he was the
father of his son.   Nor was the reputation of the play
confined to France itself.   "The *Cid*, translated and
slightly altered by Joseph Rutter," tutor in the family
of Lord Dorset, was represented before the English
Court at Whitehall, and soon afterwards at the Cock-
pit in Drury Lane.   King Charles himself requested
the author to publish his translation or adaptation.
Madrid, too, brought the *Cid* upon her stage, but as at
the outset Corneille had frankly acknowledged that
he was indebted to the play of Guillen de Castro for
the essence of his plot—and this was the full extent
of his obligation—the Spaniards had reason to credit
him with honourable candour as well as dramatic genius.
I suspect, however, that the gravest Spaniards must
have given way to some merriment when they found
that he had laid the scene at Seville, a city which for
two centuries after the time in question remained in
the hands of the Moors.   Señor Corneille, certes, was
not well versed in Spanish history, however familiar

he might be with the old chronicles relating to his hero. In no very long time, it has to be added, the *Cid* was translated into every European language save Sclavonic and Turkish—an honour entirely without precedent.

Parisian society, of course, was not backward in doing homage to the man who had written the *Cid*. He was sought after, induced to enter the most exclusive *salons*, and half-suffocated with praise. The shadowy figure of the author of *Mélite* and *L'Illusion* is thrown into clear relief by the light now shed upon it. Those who had never seen him before must have gazed at him with mild astonishment on his first introduction among them. In all probability they had pictured him to themselves as a poet *à la* Scudéri—a cavalier of agreeable presence, courtly manners, and sprightly conversation. As it was, they found him to be of less than medium stature, dignified, indeed, by a fine intellectual countenance, but awkward in demeanour, inelegant in speech, slovenly in dress, and somewhat morose in temper. Vigneul-Marville took him at first to be ·a tradesman, while a lady of high degree declared that for his own sake he should never be heard except at the Hôtel de Bourgogne. In verses addressed to Pelisson he himself confesses that

> En matière d'amour je suis fort inégal ;
> J'en écris assez bien, et le fais assez mal ;
> J'ai la plume féconde et la bouche sterile,
> Bon galant au théâtre et fort mauvais en ville.

Et l'on peut rarement m' écouter sans ennui,
Que quand je me produis par la bouche d'autrui.

Nor was he at pains to correct his defects. "Je n'en
suis pas moins pour cela Pierre Corneille," he would say
to those who ventured to hint at them. The self-con-
tentment displayed in this remark frequently led him to
recite at the Hôtel de Rambouillet some of the best
scenes of his plays, although he must have seen that by
doing so he fatigued rather than gratified his hearers.
"Cadédis!" exclaimed Boisrobert, being reproached by
Corneille for having decried one of his earlier pieces at
the Hôtel de Bourgogne, "did I not applaud it when
you blurted it out in my presence?" But much was
forgiven the "grand Corneille," as from this time he
seems to have been called. In addition to having
written *Le Cid*, he was of good birth and education, and
some of the butterflies among whom he moved may
have been kind enough to suggest that the city in which
he had passed his early days was as yet without the pale
of Parisian influence. Had the tone aimed at in the
salons been less artificial than it was, the dramatist, I
think, would have appeared in them to better advantage.
Nothing like awkward constraint was apparent in his
demeanour when he found himself among chosen friends,
such as Rotrou and Pelisson. In a discussion with them
his ungainliness disappeared; his dark eyes acquired a
new force of expression, and a brusque humour peculiar

to himself gave point and pungency to what he said. It was easy at such times to perceive that to bluntness of manner and speech he united many high qualities— a humane disposition, a proudly independent spirit, a strong reverence for all that is great and good.

His claim to the honours bestowed upon him was to become a matter of fierce dispute. Except Rotrou, who at once recognized the merits of the play, every dramatist in the town endeavoured to turn the *Cid* into ridicule. It seemed as if they believed that unless the general verdict were reversed or modified they could never venture to put pen to paper again. For some time, however, they did not resort to open hostilities, probably fearing that Richelieu would espouse the cause of Corneille. Any misgivings on this point were soon cast to the four winds. The Cardinal manifested a rooted prejudice against the play. I have somewhere read that he offered Corneille a large sum to allow him to pass for its author, but that the dramatist, prizing fame above any other consideration, declined the bribe. I place no faith in this story, in the first place because such an imposture could not have been maintained, and in the second because the Cardinal was too good a judge of men not to know that such an overture would be abruptly rejected. Be that as it may, the *Cid* excited in his mind what Tallemant des Réaux calls a "jalousie enragée." He was "as profoundly

agitated by its success as if the Spaniards had appeared
before the walls of Paris." He was exasperated beyond
measure that so beautiful a piece should have been
composed without his assistance. Boisrobert, perceiving
as much, had a burlesque of the *Cid* played in the
theatre of the Palais Cardinal by a number of lackeys
and scullions. One line of this precious effusion has
·been preserved. Rodrigue, asked by his father whether
he has a heart, replies—

Je n'ai que du carreau.

This and similar pleasantries hugely diverted his
eminence; and the envious dramatists, connecting the
fact with the sudden withdrawal of Corneille from the
Palais Cardinal in the previous year, saw no reason
to stay their hands.

A paper war followed. Scudéri led off the attack
with a pamphlet designed to prove that the *Cid* violated
all the rules of dramatic composition; that its subject
was bad, its action ill-conducted, its versification con-
tinually faulty, and the little excellence it possessed
stolen. He was astonished, he said, that beauties so
fantastic as those of this play, which turned upon a
" méchant combat de l'amour et de l'honneur," should
impose upon the learned as well as the ignorant, upon
the Court as well as the masses. He hoped the
public would not condemn without consideration such
tragedies as *Sophonisbe*, *César*, *Cléopatre*, *Hercule*,

Mariamne, and *Cléomédon.* The second-named piece, it
should be remarked, was by Scudéri himself. Had
he wished to acknowledge in the directest manner that
the *Cid* eclipsed all those plays he could hardly have
been better advised. Corneille published a piece of
verse under the title of an *Excuse à Ariste,* ostensibly
declining a proposal to set words to a piece of music,
but really as a reply to his assailant. In this lucu-
bration, as though to emphasize his success, we are
pointedly told that he had brought out the *Cid* " sans
appui," owed nothing to " illustrious advice," and had
acquired renown by his own unaided exertions. Effective as his *Excuse* was as a retort, it can hardly be
deemed judicious, as it could not fail to still further
incense the Cardinal against him. Mairet more than
once entered the lists against the man whose *Veuve* he had
pointedly praised ; Claveret fed fat the ancient grudge
he bore the author of the *Place Royale ;* while an
anonymous scribbler, in a pamphlet called *L'Auteur du
Vrai Cid à son Traducteur Français,* makes Guillen de
Castro claim all the " renown " to which Corneille had
just referred. The pamphleteer obviously knew nothing
of *Las Mocedades del Cid,* and in all probability, like
the whole of the attacking party, would never have
heard of De Castro at all if Corneille had not avowed
the source of the plot. The other side did not lose
courage ; a cogent *Défense du Cid* appeared, and Balzac,

in a letter to Scudéri, espoused the cause of the persecuted author with equal skill and discernment. Corneille, however, derived most of his strength in the contest from the errors of his adversaries. In their virtuous impetuosity they applied to him the term "vile," classed the *Cid* with "vermisseaux," and declared that he had received letters of nobility on behalf of his father only to degrade them. The playgoers who applauded the piece—and their number was legion—must have resented this language as an insult to their own judgment, and have seen that such an outburst could not have been conceived in a spirit of unbiased criticism.

Richelieu, perceiving that the assailants of the play had gone too far, threw the gold wand into the arena; but his bitterness against Corneille, aggravated by the boasts in the *Excuse à Ariste*, led him to continue the crusade against the *Cid* in another form. He referred the "question between the Sieurs Scudéri and Corneille" to the Academy, nothing doubting that that body would condemn any production he disliked, and that their verdict would have considerable weight with Paris at large. The Forty, to do them justice, manifested a strong disinclination to undertake so invidious a task. It was sufficiently obvious to them that by doing so they would either offend the Cardinal or lose in the estimation of the world. At the outset they sought to excuse themselves on the ground that the decision of such a question was beyond their province. Richelieu, of course, at once treated the objection as frivolous. They next urged that by the constitution of the Academy they could not proceed without the consent of the author. Boisrobert was forthwith instructed by his eminence to induce Corneille to remove this obstacle. The dramatist, in reply, said he thought that a " libelle " did not merit the notice of so distinguished a body. " However," he added, " MM. de l'Académie may do as they please, since you tell me that Monseigneur would like to have their opinion on the subject." Nevertheless, the Forty continued to hold out. Every imaginable reason why they should not comply with the Minister's request was put forward. Richelieu at last lost his temper. " Faites savoir à ces Messieurs," he said to Boisrobert, " que je le désire, et que je les aimerai comme ils m'aimeront." Cowed by this imperious message, the Academy then entered upon their unwelcome task, which occupied some time. " It is with considerable impatience," Corneille ironically wrote during the deliberations, " that I await the judgment of the Academy as to the *Cid*, for until it is pronounced I am uncertain what to do in the future ; I cannot employ a single word with confidence." Eventually, after being read by the Cardinal at Charonne, the *Sentiments de l'Aca-*

démie Française sur le Cid came out. It is needless to
say that on all material points they were unfavourable
to Corneille.

The result was not what Richelieu anticipated. He
had the mortification to see the verdict of the Academy
set aside, if not turned into biting derision, by the
many-headed public. As the familiar quotation has it,

Tout Paris pour Chimène *eut* les yeux de Rodrigue,

and the enthusiasm aroused by the *Cid* seemed to
increase rather than abate with lapse of time. In
comparison with this tragedy, indeed, everything that
preceded it, the *Juives* of Garnier not excepted,
seemed to be without life and spirit—a *corpus sine
pectore.* Not that Corneille possessed all the gifts
necessary to do full justice to his theme. Over the
world of passion and emotion he held only a divided
sway. Some of the springs of human sensibility
were beyond his reach. In the atmosphere of pathos
and tenderness he was certainly in an uncongenial
element. It was not for him to engage the softer sympathies, to move a reader or auditor to pity and tears.
Happily for his own fame, as well as for the future
of the French drama, he had the sagacity to perceive
and the wisdom to keep within the limits assigned
to his gifts. He affected to think it inconsistent with
the dignity of tragedy to employ love except as a
minor feature of a plot, and then only as a spur to

great deeds. He deliberately appealed to the head
rather than to the heart. He sought to excite admiration by a portraiture of moral heroism, of the human
mind in its noblest and most commanding aspects.
And in this comparatively narrow walk of art he rose
to the level of the greatest. Imaginative force, grandeur and piercing vigour of thought, unfailing grasp
of character, a high appreciation of dramatic effect,—all
these qualities are largely present in his work. His
style is unequal enough, but it has the unquestionable advantage of being free from the jargon of the
précieuses, and its defects have scarcely occurred to us
when they are driven out of our thoughts by some
majestic image, some overwhelming burst of passion,
some lightning-like flash of a might peculiar to himself.
It is lamentable that such a man should have been
won over to the side of the classicists; for his new
faith, if not dissonant with his genius, certainly ham-
pered him in his choice of materials, diminished the
breadth and force of his painting, and led him into
more or less offensive improbability. His influence
upon the drama it would not be easy to over-estimate.
He raised the accepted ideal of tragedy, generated a
spirit of healthy emulation among even his detractors,
diffused a taste for nervous and genuine eloquence in
preference to the mystic hyperbole then in fashion,
communicated a powerful impulse to the reaction in

favour of the antique model, and directed attention to the dramatic treasures of Spain. In comedy, too, he had already effected a salutary change by proving that an audience could be amused by something better than impossible incident, vapid dialogue, and grotesque personages. It is not without good cause that he is commonly styled " le créateur de l'art dramatique en France."

CHAPTER IV.

1637—1642.

His triumph assured, Corneille returned to Rouen, to be received there, no doubt, with pride and pleasure by his ennobled father, by genial old M. de Chalons, by the demoiselle whose fickleness had caused him to turn his attention to the theatre, and by many of his fellow-citizens. The selection of subjects for his next plays must have cost him much anxious thought. The eyes of France were upon him, and to realize the expectations he had raised it was necessary to exceed them. His sympathies really lay with the picturesque scenes and characters of the Middle Ages, but it was more than probable that if he utilized one of them the Scudéris would accuse him of availing himself of a Spanish plot without acknowledgment; and eventually, anxious to prove that the invention of a plot was not above his capacity, he turned his attention to the history and legends of antiquity. In this well-trodden field he found four themes which, in addition to being susceptible of effective treatment, had not yet been worked by French dramatists—the contest between the Horatii

and the Curiatii, the conspiracy of Cinna against
Augustus, the martyrdom of Polyeuctes, and the death
of Pompey.   Nevertheless, he did not entirely abandon
his Spanish studies.   In a comedy by Don Juan de
Alarcon, *La Verdad Sospechosa*, the importance of com-
bining character with intrigue had at length been
shown ; and Corneille, alive to the importance of the
innovation, resolved to adapt the piece to the Paris stage.

The *Cid*, I believe, was followed at the Hôtel de
Bourgogne by Rotrou's tragi-comedy *Laure Persécutée*,
in which a story akin to that of Inez de Castro is told
with a force not previously displayed by the same pen.
Even thus early, it would seem, the success of Corneille
was tending to stimulate the genius—and the term is
not lightly used—of his friend.   Mairet, intimidated
rather than spurred to fresh exertion by that success,
was represented by *L'Illustre Corsaire* and *Sidonie*, and
Calprenède by a tragedy on the fate of the nine-days'
queen, *Jeanne d'Angleterre*.   Then came two untried
dramatists—Guérin de Bouscal, Avocat au Parlement,
and Desfontaines, man of letters pure and simple.   The
former was less successful than the latter, though
superior to him both in art and taste.   Tristan,
anxious to confirm the advantage he had won by
Mariamne, took to the Marais his tragedy of *Panthée*,
the leading character of which had been written for
Mondori.   A cruel disappointment was in store for

the author. During a performance of *Hérod* Mondori
was seized with apoplexy, and as symptoms of paralysis
followed the doctors ordered him to take a long rest.
Tristan, too impatient to await the actor's recovery,
transferred the chief part to another member of the
company, in whose hands it created so little effect that
Panthée failed.

Boisrobert here induced the authorities at the Hôtel
de Bourgogne to accept a piece by his brother, Antoine
le Metel, Sieur d'Ouville. *Les Trahisons d'Arbiran*, as it
was called, had little to recommend itself save a veiled
satire upon a tendency then shown by all classes to
give themselves airs inconsistent with their lot in life.
Even, we are told,

> Un simple bateleur, quoique léger d'aloi,
> Se dit Comédien Ordinaire du Roi,
> Il fait le fanfaron, et croit qu'il se ravale
> S'il cède d'un seul point à la Troupe Royale.

For some years the players of the Hotel de Bourgogne
had been styled the *Troupe Royale* and *Comédiens
Ordinaires du Roi*. Boisrobert was often credited with
the authorship of his brother's pieces, although the only
point of resemblance between them as writers was that
each borrowed plots from the Spanish and Italian stage.
Les Trahisons d'Arbiran soon gave place to Duryer's
Lucrèce, probably written some time previously. Here,
poignard in hand, Sextus prosecutes his nefarious purpose; Lucrece rushes away, her persecutor follows, faint

cries are heard behind the scenes, and the heroine
reappears with a significant speech in her mouth. No
better illustration of the depths to which the tragic
drama occasionally fell at the period when the *Cid*
appeared could be found.

The vitality of that play was to be illustrated in
a manner which Corneille could not have approved.
The *salons* had just discovered a youthful prodigy in
the person of Urbain Chevreau, son of an advocate in
Poitou. Not yet twenty-four years of age, he was
versed in many languages, had thrown off poetry and
romances, and was engaged upon nothing less than
a history of the world. Even this task, however, was
not so formidable as one to which he now addressed
himself. With amusing temerity and self-confidence,
he produced *La Suite et le Mariage du Cid*—*i. e.*, a continuation of Corneille's play. The Infanta, actuated
by jealousy, opposes the union of the lovers; but
Rodrigue, after being arrested on suspicion of daring
to look with eyes of affection on that royal lady,
becomes the husband of Chimène in reward for another
victory which he gains over the redoubtable Moors.
Moreover, as though to make things additionally
pleasant for the young pair, the troublesome princess
agrees to marry a king. The inevitable comparison with Corneille must have told severely against
Chevreau; but as Rodrigue was a popular figure

the piece had several representations. The author, attributing its success to its own merits, brought out two more plays, *L'Avocat Dupé* and *La Lucrèce Romaine*. In the latter, notwithstanding his historical researches, he calls Tarquin Emperor of Rome.

L'Aveugle de Smyrne, concocted two years previously by Richelieu and the Cinq Auteurs, was played at the Palais Cardinal on the 22nd February, the interest it excited for its own sake being increased by the appearance of Mondori as the hero. The illustrious actor was now partially paralysed, but at the instance of the Minister, who was naturally anxious that the piece should be well played, he undertook to do what he could. The audience, as may be supposed, included the flower of the Court, or rather that section of the Court which Richelieu held in favour. The plot of *L'Aveugle de Smyrne* may be very briefly described. Philarque, son of Atlante, Prince of the Senate of Smyrne, loves and is loved by Aristée. His father, in order to prevent what would be a *mésalliance*, has recourse to a magician, who, mistaking his instructions, blinds Philarque with a mysterious powder. In the mean time, however, Aristée has entered the Temple of Diana, Philarque having suspected her fidelity. Eventually, with the consent of the afflicted Atlante, the lovers are united, and the husband's sight is restored by the tears of his wife. *L'Aveugle de Smyrne*, it must be added, was represented under far

rom favourable conditions. Mondori, after struggling
painfully through two acts, found it impossible to go on,
and his place had to be taken by an "understudy."
The performance over, the Cardinal awarded the stricken
actor a pension of two thousand livres per annum, and
the gifts made to him by the nobles present were large
enough to bring him eight thousand more. In any case,
however, it may be doubted whether the play would
have attained its end. It fell an easy prey to criticism,
and went with *Les Tuileries* to show that the five
poets, individually excellent, could not work together
with a very happy result.

Richelieu, annoyed at the failure of the play, abruptly
disbanded the brigade, but did not relinquish his hopes
of dramatic distinction. He resolved that in future
his plots should be executed by one head only, and
Desmarets was selected for the office so created. The
first-fruit of this new compact was a comedy entitled
Les Visionnaires, brought out at the Hôtel de Bourgogne.
Many conspicuous figures in French society are here
portrayed under a thin disguise. Madame de Rambouillet and Madame de Chavigny are easily to be recognized, while Madame de Sablé, who allowed the Cardinal
to believe that if she kept him at arm's-length her
heart was really his, is introduced as a girl enamoured
of Alexander the Great. Curiously enough, Desmarets,
" le plus bel esprit de tous les visionnaires et le plus

visionnaire de tous les beaux-esprits," did not appear
among the personages. The comedy was received with
loud applause, qualified, however, by derisive laughter
as to many of the details. Desmarets was so far carried
away by a sense of his own importance as to reply to his
critics in these terms—

> Ce n'est pas pour toi que j'écris,
> Indocte et stupide vulgaire :
> J'écris pour les nobles esprits ;
> Je serais marri de te plaire—

language which scarcely disposed playgoers in general
to give other works by the " first clerk in the depart-
ment of poetic affairs at the Palais Cardinal" a very
indulgent hearing.

The arrogant dramatist presently found it prudent
to modify his tone. Richelieu testified the liveliest
interest in a new tragi-comedy by Scudéri, *L'Amour
Tyrannique.* "Monsieur," he said to him after the first
representation, probably referring to a line in the prologue, "your work requires no apology ; it more than
justifies its existence." Nor was he content with paying
merely verbal compliments. He asked Sarrazin to
prepare a *discours* to the effect that M. de Scudéri was
the greatest dramatic poet of the time. The essayist,
whose judgment in literary matters, as the Cardinal knew,
had great authority in Paris, was not ashamed to comply
with the request. In a letter nominally addressed to
the Academy, but really designed to serve as a preface

to the play, he glanced at the antiquities of the French
stage, spoke approvingly of Mairet, and then awarded
the author of *L'Amour Tyrannique* the distinction
dictated by Richelieu.   It must have been with no
ordinary feeling of astonishment that literary Paris
waded through this *discours*.   *L'Amour Tyrannique* was
not worthy even of Scudéri, although it proved so
attractive at the outset that on one occasion two of the
doorkeepers· of the theatre were crushed to death by the
crowd.   Moreover, several plays of greater value appeared
at about the same time without exciting a word of praise
from the Cardinal—notably Rotrou's *Captifs*, a clever
imitation, with original details, of Plautus; *Lizidor*,
suggested by the Arcadia of Sir Philip Sidney, to whose
nephew, the then Earl of Leicester, the piece was dedicated; and last, but not least, Calprenède's *Comte de Essex*,
an unusually effective tragedy.   How, then, are we to
account for this excessive praise of *L'Amour Tyrannique?*
Richelieu may have thought such praise deserved, but
there can be little doubt that in view of Corneille's
reappearance on the scene he wished to induce fashion
to declare itself in favour of some other poet, and that
he regarded Scudéri, the idol of all the *salons*, as more
likely than any of the contemporary dramatists to make
the proposed imposture succeed.

Again did the force of public opinion prove too great
for the Cardinal.   *Horace*, the first of the tragedies

undertaken by Corneille at Rouen two years previously, came out at the Hôtel de Bourgogne early in 1639. If the hangers-on at the Palais Cardinal attended to prevent or at least qualify the apprehended triumph, as was probably the case, their labours were completely thrown away. But few could resist the spell thrown over them by this tragedy. In dealing with the heart-struggles incident to the combat between the Horatii and the Curiatii the dramatist displayed a power beyond that of the *Cid*, besides demonstrating his ability to construct a plot with the simplest materials. Especially impressive is the figure of the elder Horace (Bellerose). He seems to concentrate in his person the whole grandeur of the Roman character. His love for his children, deeprooted as it is, at once yields to his patriotism. The audience were sensibly moved when, parting from his son and the affianced lover of his daughter, soon to face each other in deadly strife, he said—

Moi-même, en cet adieu, j'ai les larmes aux yeux ;
Faites votre devoir, et laissez-faire aux dieux ;

and a thunder of applause shook the theatre when, after cursing his third son for having, as was supposed, fled from the field as the other Roman champions fell, he fiercely replied to the question, " Que vouliez-vous qu'il fît contre trois ? " by exclaiming, " Qu'il mourût ! " The imprecation launched against Rome by Camille— the daughter of the elder Horace and the mistress of her brother's foe—had a similarly powerful effect. In a word, the tragedy realized the high-flown expectations which the announcement of its coming had raised, and the eulogies lavished by Sarrazin upon Scudéri became the laughing-stock of Paris.

Corneille, probably at the instigation of his friend Madame de Combalet, dedicated *Horace* to the Cardinal, who, however, was not in the mood to receive it in a gracious spirit. Evidently in the hope of neutralizing its success, he bégan to sound the praises of a. tragi-comedy entitled *Mirame,* in the composition of which he is believed to have had an important share, although it was put forward as the work of Desmarets alone. My Lord Cardinal manifested what Pelisson describes as a " paternal tenderness " in its behalf. In his palace there was a room large enough to hold six thousand persons. He now converted it into a theatre, decorating it throughout in most beautiful style, and providing the stage with all the machinery then deemed necessary to scenic illustration. *Mirame* was played here in the spring of 1639, before an audience judiciously chosen by the Cardinal himself. His eminence, as may be supposed, was by far the most interested spectator of the performance. At every murmur of applause his stern features were lighted up by a look of gratification ; but immediately afterwards, in his anxiety that no line should be lost, he would project himself

half-way out of his box to restore silence by a
gesture. The piece, however, was · in all respects
feeble, and it was only too obvious that the demonstrations of delight which followed the fall of the curtain
were insincere. Richelieu, vexed beyond measure, withdrew to Ruel, whither he was followed by Desmarets
and a certain Petit. "Alas!" exclaimed the Cardinal
on seeing them, "the French will never acquire true
taste." "Monseigneur," said Petit, "the fault lies
not with the play, which is really admirable, but with
the players, who were both ignorant of their parts and
half-drunk." "I remember," said the Cardinal, "that
they all played in the most pitiable style." This idea,
we are told, "le calma;" his two visitors were invited
to supper with him in order that they might speak
further on the subject, and a second performance of
the piece was decided upon. The players must have
had too keen a sense of their own interests to be otherwise than good at the outset, but it is beyond doubt
that the second performance succeeded better than the
first, and that *Mirame* was spoken of as a "parfaite
réussite." At the best, however, it was an expensive
amusement to the Cardinal, seeing that the production
cost him a hundred thousand crowns, a considerable portion of which was expended in bringing abnormally high
oaks from the Forest of Bourdonnais to furnish material
for the decorations of the interior of the new theatre.

Boisrobert had even less reason to look back to *Mirame*
with pleasure.   Having brought two women of doubtful
reputation to witness the first performance, he was
exiled from Paris at the instance of the Duchesse
d'Aiguillon, and .was not allowed to return until the
Cardinal became so ill as to compel his physicians to
prescribe the "recipe Boisrobert."

In addition to *Mirame*, Desmarets wrote at this time
an *Erigone* and a *Scipion*, poor pieces both.   His continued failure as a dramatiŝt seems to have encouraged
more than one of his rivals to strive for at least a
share of the favour he enjoyed at the Palais Cardinal.
Calprenède, while engaged on an *Edouard III.* (in which
the victor of Crécy makes dishonourable advances to
the Countess of Salisbury, and, finding her virtue im-
pregnable, marries her), obsequiously laid at Richelieu's
feet *La Mort des Enfants d'Hérode*, a sequel to Tristan's
Mariamne.   Duryer, in giving to the world an *Alcionée*,
declared in effect that as it had pleased his eminence there was no doubt it would live.   If this confidence proved unfounded it must not be assumed
that the tragedy was without signal merits.   The
character of Alcionée is finely drawn, and in the selection of his materials the author practically recognizes
the value of heart-struggles akin to those employed
with such good effect in the *Cid* and *Horace*.   In his
next tragedy, *Saul*, Duryer again bears silent testimony

to the influence of Corneille. The story is handled
with a reverence and grace which had not characterized
any other play upon a sacred subject, and which could
hardly have been looked for at the hands of the author
of the broadly indelicate *Lucrèce*.   Strangely enough,
Saul elicited no commendation from Richelieu, possibly
because it was deemed prudent not to encourage any
tendency to turn Scriptural scenes and characters to
theatrical uses.   No less industrious than the needy
Duryer, Guérin de Bouscal · constructed two comedies
of five acts each out of *Don Quixote*, but only to find
that he had taken much trouble to little purpose.
Doubtless the spirit of the original had evaporated
in the process of translation ; but even in the contrary
case the result would have been the same.   *Don Quixote*
could hardly prove popular at a time when the romantic
spirit it held up to ridicule was yet alive in Paris,
and when the writings of Mdlle. de Scudéri were
the admiration of nearly all sorts and conditions of
people.

Cinna followed.   Based upon a page of Seneca (*De
Clementia*, lib. I. cap. 9), but original in regard to many
incidents and figures, it exhibited a majesty of thought
and language for which *Horace* itself had not prepared
the town.   Especially striking was the opening of the
second act, where Cinna urges Auguste to restore the
liberties of Rome, and Maxime seeks to impress the

emperor with a sense of the danger of abdication. It is not too much to say that Demosthenes himself might have envied the depth and force with which they sustain their positions. Eventually, finding that Cinna, whom he has educated with paternal care, is engaged in a conspiracy against his life, Auguste (Bellerose) summons him to his presence, reminds him of his obligations, shows that the plot has been discovered, and, at the moment when spectators unacquainted with Roman history were trembling for the fate of the culprit, says—

> Je suis maître de moi comme de l'univers;
> Je le suis, je veux l'être. O siècles! O mémoire!
> Conservez à jamais ma dernière victoire:
> Je triomphe aujourd'hui du plus juste courroux,
> De qui le souvenir puisse aller jusqu'à vous.
> Soyons amis, Cinna; c'est moi qui t'en convie.

This magnanimous clemency, free from any suggestion of the prudential motives by which the Augustus of history was actuated in the matter, created a profound impression. The great Condé, then twenty years of age, was "affected even to tears." Moreover, as has already been pointed out, the complexion of the age was eminently favourable to the success of a play which, like *Cinna*, abounded in generous sentiments and threw a broad ray of light upon the constitution of the Roman Empire. The minds of men had been directed to the principles of government by the extension of regal authority, and the spirit of faction was everywhere raising its head.

The effect of *Cinna* at the Palais Cardinal was very different from what might have been expected. The fame of Corneille, it now became evident, was not only proof against the machinations of the Minister, formidable as they might be, but was steadily increasing with each tragedy he produced. More than one passage in *Horace* and *Cinna* was inimical to the political system now being established. In these circumstances, it would seem, the Cardinal thought it advisable to establish an *entente cordiale* with the poet, probably as a means of at once gathering a sort of reflected glory from his works and bringing him under the influence of the Court. Whatever his reasons may have been, he made friendly overtures to the man whom but five years previously he had treated as a mere hack, and whose progress in public estimation he had laboriously striven to impede. Nor were these overtures ill-timed. The wolf was at the poet's door. His father dying in straitened circumstances, the burden of supporting the whole of the family had fallen upon his shoulders, and in default of large practice as a lawyer his means were of the slightest. The poverty to which he was reduced may be illustrated by a well-known incident. *Cinna* was to have been dedicated to Mazarin, but the author, knowing that he was not likely to receive any money-present in return, bestowed that honour upon an obscure person who was wise and wealthy enough to offer a thousand pistoles for it, and the language employed on the occasion is expressive of the liveliest sense of gratitude. In such circumstances, therefore, he was in no position to add fuel to the feeling against him. His dignified demeanour towards Richelieu, joined to his resentment of the persecution he had suffered since the production of the *Cid*, leads us to believe, however, that he was tempted at the outset to resist the Cardinal's advances, especially as it was very improbable that the doors of the Hôtel de Bourgogne would be closed against him. On the other hand, Richelieu was no stranger to generous impulses ; and to Corneille, as to others, the step taken by the Minister may well have been interpreted as an acknowledgment of, and a desire to make amends for, an error. The dramatist had also to remember that the pension conferred upon him in 1635 had never been withdrawn. In the result, evidently not perceiving the *arrières pensées* of the Cardinal, he took the extended hand.

This treaty of peace and amity had scarcely been concluded when Richelieu found himself able to lay Corneille under a lasting obligation. Notwithstanding his pecuniary embarrassment, the poet was in love with and loved by Marie de Lamperière, daughter of the Lieutenant-Général of the Andelys, within a day's drive of Rouen. The lady's father, perceiving that M. Corneille was as poor as a church mouse, and not being in a position to provide her with a dowry, sternly set his face against the proposed match—nay, insisted upon its being broken off without any prospect of renewal. Corneille, who was now engaged upon *Polyeucte*, took his disappointment to heart. The pen dropped from his hands. His occupation was gone. The pleasant visions which had nerved his brain were dispelled. Before he won a competency Mdlle. de Lamperière might become the wife of somebody else. Dejected by reflections like this, he one day presented himself at the Palais. Richelieu asked what progress he was making with his next play. " None," was the reply ; " my mind is too much disturbed to permit me to work." The Cardinal inquiring the cause thereof, the poet, at the risk of exposing himself to a little raillery, told the whole story. " Is that all ? " the iron Minister seems to have said with the most provoking calmness ; " well, your troubles will soon be over." And forthwith he despatched to M. de Lamperière a letter commanding him to present himself at the Palais Cardinal. The Lieutenant-Général of the Andleys, doubtless apprehending many terrible things, lost no time in obeying. The Cardinal briefly signified his pleasure in the matter ; the father bowed acquiescence, and Marie de Lamperière became Madame Corneille.

The honeymoon over, the happy husband returned to

Polyeucte, which in the course of a few weeks was ready
for the actors.   It may be doubted whether the old
ecclesiastical legend could have been turned to better
account than it was here.   Pauline, daughter of Félix,
a Roman patrician, is obliged to follow him to Armenia,
where, in obedience to his commands, she consents to
marry Polyeucte, a worthy descendant of the ancient
kings of the country.   Her affections, however, are
really fixed upon Sévère, a high-souled Roman citizen,
but too poor to find favour in her father's eyes.   By the
irony of fate, this same Sévère becomes the General of
the Emperor Decius, and now, full of hope, follows
Pauline to claim the fulfilment of her promise.   How
cruelly his hopes are shattered need not be said.   At
this juncture Polyeucte is converted to Christianity, and,
having thrown down the idols in the midst of a solemn
sacrifice, is condemned to death.   Pauline has only to
let justice take its course to secure her own happiness,
but her duty as a wife prevails over all other considerations.   She strives to move her father to forgiveness,
to induce Polyeucte to purchase life by renouncing his
new faith.   It is all in vain, though Sévère, in response
to her tearful entreaties, nobly seconds her exertions to
save the life of one whose death would set her free.   The
martyrdom of Polyeucte is not without good fruit.   In
her first burst of anguish Pauline receives a ray of divine
light.   She becomes a Christian ; her father, touched by

grace, follows her example, an'd Sévère, so far from persecuting them, appears as an incarnation of the spirit of religious tolerance. This beautiful story, it remains to be said, is told with all the wealth of idea and feeling which distinguished Corneille's two previous works. The religious enthusiasm of Polyeucte, the unselfish devotion of his wife, the self-abnegation of Sévère,—all are exquisitely drawn pictures, each gaining by contrast with the dark shades assigned to the character of Félix.

More than once did it seem probable that this tragedy, in spite of its high merit and the eagerness with which it was looked forward to, would not dignify the repertory of the Hôtel de Bourgogne. The troupe at first returned it to the author, evidently on account of the nature of the subject. They saw only the martyr ; the character of Pauline, the finest yet delineated by a French dramatist, attracted but little attention. Before long, however, and not, as stage tradition has it, after an interval of eighteen months, during which the manuscript lay unheeded on the canopy of a bedstead, *Polyeucte* was put in rehearsal. The author then read it at the Hôtel de Rambouillet, that " souverain tribunal des affaires d'esprit." The audience, which probably included the whole of the Marquise's " set," praised the piece without reserve, but as a matter of fact were greatly shocked by its " Christianisme." Having been good-naturedly apprised by Voiture of their real opinion, Corneille timorously resolved to withdraw the play, and would have done so if an actor who had been deemed unworthy of filling any of the important parts had not induced him to let it take its chance. The player had better judgment than the *précieuses*. The public hailed *Polyeucte* as M. Corneille's *chef d'œuvre*, and in this, as in other instances, anticipated the verdict of posterity. Corneille was so elated by his new triumph that he requested permission, through the Duc de Schomberg, to dedicate the tragedy to the King, though well aware that his majesty's appreciation of the compliment was not likely to take a substantial form. " No, no," said Louis, who happened to be in one of his parsimonious fits, " it is unnecessary." " Sire," said the Duc, " it is not from interested motives that Corneille seeks this honour." " In that case," said the King, " il me fera plaisir.".

Passing over a tragedy by Benserade, *Méléagre*, in which Atalante, reproached by Déjanire with courting dangers their sex should not meet, says :

Pour vous, vous êtes fille, et fille infiniment ;
Et moi, si je la suis, c'est de corps seulement—

we come to a brace of new dramatists. First in order of time was Gabriel Gilbert, at present secretary to the Duchesse de Rohan, and subsequently " des commandements de Christine, Reine de Suède, et son résident en France." His duties do not appear to have occupied much of his time. He aspired to literary honours of nearly all kinds, and if such honours were to be gained by mere industry he would have been more than satisfied. But, like Hardi, he wrote too much to write well. He was fortunate in his choice of subjects, but not in his method of handling them. His first play was *Marguérite de France*, in which Henry II. of England appears on the stage. The next new dramatist, Jean Puget de la Serre, librarian and historiographer to Monsieur the King's brother, was also indebted to English history for the subject of his first piece. In *Thomas Morus*, a tragedy in prose, he introduces Henry VIII. and Anne Boleyn, ascribing to the latter almost every womanly virtue under the sun. This piece, it is certain, met with great success. The whole of the Court sang its praises. The sorrows of the heroine wrung tears even from Richelieu. The public were so eager to get into the theatre that on one occasion four doorkeepers were crushed to death. "Voilà," writes the author triumphantly in reference to the last incident, "ce qu'on appelle de bonnes pièces! M. Corneille has no such proof of the excellence of his, and I shall not allow myself to be inferior to him until he has five doorkeepers killed in one day!"

La Mort de Pompée was another novelty of the year. It must be admitted that none of the servants of the

theatre perished in consequence, but it is equally true
that Corneille had no reason to complain of any abate-
ment of public interest in his work. Nor was *Pompée*
unworthy of the attention it obtained. The events
leading up to the death of Pompey, as narrated by
Lucan, are dramatized with both skill and grandeur.
In Cornélie the energy of the Roman character is again
shadowed forth ; César, except when he is making love,
is all that history represents him to be. Pompée himself does not appear, but the keenest interest is awakened
in his behalf. The chief defect of the play was aptly
pointed out when a lady remarked that there were too
many heroes among the personages, and that, consequently, the impression made upon her by each was not
so distinct and vivid as she would have wished. Ninon
de l'Enclos was to aptly quote one day a line in this
piece. Her smiles were sought after by a man who
possessed many admirable qualities, but who, owing
to a natural shyness, was not an adept at love-making
—who could only look at her with a yearning expression, place his hand upon his heart, and heave a
succession of sighs.

Ah ! ciel, que de vertus vous me faites haïr !

she said to him one day, quoting words addressed by
Cornélie to César. Before long she transferred her
affections to Pécourt, the dancer. Meeting the latter
one day, and noticing that his dress had something of

the character of an uniform, the discarded lover ironically asked him to what corps he belonged "Monsieur," was the cool reply, "I command a *corps* that once belonged to you." *Pompée*, it should be added, was translated into English by Mrs. Phillips ("matchless Orinda") at the instance of Lord Orrery, and on the completion of her labours received from him some lines to the effect that if Corneille could read the copy he would probably deem it greater than the original. M. Corneille, fortunately for his peace of mind, was not sufficiently acquainted with English to determine the question.

It was at this time that the State first recognized the existence of the stage, took measures to maintain the high tone the drama had lately acquired, and began to relieve the players from the stigma which the Church had so long cast upon them. In the spring of 1641, at St. Germain-en-Laye, Louis· XIII., or rather Richelieu, issued an important declaration on the subject. "The continual benedictions which had been showered upon the present reign," the document said, "made it more and more necessary that his majesty should do all that in him lay to suppress anything in the shape of an abuse. Now, it was to be feared that the plays so advantageously represented for the amusement of the people might at times be performed in a manner *peu honnête*, and calculated, therefore, to debase the mind. Accordingly,

the players were forbidden, on pain of being declared
infâme and subjected to other punishments, to give
indelicate scenes, or to use words which, either from
being of a lascivious nature or susceptible of *double
entente*, might be at variance with the public weal. The
Judges were to carry out this order, and in case it
should be contravened by the said players should forbid
them the theatre, and proceed against them by such
means as, considering the nature of the offence, they
should deem meet. The severest punishments in the
power of the Judges to inflict were to be the *amende*
and banishment. In the event of the said players so
regulating the work of the theatre as to render it
altogether exempt from impurity, the King desired
that their calling, which might innocently divert his
people from various dull occupations, should not expose
them to blame or prejudice their reputation in public
intercourse. This was decreed in the belief that their
desire to avoid the reproach they had hitherto incurred
would have as much effect in inducing them to do their
duty as a fear of the punishments that would inevitably
overtake them if they infringed the present ordinance."
By this declaration, it need hardly be pointed out, the
social status of the player was materially raised, and
the additional self-respect it spread amongst them was
in itself a guarantee that the object of the measure
would be achieved. It is ungracious enough to look a

gift horse in the mouth, but it must be added that the
Cardinal would have been wiser and more consistent if,
going a step further, he had exerted his influence at
Rome to restore the rights of the humblest citizen—
communion and a hallowed burial—to the followers
of an art which he, a member of the Sacred College,
so frequently countenanced and patronized.

Elated, no doubt, to find their long-condemned
profession declared by the King to be worthy of respect,
the troupe of the Hôtel de Bourgogne addressed themselves with new ardour to their work, though only to
meet with more or less disheartening reverses until,
early in the following year, Corneille's adaptation of
La Verdad Sospechosa—now tersely called *Le Menteur*—
appeared. ' The only noteworthy pieces brought forward
in the interim were *Clarice*, a clever adaptation by
Rotrou from the Italian of Sforza d'Oddi, and *Andromire*,
an equally clever vindication by Scudéri of the now
discredited doctrine that tragedy and comedy might be
amalgamated with advantage. The *Menteur* was an
agreeable surprise to the playgoers. Hitherto, as we
have seen, the importance of character to comedy had
not been sufficiently recognized. The paramount end
of the dramatist had been to weave an exciting intrigue.
Le Menteur relied in a large measure upon the delineation of a special idiosyncracy. The mendacity of Dorante
forms the chief source of effect, the pivot on which

the whole piece turns. Moreover, the plot was excellent—so excellent, indeed, that Corneille said he "would have parted with his two best tragedies for the honour of being its inventor." Richelieu, in order to heighten the effect of the performance, gave Bellerose a superb coat to play Dorante in—a step which at first seemed likely to defeat its object, as Beauchâteau, fearing that he would attract less attention on the stage than his better-dressed brother, sadly exaggerated the part of Alcippe. Notwithstanding the want of harmony in the acting, the piece was hailed as a masterpiece of comedy art, and its success encouraged the author to write what proved a rather uninteresting continuation of it under the title of *La Suite du Menteur*.

Richelieu, whose interest in the success of *Le Menteur* has a pleasing significance, continued to devote most of his spare thoughts to stage-work. In conjunction with his Minister for Poetic Affairs, the ever faithful Desmarets, he framed a comedy in which the powers of Europe are personified, and which, as may be supposed, bore strong testimony to the greatness attained by France under his rule. The work completed, he sent it by Boisrobert to the members of the Academy, with a note requesting them to alter the dialogue as they thought fit. The Forty, perhaps desirous to make amends for their complaisance in regard to the *Cid*, examined *Europe*—for that was the name of the piece—in a severely critical spirit. In every page they made excisions or other improvements. The Cardinal, irritated by their excessive candour, tore up the manuscript as soon as it was returned to him ; but a few hours later he had the fragments put together, dispensed with all but a few minor corrections, and again referred *Europe* to the Academicians. " In profiting by their lights," he said to Boisrobert, "I have not adopted all their suggestions, as nobody is proof against errors of judgment." The Academicians, learning that he resented their boldness, wisely sent back the MS. as it last left his hands, adding that in its present state it had received their "approbation unanime." Fortified by this approbation, which was promptly noised about, *Europe* appeared at the Hôtel de Bourgogne as the work of Desmarets. Its fate was that usually reserved for politico-allegorical plays without plot or wit ; and at the fall of the curtain, when an actor came forward to announce a second performance, the pit, unconsciously stinging the Minister to the quick, demanded that the *Cid* should be given instead.

The Cardinal did not long survive the production of *Europe*. He died towards the end of the year, having succeeded in all his ambitious projects except that of destroying or impairing Corneille's reputation as a dramatist. His connexion with the drama reveals the weakest side of his character, but it must be pointed out that the ire excited in his mind by the triumph of *Le Cid* and *Horace* never betrayed him into the meanness of withdrawing the pension he had awarded to the author, and that after their reconciliation he seemed to be animated by a generous wish to make atonement for his folly. Corneille, unable to forget either a wrong or a benefit, thought of his sometime persecutor with mixed feelings. Being asked to lay a leaflet of verse on the Cardinal's grave—and no poet of the time could have fulfilled the office so well—he said :

> Qu'on parle mal ou bien du fameux Cardinal,
> Ma prose ni mes vers n'en diront jamais rien :
> Il m'a trop fait de bien pour en dire du mal ;
> Il m'a trop fait de mal pour en dire du bien.

The "bien," it may be thought, should have had more weight with him than the "mal," especially as it was by the instrumentality of Richelieu that he had gained the hand of Marie de Lampèrière. In this lukewarmness he probably stood alone among the votaries of the theatre. Nearly every dramatist was indebted to the Cardinal for encouragement or practical assistance, and the players could not forget that he had treated them as artists, had formally declared their vocation to be worthy of respect, and had even made them share his hospitalities. Shortly before his death, too, the Troupe Royale began to receive an allowance of 12,000 livres per annum from the State. One instance of his regard for the profession may well be mentioned. In 1638, hearing that Montfleuri was about to marry the daughter of an obscure comedian, he expressed a wish that the ceremony should be performed in his presence in the stately *salon* at Ruel. Elated by the compliment his brethren had received in his person, Montfleuri signed the register, not as Zacharie Jacob, gentleman of Anjou, but as " Zacharie Jacob de Montfleuri, Comédien du Roi."

The death of Richelieu is coincident with the close of an important period in the history of the stage. By an unrelenting irony of fate, the lustre of his administration had been appreciably enhanced by the gifts which he had done his best or worst to disparage. In Corneille's last four tragedies, it will have been observed, the principle underlying the *Cid* had been closely adhered to. *Horace* exhibits the heroism of patriotism, *Cinna* the heroism of clemency, *Polyeucte* the heroism of Christian faith and marital honour, *Pompée* the heroism of conjugal affection. Each of these noble plays had justified or augmented the fame previously won by the author, for each had served to reveal his genius in a stronger, though not more attractive, light than the *Cid*. If anything, that genius reached its full height in *Polyeucte;* in the portraiture of the wife who, sustained by moral energy and a sentiment of duty, wrestles with and subdues a passion

which forms a part of her being. It is also true that
the limits set to his powers were increasingly apparent;
the softer and lighter feelings found no mirror in his
page, and his heroines, the "adorables furies" spoken
of by Balzac, have a more or less masculine aspect.
Many playgoers must have seen how narrow the sphere
of the dramatist was, but the undeniable grandeur and
beauty of his work had by this time given it supreme
authority as a model. Nearly every dramatist thought
it necessary to observe the unities, to portray the sterner
rather than the softer passions, to keep the grave free
from any suggestion of the gay, to aim at marked individuality in the delineation of *dramatis personae*, to
alternate the play of imagination with depth of reasoning, and, so far from enervating dialogue by the jargon
of the *salons*, to copy the severe style of *Horace* and
Cinna even in its occasional bluntness. Moreover,
probably as a consequence of the direction Corneille
had lately taken in his search for subjects, it came
to be thought that modern history, rich as it was in
dramatic elements, should be avoided as incompatible
with the dignity of tragedy. Hardly less important
was the new turn which comedy had taken under his
auspices, particularly after the appearance of the *Menteur*.
Farce did not disappear, but it was henceforward to be
overshadowed as a source of diversion by a species of
play *raisonnable* in form, elegant in language, and com-

bining interest of story with distinctness of character. In most cases the plot came from the Spanish stage, a knowledge of which was now deemed an indispensable part of the equipment of the dramatist. Italian influence, on the other hand, appreciably waned; the pastoral relaxed its hold of the theatre, and farce began to resume a purely national character. It may appear strange that at such a time the classic should have overborne the romantic school, but the genius of Corneille was great enough to endow the former with long-enduring life. Nor is it simply as the regenerator of tragedy and comedy that he comes before us. His recent works, joined to the support extended to the stage by one who was at once a powerful Minister and a Cardinal, relieved the drama from a world of unreasoning prejudice, elevated it to the first place in literature, and gave it an importance which it can hardly be said to have enjoyed since the death of Euripides.

CHAPTER V.

1643—1659.

THE supremacy attained by Corneille in both tragedy
and comedy was to be shown in diametrically opposite
ways by his contemporaries. Most of them surrendered
to the influence of his example; others, consulting
only a mortified vanity, sullenly brought their connexion with the theatre to an end. In the latter
group we find Mairet, Benserade, Scudéri, Calprenède,
and Chevreau. Retiring to Besançon, the first, whose
Sophonisbe had done much to aid the cause of the
classical form, gave himself up to severe study, and
might have passed the remainder of his life in seclusion
if the Queen had not employed him in more or less
important missions. Benserade, having gained a footing at the Louvre, devoted himself to the composition
of court ballets, in which he adroitly confounded " le
caractère des personnes avec celui des personnages."
Scudéri's secession may not have been exclusively due
to a sense of his littleness in comparison with the poet
to whom he had been set up as a rival. Educated in
the school of Hárdi, he chafed against the laws laid

down by the classicists, and the rigour with which those laws were now upheld must have given him an additional distaste for the stage. It is true that he was in no position to despise the money paid by the actors for plays, but the phenomenal success of his sister as a romance writer tended to reassure him as to the future. His subsequent history may be briefly told. He became Governor of Notre Dame de la Garde at Marseilles, a post which made so few demands upon his time that, according to the wags of the day, he repaired to the place with his sister, heard a salute of ten guns fired in his honour, shut up the fort, put the key in his pocket, and returned to Paris by the coach. He next fought with conspicuous bravery in Condé's early campaigns, from Rocroi to Lens inclusive. Identifying his fortunes with those of his general, he soon embroiled himself with the Government, and for some time was an exile from Paris. During this period, thanks to his literary and military reputation, the middle-aged spendthrift won the heart and hand of a young heiress, Mdlle. de Martin Vost, and thenceforward lived in Normandy in the style of a *grand seigneur*. Madeleine de Scudéri did not profit by her freedom to marry, although one of her suitors, the renowned Pelisson, who "abused the privilege of the clever to be ugly," inspired her with a warmer feeling than friendship. Heroic romance seemed to absorb all her thoughts except on Saturdays, which she devoted to the reception of friends. Her house, situated in the old Rue du Temple, then open to the country, became a resort of all that was best in Parisian society—a Rambouillet on a smaller scale. Ever "un peu fanfaron," but "très chevaleresque," her brother was to be found at these gatherings to within a short time of his death, which occurred in his sixty-sixth year. Despite his long dependence upon her earnings, the "fou solennel," as Corneille termed him in the heat of the contest over the *Cid*, was not without a true manliness of spirit. Before his marriage, among other things, he wrote a heroic poem, *Alaric*, and inscribed it to Christina of Sweden. On the eve of its appearance, her majesty, through a third person, gave him to understand that by retaining in it a panegyric upon a nobleman who had done him a service, but who in some way had displeased her, he would lose the promised reward of his homage—a valuable gold chain. "Not for all the chains worn by the Incas of Peru," he exclaimed, "would I expunge that passage.!" He kept his word,—and the Swedish Queen kept hers. For the rest, his plays often show considerable dramatic talent, and might have kept alive the lamp of romanticism in France a little longer if he had not piqued himself upon what proved a fatal rapidity of production. The last of the number, *Axiane*, a tragi-comedy in prose, was, like its predecessor, founded upon his sister's first romance, *Ibrahim.* But few words have to be said of the other dramatists who ceased with him to write for the stage. The fiery and elegant Calprenède gathered new laurels in the field opened out by Madeleine de Scudéri; Chevreau acted as secretary to high and puissant personages, completed his *Histoire du Monde,* and gratified a taste for foreign travel. By all these secessions the theatres suffered an appreciable loss, but a material set-off against it was found in the increasing willingness of the remaining dramatists to derive inspiration from Corneille. Rotrou and Duryer particularly distinguished themselves in this way; the latter, in a tragedy on the story of Esther, reaching a degree of strength and beauty for which *Saul* itself had scarcely prepared his audience.

In the prime of life, but each a prey to bodily affliction, the players who above all others had been associated with the early triumphs of Corneille here disappeared from the stage. Mondori died at Orleans, never having recovered from the paralysis which struck him down a few years previously. It was suggested that the theatres should be draped in mourning on the day of his funeral, and there can be no doubt that in him the playgoers lost the first of the long line of great tragic actors in France. Bellerose had yet twenty-seven years of life before him, but was constrained by some painful malady to give up the exercise of a

profession in which he had occupied the highest rank for
at least a decade. His acting had steadily improved
with lapse of time, although to the last it was occasionally found to be affected and wanting in colour.
According to the Retz memoirs, Madame de Montbazon
was induced to reject the heart and hand of M. de
Rochefoucauld because he resembled this player in
having *l'air fade*. Whatever the shortcomings of Bellerose may have been, his position shows that he possessed no ordinary talents, and his name is immortalized
by the fact that he was the original representative of
the elder Horace, Auguste, Sévère, and Dorante.

In their selection of his successor the company were
eminently fortunate. The Théâtre du Marais had recently acquired a well-graced actor in the person of one
Josias de Soulas, known to playgoers as Floridor. The
son of a German Protestant who early in the century
had settled in La Brié, prudently allowed himself to be
converted to Roman Catholicism, and married a French
lady, the new-comer, after receiving a good education,
joined the Gardes-Françaises. We next find him in
the Régiment de Rambures as an ensign, but instead
of aiming at military distinction he became a strolling
player. In his thirtieth year he was a manager as
well as actor. "I have seen," writes Chappuzeau,
" companies form themselves into one ; I remember that
in 1638 such a thing was done at Saumur by two

known as those of Floridor and Filandre." Emerging
from obscurity at one bound, he came to the Théâtre
du Marais, officiated there as "orator," and on the
retirement of Bellerose was elected to fill his place.
Every gift required by the actor, it seems, was possessed by Floridor—ardent feeling, trained judgment,
fine presence, graceful manners, and elastic voice. Like
Bellerose, he was great in both branches of the drama,
while the education he had received gave him an advantage in declamation which his predecessor had not
enjoyed.

Other players were added at about the same time to
the troupe. First came Michel Boyron, son of a mercer
at Issoudun. Delighted with the antics of a few
strollers at Bourges, whither his father had sent him
on business, he forthwith joined them, and his success was such as to prove, that he had not made a
mistake. He excelled as a hero, prince, or lover.
Before long he became known as the Sieur Baron, for
the reason that Louis XIII., now on the brink of the
grave, chanced to call him by that name at the end of
a performance given by the Troupe Royale at Court.
Another source of strength at the Hôtel de Bourgogne
was Mde. Baron, wife of the runaway from Issoudun.
Few characters came amiss to her; and her personal
attractions were so great that when she presented herself
to Anne of Austria, who quickly became one of her

admirers, some of the ladies in attendance, not being favoured by nature to the same extent, found it convenient, we are assured, to retire.

More than a year elapsed before an original and effective character fell to the lot of Floridor. Many novelties came out without affording him that advantage—among others, *La Folie du Sage* and *La Mort de Sénéque*, by Tristan, *Stratonice*, by Debrosse, *Thesée*, by La Serre, and *Rodogune*, by Gilbert. If the last of these pieces has never been forgotten it is for reasons far from honourable to the author. Corneille had written four acts of a tragedy dealing with the heroism of fraternal affection—to wit, *Rodogune*. From indiscretion or treachery, a person in his confidence gave a minute description of it to Gilbert, who forthwith wrote a *Rodogune* bearing a close resemblance to the other in plot, situations, and even speeches. The plagiarist made but an ill use of his materials. He enfeebled the interest of the plot, frequently confounded one character with another in the distribution of the purloined speeches, and heaped verbiage of his own on beauties of thought and language until they were all but lost to sight. Moreover, the fifth act, in the composition of which he had to rely exclusively upon himself, formed as lame and impotent a conclusion as could well be imagined. It is hardly necessary to say that the play failed to please, especially as its borrowed

charms served less to redeem its dulness than to make
that dulness more conspicuous. Corneille now found
himself in a somewhat embarrassing position. By producing his own *Rodogune*—and this consideration may
not have been overlooked by Gilbert—he would allow
the public to suppose that he had borrowed at least a
plot and a set of *dramatis personae* from M. Gilbert,
unless, indeed, he exposed his indiscreet friend to the
suspicion of treacherous conduct by revealing the whole
story. In the end, with rare moral courage, he had
the piece played (Floridor, of course, being the hero),
and preserved absolute silence as to the wrong inflicted
upon him. It would be clear that one of the plays
was modelled upon the other, but he relied upon the
superior strength of his own. Nor did this self-confidence prove misplaced. *Rodogune*, if it did not quite
reach the level of *Polyeucte*, was an exquisite tragedy,
abounding in dramatic effect, and characterized by a
greater regard for the play of intrigue than the author
had previously shown. The character of Cléopatre,
Queen of Syria, is one of the most terrible ever created
for the stage; and the fifth act, in which Gilbert had
cut so sorry a figure, may well have fascinated the
most apathetic spectator.

Another novelty at the Hôtel de Bourgogne, *Jodelet,
ou le Maître Valet*, a broad comedy in five acts, by Paul
Scarron, may be said to deserve more attention than

it usually receives. As yet, except in tragedy, which depended in a large measure on merits of style, the value of dialogue to a play had not been fully understood. It was chiefly by means of character and incident that the suffrages of the audience were sought. *Jodelet* was written on a wholly different principle. Destitute of strongly-marked personages, and having no more interest than could be awakened by a commonplace love intrigue at Madrid, in the course of which a valet is induced for divers reasons to pass himself off as his master, it relied almost exclusively for effect upon verbal pleasantry—on a rapid succession of quips and cranks, often pregnant with wit and gaiety. It instantly proved successful, especially as Jodelet, for whom it had been written, took care to do justice to the good things put into his mouth. In substance the play belonged to the pre-Corneille school of comedy, but any reactionary tendency it may have had by virtue of its special attractiveness was checked by a practical willingness on the part of the dramatic authors to profit by the lesson it conveyed. Henceforward, in a word, dialogue became a prominent feature—occasionally, perhaps, too prominent a feature—in the lighter drama.

Scarron, as the complexion of his work would suggest, was a joyous devil-may-care, in spite of circumstances which might have soured the finest temper and disposi-

tion. He was born in Paris about 1610, his father
being an opulent Conseiller au Parlement. In his youth
a dark cloud came over his worldly prospects. Madame
Scarron died; the Conseiller married again, and the
second wife, having two children herself, exerted her
influence over her husband—"the best of men,"
Scarron once remarked, "but not the best of fathers"
—to the detriment of the issue of the first marriage.
Incapable of dissimulation, Scarron had the temerity
to upbraid his step-mother for her self-seeking, a
course which raised so great a storm in the household
that the unhappy Conseiller found it expedient to send
him away from home. During his exile he passed
some months in Italy, returning with a lively admiration of the peculiar farce invented in that country.
Though distinguished by a love of wild frolic and a
turn for drollery which prevented him from putting two
serious ideas together, yet, at the instance of his father,
who seems to have had a curious notion of what was
due to the ecclesiastical state, he took the *petit-collet.*
The result was precisely what might have been anticipated. He gave himself up with but little reservation
to riotous living. In more than one mad freak which
startled Paris from its propriety he was the leading
spirit. His connexion with the Church, however, did
not last beyond his thirty-fourth year. As the story
goes, in the course of a carnival at Mans, whither he

had been sent to act as Canon, he stripped himself to
the skin, smeared himself from top to toe with honey,
rolled himself on a heap of light feathers until he was
thickly covered with them, and then, accompanied by
two boon companions similarly attired, started on a
tour of the town. On the bridge they were stopped
and closely surrounded by a swarm of merrymakers,
who thought it an excellent joke to pick the feathers
from their faces. No sooner was Scarron recognized
than the crowd assumed a menacing aspect. In the
escapade of the Abbé they saw only a deep affront
to religion ; and some of their number, regardless
of the divinity that hedges the priesthood, proceeded
to belabour him with right good-will. In this dire
extremity, the feathered bipeds, disengaging themselves from the grasp of their assailants, jumped over
the bridge—long afterwards denominated the Pont de
Scarron—and sought a refuge among the rushes of the
Sarthe. The Canon got away in safety, but his friends
were drowned. It would have been a mercy to Scarron
if he had shared their fate. The chill of the immersion,
acting upon a system already enfeebled by an ill-
regulated life, struck to his very bones ; rheumatism in
its worst form supervened, and in a few months we find
him paralysed beyond hope of cure—"an epitome," as
he himself said, " of human misery."

His bodily affliction, however, neither impaired his

mind nor depressed his spirits. Temporarily expelled from the Church, and all but entirely dependent upon himself for the means of living, he became a man of letters. His pen was at first employed in the service of the theatre, for the actors paid what in those days was regarded as a good price for a play, and to him such work was both congenial and easy. The gaiety and humour thrown into his writings were still characteristic of the man. Bent almost double in an invalid's chair, with his head bowed down on his chest, and with an expression of pain frequently darkening his face, he would keep his hearers in a roar by the drollest of talk. In front of his chair were a desk and writing materials. His fame as a wit having spread abroad, his domicile, situated in the Rue de la Tixeranderie, soon became a resort of the liveliest company in Paris, and for a time eclipsed the glory of the Hôtel de Rambouillet itself. Corneille, Saint-Evremond, Sarrazin, Chapelle, Voiture, Calprenède, Scudéri, Benserade—all these were to be looked for there. Nor, as may be supposed, was the fair sex excluded. In the group at the Abbé's we find Mdlle. de Scudéri, who has just completed another ponderous romance ; Ninon de l'Enclos, who drives away *ennui* by regularly changing her lover with the new moon ; Marion Delorme, who is now an object of adoration to young abbés instead of old cardinals ; and the

Comtesse de Suze, who has forsaken the religion of her fathers in the hope that she may not see her husband again in either this world or the next. Scarron's earnings were not equal to his expenses, but it is not improbable that he received some pecuniary assistance from his father, and before long a pension was given to him by Anne of Austria in testimony of the delight his writings afforded her. In one of those writings he speaks of himself as

> Scarron, par la grace de Dieu,
> Malade indigne de la Reine.

Far less fortunate than the unlaboured *Jodelet* was a carefully-written tragedy by a new dramatist of some distinction in other walks of letters. The eldest son of a Lieutenant-Général of Nemours, François Hédelin begun life as an advocate, but soon afterwards devoted himself to the Church. He then became tutor to Richelieu's nephew, the Duc de Fronsac, and acquitted himself so well that the Cardinal made him Abbé d'Aubignac. Much of his time, however, was taken up in literary pursuits, especially dramatic criticism. Impressed with a deep veneration for the "rules," he insisted that they should never be departed from in any circumstances, and it was said that his critiques would have as much effect in imparting regularity to French tragedy in general as the plays of Corneille themselves. Not that he was listened

to with much docility by the criticized. He wrote
in so captious a spirit that most of them came to
hold him in mingled fear and detestation. It was
obvious enough that a man in this position would
not be well advised to run the gauntlet of criticism
himself, but the Abbé's vanity was greater than his
prudence. *Zénobie*, a prose tragedy now favoured by
the actors, was of his invention. His victims naturally
did not fail to use the weapon thus placed in their
hands. Backed by many friends, they attended the
first representation with a determination that it should
be the last. They laughed at every fine speech, they
roared outright at a scene which the author intended
to be particularly impressive, they declared with startling unanimity—and also with much justice—that
Zénobie exhibited all the shortcomings with which
M. l'Abbé d'Aubignac had reproached his brother
dramatists. The company, overawed by this burst
of ill-will, quickly abandoned the play—a grave
warning to critics living in times when hostile demonstrations in a theatre are not uncommon. The Court
heaped fresh coals of fire upon the Abbé's head. He
boasted on one occasion that he was the only dramatist
who had faithfully observed the precepts of Aristotle.
"M. l'Abbé," said the Prince de Condé, "you are not
to be blamed for doing so; but I shall never forgive
Aristotle for having involved you in so great a disaster."

The Comte de Fiesque having termed *Zénobie* the "wife of *Cinna*,"—" Ay," chimed in another courtier, "and as far above that play as woman is superior to man."

But the Abbé was not without consolation. Even Corneille, of whom he had spoken with something like respect, and who, we may be sure, had refrained from taking part in the demonstration against *Zénobie*, was not proof against failure. His *Théodore Vierge et Martyre*, the chief dramatic novelty of the autumn, had but a brief theatrical existence. As in the case of *La Suite du Menteur*, the author frankly admitted that its condemnation was deserved. "Such a piece," he writes, "is nothing but a body without legs or arms, and consequently without action. I should be wrong to oppose the decision of a public to whom I owe so much." Moreover—and in this point of view his reverse was a triumph—he had refined the taste of his audience so far that the "idée de prostitution" was regarded as a fatal blot upon the piece by those who less than a decade previously had applauded the *Lucrèce* of Duryer. In writing this "tragédie Chrétienne," it would seem, Corneille had a presentiment of its fate. The versification is often slovenly. Two particularly bad lines—

> On la verrait offrir, d'une âme resolue,
> À l'époux sans macule une épouse impollue—

were quoted in the hearing of Fontenelle, his nephew, biographer, and uncompromising admirer. "Who," asked the latter, "could have spoiled paper with such stuff as this?" "Your dear uncle, the great Corneille, in his tragedy of *Théodore*," was the unexpected reply.

Rotrou, Guérin de Bouscal, and Douville also came forward this year, the first and last twice. Michel Leclerc, a young advocate from Albi, became known to fame as the author of *Virginie Romaine*, a tragedy of high merit. The players were anxious to have another from the same pen, but as the author was making good progress in the law he deemed it prudent to give it his undivided attention. Nevertheless, he became a member of the Academy. Another advocate of dramatic proclivities, Jean Magnon, until recently connected with the Présidial of Lyons, was not wise enough to follow Leclerc's example, although unfitted to achieve success on the stage. Having some influence at the theatre, he was prompted by a morbid vanity to persevere, to hope against hope. "But few persons," he gravely writes in a preface, "have more *belles dispositions* in the way of poetry than I." As the players often found to their cost, he wrote with surprising facility. It was once remarked that his tragedies were more easily written than read; that they gave him less trouble to write than the public had in reading them. By a mere accident, however, he unconsciously gained at the outset a sort of immortality. His first essay, *Artaxerxe*, was played by a company of amateurs including one

Jean Baptiste Poquelin, to whom we shall presently
have to devote a little attention.

The year 1646 is remarkable rather for the quality
than the quantity of plays it brought forth. First
comes *La Sœur Généreuse*, a comedy in five acts, by the
Abbé Boyer. Having failed as a preacher in Paris,
the author, whose character was dignified by all the
"amiable vivacity" peculiar to his native province,
Languedoc, proceeded to write for the theatre, but
again mistook his vocation. He afforded a proof that
occasional wit would not compensate an audience for
the want of other qualities. *La Sœur Généreuse*, however, is said to have "enleva tout Paris"—a statement
hardly borne out by the fact that the work was printed,
as it had been played, anonymously. Scarron supplied
Les Boutades du Capitan Matamore and *Jodelet Souffleté*,
rollicking pieces both. In the former, which is in one
act only, Boniface personated the hero, supported by
Beauchâteau, Beaulieu, and Alizon. The cheery humour
of Guillot-Gorju is now looked for in vain ; a few
months previously he had left the stage for good.
Boisrobert founded upon one of Calderon's dramas a
comedy entitled *L'Inconnue*, and the pens of his brother
and Magnon were not allowed to remain idle. But
the finest productions of the year have yet to be
noticed. In Duryer's *Scévole* a page of Roman history
is dramatized with a vigour which Corneille might

have envied ; while Rotrou, in his *Saint-Genest,* soared
to a height which must have surprised his most ardent
partisans.   In this tragedy, by the way, I perceive a
graceful tribute to Corneille.   The actor Genest, being
asked by Diocletian to name the finest pieces in his
repertory, speaks of the works of an author—

> A qui les rares fruits que sa Muse produit,
> Ont acquis dans la scène un légitime bruit;
> Et de qui, certes, l'art comme l'estime est juste,
> Portent les noms fameux de Pompée et d'Auguste ;
> Ces poëmes sans prix, où son illustre main
> D'un pinceau sans pareil a peint l'esprit romain.

The tribute may have been out of place, but the spirit
which prompted it can hardly be overpraised.

Corneille went far to justify that tribute by *Héraclius,*
which, if it did not attain the level of his best work,
displayed a force peculiarly his own.   Its most prominent
defect was a too complicated plot.   The source of the
play has been a subject of hot controversy.   The most
striking incidents are similar to those of Calderon's *En
Esta Vida todo es Verdad y todo Mentira;* indeed, it is
impossible to doubt that one of the two authors was
directly indebted to the other.   The question accordingly arises, who was the first in the field ?   The date
of the Spanish comedy is not known, but we are not
without the means of forming a decided opinion on the
point.   Corneille, whose veracity there is no reason to
doubt, expressly states that he was the inventor of the

plot, and it is scarcely probable that at a time when
the Spanish drama was studied by almost every poet
in Paris he would have made such a statement if it had
not been absolutely true.   In regard to Calderon, he
may have heard of the piece at Madrid, where the
achievements of the French stage were well known, or
seen it at Paris, whither he certainly went at one period
of the Regency.   The suggestion that if he had seen
Héraclius his own play would not have been disfigured by
so many " puerilities " as it is, will have no weight with
those who are aware such puerilities were looked for by
Spanish audiences.   For these reasons, I think, we may
conclude that the plot of *En Esta Vida todo es Verdad y
todo Mentira* was borrowed from *Héraclius*.   In arriving
at this conclusion, of course, I impute no dishonesty
to Calderon.   His conduct must be judged by the
ideas of the age he lived in ; and in the seventeenth
century, as for some time afterwards, a dramatist was
deemed at liberty to silently appropriate a plot if he
treated it in a distinctive manner.   Corneille, it is true,
acknowledged the source of the *Cid* and the *Menteur*,
but in this respect he had notions peculiar to himself.
For the rest, *Héraclius* is an admirable play, in spite of
the defect I have mentioned.   The scene in which Phocas
has to strike Héraclius and his son without being able
to distinguish between them is not one to be forgotten.

Héraclius had not ceased · to quicken the pulse of

Paris when another tragedy of scarcely inferior merit fell into the players' hands. Rotrou, whose passion for the gaming-table had not decreased with years, was arrested for debt. He then sent a message to the theatre, offering to sell *Venceslas*, a piece he had just completed, for twenty pistoles in ready money. The company at once closed with the offer; the dramatist regained his liberty, and the piece was put in rehearsal. Months elapsed before its turn came, as several novelties had previously been accepted. Among these were *La Mort d'Asdrubal*, by the actor Montfleuri, *Le Déniaise*, by Gillet de la Tessonnerie, *L'Intrigue des Filoux*, by L'Etoile, whose connexion with the stage therewith ceased, and two tragedies by the Abbé Boyer *Venceslas* was worth more than all these put together. Seldom had a more impressive story been framed for stage purposes; while the character of the hero, Ladislas, could not but impress itself deeply upon the imagination. Headstrong and violent, he is never entirely alienated from our sympathies, even at the moment when, in the agony of an apparently hopeless passion, he becomes something little better than a midnight assassin. Rotrou is usually spoken of as the author of this noble play, but in point of fact it is merely a translation of one by Francisco de Roxas, with such modifications as were necessary to make it congenial to the recently-acquired tastes of playgoing Parisians.

The friendly interest manifested by the author of
the *Cid* in Rotrou's success—an interest apparently
free from any tinge of jealousy—was now extended
to another writer. I speak of Thomas Corneille, a
brother of the illustrious dramatist. Born in 1625,
just before the idea of *Mélite* was conceived, he had
studied with the Jesuits at Rouen—latterly, it may be
presumed, at Pierre's expense—and had gained some
credit amongst them by writing a poem in excellent
Latin. In early life, although relying exclusively upon
his pen for the means of subsistence, he became the
husband of a younger sister of his brother's wife, an
event which shows that M. de Lamperière, if still alive,
had more respect for the profession of letters than when
Richelieu so unexpectedly summoned him to Paris.
Engaging in manners and in conversation, Thomas
Corneille soon became a prominent figure in society—
the sooner, perhaps, by reason of the contrast he presented in these respects to the awkward and taciturn
Pierre. In the theatre, however, the latter had a
decided advantage over his brother, who, if endowed
with a keen perception of dramatic effect, which study
and experience served to enlarge, could not rise to the
level of the *Cid* and *Polyeucte*. His versification was
particularly weak, the more so, perhaps, because he had
the perilous gift of facility. Indeed, the two brothers
had nothing in common except name, blood, high moral

principle, and an enthusiasm for theatrical work. Yet, despite the similarity of their pursuits and the difference between their characters, they formed a friendship which withstood the crucial test of daily intercourse for nearly forty years. They lived in adjoining houses, and the utmost harmony appears to have subsisted between them. M. Corneille de l'Ile, as the younger was called, treated and spoke of his brother with something like reverence ; Pierre, on his part, used to declare that he would give much to be the author of the other's best work. In a wall separating their studies there was a sliding panel, and when the great Corneille found himself at a loss for a word or a rhyme, as was not unfrequently the case, he would unceremoniously avail himself of this means of communication with his brother to get out of the difficulty. Thomas Corneille's first essay in the drama, *Les Engagements du Hasard*, was suggested by the same play as Boisrobert's *Inconnue*, but was written before that piece made its appearance.

Simultaneously with the production of *Les Engagements du Hasard* a graceful compliment was paid by the Court to the elder Corneille. The opera, a form of composition which admitted of a variety of spectacular effects, had been invented at the end of the previous century by a little band of Florentines, and, favoured by influential personages, Popes and Cardinals not excepted, was now firmly established in Italy. In

1645, a piece belonging to this category, *La Festa teatrale della Finta Pazzia,* was played at the Petit Luxembourg by a company of actors collected from various parts of Italy for the purpose ; Cardinal Mazarin, who occupied without filling the place of Richelieu, having, as the story goes, been urged by Urban VIII., the poet-pontiff, to try the effect in Paris of a product so honourable to the genius of their country. The libretto was by Jacques Torelli, a Venetian architect of literary and theatrical proclivities, and the score by Giulio Strozzi. Had the Minister foreseen how the experiment would turn out he would not have ventured to make it. Most of the spectators testified no pleasure with the entertainment, some in order to mortify the much-hated Cardinal, some on account of knowing little or nothing of Italian, and some because they objected to opera on principle. In the last-mentioned class we find no less cultivated a critic than Saint Evremond. He thought that " a play sung from beginning to end, as if the persons represented had come to the absurd under-standing to discourse in music on the most ordinary as well as the most important affairs of life, was contrary to nature, hurtful to the imagination, and offensive to the understanding." St. Evremond, it is clear, had but narrow views as to the prerogatives of poetry and art; and he might well have been asked whether French tragedy, with its rhymed alexandrines and stately declamation, was less "contrary to nature" than what he denounced for that reason. In 1647, piqued at his ill-success, Mazarin had an *Orfeo* played three times a week for two successive months in the small *salon* of the Palais Royal by another Italian company, headed by a Signora Leonora. Anne of Austria, to humour the Minister, was present at each performance, but on one occasion, when the opera was so timed as to clash with her devotions, she went away early—a circumstance which seems to have caused him the greatest annoyance. Notwithstanding the interest which the Queen feigned to take in it, *Orfeo* became a subject of derision at Court, and the Cardinal, whose chagrin thereat was aggravated by the surreptitious publication of a satire entitled *Le Ballet et le Branle de la Fuite de Mazarin, dansé sur le Théâtre de la France par lui-même et par ses adhérents*, deemed it expedient to give the Italian actors their *congé*. In yielding to the force of circumstances, however, he did not entirely relinquish his purpose. He resolved that a piece of an operatic character, but bearing a different designation, should be written by a French dramatist for the Court; and Corneille was selected to execute the work.

The result was *Andromède*—a graceful poem in action, with musical embellishments here and there, and so constructed as to allow of a variety of stage pictures being presented. The Court was on tip-toe with expectation, but at the eleventh hour the performance was indefinitely deferred. " In the Palais Cardinal," writes Conrart to Félibien, "great preparations have been made to play this carnival a *comédie en musique*, with words by M. Corneille. He has taken the fable of Andromeda as his subject, and, I believe, has treated it more to our taste than have the Italians; but since the recovery of the King," young Louis XIV., now ten years of age, from his late illness, " M. Vincent has turned the Queen against such amusements, the consequence being that" at Court "all such vanities have been dropped." This M. Vincent, if I am not mistaken, was the curé of St. Germain l'Auxerrois, who, not to be deterred by the frowns of the Court from doing what he conceived to be his duty, boldly admonished the Queen for countenancing such pernicious things as stage-plays, especially the " comédie à machines." Her majesty, taking the admonition to heart, referred the question to the Bishops, who, evidently aware of her predilection for the drama, promptly decided in her favour. In regard to amusements, they said, kings and queens must have more latitude than humbler individuals. Historical and serious plays might be represented at Court without scruple. By assisting at such performances, moreover, the courtiers in attendance upon her majesty might be withdrawn from more questionable amusements in the town. The curé of St.

Germain l'Auxerrois, however, was not easily beaten. Supported by seven doctors of the Sorbonne, he held the Queen to be guilty of nothing less than *péché mortel*, and the Sorbonne itself was requested to determine the point thus raised. The result need hardly be stated. Eleven or twelve doctors out of nineteen decided that the ideas of the apostolic age were not binding upon persons living in the seventeenth century (although even now the pleasures of a worldly mind were not to be freely indulged in), and that the Queen was at liberty to witness the performance of any play void of offence to morality. But the complaisance of the Bishops and the Sorbonnists was not attended by any change in the attitude of the Church towards the stage ; at the very moment when they gave judgment, perhaps the remains of some player who had enlivened the Queen in the theatre of the Palais Royal were being interred in an unconsecrated grave.

The Court was now free to see *Andromède ;* but the insurrection of the Fronde, which broke out soon afterwards, and in the course of which Anne of Austria found it necessary to fly from the capital with her son and Mazarin, led to another postponement of the play. The agitation produced in Paris by this contest between the Parliament and the royal authority was naturally inimical to the interests of the theatres. The number of new pieces brought out during the two years which

followed the Day of the Barricades may almost be
counted upon the fingers. The actors of the Marais,
anxious to ascertain how far a *comédie à machines*
would suit the popular taste, had recourse to the Abbé
Boyer, who thereupon devised for them *Ulysse dans
l'Ile de Circé*. Thomas Corneille, following up his first
success, adapted Calderon's *Astrologo Fingido* under the
precisely similar title of *Le Feint Astrologue*, and Francisco
de Roxas's *Entre Bobos Anda El Juego* under that of *Don
Bertrand de Cigarral*. Precisians exclaimed against the
latter as outrageously farcical, but could not keep it
out of the repertory of the players. Boisrobert was
indebted to Lope de Vega for the substance of a *Jalouse
d'Elle-méme*, which also succeeded. Two comedies by
Rotrou, *La Florimonde* and *Don Lope de Cardonne*, also
came from the other side of the Pyrenees, but in the
interval between them he vindicated his right to the
title of an original and effective dramatist by a tragedy
having Cosrhoes for its hero. Duryer, too, had three
plays accepted—*Nitocris*, *Dynamis*, and *Amarillis*. The
merry humour of Scarron again shone forth in *L'Héritier
Ridicule*—a humour in remarkable contrast with the
bitterness of the lampoons he launched against Mazarin
at this period.

The political and social storm began to pass away ;
the Court returned to Paris, and *Andromède* was
represented before it on a stage fitted up for it in

the Hôtel du Petit Bourbon, situated in the Rue des
Poulies, opposite the cloister of St. Germain l'Auxerrois.
" The most critical," says Renaudot, " must confess that
the *Andromède* of the Sieur Corneille is produced in
a manner to charm every spectator." But then the
scenery was under the management of Jacques Torelli,
who, to say nothing of other improvements he had effected
in this branch of theatrical art, had devised the means
of changing an elaborate set in almost less time than
it takes to record the feat. The circumstances under
which he had left Venice are not a little curious. His
achievements as a stage mechanician gave rise there to
the dark suspicion that he had dealings with the Devil ;
and one night an attempt was made by a party of
men in masks to assassinate him. He defended himself
so well that his assailants—more than ever convinced,
perhaps, that their suspicions were not without cause
—took quickly to their heels, though not before one of
them had badly wounded him in the hand. Finding
his native city was becoming too warm for him, the
" great sorcerer," as he was styled, took up his quarters
in less superstitious Paris, where he seems to have
been cordially received by Mazarin. The success of
Andromède was due in a large measure to the scenic
effects devised for it by this versatile Venetian, but the
piece appealed to the ear almost as much as the eye.
Not to speak of the music engrafted upon it, the verse

displayed a grace of fancy for which even the *Cid* had scarcely prepared the audience.

The satisfaction derived by Corneille from the result of his labours was soon to be qualified by the loss of the oldest and most valued of his Parisian friends. For some time past Rotrou had filled the posts of Lieutenant-Particulier and Commissaire-Examinateur au Comté et Bailliage of Dreux, his native place. Here, except when he had a play in rehearsal, he invariably resided—a circumstance which served to exclude him from the Academy, as by the rules of that body any one living out of Paris could not be made one of the Forty. In the summer of this year a terrible epidemic visited the town, and, setting all medical science and skill at defiance, seemed likely to carry off the whole of the population. Most of the local officials sought safety in flight, but Rotrou, disregarding the entreaties of many friends, would not follow their example. Holding the offices he did, he thought it was incumbent upon him to assist in checking the progress of the disorder, to mitigate suffering, and to comfort the bereaved. " The peril in which I stand," he writes to his brother, " is imminent. The bells are at this moment tolling for the twenty-second death to-day. Before long, perhaps, they will toll for me; but my conscience tells me I am only performing my duty. The will of God be done!" He accord-

ingly remained at his post; and three days after the
foregoing letter was written, on the 27th of June,
the gloom which hung over the unfortunate town
was deepened by the announcement that M. Rotrou
had fallen a victim to the scourge. Prone as Frenchmen are to forget public services, the name of this
intrepid magistrate is still held in affectionate veneration by the good people of Dreux, although more than
two centuries elapsed before a monument to his memory
was erected on the scene of his self-sacrifice. In his
case, perhaps, no such tribute was required. His chief
tragedies, with all their inequalities and shortcomings,
occupy a permanent place in French literature; and
the heroism which marked his premature end would
show that if he excelled in the portraiture of generous
impulses and sentiments it was because he was no
stranger to them himself.

Corneille may have found 'some relief from the
sorrow into which he was plunged by Rotrou's death
in the composition of a new play. *Don Sanche d'Arragon*,
heroic comedy, appeared at the end of the year. At
the outset it was received with great favour, but in
the course of a few nights the actors found themselves
playing it to thin audiences. The cause of its failure
is not far to seek. The hero, a man of unknown
origin, but graced with every virtue and accomplish-
ment, is loved by two Queens, and eventually, by means

of a *deus ex machina,* turns out to be the brother of one
and the husband of the other.   How Corneille could
have persuaded himself that such a story would serve
the purpose of a heroic comedy it is not easy to understand.   In his remarks on the play, however, he ascribes
the failure of *Don Sanche* less to its demerits than
the " refus d'un illustre suffrage."   The person here
glanced at, it has been suggested, was Anne of Austria,
before whom the piece was played immediately after its
first production at the Hôtel de Bourgogne.   Don Sanche,
by reminding her in some respects of Cromwell, could
find little favour in her eyes, especially after the
Fronde, says one commentator.   But the refusal of the
Queen's suffrage could have had no prejudicial effect
upon the fate of the play in the Rue Mauconseil.   If
anything, the fact that a play had been frowned upon
at Court would just then have afforded a potent reason
for applauding it in the town, and even in a different
state of public feeling the playgoing community would
hardly have reversed their original verdict because
it was not in unison with the Queen's.   For these
reasons I believe that the failure of *Don Sanche
d'Arragon* was due exclusively to its own defects,
which, however, did not prevent it from succeeding
in other parts of France.

   Don Sanche d'Arragon was followed by a comedy
from Thomas Corneille, *L'Amour à la Mode,* with

Floridor as Oronte, the chief personage, and Jodelet as Cliton, a diverting valet. In the first of these parts a typical Frenchman is described :

> Si chaque objet me plaît c'est sans inquiétude ;
> Jamais de préférence et point de servitude.
> Ainsi quelque beau feu que je fasse paraître,
> Pour ne rien hasarder j'en suis toujours le maître ;
> Ainsi divers objets m'engagent tour à tour,
> Je me regarde seul dans ce trafic d'amour ;
> Et chassant de mon cœur celui qui m'incommode,
> Si je sais mal aimer, du moins j'aime à la mode.

The same piece exhibits a lively coquette, by name Dorothée. Next came *La Folle Gageure*, a comedy by Boisrobert, or rather by Lope de Vega, and *Séleucus*, a tragedy by Montauban. Eighteen or nineteen years previously Rotrou wrote an *Amarillis*, but as the pastoral was then going out of fashion he turned it into a comedy under the title of *Célimène*. Edited by Tristan, the piece was now represented in its original form, with Mdlle. Baron, doubtless looking very picturesque in her male attire, as Bélise. It seems to have made some noise in the world, for Tubeuf, the Intendant des Finances, had it played in the course of a *fête* which he soon afterwards gave at Ruel to the King.

In the cast of *Amarillis* I find a new actor, Jean Villiers, who did well as youthful heroes of tragedy. Nor was he the only recruit secured at this time by the Hôtel de Bourgogne. Eldest son of a learned mathematician, Raimond Poisson received an excellent

education, and on approaching manhood had the good
fortune to win the friendship of the Duc de Créqui. His
family wished him to be a surgeon, but a passion he
had conceived for the stage led him to go into the
country as a strolling player. He was not ill-advised ;
in the delineation of quaint character he quickly
established a high reputation, and the doors of the
Hôtel de Bourgogne were opened to receive him.
But for a slight stutter he would have been deemed
faultless as a comedian. He also became the delight of
the Court, in some measure, perhaps, because the King
liked both his acting and his conversation. In an
engraving by Edelinck the new-comer is shown to have
been of good presence, with good eyes, large mouth,
and fine teeth. Not content with his fame as an
actor, he coveted the laurels of the dramatist, and if
his taste in this respect was not born of talent he did
not wholly fail. His first play was a farce entitled
Lubin, ou le Sot Vengé.

And now we have to speak of another tragedy by
Corneille. *Nicomède* is of almost exclusively political
interest, and even in the middle of the seventeenth
century might have been pronounced dull if the author
had not shot a thread of fine irony through the speeches
of the hero, dignified several scenes with new traits
of highmindedness, and clothed the whole with the
distinctively energetic language of which he was the

great and unrivalled master. The time fixed upon for
its production proved opportune enough. For some
time past the great Condé and the Prince de Conti
had been under lock and key on account of the attitude
they had assumed towards the Court. They were now
released; and the populace of Paris, who not long
previously had loaded them with execrations, went into
transports of joy on hearing the news. *Nicomède*, which
appeared before this effervescence had subsided, contained more than one passage in harmony with public
sentiment, the consequence being that the progress of
the play was frequently interrupted by significant
bursts of applause. If these demonstrations occasioned
annoyance to Corneille it was not simply from a fear
that they would expose him to the ill-will of the Court.
He seems to have carefully held aloof from the political
warfare of the time, however frequent his visits to the
house of the " Abbé " Scarron might be.

By the way, that eccentric invalid, of all men in
the world, had just entered into the matrimonial state.
In the train of one of his habitual guests he had
perceived a beautiful girl of sixteen summers, by name
Françoise d'Aubigné. Her previous history and present
position could not but give her great interest in his
eyes. Of good birth, but a penniless orphan, she had
fallen into the hands of a distant relative, Madame
de Neuillant, who induced her, though not without

considerable difficulty, to abjure Calvinism, the faith in
which she may be said to have been brought up, and
who was now looking for a religious community that
would receive her without the customary *dot.* Meanwhile, Cinderella-like, the girl was reduced to the most
menial occupations, but on one occasion was allowed to
attend her kind protectress to the house in the Rue de
la Tixeranderie. Scarron was sensibly impressed by her
beauty, her charm of manner, her cruel degradation.
Suddenly becoming poetic, he sang of her under the
names of Sylvia and Chloris. In the result, moved by
passion and compassion, he resolved to provide for her
himself. Did she wish to enter a convent ? In that
case he would pay the necessary money. Did she wish
to marry ? As for himself, he could offer only a limited
fortune and a very ugly face. For once the jester was in
earnest ; and Mdlle. d'Aubigné, after a little hesitation,
accepted the second proposal. " Immortality," he said
to the notary as the marriage contract was being prepared, " is what I settle upon her. The names of kings'
wives die with them ; that of the wife of Scarron will
live for ever." The prediction was to be verified,
though not exactly in the way which the grotesque
poet—long since divested for good of his clerical
functions—could have anticipated.

Madame Scarron imparted a new charm and a new
character to the meetings at her husband's house. Her

timidity as a girl soon wore off, revealing a woman of
infinite *savoir-faire*, grace of manner, and even wit.
Her *salon* became nothing less than a temple of fashion.
The proudest cavalier or dame seemed to think it a
privilege to be included in her set. Gilles Boileau,
whose election to the Academy had been opposed by
Scarron, maliciously proclaimed that this social success
was due exclusively to the lady, and her husband
gallantly declared that such was the fact. The tongue
of scandal, as may be supposed, was busy enough with
her name; but there is absolutely no reason to suppose
that her conduct justified the aspersions cast upon her.
Nor does her claim to our respect end here. From the
hour of her marriage a change stole over the tone of
the gatherings in the Rue de la Tixeranderie. The
conversation became decent without losing any of its
brightness—as void of offence to ears polite as any
to be heard in the refined atmosphere of the Hôtel de
Rambouillet.

Scarron himself was to yield to the purifying
influence exerted by his wife. Both at the table and
in his writings he ceased to indulge in unclean jests
and expressions. The first comedy he wrote after
his marriage, *Don Japhet d'Arménie*, bears emphatic
testimony to the change thus wrought in him. Barely
inferior in liveliness to what had gone before it, this
piece, in which a fool by profession appears for the first

time on the French stage, was comparatively free from the taint of indecency. Not until he had finally put off the garb of the Abbé did the poet seem worthy to wear it. *Don Japhet*, indeed, caused so little scandal that the author obtained permission, doubtless through Anne of Austria, to dedicate it to the King—a privilege of which he availed himself in a characteristic manner. " On occasions such as these," he writes, " it is usual to say in fine language that you are the greatest monarch in the world ; that at the age of fourteen or fifteen you are more learned in the art of government than a gray-bearded ruler; that you are the handsomest of men, to say nothing of kings, who are a limited class, &c. I do not propose to do any such thing ; all that may be taken for granted. I simply seek to persuade your majesty that if you extended to me a little practical encouragement (*me faisait un peu de bien*) you would not be doing a great wrong ; that if you gave me a little practical encouragement I should be gayer than I am ; that if I were gayer than I am I should produce lively comedies ; that if I produced lively comedies your majesty would be amused ; that if you were amused your money would not be wasted." M. Scarron, who about this time had lost an action against his mother-in-law for the recovery of his rights, was evidently in want of money ; and it is also worthy of note that the first play he wrote after his marriage with Mdlle. d'Aubigné

—a play which probably owed something to her—should have been associated with the name of Louis XIV.

In the circle at Scarron's house we perceive a man who never appeared in the streets of Paris without striking terror into the hearts of many passers-by. Cirano de Bergerac, of the Regiment des Gardes, was commonly known as a "démon de la bravoure." There was scarcely a day on which he had not a duel on his hands. In one of his letters he says, "Quand tout le genre humain serait erigé en une tête, quand de tous les vivants il n'en resterait qu'un, ce serait encore un duel que me resterait à faire." Most of these little "affaires" were due to a singular cause. His nose was strangely deformed; and if any one inconsiderately stopped in the street to laugh or even stare at it, as was not unfrequently the case, a challenge was sure to follow. Before long, we are told, persons less bellicose than himself passed him with carefully-averted eyes. His sword, too, appears to have been at the service of friends, as a well-attested incident will prove. Sinière, the poet, was once assailed near the Tour de Nesle by no fewer than twenty bravos, probably at the instigation of a noble whom he had lampooned. Cirano, happening to come up at the moment, attacked the ruffians single-handed. In the twinkling of an eye he killed two and put seven *hors de combat;* the residue, recognizing in him the "devil for

courage" (his nose left no doubt as to his identity),
took to flight in a body. From this moment he was
called the "intrepid." He also distinguished-himself in
the sieges of Mouzon and Arras, though at the cost of
receiving a severe wound on each occasion. Hitherto
he had led an ill-regulated life ; but a fear that his
injuries would prove mortal, joined to the exhortations
of a nun from the Faubourg St. Antoine, brought him
to a better way of thinking. He left the army,
returned to Paris, and, without ceasing to cross swords
with those who gave him offence, especially in regard
to his nose, devoted himself to literature.

Nor were his hopes disappointed. He quickly gained
renown as a writer on scientific subjects. Eight years
previously, at the age of twenty-six, he had induced
Gassendi to receive him as a pupil, and the instruction
so gained was now to bear good fruit. Among other
works he wrote a *Histoire Comique des Etats et Empires
de la Lune et du Soleil,* in which more than one sign
of original thought is to be found. "Je crois," he
says, "que les planettes sont des mondes autour du
soleil, et que les étoiles fixes sont aussi des soleils, qui
ont des planettes autour d'eux—c'est à dire, des mondes
que nous ne voyons pas d'ici, à cause de leur petitesse,
et parce que leur lumière empruntée ne saurait venir
jusqu'à nous. De sorte que tous ces autres mondes
qu'on ne voit point, ou qu'on ne voit qu'imparfaitement,

ne sont rien que l'écume des soleils qui se purgent."
He adds—"and as a fire throws out its cinders, so the
sun throws out some of the matter which nourishes
their fire." How remarkable this passage is I need
not stay to point out. Not content with pursuing
one walk of literature, Cirano wrote *La Mort d'Agrip-*
pine, a tragedy dealing with Sejanus's conspiracy against
Tiberius. It was played at the Hôtel de Bourgogne
under the patronage of the Duc d'Arpajon, in whom the
author had found an influential friend. Cirano's success
as a scientific writer was to interfere with his success as
a dramatist. His views on astronomical matters
brought him into collision with the priesthood, and at
the first performance of his tragedy a large section of
the audience assembled in a hostile spirit. In the fourth
act, where Séjan, in view of his triumph over Tibère,
delivers these words—

Trappons ; voilà l'Hostie !

the storm broke. The voices of the actors were drowned
in screams of "athée !" "méchant !" "comme il parle
du Saint Sacrement !" One of the scenes between Séjan
and Terentius also gave rise to a display of indignation.
The Duc d'Arpajon, dismayed by the tumult, took less
interest in so impious a writer as Cirano was supposed
to be ; but as the latter belonged to an opulent family
in Périgord, and was accordingly above want, the loss
he suffered could hardly have preyed deeply upon his

mind. To him it was a matter of far greater importance that his play had failed.

A still greater disaster than this was soon to befall the Hôtel de Bourgogne. The players appeared in a new historical tragedy by the author of the *Cid*, entitled *Pertharite, Roi des Lombards.* Any hopes they may have entertained as to the result of their labours were doomed to disappointment. Not only was the poetry comparatively poor, but the subject, as Fontenelle himself is constrained to admit, was singularly ill-chosen. The spectacle of a husband ransoming his wife at the price of a kingdom could not be very impressive—could not but excite ridicule—at a time when marital obligations were incurred only to be set aside. In the result, *Pertharite* did not survive a second representation, and as far as I am aware no one has ever maintained that it deserved a better fate. For reasons unexplained, Corneille, who had cheerfully acquiesced in the popular verdict upon *Théodore*, was so irritated by his last reverse that he resolved, as Ben Jonson had done in like case, to write no more for the stage. " It is better," he said, " that I should take leave of my own accord than wait to receive it. It is right that after " more than " twenty years of work I should begin to see that I am getting too old to be still in vogue. In taking this step I have this satisfaction, that I leave the French stage in a better state than I found it, as regards both art and morals "—a justifiable piece of self-flattery. The Parisian world probably attributed this resolution to a temporary fit of pique, especially as he was only forty-seven years of age, and as none of his contemporaries, Duryer not excepted, were able to contend against him. Events, however, showed that he was terribly in earnest. Withdrawing to Rouen, he proceeded to translate Thomas-à-Kempis, a work in which the Queen appears to have taken a practical interest, and to write the *Examens* which form so interesting an adjunct to his works.

It is not improbable that the undignified vexation exhibited by the great dramatist was due in some measure to the favour accorded at about the same time to a play of decidedly inferior merit, and written, more-over, by one for whom he entertained no particular respect. This was a *Cassandre Comtesse de Barcelone*, by Boisrobert. For some nights it drew large audiences, and the Queen had it played at the Palais Royal for her diversion. Before long it appeared in print, with a characteristically modest preface from the delighted author. " I am assured, reader," he writes, " that this tragi-comedy, which at the theatre has been deemed so fine by the whole of the Court and town, will prove scarcely less agreeable on paper—that thou wilt find it as effectively sustained by the delicacy and majesty of its versification as by the dignity of its subject.

If Villegas, a somewhat obscure Spanish poet"—this
obscure poet, if I may presume to interrupt the Abbé
for a moment, was the Anacreon of Spain, a fact long
since acknowledged—"had Villegas been as fortunate
in the *dénouement* as in the central idea of the piece,
he would have doubtless equalled the most famous
poets of his nation and time." In plainer language,
Boisrobert and . Villegas together were a match for
Lope de Vega or Calderon, and *Cassandre* was fit company for *La Vida es Sueño* and plays of similar calibre.

With another novelty of this year a curious little
story is connected. Hitherto it had been the custom
of the players to buy pieces outright, the amount
paid for one being determined by the reputation of
the dramatist. The sum received by Corneille had
been about two hundred crowns. One morning, by
appointment, Tristan appeared in the green room to
read a tragi-comedy entitled *Les Rivales*, "copiée de
Rotrou." Every one was pleased with it, and the
authorities, believing that it had been written by
the author of *Mariamne*, offered a hundred crowns for
it. Tristan gladly accepted these terms, at the same
time revealing what until that moment had been a
dead secret. The play was from the pen of a youth
named Philippe Quinault, in whose fortunes he had
come to feel considerable interest. He presumed that
this fact would not interfere with the completion

of the arrangement just made ? The amiable device
employed by Tristan in the interests of his *protégé*
did not succeed.   The players declared that they
could not afford to risk more than fifty crowns on a
piece by an untried hand.   Tristan, satisfied that
the piece was worth more than this, and unwilling,
perhaps, to acknowledge his defeat, suggested that a
system of payment by results should be adopted.   For
example, the author might be allowed a ninth of the
receipts during the first run of his piece, which there-
after should belong exclusively to the theatre.   Now,
the old system was not without some drawbacks.   If
a piece failed, the players were much out of pocket
by the transaction ; if it proved more than usually
successful, they were expected to make the author
a substantial present.   The system proposed by Tristan
seemed better than this, and was almost immediately
adopted.   Le Sieur Quinault had good reason to con-
gratulate himself upon the change.   The *part d'auteur*,
as the dramatist's share of the receipts was termed,
must in his case have been a great deal more than fifty
crowns.   The applause bestowed upon *Les Rivales* was
so uproarious that it could be heard two streets away.

It has been stated that Quinault was a native of
Feiblin, in La Marthe, and that in early life he was
in the service of Mondori.   Neither of these assertions
is true.   He was born in Paris in 1635, his parents,

as we learn from an entry in the registers of St. Eustache, being "Thomas Quinault, maître boulanger, et Perrine Riquier, sa femme, demeurants Rue de Grenelle." More fortunate than many of the bourgeoisie at that period, he received a good education, a circumstance which proves that Quinault père was not under the necessity of sending him out to service. Before entering his teens he attracted the notice of Tristan, who, alive to his precocious intelligence and engaging manners, treated him with almost paternal tenderness. Naturally enough, he soon came to sympathize with the poet in his tastes and pursuits, and in the result *Les Rivales* was written. By means of the money he received for this work, with some added by Tristan, he was placed with an Avocat au Conseil. Nor was it simply by the success of this comedy that he justified the interest which Tristan took in the development of his youthful promise. Handsome, vivacious, sociable, and modest, Quinault was esteemed by all with whom he came into contact, or at least with all those who were not induced by jealousy of his natural and acquired advantages to disparage him.

No less successful than *Les Rivales* was a comedy by the author of the disastrously unsuccessful *Agrippine* of a few months before. *Le Pédant Joué*, as it was called, had two noteworthy features. It was written in prose, and a peasant in the piece, contrary to al¹

precedent, was made to speak in the jargon of his
native province.   The dialogue is often bright and
amusing, but what rendered the piece particularly acceptable was the fact that the pedagogue-hero closely
resembled a person well known in Paris—namely, M.
Granger, Principal of the Collége de Beauvais, Cirano's
Alma Mater.   For the best scene of all, that of the
Turkish galley, with an expression which soon got
into everybody's mouth—" Que diable allait-il faire
dans cette maudite galère ? "—he was indebted to a
piece lately played in the country.   The production of
Le Pédant Joué gave rise to a singular incident.   Montfleuri, who played in it, had the misfortune to offend
the author, who took a characteristic revenge.   " Enfin,
gros homme," he wrote to the player, " je vous ai vu !
Mes prunelles ont achevé sur vous de grands voyages ;
et le jour que vous éboulâtes corporellement jusqu'à moi
j'eus le temps de parcourir votre hemisphere, ou, pour
parler plus véritablement, d'en decouvrir quelques can-
tons.   Si la terre est un animal vous voyant aussi rond
et aussi large qu'elle, je soutiens que vous êtes son mâle,
et quelle a depuis peu accouchée de l'Amérique dont
vous l'avez engrossée."   This was bad enough, but worse
remained behind.   The hot-tempered poet commanded
the actor not to appear on the stage for a month.
Montfleuri disregarded the injunction, evidently be-
ieving that Cirano could not be in earnest, or that,

even if he were, the result would be the same.   He was
soon undeceived.   In the front of the pit, with grim
determination in his looks, stood his terrible enemy, who
in a voice of thunder told him to retire or abide the consequences.   He tremblingly obeyed ; and the audience,
either lost in astonishment or afraid of provoking the
" démon de la bravoure," manifested no resentment at
this unheard-of act of tyranny.

Le Pédant Joué had scarcely been withdrawn when
the Hôtel de Bourgogne found itself engaged in a trial
of strength with the Théâtre du Marais.   One evening
Scarron read to some guests in the Rue de la Tixeranderie a piece destined for the latter house, *L'Ecolier de
Salamanque*.   It was an adaptation by himself of a
Spanish piece, which he named.   The Abbé Boisrobert,
who was one of the company, immediately procured
the original, adapted it in his own fashion, and had
it brought out at the Hôtel de Bourgogne, under the
title of *Les Généreux Ennemis*, a short time before
L'Ecolier de Salamanque appeared at the other theatre.
Moreover, when *L'Ecolier* did appear, the Abbé, not
content with speaking ill of it, took no pains to remove
the very natural impression among playgoers that
Scarron had trod in his footsteps.   For this breach of
the laws of honour he did not go unpunished.   The
inevitable comparison between the two plays told heavily
against him.   *L'Ecolier de Salamanque* was written in

Scarron's distinctive style, and, unlike *Les Généreux
Ennemis*, introduced a character which at once caught
the fancy of the town.   I refer to Crispin, the parent of
a numerous progeny of stage valets.   The origin of this
unique figure is not far to seek.   Many deserters from
the Spanish army had found employment in the houses
of wealthy French families, chiefly in the midlands.   In
Crispin, I think, we have one of these deserters turned
into a valet.   His dress resembles that of a Spanish
soldier, his speech abounds in allusions to war.   If in
one respect he seems to belong to Paris rather than
Madrid—if he puts off the saturnine gravity peculiar
to his nation and becomes a wit—it was because the
conditions of his existence required him to be amusing.
However that may be, he quickly ingratiated himself
with every playgoer, and *L'Ecolier de Salamanque* drew
large crowds to the often deserted pit of the Marais.
Scarron showed his sense of Boisrobert's conduct in
more than one acrid epigram ; indeed, to judge from
a letter he wrote to Marigny on the subject, even the
influence of his wife could not prevent his indignation
from leading him into repelling coarseness.

During its brief existence *Les Généreux Ennemis* was
played alternately with *Les Illustres Ennemis*, by Thomas
Corneille.   Quinault was now deep in law-studies, but
he found time to write *L'Amant Indiscret*, the incidents
of which seem to have been suggested by a piece

represented at Lyons in the previous year, *L'Etourdi*. The stage-spectators at the first performance overwhelmed him with congratulations, but one of the group, a client of his, was silenced by force of sheer astonishment. Could the author of these pretty and flowing lines be the budding lawyer who but a few hours previously had proved himself a master of the details and phraseology of litigation? The Abbé Boisrobert, it would seem, was occupied in a less worldly manner on the eve of his hour of trial as a dramatist. One morning he was seen at a church in an attitude of deep devotion, with an enormous breviary open before him. "Who is this excellent man?" somebody asked M. de Coupeauville, Abbé de la Victoire. "The Abbé Boisrobert, who is to preach this afternoon at the Hôtel de Bourgogne," was the reply. In other words, a comedy by the unctuous Abbé, *Les Apparences Trompeuses*, was to be played for the first time that day. Not long afterwards Coupeauville met Boisrobert leaving the theatre on foot. "Where," he asked, "is your coach?" "Stolen while I was inside the theatre," answered Boisrobert. "What!" exclaimed Coupeauville, "at the very doors of your cathedral? The affront is unendurable." Another piece written by Boisrobert at this time was *L'Amant Ridicule*, which included a Ballet des Plaisirs. The lover in question, learning that his mistress deems valour, a quality in which he is unfortunately deficient, the highest grace of man, induces a cousin to feign a duel with him at a moment when she must chance to witness it. The advantage, of course, is to be on his side; but the cousin, who happens to be desperately enamoured of the lady himself, takes particular care that this part of the stratagem is not carried out. It must have been a source of considerable gratification to the Abbé that *L'Amant Ridicule*, which pleased everybody, should have come out at almost the same time as another adaptation by Scarron from the Spanish, *Le Gardien de Soi-Méme*, which deservedly failed. By this coincidence he gained an advantage over his now inveterate enemy, but in justice to the latter it should be pointed out that a play by Thomas Corneille on the same subject, *Le Géolier de Soi-Méme*, met with a similar fate. In *La Comédie sans Comédie*, a strange medley by Quinault of every known form of the drama, the Théâtre du Marais again lighted upon a little mine of wealth, thanks in some measure to the efforts of two players new to the town—Laroque and Hauteroche.

La Comédie sans Comédie, which did not justify its appellation, was the last of Quinault's plays which had the benefit of being revised by the author of the still popular *Mariamne*. In the autumn of 1655 Tristan died at the Hôtel de Guise from consumption, probably aggravated by his irregular habits, his devotion to the gaming-table, and, above all, his grief at the loss of an idolized wife and son. But few of the day-dreams of his youth had been realized. In the following lines, which he is said to have written as an epitaph upon himself, we seem to have the echo of a wasted life—

> Ebloui de l'éclat de la splendeur mondaine,
> Je me flattai toujours d'une espérance vaine ;
> Faisant le chien couchant auprès d'un grand seigneur ;
> Je me vis toujours pauvre, et tâchai de paraître ;
> Je vécus dans la peine attendant le bonheur,
> Et mourus sur un coffre en attendant mon maître.

Nor was this the only scrap of autobiography he gave us. Nominally a romance, his *Page Disgracié* presents us with a vivid narrative of his early career. But even in his most self-reproachful mood he must have felt that he had not lived wholly in vain. The success of *Mariamne* had "balanced" that of the *Cid.* In the delineation of the softer passions he had illustrated the superiority of the language of the heart to the jargon of gallantry. The much-coveted honour of a seat in the Academy had been conferred upon him. It is probable, however, that these circumstances afforded him less comfort in his closing hours than the almost filial affection of Quinault, whose gratitude to his old benefactor could not have proceeded from a sense of favours to come.

In the same year, to the intense relief, perhaps, of Parisian society in general and Montfleuri in particular, Cirano de Bergerac was gathered to his fathers. Entering the Duc d'Arpajon's house one evening, he was struck on the head by a piece of wood, possibly hurled at him from somebody who had felt the point of his invincible sword. The wound assumed a threatening aspect; and the Duc, perhaps anxious to dissociate himself from the author of *La Mort d'Agrippine,* counselled him to seek rest away from Paris. In the result he went to the house of a brother, Cirano de Mauvières, where, although watched over with the greatest care, he died. He was then in the prime of manhood, having been born as recently as 1620. His innumerable duels had prevented him from doing justice to his intellectual gifts, but the little he had written was to keep his name alive. The influence of *Le Pédant Joué* was strong with a great dramatist of after years; and the fantastic treatise on the sun and moon, itself a faint imitation of Rabelais, is supposed to have suggested the idea of *Gulliver's Travels* to Swift.

Baron, too, was now to disappear. Impersonating Don Diègue in the *Cid,* he was wounded in the foot by the sword of Chimène's father, and as gangrene supervened the doctors found it necessary to amputate the injured member. Exclusively dependent upon his earnings as an actor, and reluctant, perhaps, to live upon the charity of his comrades, he refused his consent to the operation. "A pretty figure," he is reported to have said, "an actor with a wooden leg would make on the stage!" In a similar emergency, it seems, Marshal Fabert came to a similar resolution. "What!" he exclaimed, "allow my foot to be cut off? No; death shall have me all at once or not at all." M. le Maréchal, to the discomfiture of his medical advisers, recovered without the aid of so violent and costly a remedy; but Baron was less fortunate. In Loret's *Gazette* for the 9th October (this little work, which had been begun about two years previously, was a news-letter in burlesque verse, addressed to Mdlle. de Longueville) I find these lines—

> Baron, fameux comédien,
> Qui récitait des vers si bien,
> Et qui, dans l'Hôtel des Bourgogne,
> Par son organe et bonne trogne,
> Représentait parfaitement
> Le héros, le prince, et l'amant,
> Est décédé cette semaine
> D'une impitoyable gangrène.

In their hour of mourning the players of the Hôtel de Bourgogne had recourse to a new dramatist, by name Samuel Chappuzeau, who had practised medicine at various German Courts, but was now director of a troupe of French comedians established at Hanover. His first dramatic essay was a comedy concerning *Damon et Pythias*. Effectively constructed, it failed most lamentably in regard to dialogue, and before long

was consigned to the " dread repose " of the shelf.   The
counter-attraction at the Marais was a comedy by Boisrobert, *Les Coups d'Amour et de Fortune,* an unacknowledged adaptation of *Il Credito Matto.*   The unctuous
Abbé was at this time under sentence of banishment
from his beloved Paris, having inadvertently broken the
Third Commandment on losing some money at cards to
Mazarin's nieces.   By a not uncommon coincidence, the
subject of *Il Credito Matto* was treated by Quinault in
a comedy produced almost simultaneously in the Rue
Mauconseil; and Boisrobert, finding that the source of
the plot had not been avowed, had the effrontery to
maintain that his young rival had " imitated " him, and
that " de mauvaise grâce."   Scarron soon afterwards
came out with a startling statement.   Both dramatists,
he alleged, had stolen the plots of these pieces from an
unacted piece by Tristan, the story of which had been
devised by Mdlle. Beauchâteau.   " In this matter," continued the triumphant Scarron, " I speak with authority,
as the comedians induced me to supply what was wanting in the play—namely, the fifth act."   Mdlle. Beauchâteau, as may be guessed, had herself been indebted
for her materials to *Il Credito Matto,* which had not
come in Scarron's way, and Quinault was unaware of
the existence of his old benefactor's piece.   In any
case the two dramatists would have saved themselves
much annoyance if at the outset they had frankly

confessed their obligations to the foreign comedy. The incident just recorded may have given interest to a post-humous tragedy by Tristan, *La Mort du Grand Osman*, which stood sadly in need of such adventitious support. It was followed by *La Belle Invisible*, a gross plagiarism by Boisrobert of one of Douville's pieces, and *Le Marquis Ridicule*, another attempt on the part of Scarron to make his audience ill with laughter.

The Théâtre du Marais, though not very powerful in a histrionic point of view, had long been a formidable rival to the Hôtel de Bourgogne, and was now to achieve the greatest commercial success exhibited in old French theatrical history. Quinault and Thomas Corneille, who had hitherto written nothing but tragi-comedies and comedies, suddenly essayed their powers in tragedy. The first gave the town a *Mort de Cyrus*, the second a *Timocrate*. Neither elevated nor energetic, *Cyrus* did not hold the audience for a moment, and the ridicule excited by such lines as one put into the mouth of Thomiris—

Que l'on cherche partout mes tablettes perdues —

quickly stamped it as a failure. Very different was the fate of *Timocrate*. The walls of the theatre shook with applause. Louis XIV. himself deigned to be a spectator of one of the performances. The author, in addition to being told that he had surpassed his brother, was seriously recommended to lay down the pen for good, as he had nothing to add to his glory, and might imperil it by other works. In all, *Timocrate* was represented eighty-four times in succession, by far the longest run yet achieved. It is próbable the piece would have remained on the bills for some time after that if the actors had not by degrees found their task intolerably monotonous. "Messieurs," said the orator of the troupe to the audience, "it would seem that you are never tired of listening to *Timocrate.* For ourselves, we are utterly tired of playing it. If we go on doing so we shall run the risk of forgetting our other pieces. Permit us, then, to withdraw it." It was evidently believed behind the scenes that the tragedy might be revived at no distant period with equal success; and the audience, perhaps holding a similar opinion, granted the request. Curiously enough, *Timocrate* was never seen on the stage again. Extravagantly praised, it had to face the ordeal of extravagant censure, and its merits were not sufficiently rare to carry it through so trying an ordeal.

In his anxiety to qualify the effect created by *Timocrate*, the exiled Abbé Boisrobert, who was not fertile in original ideas, fell back upon a play written some ten years previously by one Delacaze, re-wrote it with scarcely an alteration except in the nomenclature of the characters, and, dubbing it *Théodore*, had it

played at the Hôtel de Bourgogne as his own. He
evidently supposed that the original was not known
in Paris, but a pamphlet entitled *Remarques sur la
" Théodore," dediée à M. de Bois-Robert Métel, Abbé de
Châtillon, par A. B., Sieur de Saumaize,* undeceived him
somewhat roughly on this point. After a long absence
from Paris, during which he had visited Rome in the
suite of Christina of Sweden, another dramatist who
had been guilty of barefaced plagiarism, Gabriel Gilbert,
reappeared with two tragedies of his own invention—
Cresphonte and *Les Amours de Diane et d'Endymion.*
The latter is said to have been composed at the request
of his royal mistress, who may have alarmed him into
returning to Paris by the assassination of Mondaleschi.
Quinault also figured at this time as the author of
two plays; but neither *Le Mariage de Cambyse* nor
Amalazonte, as they were called, justified his reputation.
Thomas Corneille, in order to follow up the success
of *Timocrate,* here wrote a *Bérénice,* for the outline of
which he was indebted to Madeleine de Scudéri's
Cyrus.

In the words of Loret, the "jeune Corneille" was
now "la merveille du théâtre," especially as Duryer,
after a long and not wholly abortive struggle with ill-
fortune, had just gone to his rest. But the young
poet was not to enjoy this distinction very long. Pierre
Corneille, who was now in his fifty-third year, and

whose moroseness had not been lightened by the dull routine of his Rouen life and the labour of translating Thomas-à-Kempis, began to cast wistful glances at the scene of his early triumphs. The pique he felt at the condemnation of *Pertharite* had passed away, while the longing to figure again as the hero of a first night— to have his verse declaimed by a trained stage artist, to hear the shower of applause that would follow each noble speech, to receive the homage due to the greatest dramatic genius of his time—took possession of his mind. His altered resolution was to be guessed at by some lines addressed to the magnificent and lettered Fouquet, who, delighted to be the means of restoring the author of the *Cid* and *Polyeucte* to the boards, left no stone unturned to confirm it. He loaded the poet with delicately-rendered benefits,. at the same time suggesting that he would do well to treat the finely-tragic legends of Œdipus and Camma. In the former, by far the more difficult of the two, Corneille found an acceptable theme ; and an *Œdipe* from his pen, with Floridor as the fate-driven hero and Mdlle. Beauchâteau as Jocaste, was brought out at the Hôtel de Bourgogne early in 1659.

As may be supposed, the news that he had re-entered the lists created no little excitement. The audience assembled in a pleasantly sanguine mood, for it was probable that the contemplation which comes of

leisure had reinvigorated his mind, and he was reported
to have elaborated the play with patient care. Unfortunately, their hopes were only partially realized.
Executed under the most favourable conditions, *Œdipe*
yet fell short of anything like greatness, dramatic or
poetic, and must have gone with the succession of plays
beginning with *Rodogune* to suggest that Corneille was
no longer capable of producing a *Cid*, a *Cinna*, or a
Polyeucte. In truth, his genius seems to have decayed
soon after his marriage. It was a plant which attained
a precocious maturity, put forth the richest fruit, and
then passed into a state of comparative unproductive-
ness. In all that he had conceived during the last
seventeen years a gradual decline of force is apparent.
Here and there we are reminded of what he had been,
but the effect is like that of a flash of lightning in an
ever-darkening sky. Unlike Sophocles, whose *Œdipus*
he had lately striven to surpass, he fell short of himself as time went on. " Believe me," the outspoken
and misanthropic Duc de Montausier said to him,
" verse-making is the prerogative of youth only ; " and
in this instance, it must be allowed, the proposition
was not unsupported by the logic of facts. Nor did he
retard his downward course by making full use of the
residue of his power. He now wrote in the spirit of a
statesman rather than of a poet. He aimed at political
instead of ethical interest. He subordinated passion

and imagination to force of reasoning. He appealed more than ever to the sentiment of admiration. He relied upon ingenious complexity·of plot in preference to transcripts of human nature. If his object in all this was to disguise his weakness, to prove that

la main qui crayonna
La mort du grand Pompée et l'âme de Cinna

had not lost its cunning, he could not have been worse advised. His change of policy led him to select subjects unsusceptible of the best kind of dramatic effect, and it was not in his power to redeem or gloss over their poverty by beauties of detail and diction. Broadly speaking, his later plays are heavy, uninspiring, and lifted above mediocrity only by the dignity and keen insight with which he treated his ill-chosen materials. Nevertheless, his popularity outlived its cause. The announcement of a novelty from his pen did not fail to bring together a large and well-disposed audience, and the voice of criticism was softened by a grateful remembrance of the intellectual enjoyment derived from his best work. *Œdipe*, with all its short-comings, was applauded so vigorously that Louis XIV. appeared in the Rue Mauconseil to see it—an honour not frequently done to the theatre. From this time, however, the sway Corneille had so long held in the realm of the drama was to be divided with another.

His supremacy as a tragic poet was still unshaken by rivalry, but in comedy he had to yield the palm to one of a troupe of strolling players who had just received the King's permission to establish themselves at the Hôtel du Petit Bourbon.

CHAPTER VI.

1658—1661.

In the Rue Saint Honoré, at the corner of the Rue des Vieilles Etuves, there had long stood a house bearing the sign of the Pavillon des Cinges, and appropriately ornamented over the doorway with an old sculpture representing apes in an apple-tree. Soon after the assassination of Henri Quatre this house fell into the hands of an upholsterer named Poquelin, thenceforward one of the most prosperous of the Parisian bourgeoisie. Besides doing well in business, he held the appointment of *valet-tapissier* to the King— that is, had to accompany his majesty about the country, look to the draperies of the apartments occupied by the Court in the châteaux, and in particular circumstances to make the royal bed. He married one Marie Cressé, who possessed a little fortune, and who, although her father was a tradesman, seems to have been of good descent. Four or five children were the issue of the union, the eldest, Jean Baptiste Poquelin, coming into the world on the 15th January 1622.

As a boy, it is said, this Jean Baptiste displayed a

surprising turn for mimicry. He took off with both accuracy and humour the peculiarities of servants, customers in the shop, and the priests and worshippers at the church to which his mother, one of the most pious of women, led him every Sunday for mass and vespers. Madame Poquelin, proud as she may have been of his precocious intelligence, sternly set her face against such amusements, especially when they were indulged in at the expense of the clergy. "Lisette," said Jean Baptiste to a work-girl in the house, after receiving a sound chastisement for such an offence, "can you tell me why my imitations of the priest make them so furious ? " "Certainly," was the reply ; "you succeed only too well, my little Jean." It is obvious that if the young mimic was to become a respectable citizen he should have been kept away from the theatre ; as it was, a good-natured relative—usually supposed to have been his maternal grandfather, who, however, died in 1626— frequently carried him off to see Bellerose and the Trois Farceurs at the Hôtel de Bourgogne. Before long he had theatricals on the brain, and neither threats nor caresses could induce him to initiate himself into the mysteries of his father's business. "I verily believe," M. Poquelin exclaimed, "that the boy will turn actor" —a suggestion which at that time was made only to send a shiver through the frames of all right-minded persons, playgoers not excepted. Modern criticism has rejected these stories as apocryphal, but at least they are old enough to justify us in accepting them as the echo of reminiscences from Jean Baptiste's lips of a not uneventful early life.

In his fourteenth year, after losing his mother, M. Poquelin's heir was sent as a day-boarder to the Collége de Clermont, Rue St. Jacques. Here, as a means of extending their influence and gaining valuable recruits, those *pères de la ruse*, the Jesuits, educated a large number of boys gratuitously, or at all events for a merely nominal sum. Consequently, the pupils represented many grades of society, and the variety of character they exhibited must have brought much food for reflection to so quick an observer as Jean Baptiste is reported to have been. His chosen companions at the Collége were four youths destined to attain eminence in different ways—the Prince de Conti, Chapelle, Bernier, and Hesnault. According to biographical tradition, he made rapid progress in his humanities and rhetoric, the more so because the Jesuits industriously fostered a spirit of emulation amongst their flock. Nor was his education confined to what he learnt in the Rue St. Jacques. Chapelle, at the instance of his father, entered upon an independent course of philosophy under Gassendi; and Poquelin, with Hesnault and Bernier, was allowed to accompany him therein. It is significant that in a short time he should have set to work upon a translation of Lucretius, but we may reasonably doubt whether the strangely qualified epicureanism of the tutor exercised more than a passing influence over his mind. Bellicose de Bergerac, as the story goes, obtained admission to the little class by bursting in upon them, laying his hand upon his sword, and threatening the philosopher with an early grave if the favour were denied him. In 1641, owing to the illness of his father, Poquelin went with Louis XIII. and the Court to the south as *valet-tapissier*, the reversion of which office had previously been secured for him by purchase. But M. Poquelin did not intend his son to have only one string to his bow. Jean Baptiste devoted himself to law studies ; and a satirical ballad against him in after years, referring to his appearance at the Palais de Justice in the robe of an advocate, may be taken as a proof that he was actually called to the bar.

His liking for the stage, however, had not been destroyed by the distractions of the Collége de Cler-mont, upholstery, or the law. He joined a company of amateur actors who, collectively known as the "Illustre Théâtre," played upon a stage supported by trestles on a racket-court in the Fosses de Nesle or the Quartier de St. Paul. These performances were well attended, for the simple reason, perhaps, that no one had to pay for looking on. The amateurs, attributing their success to another cause, set up their theatre in a tennis-court in the Faubourg St. Germain, and, in defiance of the privileges of the comedians by profession, charged a small fee for admission. Magnon's *Artaxerxe*, as already stated, was one of the pieces they played. The self-confidence of the little band was somewhat rudely dispelled. By ceasing to act gratuitously they at once lost ground in public estimation. If anybody witnessed their performances it was only to decry them. In this emergency, Poquelin, assuming the command of the troupe, summoned to his aid a few players who chanced to be in Paris at the time—two brothers and two sisters named Béjart, apparently of good birth, and a buffoon named Duparc, better known as Gros-René(e). Madeleine Béjart, the elder of the two sisters, is described by a contemporary, Tallemant des Réaux, as one of the best of living actresses : she was certainly one of the most beautiful. Even her charms, however, did not restore the fortunes of the Illustre Théâtre. The enterprise ended in disaster, Poquelin being proceeded against and imprisoned for debt by the costumier, the tallow-chandler, and other creditors. Happily, this cruel experience did not make him disgusted with the stage. By this time, indeed, his taste for it had become a passion ; and at length, giving way to an overmastering impulse, he took possession of a little fortune bequeathed to him by his mother, formally relinquished his

right to the reversion of his father's office at Court,
resigned his chances of forensic distinction, and determined to go into the country with the Béjarts and
Duparc as a strolling player. His family, of course,
were greatly distressed at the news. In their view
he was deliberately foregoing excellent prospects to
adopt a calling held in but scant respect, the decree
of 1641 notwithstanding. In order to diminish their
annoyance he exchanged the name of Poquelin for that
of MOLIÈRE, the origin of which is a matter of specula-
tion. But any entreaties that may have been made
to him to reconsider his intention fell upon deaf ears.
In 1646 he left Paris with his new-found friends ;
and Tallemant, manifestly unable to believe that a
passion for the stage could account for such an act of
self-sacrifice, said that the young advocate had deserted
the benches of the Sorbonne to follow Madeleine Béjart
—a notion which in years to come obtained some
currency, but which, as every well-informed person can
see, is not borne out by a scrap of evidence worthy of
the name.

Molière, to whom his companions looked from the
outset for guidance, may have been induced by an
almost proverbial generosity to make good the defici-
ences of the theatrical exchequer from his own pocket,
but even in that case the troupe could hardly have
escaped many of the hardships inseparable from the

course of life they were taking. It was truly a changeful life—one of constant tramping from place to place, of alternate success and disappointment, of steady perseverance in all circumstances, and also, perhaps, of more or less stirring adventures. Now the strollers find themselves in a district scourged by civil war; now they deferentially seek the sanction of some upstart *maire* to perform within his jurisdiction; now they declaim the stately verse of Corneille in a barn or on a stage improvised in the street; now they look ruefully at each other as the keeper of the inn in which they have put up lays his reckoning before them. Scarron's *Roman Comique* enables us to realize in some measure the conditions of their existence; indeed, it is not improbable that this whimsical picture of itinerant players in the seventeenth century —a work destined to outlive the drollest of its author's farces—was suggested in part by a chance encounter with the Illustre Théâtre at Mans, where the scene of the story is laid(*f*). "Molière," writes a contemporary, "was neither too stout nor too thin. He was rather above than below the medium height; his carriage was noble, his leg finely formed; he had a serious air, and walked gravely. His complexion was dark; his nose and mouth were rather large, his lips a little thick, his eyebrows very black, and the changes of his facial expression incessant. As to character, he was gentle,

P 2

kind, and generous." Destin, the hero of the *Roman Comique*, is a man of similar stamp—"sympathetic, refined in manner. brave, contemplative, amiable, a personification of pleasant *insouciance*, by turns grave and gay, full of noble impulses." Whatever may have been the source of Scarron's inspiration in this instance, the district particularly favoured by Molière and his companions was the south and the south-east of France, the heart of the territory in which the Troubadour of old had sung. Their names became as familiar as household words to the vivacious inhabitants of Lyons, Narbonne, and other hives of industry in that part of the country. One of these towns was to be associated by a curious tradition with the memory of the leader of the company. In those days, *cafés* not having been invented, the favourite resort of the gossips was the barber's. Molière, ever ready to amplify his knowledge of human nature, would repair to such places on market-days in the most observant mood; and an antique arm-chair which he is said to have occupied in the shop of a popular Figaro at Pézénas, by name Gély, is still preserved in the town with pious care.

It was not long before fame began to mark him for her own. He achieved considerable distinction as an actor. In tragedy, it is true, he was not at home; but a keen sense of humour, aided by experience, study,

attention to by-play, and a striking naturalness of recit-
ation and manner—a naturalness in direct contrast to
the style cultivated on the Paris stage—seems to have
given life and spirit to all his essays in comedy. "The
delicacy with which he embodied a character and
expressed a sentiment," says Grimarest, "proved that
he was profoundly versed in the art of declamation.
He entered into the smallest details of a part, and, unlike those who have no fixed rule or principle for their
acting, did not recite at hazard." Fortunately, the applause he won in this way did not satisfy his ambition.
He wrote at least eleven farces :—*Le Médecin Volant, Les
Docteurs Rivaux, Le Docteur Pédant, Le Maître d'Ecole,
Gros-René Ecolier, Le Docteur Amoureux, La Jalousie de
Gros-René, Gorgibus dans le Sac, Le Fagotier, La Casaque,
Le Grand Benét de Fils aussi Sot que son Père*, and *La
Jalousie du Barbouillé*. These pieces, of which only the
first and last have come down to us, were *baissers du
rideau* of the Italian school, replete with diverting incident, often lighted up by a flash of wit, and depending
in a large degree upon the resources of the players. In
Molière's own words, they "procured him some little
reputation," though not of a kind to afford him the
highest pleasure. He longed to follow up the path
opened in the *Menteur*, which, as he frankly avowed in
after years, fixed his ideas on the subject of comedy.
It was to be feared that a play of this order would be

received with less favour by provincial audiences than
one like the *Médecin Volant,* but the young dramatist
was not deterred by the prospect of a little temporary
loss from making the experiment. In *L'Etourdi,* working upon a story taken from *L'Innavvertito,* he produced
a work which, if not entirely free from the rough fun
in vogue, was remarkable alike for spirit, truth, and
the individuality of at least one of the characters.
Mascarille, a clever valet, possibly suggested by Davus,
devises a variety of schemes to aid his master, Lélie, in
a love pursuit. He is foiled at almost every step by
the blundering interference of the latter, who, however,
wins our respect by, among other good qualities, the
very straightforwardness that causes his discomfiture.
Molière was soon reassured as to the result of his new
departure. *L'Etourdi* evoked extraordinary applause,
and the use made of it by Quinault in *L'Amant Indiscret*
would suggest that its fame was not confined to a
narrow area.

At Lyons, where this delightful little comedy first
appeared, the troupe seems to have been reinforced by
five new players—Mdlle. Duparc, Ducroisy, Lagrange,
and the Debries. The first was a sister of Gros René,
for whom Molière had written at least two of his
Italian-like farces. Nothing could have been more
queenly than the way in which she filled the most
dignified characters, such as the heroines of Corneille.

Philibert Gassaud, Sieur Ducroisy, was a gentleman of Beaure, and might have withstood a strong *penchant* for the stage if it had not been for the Declaration of 1641. In tragedy and anything like serious comedy he proved an important recruit. Charles Varlet, Sieur de Lagrange, had come from Amiens. He had rare intelligence and taste, which Molière cultivated to the highest point. Edouard Wilquin, Sieur Debrie, an inveterate drunkard, was obviously engaged on account of his wife, Catherine Leclerc, a woman of finely sympathetic nature, on whom he relied for subsistence, but whom he often subjected to brutal ill-treatment. Any affection she may have had for him had long since died away; she lived only for her art. And to that art she proved a distinguished ornament. "Mdlle. Debrie," writes one who saw her, "was tall, slender, and graceful; noble in her manner and natural in all her attitudes, with something particularly delicate in her face and features, which rendered her most fitting for the part of an *ingénue*. Her eyes had a peculiar charm, derived from an expression of mingled candour and tenderness."

The accession of Mdlle. Duparc and Mdlle. Debrie serves to throw new light on the character of Molière. If tradition may be credited, he fell desperately in love with the former—offered her his hand as well as heart. Mdlle., however, deliberately repelled his advances. Her beauty led her to believe that she might make what the world would deem a good marriage, and in Molière she saw only a moderately successful author and strolling player. Had a presentiment of his future greatness crossed her mind she might have returned a different answer. It was in vain that Molière endeavoured to forget his disappointment. He fell a prey to melancholy. He ceased for a time to feel any interest in the present or the future. Mdlle. Debrie, who from the outset had understood him better than any one else, endeavoured to dispel his sadness. By degrees she induced him to make her his confidant, to feel that her sympathy was dear to him. "I fear," he said to her one day, "that you have done me a cruel kindness. My malady seems to have left me, but in reality it has only changed its form. I now require a physician to heal the wounds you have yourself caused." No music could have been more grateful to the ears of the long unhappy woman than these words. Considerations which even in that age must have had weight with her —the obligations of a wife, self-respect, her regard for the opinions of others—all were scattered to the four winds. "Those wounds," she said, "have been more fatal to myself than to you."

Mdlle. Debrie may well have been regarded by Molière as a personification of Fortune. From this moment he struck into the current which swept him to his goal. His fellow-pupil at college, the Prince de Conti, now at peace with the Government, was holding the States of Languedoc, and, having taken up his quarters at the château of La Grange, near Pézénas, resolved to be diverted by the players. His highness's secretary, De Cosnac, afterwards Bishop of Aix, sent for the troupe of Molière and Bejart, then in Languedoc. Accompanied by M. Debrie, who bore the loss of his wife like a man of the world, and who did not allow any resentment he may have felt on that head to interfere with his interests, the troupe promptly set out for Pézénas. In the mean time, however, the Prince had impatiently engaged another set of players, headed by one Cormier. Molière arrived, and, being told that his services were not required, asked that the expenses he had incurred by the journey should be defrayed by the Prince. The request was reasonable enough, but the Prince, " obstinate about trifles," would not accede to it. " This injustice," writes Cosnac, " had so much effect upon me that I decided to have a representation by Molière's troupe in the theatre at Pézénas, and to give them 2000 crowns from my own pocket rather than not keep faith with them. M. le Prince, touched in his honour by my conduct, consented that they should play once in the theatre at La Grange," the result being that they were kept there during the whole of his stay. Molière's stock was now enriched by another pretty comedy, *Le Dépit Amoureux*, written in the style of *L'Etourdi*. It had two distinct plots, one suggested by Nicolo Secchi's *Filia Credata Maschio*, and the other, which turns upon the love-tiff in question, invented by himself. Lucile was played by Mdlle. Debrie, the valet by Gros-René, Marinette by Madeleine Béjart, and Eraste by the author. Mdlle. Duparc was probably the young lady who plunges herself into so much embarrassment by donning male attire. The play, I imagine, afforded much delight to the household at La Grange, thanks to the humour and spirit and grace of the dialogue. Did the Prince de Conti recognize in the author-actor whose claim for expenses he had cavalierly laughed at the Jean Baptiste Poquelin of old college days? History does not say; but tradition has it that from this time the Prince took a practical interest in Molière's prosperity. At the outset, as the story goes, he offered a secretaryship to the dramatist, who, dominated by the love of his profession, and learning that a former occupant of the office, Sarrazin, had died from a blow inflicted upon him with the tongs by his master, the most irascible of men, excused himself from accepting it. However that may be, it is certain that after leaving the Grange Molière literally had a friend at Court. In a few months he was advised to change his circuit so as to be within reach of Paris; and in the autumn of 1658, at Rouen, the troupe received a summons to act in Paris before the King.

The performance took place in the guard hall of the old Louvre on the 24th of October. The players may well have been unnerved as they peeped through the little hole in the curtain at the audience. No such gathering had ever assembled to watch them. The Court of France—the most splendid in history—was present in all its strength. Here was Louis XIV., now twenty years of age, an ardent votary of pleasure, yet stately and reserved, with strength of character plainly written in his face; here was Monsieur his brother, dressed more like a girl than a boy; here was Anne of Austria, still Regent of France, and, though not without *embonpoint,* retaining much of her celebrated beauty; here, conspicuous by his red robe, his finely-cut features and long white hair, was the man who for many years had guided the vessel of the State, Cardinal Mazarin. To the rear was a host of the butterflies belonging to the Court, to-gether with a few actors of the Hôtel de Bourgogne, all anxious to see of what stuff these favoured rivals were made. The play bespoken for the evening was Corneille's *Nicomède.* I suspect that as the per-formance went on a feeling of disappointment stole over the audience, the actors from the Hôtel de Bourgogne excepted. Molière and his companions,

to say the least of it, were less at home in the stately
lines of Corneille than in the quick and vivacious
dialogue of *L'Etourdi,* and the trepidation incident
to the occasion must have rendered them unable to
do anything like justice to themselves. *Nicomède*
finished, Molière, perhaps sensible of their shortcomings, took a very unusual step. He made a
speech from the stage. He thanked his majesty for
his goodness in bearing the defects of the troupe,
who had naturally felt some agitation on finding
themselves before so august an assembly, and who,
in their eagerness to have the honour of playing
before the greatest King in the world, had forgotten that he had already much better actors in his
service. As," continued Molière, " his majesty has
so far endured our country manners, I venture, very
humbly, to hope that I may be permitted to give one
of the little pieces which have procured me some
reputation, and with which I have been fortunate
enough to amuse the provinces." The King assented
by retaining his seat; the audience, who but a few
moments previous had been preparing to disperse,
resumed an attitude of attention. The little piece
referred to was *Le Docteur Amoureux,* one of Molière's
earliest farces. The result must have more than
equalled his most roseate anticipations. He quickly
converted a failure into a triumph. Everybody

present had much ado to restrain the merriment produced. The actors from the Hôtel de Bourgogne must have felt that in Molière they had a dangerous rival in comedy—an impression considerably deepened when, an hour or two later, it was found that the King had requested him and his comrades to establish themselves in Paris under the style and title of the "Troupe de Monsieur."

Yes, the goal was won. After a probation of twelve years, representing the best period of his life, Molière had done much to justify his abandonment of the career once prepared for him. His self-imposed exile from Paris—an exile which, as might have been expected of a Frenchman born and bred there, he had felt very deeply — was at an end. He had appeared before the King, had won his favour, had received from him a substantial guarantee of future support. No longer was it necessary for him and those who had cast in their lot with his to trudge from one provincial town to another, to bow low for permission to regale the populace with the choicest productions of French dramatic genius, and then, as was too often the case, to experience disheartening apathy by a throng incapable of appreciating the value of what he set before them. Nor was his exultation materially damped by a want of cordial recognition from his family. Even after he had

become famous, it is true, his brother omitted his
name from a genealogy which, in the pride of their
mother's descent, they caused to be drawn up; but
old M. Poquelin, actuated by an almost superstitious
faith in the judgment of Kings, to say nothing of
paternal affection, welcomed him with open arms.
Next came social recognition; the doors of many
exclusive houses, as may be supposed, were open to
the man on whom the sun of Court favour had begun
to shine. If his mother, the devout Marie Cressé of
thirty years before, who had been pious enough to
thrash him for imitating a priest, could have lived
to join in the welcome! As for the troupe, he had
endeared himself to them by his great *bonhomie* and
generosity, and a sense of the fact that they owed
their present position to his gifts served to strengthen
the ties which bound them to him. No leader was
ever regarded with more affectionate loyalty by his
followers than Molière.

The theatre assigned to him was that of the Hôtel
du Petit Bourbon, where, by the influence of Mazarin,
a new troupe of Italian players had begun to appear
three times a week in farce. The rivalry of these
foreigners was not to be despised, especially as they
showed a very natural tendency to use French in preference to their own language. From one point of
view, no doubt, their *théâtre* had a rather monotonous

aspect. Its personages, as in bygone times, were nearly always the same—Scaramouche, Arlequin, the Dottore, Isabelle, Colombine, Pantalon, Mezetin, &c. But, to the extreme delight of the Cardinal, who probably supported it as a means of establishing the opera in France, the more it was known the more it seemed to be liked. Frequently novel in plot, it was animated throughout by a joyous spirit, to which ample effect was given on the stage. Fiorelli, the Scaramouche, and Dominique Biancolelli, the Arlequin, are said to have risen high above their comrades. Dangeau goes so far as to describe the former as " le meilleur comédien qui ait jamais été." In the words of his biographer, " Scaramouche had the extraordinary power of expressing any sentiment by contortions of body and face," and could hold an audience spellbound without uttering a word. Molière, ever ready to overrate his obligations to others, avowed that he owed all his success as an actor to the great Italian *mime*—an avowal which may have given rise to one of the lines to be found under his portrait;

> Cet illustre comédien
> De son art traca la carrière,
> Il fut le maître de Molière,
> Et la Nature fut le sien.

Favoured by the King, before whom he often sang Italian songs to the music of a guitar, with a trained dog and parrot chiming in at particular places, Scara-

mouche, though not the most estimable of men, became
a sort of idol among all classes, and his bust was to be
seen in more than one *salon*.   Dominique seemed to be
composed of two different natures ; on the stage he was
the personification of gaiety ; in private life he invariably fell into a profound melancholy.   On one occasion,
having consulted a physician as to this ailment, he
was told that all the medicine in the world would not
do him half so much good as a few of Dominique's
performances.   " In that case," he groaned, " I am lost ;
Dominique himself is before you ! "

Molière took the off-days of the Italian comedians—
Tuesdays, Thursdays, and Sundays.   Before his cam-
paign opened he was joined by L'Epi, of the Marais,
and an actor of high excellence in both tragedy and
comedy, Guillaume Marcoureau, Sieur de Brécourt,
formerly an officer in the army.   Unfortunately, the
latter had an ungovernable temper, and his engagement
in the troupe had scarcely been signed when, having
run an insolent coachman through the body on the
Fontainebleau road, he sought refuge in Holland from
the vengeance of the law.   From some contemporary
doggerel we learn that Molière began with *Héraclius*
and other tragedies by Corneille, but it was not until
L'Etourdi and *Le Dépit Amoureux* were played that the
Comédiens de Monsieur won the town they were permitted to woo.   The charms of these pieces, set off by

clever and disciplined acting, were acknowledged with enthusiasm. If anything was wanting to the triumph of the dramatist it was the presence of the King, who had gone to Lyons for the purpose of meeting Marie de Mancini. Molière, alive to the mistake he had made in giving at the outset a succession of tragedies, instantly proceeded to confirm the advantage he had gained. He would write another comedy, and it occurred to him that by importing into his work some genial yet incisive ridicule of a popular folly he would do himself no harm.

He had only to look out upon the world around him to find an inviting subject. In one respect, it may be said, Parisian society had taken leave of its senses. The ultra-refinement introduced by the Marquise de Rambouillet was being carried to an almost incredible extreme. Every frequenter of the *ruelles* and *salons* of fashion adopted a style of speech in comparison with which the euphuism of yore was lucidity itself. Extravagant metaphor and emblems were employed to designate the merest trifles. The *précieuses* and their worshippers would not have been content to call a spade an oblong instrument of manual industry. In their mouths a nightcap was a " complice innocent de mensonge ; " water, " humeur celeste ; " a chair, a " commodité de la conversation ; " a thief, a " brave incommode ; " a scornful smile, a " bouillon d'orgueil ; " a mirror, a " conseiller des grâces." If in their laborious

attempts to coin new phrases they often became
unintelligible to each other, as was probably the case,
they deemed it only another proof of their delicacy of
thought and expression. Blended with this curious
neologism, too, was a studied and elaborate affectation
of chaste romantic sentiment. Nothing could be more
beautiful than Platonic love, but as "the world must
be peopled" it was necessary to enter into the holy
state of matrimony, though not with any appearance
of haste. Only by slow and barely perceptible degrees
should a female heart "yield to its assailant." No
lover should have a chance of being made happy until
he had traversed the whole of Loveland, as mapped
out for the instruction of the sterner sex by Madeleine
de Scudéri. Beginning at Indifference, he would
have to gradually make his way through Disinter-
ested Pleasure, Respect, Assiduity, Empressement, and
Sensibility to the city of Tenderness, whence the river
of Inclination would bear him to the Dangerous Sea.
Proposals of marriage should be met at first by a
blank refusal, however deeply engaged the affections
might be. Many of the fantastic ideas thus cherished
were favoured by romances of the *Clélie* and *Cyrus*
type, from which, indeed, a new code of social laws
was deduced, and which, with a mass of madrigals and
sonnets remarkable at best for dainty gallantry, were
accepted by the elegant contemporaries of Corneille

and Pascal as literature of the first water. Naturally enough, the folly of the *précieuses* found imitators among the younger section of the bourgeoisie. More than one citizen woke up some fine morning to find himself an object of derision and scorn to his women-kind on account of his honest directness of utterance, his unpolished manners, his profound want of sympathy with what they called poetry.

Molière, with a courage not to be justly estimated unless we bear in mind that he, a rather obscure comedian, as yet uncertain of his footing in his capital, would inevitably provoke the hostility of an influential sect by such an act, determined to arrest this increasing corruption of taste, sentiment, and language, by force of satire. He wrote a comedy in one act, *Les Précieuses Ridicules*. Madelon and Cathos, respectively the daughter amd niece of Gorgibus, a plain-speaking citizen, have been bitten by the prevailing rage. They give themselves up to the romances of Mdlle. de Scudéri, call themselves Polixene and Aminte and their maid Almanzor, and generally behave in a way which leads the old man to suspect their sanity. To crown all, they reject with ineffable disdain the proposals of two suitors of good worldly position, but unfortunately unversed in the ways of the Hôtel de Rambouillet. "How," asks Madelon, "could we be expected to endure such irregular proceedings as theirs?

To begin point-blank by proposing marriage!" "Well," says the exasperated Gorgibus, "and is not that a proof of the honourable nature of their intentions?" "Ah," exclaims the shocked Madelon, "how terribly commonplace you are! You really should get some one to make you express yourself fashionably. The idea of Cyrus," in Mdlle. de Scudéri's romance, "marrying Mandane at once, or of Aronce being wedded to Clélie straight off! If everybody had such opinions as yours a novel would soon come to an end." The lovers, indignant at the lofty scorn with which they have been repelled, cause their valets, Mascarille and Jodelet, to lay siege to the hearts of the *précieuses* in the guise of men of quality. The scheme is as successful as they could wish. Poor Madelon and Cathos mistake the lively impudence of the two valets for the quintessence of Parisian gallantry, and are lost in admiration of a wretched impromptu composed by Mascarille. But from this seventh heaven of delight they are abruptly lowered. The rejected lovers appear, the valets are literally stripped of their " borrowed plumes," and the *précieuses* have reason to devoutly wish that the earth would open under their feet to hide their confusion. It is interesting to see that while holding up their affectation to laughter Molière does not alienate them from our sympathies, which are never with the authors of the deception

practised upon them.   He indirectly suggests that so
far from being blue-stockings in the ordinary sense of
the term they are mere girls under the influence of
a passing mania.   But while showing this tenderness
for them he does not lose sight of his chief object.
The model they set before themselves is assailed with
a humour and satirical power previously unknown to
the stage.

Les Précieuses Ridicules appeared on the 4th November, with Molière as Mascarille, Madeleine Béjart and
Mdlle. Dubrie as Madelon and Cathos, Ducroisy and
Lagrange as the unchivalrous lovers, and Béjart as
Gorgibus.   Evidently unaware of the castigation in
store for them, several well-known *précieuses*, such as
Mdlle. Deshoulières, Ménage, Chapelain, and Ninon de
l'Enclos, were among the audience.   No sooner did the
meaning of the comedy become manifest than the
theatre rang with laughter and applause.   Many a
man present had a Madelon or a Cathos at home ; all,
" like children admitted behind the scenes, saw with
wonder and mirth the tinsel which from a distance they
had admired as crowns and royal robes."   " Courage,
Molière," cried an old man, starting up in the *parterre ;*
" voilà la vraie comédie ! "   Ménage had the sagacity to
perceive that the purpose of so vivacious a satire would
be attained.   " Monsieur," he said to Chapelain, " we
have approved too much the follies which M. Molière

has so pointedly and sensibly ridiculed. As Saint-Remi remarked to Clovis, we must 'burn what we have adored and adore what we have been disposed to burn.'" By others of its victims, however, the piece was taken in a different way. Scarcely had the first representation ended when powerful influence was exerted to prevent a second. Molière received an official order not to play the piece again. In two or three weeks, however, the prohibition was withdrawn, probably at the instance of the King himself, before whom *Les Précieuses Ridicules* was played during his sojourn in the Pyrenees, and who, although an ardent admirer of Madeleine de Scudéri's romances, was induced by a curious love of tormenting others, one of the most remarkable traits in his character, to take part with the audacious dramatist. *Les Précieuses Ridicules* accordingly reappeared in the bills of the Hôtel du Petit Bourbon, where, notwithstanding a considerable advance in the prices of admission, it remained for four months. According to Loret, it "was much visited by all sorts of people. It cost me thirty sous to see it," he adds, "but I laughed for more than ten pistoles."

Les Précieuses Ridicules sounded the knell of the mania it assailed. The worshippers at the shrine of Madame de Rambouillet resumed their baptismal names, condescended to use fairly intelligible language, and otherwise showed that the satire of Molière, with

MOLIÈRE.

the merriment it excited, had the power to alter
them for the better. But, as may be supposed, they
exhibited no little resentment of the indignity to which
they had been exposed. The dramatist was loudly
reproached with a disregard of the courtesy due to
women, of the charms of refined thought, of the
decencies of speech and conduct. It seemed to be
thought that if such plays as *Les Précieuses Ridicules*
were to be tolerated the end of all things was at
hand. Molière was in a position to behold the
storm without apprehension, but his proverbial good
nature prompted him to lessen the pain he had inflicted. "The most excellent things," he wrote in
the preface to the authorized edition of the comedy,
" are liable to be copied by apes, and the true *précieuses*
are wrong to take offence at a representation of those
who imitate them so badly." If the wrath of the
blue-stockings was turned away by his courtesy they
could not have been very keen-sighted, as the butt
of the satire was not so much the eccentricities of
Madelon and Cathos as the model to which those
unhappy girls conform — the "excellent things" to
which reference is made. In truth, Molière had no
intention to abandon the unofficial censorship he had
assumed. His strength, as he now saw, lay partly in
satirical comedy, in holding up the mirror to the Paris
of his own time. "Henceforth," he said, "I shall do

better to study the world than Menander, Terence, Plautus," and the modern Italian drama.

In the mean time the players of the Hôtel de Bourgogne had done much to counterbalance the increasing popularity of the new troupe. *Œdipe* gave place to a version by Villiers of *El Convidado de Piedra*, already played with good effect by the Italian comedians at the Petit Bourbon. *Le Festin de Pierre*, as it was incorrectly and absurdly called, drew many large houses, and the striking figure of Don Juan became deeply impressed upon the popular imagination. The other novelties of the year were less remunerative. The Abbé Boyer, who for some time had held aloof from the stage, was induced by the circumstances under which Corneille had reappeared before the public to take up his pen again. He produced a *Clotilde*, dedicating it to the apparently all-powerful Fouquet. It had only two representations ; and the author, according to an epigram by Furetière, ascribed his failure to the fact that the weather on the first occasion was very bad and on the second very fine. Next came *Ostorius*, a tragedy by Michel de Pure, an ecclesiastical student from Lyons, where his father was prévôt des marchands.

> Quant je veux d'un galant depeindre la figure,
> Ma plume, pour rimer, trouve l'Abbé de Pure,

said Boileau, who for reasons unexplained became his mortal enemy. Ugly he certainly was, but the disadvantage was to a large extent redeemed in him by agreeable manners and pleasant wit. His intellectual qualities, however, did not include those which go to make a successful dramatist. *Ostorius* deservedly failed ; and a piece entitled *Les Précieuses*, possibly another hit at Molière's victims, is said to have shown that he had as little turn for the gay as for the serious.

Molière, with a practical wisdom seldom absent from his doings, did not fail as a manager to think of the morrow, and in view of the withdrawal of *Les Précieuses Ridicules* he began to look about for new plays by old hands. Marked as his success as a dramatist had been, and great as was the facility with which he wrote, he did not shut his eyes to the impolicy of allowing the fortunes of his theatre to depend exclusively upon his own productions. In tragedy his troupe might not be so effective as other actors, but then it was not so much the acting as the play that people came to see. From the outset, however, he attracted no dramatist of repute to his standard. The troupes of the Hôtel de Bourgogne and the Marais made it known that if any one wrote for the Petit Bourbon he would forfeit their good-will. No rising author could afford to disregard such a menace ; while those who were in a position to do so may well have hesitated to intrust their manuscript to a body of players who, as far as tragedy was concerned, were the least efficient in the capital. Beset in this way, Molière, in his anxiety to show how ready he was to accept novelties, brought out a worthless tragedy by Magnon, entitled *Zénobie*, in the composition of which the Abbé d'Aubignac is believed to have had a hand.

Having effectually blockaded Molière, the players of the Hôtel de Bourgogne, as a means of competing with him on his chosen ground, induced a number of the actors of the Marais to join them. In their selection of novelties, however, they still manifested a preference for tragedy. Thomas Corneille, who for some years past had devoted himself to the Marais, wrote for them a *Darius*, perhaps the least interesting of all his works. The leading characters are finely contrasted, but the story is not strong enough to bear the weight of five acts. Very soon afterwards the author redeemed this failure by *Stilicon*, a tragedy admirable in point of construction, and forming altogether a vivid picture of Rome at a striking period of her history. Quinault was less fortunate in a *Stratonice*, while another effort of the Abbé Boyer, *La Mort de Démétrius, ou le Rétablissement d'Alexandre, Roi d'Epire*, is worthy of remembrance only by the length of its title. In the way of comedy the troupe had nothing better to produce than *Le Mariage de Rien*, which may be described as an attempt to relieve the most oppressive dulness by indecency. It was from the pen of Antoine

Jacob de Montfleuri, eldest son of the actor of that name. Educated for the legal profession, which he entered this year, Montfleuri *fils* yet devoted himself at the outset to dramatic authorship, apparently with the object of proving that the most sacred ties are fit subjects for indecent mirth on the stage. In the midst of these pursuits he espoused a daughter of Floridor, a model of every virtue.

Molière was now to show that with all the dramatists of the day at their back the Troupe Royale could not equal him in popularity. The second comedy he wrote in Paris, *Sganarelle, ou le Cocu Imaginaire*, appeared at the Petit Bourbon on the 28th May. Here, working upon a story derived from an Italian farce, *Il Cornuto per Opinione*, he painted a humourous picture of bourgeois life, brightened in many places by touches of sarcasm at the expense of popular follies. In substance the play is one of intrigue, but at least one of the characters is original and strongly individualized. Sganarelle, whose unfounded suspicions as to his wife's fidelity forms the *raison d'être* of the plot, is a citizen of the vulgarest stamp—gross in his tastes, self-opinionated, at once cunning and credulous, too much of a poltroon to resent his fancied wrongs, and withal endowed with a certain broad humour which is really irresistible. He was as new a figure to the stage as Mascarille and Crispin had been, but far more natural. Molière himself played this part, supported by Mdlle. Debrie as the wife, Lagrange as the supposed seducer, and Duparc as the too hungry valet.   Inferior in all respects except style to *Les Précieuses Ridicules, Sganarelle* at once proved popular, and, although brought out at a time when Paris was empty, was repeated forty times.   But one voice seems to have been lifted up against the play —the voice of a worthy citizen who was notoriously what Sganarelle only believed himself to be.   Thinking he was the original of that character, he quitted the theatre one evening with a determination to thrash the unfeeling dramatist whenever an opportunity presented itself.   Before he could do so, however, a candid friend convinced him of his error by asking him a very simple question—" How can you be said to resemble a husband whose injuries are only 'imaginary?'"

The year we are now passing through was marked by great public rejoicings.   The war between France and Spain came to a close, and soon after that happy event King Louis espoused the Infanta Maria Theresa. In the midst of the transports with which the overburdened people heard of the conclusion of peace, the theatres, as we learn from Loret, were opened free:

> Les comédiens de Paris,
> Comme gens francs et bien nourris,
> Ont été d'humeur liberale ;
> Car, autre la Troupe Royale,
> Ceux du Marais, ceux de Monsieur,
> Rebutant tout homme payeur ;

> Ainsi que l'on m'a fait entendre,
> Répresentant sans rien prendre.

From the same source we find that Floridor and his comrades repaired in a body to Saint Sauveur's to join in a thanksgiving. In the summer, when the marriage was solemnised in the far south, and in the beginning of September, when the young King and Queen entered Paris in all the pomp and pride and circumstance of royalty, the enthusiasm of the populace knew no bounds. Business was entirely stopped, cheers rent the air as his majesty passed along, and at all the theatres in the capital performances were again given gratuitously. Nearly every château in the country, too, assumed a festive appearance in honour of the event. The play-loving Marquis de Sourdéac entertained more than five hundred gentlemen at Neubourg for eight days, in the course of which a new *tragédie à machines* from the pen of Corneille, *La Toison d'Or*, was played by the actors of the Théâtre du Marais. Picturesquely put upon the stage, illustrated by dances and music, and written throughout, like *Andromède*, with remarkable grace of imagery and diction, it was received with warm acclamations, although more than one seigneur present must have resented the poet's hardihood in making such an allusion as this to the existing circumstances of the country :

> A vaincre tant de fois mes forces s'affaiblissent ;
> L'État est florissant, mais les peuples gémissent ;

Leurs membres décharnés courbent sous mes hauts faits,
Et la gloire du trône accable les sujets.

In the morose Corneille, it is clear, we have less of
a courtier than a patriot with the courage of his
convictions. In due time *La Toison d'Or* was added
to the entertainments of the capital, where, aided by
the original dresses and decorations, generously given
to the comedians by the Marquis de Sourdéac, it became
"la merveille de la cité." In connexion with the royal
marriage it has also to be stated that a troupe of
Spanish comedians established themselves in Paris
under the warrant of the King, playing occasionally
at the Hôtel de Bourgogne, but more frequently, as
may be supposed, before the Court. Here is Loret's
account of them :

Il chantent et dansent ballets,
Tantôt graves, tantôt follets ;
Leurs femmes ne sont pas fort belles,
Mais paraissent spirituelles ;
Leurs sarabandes et leurs pas
Ont de la grâce et des appas ;
Comme nouveaux ils divertissent,
Et leurs castagnetes ravissent.

But when they ceased to be "nouveaux" they ceased
to attract, for the language they spoke was as unintelligible as Hebrew to ninety-nine out of every hundred
Parisians. Indeed, on the "Spanish days" the audience
often consisted exclusively of a few dramatic authors,
who, for reasons not far to seek, were never absent from

the first performance of a new piece by the foreign comedians.

It was while the rejoicings on account of the King's marriage were in progress that Jodelet died. He does not seem to have been keenly regretted by his fellow-players, for the broad humour which formerly distinguished his acting had appreciably diminished as old age came upon him, and his temper, at no time very sunny, had not been improved by the consciousness of his decline. Loret chronicles a rumour that the vacancy thus caused in the Rue Mauconseil would be filled by Duparc, but if any negotiations were entered into with that comical impersonator of valets they bore no fruit. Had he seceded from his troupe Molière would not have been without recompense. Brécourt, who excelled in both tragedy and comedy, had been permitted, in return for State services of a somewhat doubtful kind, to reappear at the Petit Bourbon, where he played the Vicomte de Jodelet in *Les Précieuses.* In Holland, it appears, he had endeavoured, but without success, to capture a person upon whose head a price had been secretly set by the French Court. No sooner did this proceeding become known than it excited a tempest of popular indignation, and in the hope that the will would be taken for the deed he made his way in disguise to Paris. "Informé de la bonne volonté dont il avait

donné des preuves," the King "lui accorda sa grâce,"
to the intense disgust, no doubt, of the relatives of the
man whom he had done to death on the road to
Fontainebleau. Nor did his majesty stop here ; the
long-exiled comedian received some special marks of
royal favour, even to the extent of being invited to
join the chase at Fontainebleau. During one hunt
he was fortunate enough to protect the party from some
danger by boldly seizing and putting *hors de combat*
a boar which rushed at them from a thicket. The
King, after declaring that he had never seen a more
vigorous sword-stroke, inquired whether he was hurt—
a question which, natural as it may seem, was regarded
by all present as a remarkable act of condescension.
Brécourt, it should be added, wrote for Molière a little
piece entitled *La Feinte Mort de Jodelet*, in allusion to
the actual decease of that once popular comedian.

The grave had scarcely closed over Jodelet when it
reopened to receive the writer whose fantastic concep-
tions it had been his mission to embody. The *salon* in
the Rue de la Tixeranderie, the resort for fifteen years
or more of the wits of Paris, was at length to be shut.
From the time of the production of *Le Marquis
Ridicule* the bodily infirmities of Scarron had visibly
increased, and as the autumn arrived it became
evident that his end was at hand. But even the
approach of death could not subdue his characteristic

levity.   In his last hours he dictated the most farcical
of wills.   He bequeathed to his wife permission to marry
again, certainly never dreaming who her second husband
was to be ; to the Academy, power to alter the French
language at will ; to his servants, pensions on the many
bon-mots he had made ; to the two Corneilles, five
hundred pounds of patience ; to Gilles Boileau, in
addition to some caustic epigrams against him, gangrene
and the *haut mal*.   The allusion to Pierre Corneille is
explained by his petulant abandonment of the stage
after the fall of *Pertharite*, but why his brother stood in
need of a bequest of patience I am unable to understand.
The jovial testator died on the 14th October, having
only a few minutes previously remarked to his servants,
who came to his bedside with tears in their eyes,
" Ah, my children, I shall never make you cry as I
have made you laugh ! "   His body, long distorted
by pain, was laid in St. Sauveur's, where a simple
tablet was erected to his memory, " Alas, poor Yorick !
a fellow of infinite jest, of most excellent fancy.   Where
be your gibes now ? your gambols ? your songs ? your
flashes of merriment that were wont to set the table "
and the theatre " in a roar ? "   He left his wife in
poverty, but eventually, after many abortive attempts,
her friends procured for her a continuance of the pension
he had received from Anne of Austria.   It is no slight
testimony to his good qualities that he won at least the

esteem of the high-minded woman who bore his name. In one of her letters she speaks warmly of his probity, his disinterestedness, his kindness of nature. In a word, she adds, " he was excellent at heart, and his licence I succeeded in correcting."

The supply of players at this time was undeniably in excess of the demand, but another troupe from the country, having had the good fortune to please Mdlle. de Montpensier, obtained permission to take up their quarters at the theatre in the Rue des Quatre Vents, Faubourg Saint Germain, under the style and title of the Comédiens de Mademoiselle. Its leader, Dorimon, wrote as well as acted, and three of his pieces—*Le Festin de Pierre, La Femme Industrieuse*, and *La Dame d'Intrigue*—were not unfavourably received. *Apropos* of the first, he received the following lines from his wife, who seems to have had a share in his later literary labours—

> Encore que je sois ta femme,
>   Et que tu me doive ta foi,
> Je ne te donne point de blâme
>   D'avoir fait cet enfant sans moi.
> Toutefois, ne me crois pas buse,
>   Je connais le sacré vallon ;
> Et si tu vas trop voir ta Muse,
>   J'irai caresser Apollon.

The Comédiens de Mademoiselle were not destined to remain in Paris very long. At the close of the Fair, finding their theatre deserted, and wisely declining to rely upon the good-will of their protectors, they returned to the provinces, never to be heard of again.

And now let us revert to the Hôtel de Bourgogne. Pierre Corneille, after finishing *Œdipe*, had given up in favour of his brother the second of the subjects suggested by Fouquet, and the tragedy founded upon it was now brought forward. The versification of *Camma* was such as to make one regret the decision of the elder poet, but it may be doubted whether he could have improved upon it in point of construction, especially towards the close. Fontenelle speaks of the *dénouement* as " one of the happiest ; " it was deferred to the last moment, and, except by those acquainted with the Galatian legend, could not have been foreseen. Camma, " in order to save the life of Sostrate, whom she loves, brings herself to espouse Sinorix, whom she justly detests. In the fifth act Camma and Sinorix return from the Temple, where they have been married. It is certain that the play will not end here, but what will the end be ? To deepen the mystery, Camma allows Sinorix to see that she is acquainted with his past, of which he has believed her to be ignorant, and declares that although he possesses her hand she loathes him as intensely as ever. Sinorix suddenly dying, Camma confesses to having poisoned the nuptial cup, from which she had also drunk. Seldom do we find a *dénouement* so little expected and yet so natural." In the result, *Camma* proved decidedly attractive—so attractive, indeed, that the Troupe Royale found it to their interest to act four times a week instead of three.

The Hôtel du Petit-Bourbon was now being pulled down to make way for the colonnade of the Louvre, and Molière's company, with the Italian players, received permission to take up their quarters in the superb theatre which Richelieu had erected in the Palais Royal for the representation of *Mirame.* Here, on the 4th February, they acted for the first time *Don Garcie de Navarre,* a *comédie héroïque* by their chief. In writing this piece, which is of Spanish origin, Molière was evidently anxious to show that his powers as a dramatist and an actor were not restricted to the domain of light or farcical comedy. He treated in an elevated spirit the passion which Sganarelle had held up to ridicule. He delineated in the character of the hero a prince with rare qualities of head and heart, but reduced to extreme misery by a sensitively jealous nature. Every scene bears the impress of thoughtful and thorough workmanship. But the result was not what he had a right to expect. Had the piece been converted into a tragedy it might have succeeded by reason of the grave and stately eloquence of the writing; as it was, the bulk of the audience, having assembled in the expectation of seeing another *Précieuses* or *Sgan-arelle,* were led in their disappointment to pronounce it gloomy and uninteresting. Moreover, the jealousy of Don Garcie, arising as it did from deep-seated affection, appeared somewhat ridiculous now that the romantic spirit was rapidly dying away. It would also appear that the acting of Molière, whose name had until now been identified with diverting characters, was not judged by reference to its merits. In the end he withdrew the play, at the same time resolving not to appear in a serious part again.

It was about this time, I compute, that Molière and his troupe received orders to give a performance of *L'Étourdi* and *Les Précieuses Ridicules* at the Louvre in the presence of Mazarin, who, followed by the King, was wheeled on a sofa into the *salle* in which the players appeared. More than one reader will think it remarkable that an amusement relentlessly persecuted by the Church of Rome should have been resorted to by a Cardinal in what he must have known were his last hours. If anything could have mitigated the distress with which the minister contemplated the approach of death it would have been the fact that something more had been done to implant the opera in France. Two years previously, the Abbé Perrin, a hanger-on of Gaston d'Orléans, had had the temerity to compose a work of this kind in French, *La Pastorale*, to which music was set by Lambert, Intendant de la Musique to Anne of Austria. It was sung at Issy, and Mazarin had it played more

than once in the presence of the King. The innovation,
however, did not find favour except in a very limited
circle, and even those who appreciated the opera
maintained that the genius of the French language
would not lend itself to the purpose in view. In the
next piece, *Ercole Amante,* played at the Tuileries during
the marriage festivities, Italian was again used ; but,
for the benefit of those who did not understand that
language, a translation of the libretto into French was
circulated amongst the audience. In the ballets accom-
panying this piece the king and queen took part,
surrounded by most of their court. Again were
Italian singers brought to Paris by Mazarin to sustain
the parts, one of which, however, was intrusted to the
Abbé Melani. Perrin next put together an *Ariadne,*
but before it could be represented the Cardinal died,
and in the absence of his powerful support the attempt
to make Paris a home of the opera was again allowed
to fall into abeyance.

Molière, who seems to have found in Mazarin a
zealous admirer, now proceeded to write a comedy in
which a young actress lately added to his company
might be introduced. This was Armande Claire Eliza-
beth Béjart, a younger sister of Madeleine. Born in
1645, just after the Illustre Théâtre left Paris to wander
about the country, she had been confided in early life
to the care of that vivacious actress, and had grown

to womanhood—for woman she already was—under the eyes of Molière. He, charmed with her girlish graces, took upon himself the cost of her education, and few tasks gave him greater pleasure than that of preparing her for the stage. Her portrait has been painted for us in one of his own dialogues. "Her eyes," he says, "are not large, but are full of fire— the most brilliant, the most piercing, the most moving that can be seen. Her mouth is large, but has attractions peculiar to itself. She is not tall, but her movements are easy and elegant. She affects a non-chalance in her speech and deportment, but there is grace in all, and her manners have a nameless charm. Her wit is of the finest and most delicate kind; her conversation is delightful; and if she is capricious, as I must admit she is,—well, everything is becoming to, and must be borne with from, the fair." And this description is substantially confirmed by contemporary testimony, from which we further learn that she had an extremely pretty voice, sang with taste in both French and Italian, dressed gracefully, was a mistress of the art of filling up the intervals of her part on the stage with expressive by-play (thanks, no doubt, to Molière), and could impersonate coquettish or satirical women to perfection.

The comedy designed by Molière in the interest of his youthful comrade was produced on the 4th June,

under the title of *L'Ecole des Maris.* It threw all
his previous achievements into the shade, whether as
regards character, plot, situation, or dialogue. In
selecting his materials he would appear to have had in
mind the *Adelphi,* Moreto's *No puede ser Guardar una
Muger,* and Lope de Vega's *Discreta Enamorada.* His
obligation to these works, however, was at best slight,
as a comparison of them with the story he set forth
would show. Two brothers, Ariste (L'Epi) and Sganarelle (Molière), are respectively guardians of two sisters,
Léonor (Armande Béjart) and Isabelle (Mdlle. Debrie).
Each intends to espouse his ward, but treats her in a
different way. Ariste, reposing implicit confidence in
Léonor, concedes her full liberty of action; Sganarelle,
suspicious and tyrannical, seeks to cut off Isabelle from
all intercourse with the world. The wisdom of Ariste
is justified by the event; but the other suitor, in
addition to forfeiting any regard Isabelle may have
had for him, is made a go-between her and a more
favoured lover, Valère (Lagrange). In many points
this groundwork is new; and for all that constitutes
the excellence of the play, especially the robust
manliness and good sense of Ariste, the delicacy with
which Isabelle is exhibited in difficult circumstances,
and the piquancy of the character of the soubrette
(Madeleine Béjart, who, by the way, had the satisfaction of seeing her youthful sister create a favourable

impression as Léonor), Molière certainly owed nothing except to his own genius. For the rest, *L'École des Maris* was triumphantly successful. Loret tells us that this

> Pièce nouvelle et fort prisée,
> Que Sieur Molière a composée,

became the "delight of all Paris." Not long afterwards it was represented by the same players before the Court at Vaux, where, as in the capital, it fixed the reputation of the dramatist.

And that reputation was already high enough to compensate him for the sacrifices he had made to obtain it. In the comedy of character and incident he had left Corneille far behind, at the same time infusing into his dialogue a vivacity and grace not to be found in that of the *Menteur*, and even more welcome to the ears of the groundlings, perhaps, than the broad jests of the cripple who had been the first to demonstrate the value of spoken words as a source of amusement in themselves. Indeed, it is not too much to say that *L'École des Maris* gave its author a place in the front rank of comic poets, and from this time a new play from his pen was looked forward to with the keenest interest. Still more rapid, perhaps, was the progress he made at Court. It required less intelligence than Louis XIV. possessed to perceive that Molière would add to the glories of the reign

just begun, and his admiration of the dramatist was
not improbably blended with a feeling of strong
personal regard for one whose noble qualities of heart
were as conspicuous as his intellectual gifts, whose
conversation and manners were those of a lettered
gentleman, and who bore himself in the presence of
his sovereign with a deference wholly free from the
taint of servility.   In the words of Bazin, " Molière
was now to enjoy something more than a disdainful
and frivolous protection at the hands of the King.
From the moment these two men—the one a monarch
freed from leading-strings, the other an unrivalled
comedian but still timid moralist—became well acquainted with each other, a tacit understanding subsisted between them—an understanding that the latter
might dare everything, with full assurance of protection,
upon the sole condition of respecting and amusing the
former.   No public treaty to which the faith of a
monarch is solemnly pledged could have been fulfilled
more sincerely ; at no time, and in no circumstances,
was the shield thrown over the poet withdrawn. He was
no poor knight-errant, pursuing his mission at his own
risk and peril, exposed to vengeance, and apprehensive
of being abandoned to his fate.   He received confidence
and strength from a caprice, for once enlightened, of
sovereign power ; his genius gave him all the rest."

CHAPTER VII.

1661—1664.

BEFORE long, as a consequence of the esteem in which Molière was held at the Louvre, the drama assumed a new importance and dignity. Emancipated by the death of Mazarin from even the semblance of tutelage, Louis XIV., already distinguished by the calculating sagacity of a practical statesman, became the real as well as nominal master of France, and it is no mere figure of speech to say that from this moment he was the cynosure of all eyes in Europe. For one thing, he made his Court one of the most splendid on record. It seemed to comprise all that was picturesque and great in the life of the nation he represented. The nobles, humbled by Richelieu as a political force, but as little able to lay aside their old insolence of demeanour as to improve their morals, came from their châteaux to bask in the sunshine of royalty ; men of approved genius, no matter in what field they had shown it, were invited to swell the throng on a footing of something like equality. His majesty became the centre of a never-ending circle of edifying or

frivolous pleasure, although he devoted himself for
several hours a day to the business of the State.
Palace life seemed to be made up of fêtes, pageants,
theatrical performances, presentations, and the most ingenious refinements of enjoyment. " In short," says
Madame de Sévigné, " it was a very whirlwind : illumin-
ation ; jewels ; dresses faced and embroidered with gold ;
dissipation ; unanswered questions; idle compliments ;
civilities without thought ; feet entangled in trains ;
traffic congested ; lighted torches; people crushed
under the wheels of coaches." It is unnecessary here
to descant upon the wide-spread misery which the
profusion of the King, joined to his insatiable thirst
for conquest and military fame, brought upon the
country at large. The line in *La Toison d' Or*—

Et la gloire du trône accable les sujets—

may be taken as a summary in one sentence of his
long and eventful reign. From the outset, however,
that reign was fraught with benefits to civilization.
Neglected as his education had been, he took a keen
and practical interest in literature and art, especially
when, as in the representation of a great play, they
went hand in hand. Until recently, indeed, the
theatrical diversions of the Court consisted almost
exclusively of Benserade's allegorical ballets, in which
his majesty, with other members of the royal family,

not unfrequently appeared. But Molière aroused in him a taste for stage work of a higher order; tragedy and comedy figured in most of the fêtes he gave or attended, and the drama could not but derive additional lustre from the homage paid to it by a prince who personified the France of his time— for he often followed where he seemed to lead—in so imposing a way as to make himself an object of reverence to his plundered and down-trodden people.

Molière was now to be associated with an incident of historic interest. Fouquet, heir-presumptive to Mazarin's power in the State, entertained the Court at Vaux on the 17th August, when *Les Fâcheux*, a comedy in three acts, by the author of *L'École des Maris*, was played in a theatre erected under the stately fir trees in the park. It may well be believed that murmurs of surprise and delight were heard among the brilliant assemblage in the *parterre* as the curtain rose. *Mirame* itself was not put upon the stage with so much magnificence as *Les Fâcheux*. The one scene of the piece, representing a garden, had been designed by Lenôtre, painted by Lebrun, and ornamented with sculptured fountains, all in play, by Puget or Couston. Contrived by Torelli, who acted as stage manager, a huge rock in the background transformed itself into a shell, from which a naiad (Armande

Béjart) came forth to deliver a prologue written by
Pelisson.

> Peut-on voir nymphe plus gentille
> Qu'était Béjart l'autre jour ?
> Lorsqu'on vit ouvrir sa coquille
> Tout le monde disait à l'entour,
> Lorsqu'on vit ouvrir sa coquille
> Voici la Mère d'Amour.

But the admiration excited by this charming picture
was soon to be displaced by a different feeling, at
least among the bulk of the audience. *Les Fâcheux*,
which had been "conceived, written, and got ready for
representation" in the short space of fifteen days,
was found to be a refined and incisive satire upon
those by whom that audience was mainly composed.
In one of Scaramouche's farces, The *Case Svaliggiate, ou
Gli Interompimenti di Pantaleone*, some amusement had
been created by the spectacle of a lover interrupted
by a succession of insufferable bores on his way to
a rendezvous. Molière made use in his new piece of
a similar ground-work, at the same time turning the
figures of those who beset his hero, Eraste (played
by himself), into full-length portraits of typical
personages in the king's train, and using them as
stalking-horses for ridicule upon more than one
conceit and folly. Now we have a beribboned and
feathered gallant noisily taking a seat on the stage
in the sight of the audience while the performance

is going on (a custom, by the way, of recent origin);
now an amateur composer insists upon singing some
dance music he has written; now a gamester per-
tinaciously enters into a description of a point in
piquet; now a pair of *précieuses* are anxious to know
whether a lover ought to be jealous; now a pedant
is anxious that a petition regarding himself shall
be presented to the king; now a duellist wishes to
prove himself cunning of fence by defending friends
from imaginary attacks; now, to crown all, a bore
inflicts upon us an account of having been himself
bored.   In writing such a piece, of course, the
dramatist acted upon an assumption that his temerity
would be applauded by the king, who, to say nothing
of his delight in annoying others, had been animated
from his boyhood by a desire to bring the authority
of the nobles within narrow limits.   Nor did this
assumption prove groundless.   His majesty, notwithstanding his ill will towards Fouquet,—an ill will
which, coupled with the jealousy aroused in his
mind by a chance discovery in the château that the
Minister aspired to the smiles of Louise de la
Vallière, would have led the royal guest to place
his host under arrest if Anne of Austria had not
interposed,—readily entered into the humour of the
piece, chiefly by reason of the speechless dismay and
confusion shown by many of his courtiers under the

castigation inflicted upon them from the stage. His
pleasure, indeed, may be said to have increased in
proportion to their pain. The only fault he found
with the satire was that it did not go far enough.
" M. de Molière," he whispered to the dramatist
at the close, looking towards M. de Soiecourt, the
master of the hounds, "there is an 'original' you
might well copy." Molière was not a master of the
phraseology of the chase, but a brief conversation with the proposed victim taught him as much
of it as would serve his purpose, and in the dead
of night, after the guests had gone to bed—many,
of course, to ponder in no very amiable mood
over the meaning of his attack upon them — he
added to his list of bores the diverting character
of the huntsman Dorante.   Thus strengthened, *Les
Fâcheux*, which presents an example of two species
of plays hitherto unknown but thenceforward popular
in France, — the *comédie-ballet*, where the intervals
between the acts are filled up with dances in harmony
with the spirit of the whole, and next of the *pièce à
tiroir*, a string of episodes,—was performed at Fontainebleau on the 27th August, and at the Palais
Royal on the 4th November.   Need it be said that
the bourgeoisie laughed consumedly at these illus-
trations of their superiors?   The indignation of
the latter was naturally very great, but as the

piece was dedicated to the highest personage in the realm, and that in a tone which indicated a sense of perfect security, they deemed it prudent, at least for the present, to hold their peace on the subject. By this time, it should be added, the once proud and flattered Fouquet, the heir-presumptive to the power of Mazarin, had fallen from his high estate, to be condemned soon afterwards to imprisonment for life in the Alpine fortress of Pignerol.

The Hôtel de Bourgogne had nothing better to counterbalance the attraction of *Les Fâcheux* than two invertebrate tragedies by Thomas Corneille, *Pyrrhus* and *Maximian*. The afterpiece to each, I think, was *Le Médecin Volant*, the first essay in dramatic composition of a rising writer. In 1651, having arrived at the mature age of thirteen, Edmond Boursault left his native town, Merci-l'Everne, between Bar-sur-Seine and Châtillon, to push his fortunes in Paris. He could neither read nor write, as his father, an unlettered soldier, was determined not to be outshone in the matter of education by his children. How the raw country lad contrived to keep his head above water in Paris we are not told, but it is certain that by dint of intense industry he repaired the heavy wrong done him at home, and that at this time he could write French with a purity and elegance which any scholar in the colleges might have envied. His first important literary enter-

prise was a *Gazette* in rhyme, *à la* Loret. Its success
was greater than he could have anticipated; he was
commanded to present a copy of each issue in person to
the king, and a pension of 2000 livres was conferred
upon him. Before long, however, the encouraging prospect thus opened was overclouded. In one of his
gazettes, at the instance of the Duc de Guise, now his
steadiest patron, he indulged in a little pleasantry at
the expense of a Capuchin who, while slumbering in the
shop of a seamstress, had been converted by irreverent
hands into something like an effigy of Guy Fawkes.
Hugely diverted the Court was by the story, but the
Queen's Spanish Confessor induced her to regard it as
a mark of disrespect to religion itself, and to appease
her resentment the king suppressed the work, cancelled
the pension, and would have sent the author to the
Bastille if Condé had not said a word in his favour.
In all probability this intercession was due as much to
interest in the man as admiration for the writer. Boursault had many estimable qualities of heart, and was
conspicuously free from the faults which too often
distinguish the self-educated and self-made man.

It is to witness a pathetic drama of real life that we
return to the Palais Royal. For the last eight or nine
years Catherine Debrie had been Molière's wife in all
but name, now consoling him under repeated disap-
pointments, anon supporting him in his aspirations by

intelligent sympathy, and generally making his happiness the chief or sole object of her existence. He was the god of her idolatry—a god at whose shrine no self-sacrifice could be too great. Nor had he failed to appreciate this devotion; his attachment to her increased as time passed away, and would have led him to give her his hand if she had been free to accept it. But in the young actress just added to the company she was to find a too powerful rival. His friendly interest in Armande Béjart involuntarily ripened into a warmer sentiment. It was in vain that his better judgment warned him not to place his peace of mind at the mercy of a girl without fixed character, predisposed to frivolity, and nearly twenty-five years younger than himself. To use his own words, "la raison n'est pas ce qui règle l'amour," and the passion he conceived for her seemed to become a part of his very being. In extreme anguish, but without uttering a syllable of reproach, Mdlle. Debrie unostentatiously quitted what she had made a home in the best sense of the word; and on the 20th February, at the church of St. Germain l'Auxerrois, from which the signal for the St. Bartholomew massacre had been given, Molière and Armande were married in the presence of old M. Poquelin, of the mother of the Béjarts, and most of the players of the Palais Royal. It was soon manifest to the dramatist that his infatuation had led him into a terrible error.

Instead of becoming what his fancy had painted, an affectionate and sympathetic companion, Armande showed
that she had married him only from motives of self-
interest.   He found her to be heartless, vain, giddy, and
shallow-minded.   She repaid his tenderness with undisguised indifference, saw nothing in his work except a
means of gratifying her love of display, and took advantage of the liberty he gave her—for he was like another
Ariste—to become one of the most notorious coquettes
on the outskirts of the Court.   If he complained of her
conduct she would upbraid him as a tyrant or resort to
impudent levity.   Being remonstrated with on account
of some undue familiarity with Lauzun, " qui préludait
par les comédiennes pour s'élever bientôt aux filles des
rois," she protested that the scandal which associated
his name with hers had no foundation,—as it was the
Comte de Guiche she preferred.   Molière, unhappily
for himself, was of too sensitive a nature not to reel
under the blow he had received.   His life from this
time was one of almost unintermittent torture.   But
his love for Armande seemed to increase as her worth-
lessness became more apparent; and accordingly, endeavouring to persuade himself that her faults were
due in great measure to the thoughtlessness of youth,
he left no stone unturned, with what success we shall
see in due course, to inspire her with sentiments resembling his own.

Five days after the solemnization of this ill-assorted marriage, a tragedy by Corneille, *Sertorius*, was produced at the Théâtre du Marais, the players there having won his confidence by the effect with which they had represented *La Toison d' Or.* "Here," writes the once great dramatist, as though to show how completely he could stultify himself, "you will find neither tenderness, bursts of passion, elaborate descriptions, nor pathetic narratives." In truth, *Sertorius* was another political tragedy, an historical dissertation in dramatic form. Viewed in this light, no doubt, it called for very high praise. It but rarely fell short of the requirements of the subject, and the scene between Sertorius and Pompée in the third act—a scene which could easily have been made worse than unimpressive—had sufficient strength to give the piece a firm hold upon public favour. In the military details, it should be added, the author was never at fault. "Where," asked one spectator, the illustrious Turenne, "where can Corneille, an advocate and man of letters, have amassed so much knowledge of the art of war as *Sertorius* displays?"

The decaying poet was soon to be the last surviving member of the group of dramatists who had borne the yoke of Richelieu. Claude de l'Etoile and Colletet had long since joined Rotrou in the grave, and on the 30th March it was found that Boisrobert—of late years

extremely corpulent, with his small eyes deeply sunk
in his face, and their merry expression forming a
whimsical contrast to his ascetic ecclesiastical garb—
had paid what is infelicitously called the great debt
of nature.   In most of the *salons,* perhaps, it was felt
that Paris could better have spared a better man than
the virtual founder of the Académie Française.   His
numerous backslidings, if ever seriously thought of,
were forgiven in consideration of the wit which had
commended him to the notice of Richelieu, and which
remained by him to the end.   Nevertheless, those
backslidings were of a nature to exclude him from
the society of good men and true.   He had lifted
himself out of obscurity by persistent toadyism, had
sought to disguise his weakness as a dramatist by
plagiarisms occasionally involving a direct breach of
confidence, and from the outset of his career had
presented an example of about everything an abbé
ought not to be.   His *liaison* with one woman was
so notorious that a friend ventured to remonstrate with
him for disregarding his vows.   " Is not the lady very
ugly ? " he asked.   " She is."   " Surely that proves
my innocence."   " On the contrary," retorted the
friend, " her ugliness only aggravates your offence."
Brought to the verge of the grave, however, the
clerical rake began to fear that he had not regulated
his doings with " sufficient exactitude," and it was in

a "profoundly repentant mood" that he went to his long account.

The news of Boisrobert's death came upon the Troupe Royale while they were preparing to introduce to the public a new authoress, Marie Catherine Hortense Desjardins, a lively and rather pretty brunette of twenty-two. Born at Alençon, where her father officiated as Prévôt de la Maréchaussée, she soon manifested a turn for literature and gallantry, and, having loved a cousin with more fervour than prudence, found it necessary, in order to save her parents from shame, to leave home. Making her way to Paris, she sought the protection of the Duchesse de Rohan, by whom Madame Desjardins had been employed as tiring woman. The hopes of the fair fugitive were not disappointed. The Duchesse received her kindly, promised to shield her from the wrath of her father, and finally gave her a home. In a few months Mademoiselle was at liberty to return to Alençon, but having set her heart upon making a good match, and in the belief that her secret would not be discovered, she remained in Paris. Now, in addition to many languishing poems, she wrote for the Hôtel de Bourgogne a *Manlius Torquatus*, which appears to have met with a by no means discouraging reception.

Manlius was the last new tragedy in which the beautiful Mdlle. 'Baron had the chance of appearing.

One night, on her return from the theatre, she found
that every article of value in her apartments had been
carried off.   Her health was too delicate to withstand
the shock, and a few days afterwards, on the 8th
September, Loret regretfully wrote—

> Une actrice de grand renom,
> Dont la Baronne était le nom ;
> Cette merveille du théâtre,
> Dont Paris était idolâtre ;
> Qui, par ses récits enchanteurs,
> Ravissait tous les auditeurs
> De la belle et tendre manière,—
> Depuis deux jours est dans la bière ;
> Et la mort n'a point respectée
> Cette singulière beauté.

Here is a rather quaint epitaph upon the deceased
actress :—

> Ici-git qui fût Indienne,
> Bohémienne, Egyptienne,
> Athénienne, Arménienne,
> Qui fût Turque, qui fût Payenne,
> Le tout comme comédienne ;
> Et puis mourût bonne Chrétienne,—

lines which suggest that her name was associated with
a large variety of characters.

Mdlle. Baron's place, if we may believe all we
read, was more than filled by the actress elected to
succeed her—Mdlle. Desœillets.   Nothing is known
of the new-comer until she joined a provincial troupe,
but it is not improbable that she was of good birth,

had received a liberal education, and was playing under an assumed name. Both on and off the stage she displayed a refinement which must have been engrafted upon her in childhood. From the moment she took the lead at the Hôtel de Bourgogne she won the affection of her audience. More than forty years of age, she yet retained a very youthful appearance, and, if not beautiful in the ordinary sense of the term, was so picturesque that the eye followed her with pleasure even while the sensibilities of the heart were awakened by her utterances. Her acting was distinguished by pathos, finesse, earnestness, everything except the power needed to give due effect to characters like Camille and Cléopatre. Her private life, moreover, was dignified by true womanliness. Even in that time— and the fact is significant enough—scandal was never busy with her name. Bright without levity, benevolent without ostentation, quick to acknowledge merit in others, she may be compared in all respects save one to the unhappy lady who was now the observed of all observers at Court—Louise de la Vallière.

In order, perhaps, to counteract this rival attraction, as well as to find relief from his domestic wretchedness in additional work, Molière wrote *L'École des Femmes*, which appeared at the Palais Royal on the 26th December. It was the first time he had taken up the pen since Armande became his wife, and there is something almost pathetic in the fact that in his new comedy, as in that which he produced as his passion for her was growing upon him, he resorted to the ethics of marriage for his materials. The chief personage in the piece, Arnolphe, a middle-aged *roué* (played by Molière himself), has arrived at the conclusion, after a wide experience of womankind, that the best safeguard of a wife's honour is extreme ignorance, that if she is not to befool her husband she must be a fool herself. No girl should know anything except how to sew, pray, spin, and love the man to whom she is pledged. Her library should consist of only two books, the Bible and the *Maxims of Marriage.* Nor does he fail to reduce these theories to rigid practice. Intending to espouse his ward Agnès (Mdlle. Debrie), he has her brought up at a convent school in complete seclusion. But the young lady, while a type of intelligent simplicity, unconsciously outwits him; she bestows her affections upon the gallant Horace (Lagrange), and the guardian, after being made the confidant of the latter, is eventually left out in the cold. The character of Arnolphe is finely contrasted with that of Chrysalde (L'Epi), in whose mouth a series of noble pleas for the cultivation of the intellect in woman is put. It has been hastily assumed by some writers that Molière and his wife are before us in Arnolphe and Agnès. Far indeed is this from the truth, Armande bearing as little resemblance to the unsophisticated ward as her husband did to the tyrannical guardian. It is not improbable, however, that some of the most emotional passages in the play derived additional intensity of feeling and expression from his own experiences. For instance, when Arnolphe, while passionately upbraiding Agnès for what he deems her duplicity, is melted by a half-tender word,—

> Va, petite traîtresse !
> Je te pardonne tout, et te rends ma tendresse ;

and again when, kneeling at her feet, he exclaims,—

> Jusqu'où la passion peut-elle faire aller !
> Enfin, à mon amour rien ne peut s'égaler ;
> Quelle preuve veux-tu que je t'en donne, ingrate ?
> Me veux-tu voir pleurer ? veux-tu que je me batte ?
> Veux-tu que je m'arrache un côté de cheveux ?
> Veux-tu que je me tue ? Oui ; dis si tu le veux ;
> Je suis tout prêt, cruelle, à te prouver ma flamme.

In all this, no doubt, the dramatist himself rather than the character is speaking. For a similar reason his acting may have gained in force and tenderness. How-· ever that may be, *L'École des Femmes,* especially towards the end, was pervaded by a depth of sensibility which he had not previously displayed, and which, joined as it was to unequalled dramatic excellence, exerted a sort of fascination over most of the audience.

His success was not without alloy. In some of the incidents and speeches of the new comedy, it would seem, the *précieuses* and the *fâcheux* saw a means of

bringing odium upon their audacious assailant, and the
temptation was not one to be resisted. Vaguely de-
nouncing the comedy as bad, they insisted that in
writing it he had ridiculed manuals of devotion, sneered
at the doctrine of punishment after death, caricatured the
forms of a sermon, and, by using such phrases as "Tarte
à la crême" and "Enfants fait à l'oreille," had degraded
national morals and the national language. "Parbleu!"
exclaimed an uncompromising detractor of the piece,
the Duc de la Feuillade, in reply to a mild suggestion
that a drama should not be judged by a chance expression or two, "how can anybody with a grain of common
sense and taste endure a play in which 'tarte à la
crême' is uttered? Execrable! 'tarte à la crême,'—
bon Dieu!" Industriously repeated every night in
the *salons*, the criticisms of *L'École des Femmes* were
soon caught up outside, especially by those who are
ever ready to calumniate an unusually successful man.
But the dramatist's assailants were not allowed to
have it all their own way. Boileau came forth
against them, and his prowess as a satirist, now placed
beyond question by the *Adieux*, ensured attention to
what he said. In a few stanzas "sur la comédie de
L'École des Femmes, que plusieurs gens frondaient," he
wrote :—

> En vain mille jaloux esprits,
> Molière, osent, avec mépris,

> Censurer ton plus bel ouvrage ;
> Sa charmante naïveté
> S'en va pour jamais d'âge en âge
> Divertir la posterité.

Finally, after pointing out that in the most burlesque expression of Molière there was often a " docte sermon," he says—

> Laisse gronder tes envieux :
> Ils ont beau crier en tous lieux
> Qu'en vain tu charmes le vulgaire,
> Que tes vers n'ont rien de plaisant.
> Si tu savais un peu moins plaire
> Tu ne leur déplairais pas tant.

Molière's cause was also espoused in a pamphlet entitled *La Guerre Comique.* Here, as elsewhere, it was conclusively shown that he had not been guilty of either immodesty or impiety. But it remained to be seen whether the attacks thus repelled would not do him some harm.

By no one were the diatribes upon Molière more persistently re-echoed in Paris than by a young ecclesiastic named Jean Donneau Devisé, who had taken the *petit-collet* at the instance of his parents, but who cared much less for the cure of souls than for the pleasures of Parisian life. In the previous year he had started *Nouvelles Nouvelles*, which differed from other newsletters of the time in at least one important respect. M. Devisé evidently wished to be regarded as a sort of Aristarchus. His hand, like Ishmael's, was against

everybody. He courted popularity by filling his pages
with the scandals of the hour, with more or less offensive
personalities, and above all, with attacks upon men who
filled a large space in the public eye. In stage work he
manifested particular interest, not only because it formed
a favourite topic of conversation in all quarters, from
the Court down to the tavern, but because the players
might be induced by a wholesome fear of his pen to
bring out some pieces which he intended to write. His
capacity as a critic, by the way, may be measured by
one circumstance. In speaking of *L'École des Maris* he
said that had it been in five acts instead of three it
would take rank with the best comedies yet written. By
parity of reasoning the Colossus of Rhodes must have
been a finer work of art than the Venus di Medici.
He now eagerly joined in the cry raised by the *précieuses*
and the *fâcheux* against Molière, holding him guilty
of what they laid to his charge, describing the noblest
of his comedies as the clumsiest ever inflicted upon
an audience, and even taunting him with the too
obvious misconduct of his wife. Nature had evidently
not formed M. Devisé for ecclesiastical life, but for the
credit of the Church it must be added that he soon
afterwards threw aside the *petit-collet* to marry the
daughter of a penniless artist—a step which led to the
discontinuance by his family of an allowance they had
agreed to make him.

Before long the attention of this enterprising free lance was diverted from *L'École des Femmes* to what he may have deemed better game.   Pierre Corneille had settled in Paris, the last of the ties which bound him to Rouen having been severed by the death of his mother.   His house from the first was in the Rue d'Argenteuil, a comparatively poor quarter.   Here, probably at the instance of Mdlle. Desœillets, whom he held in profound esteem, he undertook the subject of Sophonisba, and the tragedy based upon it was produced at the Hôtel de Bourgogne in February. The result was as favourable as could be expected. In *Sophonisbe*, as in *Sertorius*, the genius of the poet shone forth with a fitful yet often dazzling light. The story of the queen who preferred death to captivity among the Romans whom she hated so intensely is treated with a degree of force which, though not equal to that of his best days, left Mairet's tragedy far behind.   Much of the weakness now inseparable from Corneille's work, too, must have been glossed over by the acting.   Mdlle. Desœillets, of course, came forward as the heroine, and, if not possessed of all the physical energy required for her task, found in the character a means of creating a distinct and lasting impression. Massinisse was played by Floridor, Siphax by Mont-fleuri, and Erixe by Mdlle. Beauchâteau.   From this time Mairet's *Sophonisbe* lost its hold upon the stage ;

and Corneille, with a generosity not to be fully appreciated unless the persecution of the *Cid* is borne in mind, took occasion to pay an impressive tribute to the merits of his predecessor's work.

Devisé here turned his batteries against Corneille, whom he appears to have regarded as the greatest of living writers, and therefore the best possible object of attack. He pointedly decried *Sophonisbe*, ascribed its success to the acting, and accused Corneille of having written it for no better purpose than to dim the glory of a predecessor. Most people were startled at the audacity of the assailant, as he hoped and expected they would be. "I shall always think it an honour," he wrote, "to be called bold. For boldness belongs to the young; and those who do not possess it, far from deserving esteem, should be generally despised." Equal temerity, however, was to be shown by a man well advanced in years. The Abbé d'Aubignac, flouted by the players, had written a book called the *Pratique du Théâtre*—a work correctly described as "a heavy and fatiguing commentary on Aristotle, written by a pedant without wit or judgment, who fancies that he understands the drama because he can read Greek." In this treatise Corneille is highly praised, but in none of his *Examens* is any reference made to it, and the Abbé, smarting under what may have been an unintentional slight, now printed a bitter critique upon *Sophonisbe* and *Sertorius*. After maintaining that a subject effectively treated by one dramatist ought not to be treated by another, he accused Corneille of organizing a cabal against *L'École des Femmes*, the success of which, it was added, had been to him what the trophies of Miltiades were to Themistocles. Devisé, inconsistently enough, wrote an anonymous pamphlet defending *Sophonisbe* from the criticisms of the Abbé, who, satisfied that it emanated from Corneille himself, published a critique upon *Œdipe*, with a reply to the " calumnies " of its author. Devisé, dropping his mask, made an effective rejoinder, in which he explained his change of front by declaring that he went to see *Sophonisbe* in a too captious spirit. In the result he had the better of his adversary, but did not come from the fray unscathed. He had been described by the Abbé as " a poet who catered for the bourgeois of the Rue Saint Denis and the pickpockets of the Marais,"—and the burr never left him.

The *Sophonisbe* controversy over, Devisé renewed his attacks upon Molière with added bitterness, especially as the *salons* continued to resound with denunciations of *L'École des Femmes*, supplemented by unclean mirth on the subject of his great home sorrow. By this time it was evident that the attack upon him would bear lasting fruit. Neither the king nor the playgoing public was imposed upon by the affected solicitude of

précieuses and the *fâcheux* for the purity of the drama ;
but the religious section of the community, predisposed
to credit anything to the disadvantage of the stage,
and restrained by their scruples from seeing a performance of or reading the play, eagerly joined in the outcry.
In their eyes, it is certain, the mere fact that *L'École des
Femmes* had been censured as irreverent and indecent
was a sufficient reason for deeming it both.   Even one
of Molière's oldest friends, the Prince de Conti, who
had lately become a fervent theologian and Jansenist,
thought it necessary to take part against him.   " Modern
comedy," said the convert, in a treatise on the theatre,
" is undeniably free from idolatry and superstition,
but not from impurity.   Indeed, the seeming respect-
ability which has served as a pretext for bestowing
unmerited applause upon pieces of this kind is giving
place to ill-disguised immodesty.   Nothing, for example,
is more scandalous than the fifth scene of the second act
of *L'École des Femmes.*"   The absurdity of this assertion
may be seen on reference to the play, which has come
down to us as it was originally represented.   But the
attitude of the Prince was that of the devout in general.
A new and formidable body of enemies had risen up
against the dramatist, and the time-honoured prejudice
against the stage was deepened at a time when it seemed
to be yielding to the pressure of common-sense.

Molière replied to his detractors with irresistible effect.

He wrote a *Critique de l'École des Femmes* in the form
of a dramatic dialogue, to be delivered on the stage like
that of a regular comedy.   In this monument of a just
vengeance, as it has been termed, he displays a self-
command which may well excite surprise.   Intense as
was the provocation he had received—and the jeers flung
at him on account of the misconduct of his wife had
hurt him to the quick—the work is free from any trace
of anger.   He assumed his airiest and most genial
manner.   He never overstepped the limits of the severest
taste.   But within those limits he produced one of the
most telling satires on record.   Climène, a *précieuse*
(Mdlle. Duparc), a coxcomb Marquis (Lagrange), and
Lysidas, a poetaster (Ducroisy), successively assail *L'École
des Femmes* in a conversation with three clear-headed
persons—Uranie (Mdlle. Debrie), Elise (Mdlle. Molière),
and Dorante (Brécourt).   Climène's sense of decorum
has been outrageously shocked by particular passages of
the play.   " Nay," says Uranie, " you must have a sharp
nose for secluded impropriety ; I confess I saw none."
" So much the worse for you."   " So much the better,
I think.   I take things as they are presented to me, and
do not turn them round to look for what should not be
seen.   A woman's modesty does not consist in grimacing.
Nothing is more ridiculous than the delicacy which takes
everything offensively and gives criminal meaning to the
most innocent words.   The other night this affectation

was carried to such a length by some ladies in the
theatre that a lackey in the pit declared ' their ears to
be more chaste than the rest of their persons.' " The
Marquis denounces the piece as " detestable, to the last
degree detestable, what one calls perfectly detestable."
" But why is it detestable ? " asks Dorante. " *Why* is
it detestable ? " " Yes." " Because it *is* detestable."
However, the Marquis does give some reasons for his
censure. The piece has been applauded by the pit.
He could scarcely get a place. Then " tarte à la crême."
" Well," says Dorante, " what of that ? " " Parbleu ! "
replies the Marquis, " 'Tarte à la crême,' chevalier."
" Still what of that ? " " 'Tarte à la crême.' " " But
why is it objectionable ? " " 'Tarte à la crême.' " " Won't
you show us your thought ? " asks Uranie. " ' Tarte a la
crême,' " again responds the Marquis. Lysidas, after
speaking with affected moderation, declaims against
the play because, as every one acquainted with Aristotle
and Horace could see, it violated all the rules of art.
Dorante, without any want of respect for those rules,
holds that a comedy justifies its existence when it
pleases the audience, and Uranie is of opinion that
the men best versed in Aristotle and Horace are those
who write comedies which no mortal can admire.
For her part, if she is well entertained, she does not
inquire whether the rules of Aristotle forbid her to laugh.
" It is very strange," she also says, " that you writers

always condemn the plays which every one goes to see, and never speak well of any except those which fail." In the end, as all along, the defenders of *L'École des Femmes* have the advantage, one of them remarking that the author did not care how much his comedies were abused as long as the town came to see them. Brought out on the 1st June, the *Critique*, thanks to its delightful wit and irony, was represented no fewer than thirty-one times—a sure sign that Molière had not miscalculated his strength in venturing to put so singular a piece before his audience.

Most of his assailants were silenced by the ridicule here cast upon them, but the resentment it aroused was not to be repressed. Devisé led off with a piece similar in form—*Zélinde, ou la Véritable Critique de l'École des Femmes.* It produced little or no effect, as the author, unlike the man he assailed, could not keep his temper, and was accordingly led to substitute coarse invective for wit. The Duc de la Feuillade, assured that the character of the Marquis was intended as a portrait or caricature of himself—a point on which the passages in the *Critique* on "tarte à la crème" left no room for doubt—took a revenge as cowardly as it was brutal. Meeting Molière in one of the galleries of the Tuileries, he stopped as though to embrace him, seized his head, and, repeating "tarte à la crème" again and again, rubbed his face violently

against the buttons of his dress. In all probability
the Duc was well aware that an actor, however estimable he might be, could not exact satisfaction from
a peer. But the outrage did not pass unpunished :
Louis XIV., greatly to his honour, " censured with
becoming severity the courtier who, under pretence
of zeal for the eloquence and purity of the French
language, had taken an unmanly opportunity to insult
a man of genius within the precincts of his master's
palace." Nor was the Duc the only person who deemed
himself individually aggrieved by the *Critique.* In the
character of Lysidas, the champion of the laws of
Aristotle and Horace, Molière, as I think, amuses himself at the expense of the Abbé d'Aubignac, chiefly
with the object of showing that the accusation made
by that erudite but asinine man against Corneille in
reference to *L'École des Femmes* was not countenanced
at the Palais Royal. Boursault, however, imagined
that he was the person assailed, and another critique
upon the *Ecole des Femmes,* entitled *Le Portrait du
Peintre*—a critique which, if in better taste than that
of Devisé, certainly did not err on the side of moderation—figured in the bills of the Hôtel de Bourgogne.

Louis XIV., who took a keen interest in the issue
of the contest, here requested Molière to bring his
assailants on the stage, the Troupe Royale included.
The poet had no alternative but to obey, and eight

days afterwards, on the 15th October, *L'Impromptu de Versailles* was heard at the newly-made palace there —that "triumph of art over nature"—before an audience consisting in a large measure of his intended victims. The framework of the new piece is slender enough. Molière and his comrades appear under their own names to rehearse a comedy which they have yet to learn, but which the King is impatiently expecting. Brécourt is a man of quality, Lagrange a stupid marquis, Ducroisy a poet, Mdlle. Duparc an affected lady, Mdlle. Béjart a prude, Mdlle. Debrie a chaste coquette, and Mdlle. Molière an ingenious satirist. Molière himself comes forward in a character similar to that of Lagrange. In the company I perceive three new faces—Lathorillière, Mdlle. Ducroisy, and Mdlle. Hervé. Originally a captain of cavalry, the first of these recruits—a tall, handsome fellow, with remarkably fine eyes—played kings and peasants in a most creditable style, though in the former he did not invariably maintain the gravity of expression they required. The *Impromptu* is replete with fair yet biting satire upon those who had sought to injure its author. " Prenez garde," he says to Lagrange, " à bien réprésenter avec moi votre rôle de Marquis." " Toujours des marquis ! " exclaims Armande. " Oui," replies Molière, " toujours des Marquis. Que diable voulez-vous qu'on prenne pour un caractère agréable de théâtre ? Le Marquis "—and a flutter must have passed over the audience at this point—" est aujourd'hui le plaisant de la comédie ; il faut toujours un Marquis qui divertisse la compagnie." Glancing at the counter *Critiques* of the *École des Femmes*, Molière went so far as to mention Boursault by name—the only error of taste and judgment with which he can be reproached. The chief weight of the satire, as may be supposed, fell upon the players of the Rue Mauconseil. Not content with writing against them, the author, as though to give play to his inborn talent for mimicry, took occasion to imitate some of · their peculiarities. The irrepressible tendency of Mdlle. Beauchâteau to laugh in the middle of impressive scenes, the undue emphasis of Montfleuri, who by reason of the vast circumference of his body could fill a throne *de la belle manière*, as it ought to be filled —these things, for example, seem to have been pleasantly caricatured. Neither Floridor nor Desœillets is mentioned, possibly because they had no sympathy with the attack made upon their great rival. By sparing them he entitled himself to their gratitude. Applauded by the King at Versailles, the *Impromptu* was transferred to the stage of the Palais Royal on the 4th November, and the players assailed in it must have writhed under the general roar of merriment it aroused.

If Molière's latest victims had been wise they would
have affected an air of good-humoured indifference to
the attack ; as it was, they turned upon him with a
rancour which clearly showed that his shaft was quiver-
ing in the centre of its mark. In the first instance
they replied to him in a one-act piece by Montfleuri
fils, *L'Impromptu de l'Hôtel de Condé,* in which Beauchâteau and Villiers appeared under their own names to
give coarse imitations of their antagonist. During one
of the performances, it would appear, Molière entered
the theatre, took a seat on one of the forms at the side
of the stage, and eyed the movements of his mimics
with a certain languid and half-amused curiosity which
could not but have disconcerted them. Montfleuri's
Impromptu withdrawn, Villiers wrote *Le Vengéance des
Marquis, ou une Réponse à l'Impromptu de Versailles.*
He probably received no thanks from the nobles for
taking up the cudgels in their behalf ; they were not
disposed to make common cause in anything with a few
players, and the piece was abusive enough to bring
discredit upon anybody who might be defended in it.
Boursault, contrary to expectation, did not join in this
crusade, for the simple reason that, alive rather to the
injustice of his attack upon Molière than the reply it
had evoked, he had sought and obtained his friendship—a sufficient reply to the allegation that the
attacks upon him in the *Impromptu de Versailles* denote

unpardonable cruelty. Montfleuri had much less ground for complaint against Molière than Boursault, but his resentment was not to be appeased. In a memorial addressed to the King he alleged that Molière had married his own daughter—in other words, that Armande was born of an intimacy which he had formed with Madeleine Béjart soon after the Illustre Théâtre company left Paris for the country.

This revolting accusation met with the fate it deserved. Mdlle. Molière presented her husband with a son; and the King, as an indirect but emphatic answer to the memorial, was graciously pleased, in conjunction with Henriette d'Orléans, to hold the child by proxy at the baptismal font. "Du Jeudi, 28 Février, 1664," the entry in the register runs, "fut baptisé Louis, fils de M. Jean-Baptiste Molière, valet de chambre du roi, et de damoiselle Armande-Grésinde Béjart, sa femme, vis-à-vis le Palais Royal. Le parrain, haut et puissant seigneur messire Charles duc de Créqui, premier gentilhomme de la chambre du roi, ambassadeur à Rome, tenant pour Louis quatorzième, roi de France et de Navarre: la marraine, dame Colombe le Charron, épouse de messire César de Choiseul, Maréchal du Plessy, tenante pour Madame Henriette d'Angleterre, duchesse d'Orléans. L'enfant est né le 19 janvier audit an. Signé, Colombet." It is not the least doubtful indication of the generosity to which the Grand Monarque now and then rose, that on this occasion he should have so pointedly come down from the throne to throw his mantle over the grievously-insulted player. Montfleuri himself, it has to be added, escaped without further punishment, probably from a conviction at Court that the soundness of his mind was open to question. No man in his senses would have preferred such a charge until he had ascertained how far it was in accordance with facts, and but few inquiries would have sufficed to show that it was wholly destitute of justification.

It is a proof of the habitual self-command of Molière that at this stormy period of his life he should have penned a comedy in which his humour was again blended with another skilful satire. Distended to three acts by ballets, with Louis XIV. as a gipsy dancer, *Le Mariage Forcé* was performed at the Louvre on the 29th and 31st January. In the earlier scenes, perhaps, the author was not unmindful of his own experience with Armande, though the story he unfolded may have been suggested by *Le Mariage de Panurge.* By reason of his extreme wealth, Sganarelle, here a middle-aged bourgeois (Molière), is accepted as a husband by young Dorimène (Mdlle. Duparc). "This match," he fatuously remarks to himself, after conversing on the subject with a sensible old friend, Géronimo (Lathorillière), " ought to be a happy one ; everybody to whom I speak of it

laughs; me voilà le plus content des hommes!" But
his delight is abruptly checked. His future wife,
hitherto kept in extreme subjection, candidly avows
to him a passion for the most frivolous pleasures,
at the same time expressing a hope that after their
marriage they would live together like a pair "qui
savent leur monde." Is there not a reminiscence of
Armande in this? Impressed with dark forebodings as
to the consequences of allying himself to such a woman,
Sganarelle seeks the advice of two most learned seers—
Pancrace (Brécourt) and Marphurius (Ducroisy). Here,
applying some incidents in his *Jalousie du Barbouillé* to
a different purpose, but without diminishing their broad
and even riotous farce, the dramatist skilfully ridicules
the strange fanaticism which made the University of
Paris seek for a confirmation of the old decree that
all opponents of the philosophy of Aristotle should be
put to death. Pancrace, who reserves one of his ears
for the vulgar tongue, sees nothing in the world but a
"frightful licence," inasmuch as somebody has previously spoken of the "form of a hat" instead of the
"figure of a hat." Has not Aristotle said that "form"
is the external manifestation of animate bodies, "figure"
the external manifestation of inanimate bodies? Marphurius, on his part, is an uncompromising Pyrrhonian.
Everything must be spoken of in a spirit of uncertainty.
"Seigneur Sganarelle," he says, "you ought not to say

'I am here,' but 'I seem to be here.' Nous devons douter de tout." His faith is put to a severe test. Sganarelle, irritated by such galimatias; proceeds to belabour him with a stick. "Insolence," he shrieks, "I will go to the commissaire du quartier." "Nay," retorts Sganarelle, "everything should be doubtful; you should not say that I have thrashed you, but that I have only seemed to do so." For the source of the *dénouement* we must look to an anecdote of the time. The Comte de Grammont, while a guest of the English Court, paid very marked attention to Miss Hamilton, but left without having asked her to become his wife. Her two brothers, bent upon satisfaction in one form or another, overtook him at Dover. "Count," said the elder, "have you not forgotten something at London?" "I' faith, yes," replied the Count, not liking the prospect of a duel; "I have forgotten to marry your sister, and will return with you to conclude that little affair at once." Sganarelle, with the unlooked-for consent of Dorimène's father, Alcantor (Béjart), breaks his engagement with the young lady, but is cudgelled by her brother Alcidas (Lagrange) into keeping it. Reduced to the dimensions of one act by the omission of the ballets, *Le Mariage Forcé* was soon transferred to the stage of the Palais Royal, and we have no reason to doubt that it was to the taste of all save those upon whom its ridicule fell.

But a graver subject of satire than *mariages de con-*

vénance or the blind devotion of the Sorbonne to the philosophy of Aristotle was to engage the attention of Molière. No sign of the times, perhaps, was more conspicuous than a reaction against the anti-theological spirit which had found expression in the *Parnasse Satirique* of Théophile Viand, and at a later period, though in a different way, in the writings of Descartes. Daily intensified by the strife between Jesuits and Jansenists, this reaction soon bore down all opposition, and the voice of scepticism was drowned in a chorus of real or affected acquiescence in the teachings of Revelation. In nearly all quarters the odour of incense was to be perceived. The most worldly conversation was interlarded with images from and allusions to the sacred books, and every service in the churches brought together a dense crowd of worshippers. Often ready to adopt a prevalent whim, the Court of Louis Quatorze, though hardly less gay and licentious than that of Charles II., made a point of uniting devotion to "la belle galanterie." In brief, piety had again come into fashion, and a superficial observer of the phenomenon may well have deluded himself into the belief that the absorbing faith of the Middle Ages was not a thing of the past. It is almost superfluous to add that this revival was attended by at least one serious evil. The vice of self-seeking hypocrisy increased in proportion to its correlative virtue. France found itself honeycombed with men endeavouring to make a gain of godliness, even to the extent of using religion as a cloak for designs which involved the dishonour of families.

It was to the task of checking this evil that Molière now applied his piercing and victorious satire. In *Tartuffe*, a comedy in five acts, he relates the story of an attempt by an irreclaimable hypocrite to destroy the domestic happiness of a citizen who, charmed by his seeming piety, has received him as a permanent guest. In painting such a portrait, of course, the lively assailant of Parisian foibles was in a new element, but it proved even more congenial to him than that which he had hitherto breathed. His genius, as several passages in *L'École des Femmes* may have shown, had a serious side to it, and on that side was unquestionably at its best. He drew the character of Tartuffe with a strength and precision which few dramatists have equalled. By a process of self-revelation, unaided by soliloquies or addresses to a confidant, "the heart of a man who had least desired and could worse bear close investigation was discovered and ascertained in all its bearings, gradually yet certainly, as navigators trace the lines and bearings of an unknown coast." In the delineation and grouping of the other personages, too, the instincts and power of a great artist are visible. Nor did the author fail to avoid the pitfalls inseparable from such a

subject. He never confounded hypocrisy with true
religion ; on the contrary, the course of the latter is
incidentally upheld in the piece with a warmth which
suggests that he had inherited the piety of his mother,
and was animated as much by a love of the faith she
had instilled into him as by his characteristic hatred
of imposture in any shape. He also refrained from
identifying the hypocrite with either of the two parties
into which the religious world was divided. In some
respects the figure recalls the austere Jansenist to mind ;
the casuistry employed in the attempt to overcome the
wife's virtue is essentially Jesuitical. Much idle controversy has been expended upon the origin of the name
of the play, but in the obsolete verb tra-truffar, to
deceive in the extreme, an all but certain solution of
the problem, I think, has been found.

If Molière wished to produce *Tartuffe* in the first
instance at Court—and the startling nature of the
incidents afforded him a good reason for doing so – he
had not to wait long for his opportunity. Early in May
the King gave a series of dazzling *fêtes* at Versailles,
nominally in honour of the Queen and Anne of Austria,
but really to please the Maid of Honour who had
won his affections without seeking them, who was now
his unacknowledged mistress, and who instinctively
shrank from the inquisitive gaze of the world. Molière,
having been commanded to contribute to the entertain-

ments, wrote *La Princesse d'Élide*, the plot of which is
derived from a Spanish play, *El desden con el Desden*, by
Moreto. Here, by an affectation of indifference, a lover
piques a princess on whom his affections are fixed, but
who treats all pretenders to her hand with magnificent
disdain, into a resolve to win him,—with what result
I need not say. Mdlle. Molière impersonated this
character with a refinement and *verve* which may well
have surprised her husband, predisposed though he
was to overrate her charms as an actress. Her stage
father, Iphitas, was a player new to the company,
André Hubert, a most diverting representative of old
women. Molière himself appeared as the Court jester,
not the least humorous of his creations. Moron is
a character of the ignoble but often diverting type
which finds its chief illustration in Falstaff. He is a
downright coward, avoiding danger of any kind on the
ground that it is better to live a day in the world than
a thousand years in history. Molière had not had time
either to do himself justice in the piece or to clothe
more than a small portion of it in verse, but the grace
and spirit he nevertheless infused into it, joined to the
humours of Moron and the impression produced by
Armande, won for the piece the good opinion of the
audience. In all probability the dramatist received an
intimation that any other novelty he was prepared to
give would be acceptable, for on the sixth day of the

fêtes—fancifully denominated " Les Plaisirs de l'Ile Enchantée "—he put on the stage the first three acts of *Tartuffe*. I have often endeavoured to realize to myself the effect produced by this terrible picture upon its first beholders—upon the mass of revellers who, resplendent in masquerade attire, filled the theatre in every part. Not only was the entertainment of a complexion widely different from what they had anticipated, but the author, who seemed to have been born for no other purpose than to make the world laugh at itself, showed that he had the power to confront them with one of the deepest mysteries of human existence, to conduct them to the brink of a dark and unfathomable gulf, to make them seem to touch some awful secret of the cosmos. Few thinking persons could have failed to see in *Tartuffe* the work of an intellectual giant.

The King, in addition to being sensible of the genius it displayed, was clear-sighted enough to perceive that the play was aimed exclusively at hypocrisy, and Loret was probably justified in saying that the " moral comedy " by M. Molière had won the suffrages of the Court. But from the moment when the nature of this moral comedy became known in Paris a storm began to rage over the head of the intrepid dramatist. Both genuine and false *dévots* united in a bitter outcry against him. According to them, he had at length thrown aside the mask altogether, and under pretence of exposing hypocrisy was seeking to undermine the foundations of religion itself. Roullès, the curé of Saint Barthélemy, took it upon himself to "damn" the author of *Tartuffe* on his own authority, describing him as "un démon vêtu de chair habillé en homme; un libertin, un impie digne d'être brûlé publiquement." Not the least virulent denouncer of the play, perhaps, was a certain Roquette, Bishop of Autun, who was generally supposed to be the original of the stage-impostor, and a list of whose hypocrisies, drawn up by one De Guilleragues, a friend of Boileau, is said to have been on Molière's desk while he wrote. The agitation increased day by day; and the King, evidently at the instance of the pious queen-mother, determined to prohibit the performance in Paris of a play which he had almost unreservedly admired. In doing so, however, he did not entirely sacrifice his own opinions. "Although," writes the official recorder of the *fêtes* at Versailles, "the comedy written by the Sieur Molière against hypocrites is extremely fine, his majesty perceived so much resemblance between those whom a true devotion leads into the road to heaven, and those whom ostentation of good works does not hinder from evil-doing, that his extreme sensitiveness could not bear such a likeness of vice to virtue that one might be taken for the other. Having no doubt of the good intentions of the author, he has yet forbidden its representation in public, and deprived himself of this gratification in order that it might not be abused by others less capable of discerning its real meaning." Not long afterwards, as though to give further expression to his sympathy with the dramatist, the King had *Tartuffe* played in his brother's house at Villers-Cotterets, but did not succeed by doing so in allaying the excitement which the actual and supposed objects of the play had created.

Irritated by his disappointment, Molière registered a vow that sooner or later the interdiction should be set aside, and as time went on he saw a means of awakening such a friendly interest among the leaders of Parisian society in the fate of his work as would encourage the King to take that much-desired step. Everybody, of course, was anxious to taste the forbidden fruit in his possession. The *salons* vied with each other in an attempt to induce him to read his *Tartuffe* in the hearing of a select group. "No greater pleasure," we are told, "could be procured for any party of fine ladies and gentlemen." Molière complied with many of these requests, inasmuch as they gave him valuable opportunities of dispelling the prevalent misapprehension in regard to the play, of creating an interest in its fortunes, and of inspiring a wish to hear it under the more favourable conditions afforded

by its being played on the stage. His first private
audience consisted of the Pope's legate and a few
prelates, who, impressed with a belief that *Tartuffe*
was a covert satire against the Jansenists—an idea
which, erroneous as it was, he took no pains to dispel
—" en jugèrent très-favorablement." In Jansenist
circles, on the other hand, it was applauded from
a conviction that the author had designed it as a
continuation of the war opened by Pascal in the
Lettres à une Provinciale. Molière must often have
been secretly embarrassed by the questions put to
him after a reading, but it is not unlikely that he
had sympathies with each party, and was accordingly
able to win both to his side without making his
conscience uneasy. On one occasion, as a well-known
picture reminds us, we find him "lisant son *Tartuffe*
chez Ninon de l'Enclos," one of whose guests described
the piece as a sermon. "Pourquoi sera-t-il permis,"
replied the dramatist, "au Père Maimbourg de faire
des comédies en chaire, et qu'il ne me sera pas permis
de faire des sermons sur le théâtre ?"

In the course of these readings the author of *Tartuffe*
suffered a blow which may well have rendered him
indifferent for a time to the ultimate fate of that play.
Armande, intoxicated by the success he had enabled
her to achieve, had at length disregarded the first of
her obligations as a wife. Bazin has conclusively

shown that two of the men who are supposed to
have corrupted her were not in France at this period,
but it is beyond doubt that one or more of the
courtiers whom she had smitten by the charms of
her acting in the *Princesse d'Elide*—and the Abbé
de Richelieu seems to have been of the number—did
not seek her favours in vain. How keenly the husband
felt his dishonour need hardly be said. Worthless
as Armande was, she had aroused in him a passion
to end but with his life, and his nature, in one
respect unfortunately for himself, was too fine and
sensitive to permit him to regard her faithlessness
with the affected indifference, the half-condoning
sangfroid, of a man of the world in the seventeenth
century. In this painful crisis he formed a resolution
both dignified and generous—a resolution which shows
that in his mind a tender compassion could co-exist
with a just resentment and an outraged sense of self-
respect. He would cease to treat her as a wife, but
would not deprive her of the protection of his roof.
In other words, they would lead separate lives in
one house, meeting only at the theatre. Her jesses
were his dear heartstrings, and he could not let
her down the wind to prey at fortune. By this
generosity, as may be supposed, he added to the
burden of his affliction ; and before long, in order to
avoid the risk of meeting her except when it was

necessary to do so, he took a villa at Auteuil—then, as now, one of the prettiest suburbs of Paris—for himself alone.

His wound was not of a kind to be quickly healed, as the record of a conversation he had with an almost life-long friend soon afterwards will prove. One afternoon Chapelle broke in upon his solitude in the garden at Auteuil, and, finding him more than usually downcast, reproached him with betraying a weakness which he had made an object of ridicule on the stage. " I have been in love myself," the visitor lightly added, " but I should never have found it difficult to do what honour required of me." " No," replied Molière, " you have never been in love. You have taken the appearance of love for love itself. I might give you many examples of the strength of this passion, but I will give you simply a faithful account of my state of mind. If the knowledge I have of the human heart has told me that such a peril may be shunned, my experience has shown that it cannot be avoided altogether. Nature has given me an ultra-disposition to tenderness, and I thought to secure my happiness by the innocence of my choice. I took my wife, so to speak, from the cradle ; I educated her with care ; I did all I could to inspire her with sentiments which time should not destroy. As she was still young when I married her, I did not perceive her evil inclinations, and I deemed myself a little less unfortunate than the majority of husbands. With marriage I did not cease to be her lover; but she treated me with so much indifference that I began to see that all my precautions had been fruitless, and that her sentiments for me were very different from those I had hoped for. I reproached myself with a ridiculous sensitiveness, ascribing to temper what was really her want of affection for me. Unfortunately I had but too much reason to see that this was an error. The mad passion she conceived soon afterwards for Comte de Guiche created too much scandal to leave me in seeming tranquillity. I summoned all my strength of mind, called to my aid every thought that could tend to console me. I resolved to live with her as an honourable man whose wife is a coquette, and who is persuaded, whatever may be said to the contrary, that his reputation does not depend upon her conduct. But I had the mortification to find that a woman without great beauty, who owes the mind she has to the education I have given her, was able in a moment to humble all my philosophy. Her presence made me forget all my resolutions; the first words she said to me in her own defence convinced me that my suspicions were unfounded, and I begged her pardon for having been so credulous. My kindness, however, did not change her, and in the end I made up my mind to live with her as if she were not my wife. If you knew what I suffer you would pity me. My passion for her has risen to such a point as to make me sympathize with her interests; and the impossibility of suppressing what I feel for her leads me to ask myself whether she may not have the same difficulty in subduing her inclinations to coquetry, and I am disposed rather to commiserate than to blame her. No doubt you will tell me that I must be mad; but for my part I believe there is only one kind of love, and that those who have not experienced these heart struggles have never been under its influence. Everything is associated with her in my mind; my thoughts will not be diverted from her. When I see her, an emotion which may be felt but not expressed deprives me of all power of reflection. I have no eyes for her faults, but only what makes her dear to me. Is this not the extreme of folly? and do you not marvel that what reason I have serves to convince me of my weakness without giving me the power to overcome it!" Superficial as he was, Chapelle seems to have been deeply moved, as well he may have been, by the pathos of what he heard. "My prayers," he at length said, "will be for you. Do not cease your efforts to conquer yourself; they may have effect

when you least expect it. Hope the best from
time ! "

Molière's worldly position at this moment was such
as to encourage him to act upon Chapelle's advice. Not
only did his popularity in Paris seem to increase with
each successive day, but the favour of the Court,
which to him was a matter of paramount importance,
was proof against every attempt made to diminish it.
On one occasion, it is said, he was even invited
by the reserved and exclusive King to join him at
table—an honour bestowed upon but few persons
in that reign. As we have seen, the dramatist had
received the appointment which on becoming an actor
he had waived his right to inherit, that of valet-
de-chambre du roi. For a time he may well have
wished that this mark of royal approbation had been
withheld from him. Another valet-de-chambre, a peer
of long pedigree, declined to make the King's bed with
a comedian, and for a similar reason the officials of
the privy chamber treated him in such a way that
he did not eat with them a second time. Louis very
quickly proceeded to put a stop to this annoyance.
His majesty, it must be understood, had so vigorous
an appetite that a light repast was·kept in readiness
for him *en cas de nuit*—in case he should wake up
hungry in the middle of the night. " M. de Molière,"
he said one morning, " I hear that you make bad cheer

here, that my people think you are not good enough
to associate with them. Perhaps you are hungry;
I myself have got up with a very good appetite.
Let my *en cas de nuit* be served." This done, he requested Molière to sit down, helped him with his own
hands, and shared the repast with him in the sight
of any personage who might chance to come in.
Molière, while appreciating the King's motives, must
have been secretly mortified by the invitation, inasmuch
as it drew general attention to slights which, much
as they may have wounded his sensibility, he had
been too proud to notice in any way. The unintentional annoyance inflicted upon him by the King, however, was not without its advantages; the whole Court
rained invitations upon him, and if he did not again
join the noble lackeys at the table of service it was
from no want of willingness on their part to receive
him. The authenticity of the anecdote has been
questioned on the ground that the honour conferred
upon Molière had been coveted to no purpose by
prelates and generals and statesmen; but it is not
altogether improbable that Louis XIV., yielding to a
sudden impulse, adopted this effectual means of pro-
tecting from insolence a man whom he held in such
high esteem as the author of *Les Précieuses Ridicules*,
L'École des Femmes, and *Tartuffe*.(*g*)

CHAPTER VIII.

1664—1667.

IN the summer of this year the prosperous yet unhappy dramatist was enabled for the first time to bring the powers of his company in tragedy to a fair test. Bearing a letter of introduction from Lafontaine, and already known to fame as a poet of unusual promise, a young ecclesiastic, fashionably dressed, of pleasing manners, and with singularly eloquent dark eyes, submitted a *Théagène and Chariclée* for his consideration. Molière found that the plot was not strong enough to hold an audience for four hours, but the versification rose so far above the average that he asked his visitor to write for him a tragedy on the subject of the Thebais—a subject which, if tradition does not err, he had himself treated without success in his old strolling days. In less than six weeks the commission was executed. Molière, perceiving in the play a marked tendency to imitate Corneille, returned the MS. to M. Jean Racine—for that was the young author's name—with an injunction to dispense with the aid of models. In the result, *La Thébaïde*, altered so far as to receive some impress of a distinct individuality, was brought out at the Palais Royal. Neither the author nor the manager could have been dissatisfied as the curtain fell. Inferior as the company may have been in tragedy to that headed by Floridor and Mdlle. Descœillets, they yet created a deep impression by their acting, and the fact that two of the noblest speeches allotted to them had been taken almost bodily from Rotrou's *Antigone* did not prevent the critics from feeling that another original genius was enlisted in the service of the theatre.

Racine was born in 1639 at La Ferté-Milon, where his father officiated as controller of the salt magazine and of the salt-tax. This post, which conferred some social influence upon the person who possessed it, seems to have been held by the Racine family for many years, as on a tomb in the old church in the town we read—" Cy gissent honorables personnes, Jean Racine, receveur pour le roi, notre sire, et la reine, tant du domaine et duchie de Valois que de greniers à sel de La Ferté-Milon et Crespy, en Valois, mort en 1593, et Dame Anne Gosset, sa femme." Becoming an orphan in his fourth year, he was taken charge of by near relatives, and in his eleventh or twelfth year was sent to the Collége de Beauvais. Not long previously the War of the Fronde had broken out, and

Racine, having taken part with some of the scholars in one of the provincial contests, was severely wounded on the forehead with a stone. From Beauvais he proceeded to Port Royal, whither his grandmother and two aunts, almost the only friends now left to him, had retired to devote themselves to piety and the education of youth. He remained in the monastery about four years, learning Greek from Claude Lancelot, who came to treat him as a son, and Latin and the humanities from Nicole. At times, it is to be feared, he proved a somewhat untractable pupil. He one day sat down to read *Théagène* and *Chariclée*, a story hardly suited to one of his years. Lancelot, surprising him in *flagranti delicto*, angrily threw the book into the fire. The youth procured another copy, read it to the last line, and then, carrying it to the sacristan, sullenly remarked, " You may now burn this as well." But this indocility was not accompanied by a disinclination to study. His progress was rapid enough to awaken sanguine hopes as to his future. In the matter of Greek scholarship, it would seem, he learnt more than Lancelot, who was but little more than a sound grammarian, could teach him. He would bury himself in the woods to pore over Euripides and Sophocles, and at the age of nineteen, we are assured, had acquired a deep insight into the predominating spirit of their plays as a whole. Bidding adieu to Port Royal, with its picturesque and venerable associations, he entered the Collége d'Harcourt, there to go through his philosophy. He was now the ward of a cousin, Nicholas Vitart, financial secretary to the Duc de Luynes. In another year, pressed to choose a profession, he directed his attention by turns to law and theology. He liked neither ; but in the end, probably at the solicitation of the Solitaries of Port Royal, who did not lose sight of so promising a pupil, he undertook to prepare himself for the Church.

It soon became evident that he had no sympathy with his self-elected calling. Established for a time in Paris as a sort of assistant to his guardian, he gave himself up to doubtful pleasures, fell into bad company, and in some of his letters went so far as to ridicule the pious forms of expression adopted by the Port Royalists. Moreover, new ideas and aspirations took possession of his mind. In honour of the royal marriage he wrote an ode entitled *La Nymphe de la Seine*, unquestionably a meritorious production, although disfigured by such lines as

> Regnez, belle Thérèse, en ces aimables lieux
> Qu'arrose le cours de mon onde,
> Et que doit éclairer le feu de vos beaux yeux.

Chapelain was then arbiter of the royal bounties to men of letters, and Vitart judiciously sent him the manuscript. "Many of the stanzas," he wrote in reply, "could not be improved. If the few passages I have marked are set right"—especially one in which Tritons are placed in a river—"the ode will be a fine one." Naturally enough, Racine made all the alterations suggested, and in the result, on the recommendation of Chapelain, he received one hundred louis d'or from Colbert in the name of the king. This unexpected success disposed him to rely upon literature, but soon afterwards, probably in order to avoid reproaches addressed to him from Port Royal as to his mode of living and pursuits, he became the guest at Uzès of his mother's brother, Antoine Sconin, the Vicaire-Général in that town, who wished to find him a benefice. Here he wrote his notes on the Odyssey and the Olympiads—a proof that he did not allow his mind to be too much exercised upon theological subjects. In less than eighteen months, more than ever disgusted with the prospect of a clerical life, he came back to Paris, resumed his former habits, and again took to authorship. Fortune continued to smile on his efforts. For writing an ode on the happy recovery of the Grand Monarque from an attack of measles he was awarded a pension of six hundred francs —a sum which, however small it may appear now, was then sufficient for a bare maintenance. His next effusion was on a little more poetical theme, "La Renommée aux Muses." Boileau criticised it with so much good sense and kindness that Racine sought an introduction to him, and the two men became fast friends. The elder used to boast that he had taught the other how to write verse, which was probably the fact. Be that as it may, Racine soon addressed himself to one of the most trying forms of composition. He wrote for the Hôtel de Bourgogne a tragedy entitled *Amasie*, but after being accepted it was declined. " I suppose," he remarks, manifestly glancing at Corneille, " that the players do not care about galimatias in these days unless it has been written by an author of repute." Molière, as we have seen, gave him more encouragement, and was rewarded by finding in *La Thébaïde* more than one sign of imaginative power, depth of sensibility, and command of language. By this time, still pressed by Port Royalists, Racine had become Prior of Epinay, though certainly without the remotest intention to discharge the duties of the post. His mind was concentrated upon what he felt to be his true vocation— the drama.

The players of the Hôtel de Bourgogne, who for more than a year had produced but few novelties, one of which, by the way, was a tragedy by Mdlle. Desjardins, *Nitétis*, were spurred by the success of *La Thébaïde* to fresh exertions. In the previous summer, as a means of adding to the attractiveness of a *fête* at Fontainebleau, Corneille had made a play out of an intrigue at the Court of Otho. He elaborated the picture with the most patient care, writing the third act again and again, and striking off for it about twice as many lines as he ultimately adopted.   Nor was he without reward.   His audience listened to all with the pro-foundest respect.   The Maréchal de Grammont declared that the author ought to be "le breviaire des rois."   A remark made by Louvois—that the merits of *Othon* could be appreciated only by an audience composed of statesmen—is usually regarded as an unequivocal com-pliment to the genius of the dramatist ; in point of fact, as I think, it was intended to convey in the politest form an unfavourable estimate of the poem as an acting play.   In that case, it must be admitted, the minister's perception was not at fault.   Interesting enough in a political sense, especially as the problem on which it turned was treated with dignity and eloquence, *Othon* had little or nothing in it to attract a mixed audience. Evidently perceiving this, the Troupe Royale showed no haste to put it on the boards, and might have ignored it altogether if the advantage gained by Molière had not induced them to again derive a sort of reflected glory from the name of Corneille.   *Othon* appeared early in November, only to be speedily withdrawn. For this not unexpected disappointment, however, they were indemnified in some measure by a tragedy from Quinault, *Astrate*, in which some heart-struggles are depicted with considerable effect.   Boileau emptied a little vial of satire upon the piece, but it soon found a place in the repertory of the theatre.

Meanwhile a shadow had fallen upon the Théâtre du Palais Royal. Duparc, the diverting Gros-René of the troupe, died early in the new year. The sorrow of his comrades was testified in more than one way. No performance was given on the day of his death, and his share was continued to his wife until the following spring. Molière, as may be supposed, was deeply grieved at the news. Duparc had joined him with other members of the Illustre Théâtre company, had accompanied him in provincial rambles, and had endowed many of his characters with striking indi-viduality and humour. Before long another misfor-tune befell the company in the secession of Brécourt to the Hôtel de Bourgogne, but as his irascibility had not lessened with lapse of time their regret at losing him may not have been so profound as he wished. His position in the Troupe Royale was quickly improved by the death of Beauchâteau, whom he succeeded as the representative in chief of secondary characters in tragedy and comedy. Beauchâteau's career had extended over a period of about forty years, and his reminiscences of theatricals in the days of Richelieu must have been of more than ordinary interest. Molière immortalized him in *L'Impromptu de Versailles*, though not in a way which he could have entirely approved. His widow, *née* Madeleine Bouget, continued to play *amoureuses* and tragic princesses, and it is worthy of note that the elder of two sons she brought him, François Matthieu, signalized himself at the mature age of eight by composing verses in praise of various luminaries at Court.

Beauchâteau's successor left the Palais Royal in time to lose a share in an honour traditionally accorded to his old comrades—namely, that of having suggested to their leader the subject of his next play. Hitherto, except in the land of its birth, the legend of Don Juan had been strangely misrepresented, as the briefest sketch of its history will prove. In the previous century, according to the chronicles of Seville, a well-born, impious, and hardy libertine, Juan Tenorio, ravished the daughter of a Commander, one Gonzalo de Ulloa, and on being sought out by the enraged father immediately ran him through the body. The remains of the unfortunate man were buried in the cloister of the Franciscans, who erected a statue to his memory. Don Juan's rank placed him beyond the reach of the law, but not of vengeance by other means. The friars lured him into their church, stoutly put him to death, and explained his disappearance by stating that the statue, in resentment of an insult which he had the hardihood to put upon it, had descended from its pedestal, opened the earth beneath his feet, and carried him down to hell.

No one doubted the veracity of these excellent men, especially as statues were popularly believed to possess the power of accomplishing even greater miracles. In 1622, after having been illustrated in at least one Mystery, the legend was treated for the stage by a friar of the cloister in which Don Juan Tenorio lost his life—Gabriel Tellez, better known as Tirso de Molina. *El Burlador de Sevilla y Combidado de Piedra,* as he exhaustively called the piece, is precisely such a work as a pious man would write for a pious people. He sought to enforce the lesson that the hour of repentance may be put off too long. In the last scene, representing a chapel, with moonlight streaming through the storied windows, Don Juan, who is described as the slave of his passions rather than an unscrupulous seducer, cries out for a confessor, but is told that it is too late. *El Burlador de Sevilla* was so well received in Spain that in the course of a few years Giliberti brought it on the Italian stage, though not without many essential alterations. He divested it as far as was possible of its religious significance, deepened the shades in the character of Don Juan, and added to the story such diverting incidents as the production by the indispensable valet of the list (it was long enough to reach the middle of the pit) of his master's victims. Established in Paris, Torelli rewrote the piece for the purpose of giving greater prominence to the comic element,

which reached its greatest height in the versions
executed by Villiers and Dorimon. In Torelli's *Festin
de Pierre*, it may be mentioned, Harlequin appears as
the valet, and, equipped in a long cloak and sword,
with a lantern attached to the scabbard, made the
unskilful laugh, even in the scenes with the statue, by
more or less stupid buffoonery. Every *Don Juan* was
now a broad farce with a tragic ending, but a performance given by the Spanish comedians of the *Burlador de
Sevilla* in its integrity must have shown that the story
was susceptible of a more elevated treatment, and
Molière was prevailed upon by his company to take it
in hand.

It was not without some reluctance that he entered
upon his task. His *Don Juan* would have to be a
comedy of the *Tartuffe* species, and it was by no
means easy to arouse anything like serious interest
in what had served as materials for still popular
burlesques. Nevertheless, it may be doubted whether
a more grateful theme could have fallen to his lot.
In making use of the picturesque Spanish legend he
might add a great character to the French drama,
supplement his picture of hypocrisy by one of
cynically avowed unbelief, and soften the prejudices
which existed against him on account of his supposed
want of respect for religion. In the end, casting all
misgivings to the winds, he went to work with an

ardour sufficient to bring his powers as a dramatist
into full play. In the preparation of his groundwork he borrowed freely from *El Burlador de Sevilla*
and its numerous progeny, adding piquant details of
his own invention, and excluding incidents which, like
the unrolling of the list of Don Juan's victims, would
have been out of place in a philosophical drama.
Nearly every scene is irradiated by his distinctive
humour, but the tone of the piece as a whole is
precisely what its nature required. As for the figure
of Don Juan, it stands out in the finest colours,
in the strongest conceivable relief. Molière was too
great a dramatist to content himself with describing
such a man by the mouths of other personages. His
hero, if hero he may be called, reveals himself with
a candour and pointedness which remind us of Iago.
His speeches are invariably in the spirit of his actions.
He leaves us in no doubt as to the principles by which
his conduct is governed. He lays bare the primary
anatomy of his soul. He believes nothing, hopes
nothing, fears nothing. He insolently proclaims his
want of faith in the efficacy of prayer. In a new
scene, meeting a mendicant who passes his life in
prayer, but who is dying of starvation, he tosses him
a *louis d'or* "for the sake of humanity." Moreover, he
is superbly indifferent to all moral considerations. He
is unmoved by the anguish of the too-credulous beings

whose lives he has wrecked. He is perpetually on the
watch for what he terms fresh conquests. " Beauty,"
he tells his valet, here called Sganarelle, " entrances
me wherever I find it. It is in vain that I pledge my
word to one ; the love I have for her will not let me
do injustice to others. How delightful it is to ensnare
by a hundred marks of devotion the heart of a young
beauty—to overcome step by step the resistance she
makes ! But when I have once succeeded there is
nothing further to say or wish ; all the charm of passion
has vanished." Not the least characteristic of the
new scenes in the piece is one in which the libertine
appears with a pretty rustic on either arm, alternately
assuring each, of course in a tone low enough to escape
the ears of the other, that she is the sole mistress
of his heart. Nor has remonstrance the slightest
effect upon him. In reply to a long and eloquent
speech from his father, to the effect that birth is
nothing without virtue, that it is not sufficient for a
nobleman to simply bear the title and arms of one,
he coolly replies, " Sir, if you take a chair you will
speak more at your ease." But the climax of his
iniquity is not yet reached. He finds it expedient—
and the dramatist here aimed a shaft at the hypocrites
who as a matter of self-defence had originated or
swelled the clamour against *Tartuffe*—to assume a
sanctimonious aspect. " For," he says, " the pro-

fession of a hypocrite has marvellous advantages just now. Hypocrisy is a vice in vogue, and all vices in vogue pass for virtues. The imposture is always respected, and even when detected is not to be condemned. Every other human vice is amenable to censure, and may be attacked boldly. Hypocrisy has the privilege of stopping the world's mouth, and enjoys the repose of sovereign impunity. I shall not abandon my pleasures; I simply hide them. I espouse the interests of heaven, and under this convenient pretext shall persecute my enemies, accuse them of impiety, and raise up against them those unthinking zealots who, without knowing anything of the merits of the case, will declaim against them in public, heap injuries upon them, and condemn them to perdition on their own private authority." The significance of this last sentence, to which Sganarelle listens with mingled horror and consternation, is not to be mistaken. Inharmonious as the catastrophe might be with so natural a chain of incidents as that he had woven, Molière could not venture to dispense with it, and the vivid words assigned to the Guest of Stone entitle it to a place by the side of the Weird Sisters in *Macbeth*. No moral is expressly pointed in the piece, but it is sufficiently obvious that in this supernatural figure the hand of divine retribution is intended to be seen. Throughout the play, indeed, Don Juan is never permitted to enlist our sympathies. His courage, his *esprit*, his elegant and chivalrous bearing —these and other natural or acquired graces are attributed to him simply to bring his character within the bounds of humanity, to account for the fascination he exercises over women, and to deepen by force of contrast the moral blackness which they appear to relieve. In this portraiture, the most philosophical yet witnessed on the French stage, the genius of Molière, as I think, found its loftiest and most artistic expression.

Under the title of *Le Festin de Pierre*—a title which, meaningless as it was, had acquired too great a commercial value from long usage to be discarded by the practical Molière—the play so written was presented at the Palais Royal on the 15th February, Lagrange appearing as Don Juan, Molière as Sganarelle, Mdlle. Duparc as Elvire, Béjart as Don Louis, Hubert as Pierrot, Ducroisy as M. Dimanche, and Mdlles. Molière and Debrie as the pretty rustics.

> L'effroyable Festin de Pierre,
> Si fameux par toute la terre,
> Et qui réussissait si bien
> Sur le Théâtre Italien,
> Va commencer l'autre semaine,
> A paraître sur notre scène—

writes Loret, who died shortly afterwards. Before the curtain rose it must have been evident that the piece

would be criticised in a hostile spirit. The audience
included a large sprinkling of the class who execrated
the author as an enemy of religion. In their belief his
object in reintroducing Don Juan on the stage was
to exhibit atheism in an alluring light. And, naturally
enough, they found what they were predisposed to find.
In the self-revealing speeches of Don Juan they saw
only a hardy avowal of the unbelief they ascribed
to the author. In the graces which the profligate has
by right of his birth and education, and which are
necessary to explain the success of his vicious enter-
prises, they saw only an attempt to make him a hero.
In the remonstrances and arguments addressed to him
by Sganarelle they saw only a desire to bring religion
into contempt. In the closing scenes, notwithstanding
the beauty of the part of the Statue, especially where,
Juan having ordered his valet to precede it with a
torch, it says, "No need of light for one whom Heaven
guides,"—in these scenes they saw only an unavoidable
adherence to the lines of the legend. Briefly, the
drift of the play was ingeniously misunderstood, and
what might have been intended as a satire against
infidelity was taken in precisely the opposite sense.
Molière, among other concessions to this stupidity,
omitted the scene with the mendicant, which, it would
seem, had given particular offence; but nothing short
of the suppression of the play altogether would have

satisfied his censors. Indeed, the clamour against him increased with each successive representation. "Is there," the Prince de Conti asked, "a school of atheism more undisguised than *Le Festin de Pierre*, a piece in which the author, while causing a clever infidel to utter the most horrible impieties, confides the cause of God to a valet who justifies his existence by every conceivable impertinence?" A curé of Paris, writing under the *nom de plume* of Rochemont, went a little further. He called upon the tribunals to put Molière to death. In taking this extreme measure, he added, the magistrates would have more than one good precedent. Had not Augustus so dealt with a buffoon who had been wanting in reverence for Jupiter? Had not Theodosius given up to wild beasts some jesters who had turned sacred ceremonies into derision? Even Saint-Evremond could not see the play without desiring that Molière might share the fate of Juan. The hypocrites, writhing under the lash applied to them in the last act, took a prominent part in the agitation, and it was aptly remarked by an anonymous defender of the dramatist that if "the Tartuffes had never been assailed the *Festin de Pierre* would not be criminal." In the result, after fifteen performances, *Don Juan* suddenly disappeared from the bills. Not that it had failed to catch the public fancy, as is usually supposed. During its run the average of the

receipts was unusually high.   In these circumstances
we are forced to conclude that it was set aside
at the instance of the Court—a conclusion which is
strengthened by the fact that the manuscript was not
given to the printers.   But if Louis XIV. again yielded
to the outcry against his favourite player he pointedly
showed that he did not participate in it.   He bestowed
upon the Troupe de Monsieur the higher rank of
Comédiens du Roi, with a pension of 7000 francs.   He
also wished Molière to be titular chief of the company,
but to this the dramatist would not assent.   " Sire,"
he said, " I would prefer to remain the friend of my
comrades."

A riot now occurred at the Palais Royal.   For some
years the privilege of free admission to the theatres
had been enjoyed by the musketeers, body-guards,
and others.   Molière, with the sanction of the king,
put up a notice to the effect that this privilege would
be abolished.   One evening, unaware that his majesty
had authorized the new regulation, the deadheads
angrily presented themselves at the theatre when the
door was opened, made short work of a porter in their
way, and rushed on to the stage with a determination to
make the players suffer for their impudence.   It was
a trying moment for the company ; but Béjart, who was
already dressed for his part, that of a very old man, did
not lose his self-possession.   " Messieurs," he said in the

cracked voice appropriate to his appearance, " at least
spare an old man on the verge of the grave "—a plea
which evoked an involuntary burst of laughter. Molière
profited by this diversion to announce that the obnoxious notice had been authorized by his majesty; and
the malcontents, finding that they had placed themselves in a false position, expeditiously left the house.
Hubert, who had to play that evening, had in the
mean time vanished, no one knew whither. His presence was indispensable; and at that moment, perhaps,
the curtain ought to have been going up. In the end,
after a long search, he was found in a somewhat peculiar position in the garden adjoining the theatre. Unnerved by the fierce aspect of the rioters, he had tried
to escape by means of a hole in the wall, and on getting
half way through found that he could move neither
forwards nor backwards. Yes, there he was, struggling
hard to release himself, and in an agony of terror lest
some of the musketeers, surprising him in this defenceless' state, should deem it an excellent joke to play
upon his defenceless body with their swords. It may
be presumed that a short time elapsed before he heard
the last of his misadventure.

In the bills of the Palais Royal at this time I find a
tragi-comedy by Mdlle. Desjardins, *Le Favori*, which
succeeded well enough to be reproduced at Versailles.
Nevertheless, the gifted authoress did not again write

for the stage. Not long previously, it seems, she had
won the heart of a captain of infantry, by name
Villedieu, who wished to make her his mistress. Impressed in his favour, but rendered wise by experience,
she firmly resisted the proposition. All the prescribed
forms and ceremonies must be observed before they
two could be made happy. Villedieu then confessed
that he was unable to comply with this condition. In
an evil hour he had married the daughter of a notary
in the Rue Montmartre, now living apart from him.
Mdlle. Desjardins, however, did not regard this difficulty as insuperable. Might he not annul the marriage
by declaring that he had been forced to contract it?
Villedieu acted upon this advice, at the same time
announcing to the world that he intended to espouse
the poetess. The notary's daughter presented to Anne
of Austria a petition against the proposed match, but
Mdlle. Desjardins joined Villedieu at Cambrai, the then
head-quarters of his regiment, and in a few days
returned with him to Paris as his wife. Before long,
however, a cloud came over her joy. Villedieu came
to regard her with a feeling of indifference, if not of
positive dislike. It was in vain that she endeavoured
to revive his passion for her—in vain that she gave
plaintive expression to her woe, or seemed like one
distraught, or aroused his jealousy by engaging in doubtful intrigues. War breaking out, he went away on

active service, though only to fall in the first encounter
his regiment had with the enemy. His widow, impressed less by his death than by that of a worldly-
minded woman with whom she had been acquainted,
soon afterwards entered a convent ; but the nuns, doubting whether she was really penitent, sent her about her
business. She then sought and obtained the protection of a sister of Villedieu, Madame de St. Roman,
and became a rather conspicuous figure in Parisian
society. Here she met the old Marquis de la Chatté,
who, although the husband of the daughter of a citizen
in the Rue St. Louis au Marais, secretly led her to
the altar. By some means or other he must have
succeeded in cancelling his first marriage, as a child
with which his second wife presented him was held at
the font by the Dauphin and Mdlle. de Montpensier.
Again left a widow, the Marquise de la Chatté, dis-
interestedly resuming the name of Villedieu, withdrew
to Clinche-more, where she died some time afterwards
from intemperate drinking. In her closing years she
composed a few romances, but with the production
of *Le Favori* her connexion with the stage came to
an end.

The next new play in which the Comédiens du Roi
appeared was one by Molière himself. Down to the
present, it should be understood, the medical faculty
at Paris had seemed to exist for no other purpose

than to impoverish and degrade the power of healing.
Ignoring discoveries of the highest importance in anatomy and physiology, such as that of the circulation of
the blood, the doctors, one and all, took their stand upon
the *Aphorisms* of Hippocrates, or rather upon a narrow
and unintelligent interpretation of that work, and clung
with heroic tenacity to a host of exploded errors.
In this they only kept an oath which the Collége
had required them to take—namely, to shun anything
like an innovation upon the laws laid down by the
Father of Medicine. Each of them followed a particular mode of treatment, whatever the nature of the
ailment might be. They had the courage to employ
drugs without knowing precisely what the effect would
be, and were not above the suspicion of taking bribes
to kill where they were engaged to cure. In their
consultations they invariably expressed themselves in
Latin, and on returning to their mother tongue would
all but bury their meaning under a mass of pedantic
and technical jargon. Arrayed in the quaintest of
costumes—in a high conical hat, an abnormally long
peruke, and a cloak of antique pattern—they made their
way on mules through the tortuous yet picturesque
streets of the old city, nothing doubting that the singu-
larity of their appearance would inspire the vulgar with
awe, but really so many objects of ridicule to the crowd,
of lofty contempt to *les esprits positifs,* and of terror to

those who stood in need of their assistance.   In a squib of the time we are told that

> Affecter un air pédantesque,
> Cracher du grec et du latin,
> Longue perruque, habit grotesque,
> De la fourrure et du satin :
> Tout cela réuni fait presque
> Ce qu'on appelle un médecin.

If anything, the four physicians at Court, MM. Desfougerais, Guénaut, Esprit, and Dacquin, were a little worse than their fellows. Each had one great remedy for all the ills that flesh is heir to. M. Esprit, for example, invariably resorted to emetics; M. Dacquin, a converted Jew, who owed his appointment as Médecin Ordinaire du Roi to the influence of Madame de Montespan, now *maîtresse en titre*, pinned his faith to bleeding. M. Desfougerais had the credit of having killed more patients than any other doctor, but it must be confessed that in this respect he was run very hard by M. Guénaut, who, by a somewhat excessive use of antimony, his universal panacea, had sent to their last account a wife, a daughter, a nephew, two distant relations, and also, as it was currently reported, no less a personage than the powerful Mazarin himself. " Make way there for the doctor," shouted an honest citizen in the street one day, seeing Guénaut's coach impeded by a mob; "'twas he who rid us of the Cardinal." Every rule is said to have its exception, and the medical faculty just now may be said to supply an exception to this rule itself.   In the memoirs and correspondence of the period we find no trace of a doctor who deserves to be remembered save as an example of ignorance, pedantry, and empiricism. More legitimate food for satire could scarcely have been desired; and Molière, as may be supposed, did not allow the opportunity so presented to him to pass by.   In *Le Festin de Pierre* he had already done something to hold up the doctors to ridicule; now, in a comedy-ballet entitled *L'Amour Médecin*, originally contrived to grace a court *fête*, he openly declared war against the profession as distinguished from the art and science which they so sadly misrepresented.

Invented and got ready at only five days' notice, *L'Amour Médecin* was performed at Versailles on the 15th September, and at the Palais Royal on the 22nd. Nothing could be simpler than the story here worked out.   It merely turns on a stratagem employed by an ardent lover in the guise of a doctor to win the heroine from her father.   But this simple story served as a foundation for one of the most exquisite and cutting satires Molière had yet contrived.   A father, Sganarelle (impersonated by the author) calls in four doctors to cure his daughter of a strange melancholia which oppresses her.   Each of these sages—and we may easily imagine the sensation produced among the Versailles audience, and especially among the persons immediately concerned, by the discovery— was made-up to resemble one of the Court physicians, and was introduced under a name designed to render the likeness more perfect. M. Desfougerais figured as " M. Desfonandrès" (man-killer), M. Guénaut as "M. Macroton" (long speaker), M. Dacquin as "M. Tomès" (the carver), and M. Esprit as "M. Bahis" (the barker). The incidents which follow—the happy indifference to the fate of their patient with which the doctors proceed to discuss matters in general instead of her mysterious ailment, the blank refusal of one to believe that a coachman has died in six days from a malady which Hippocrates had said could end in only fourteen or twenty-one, the elaborate ceremony they observe in expressing to Sganarelle an opinion on a point they have not considered, the Babel of sound they produce by speaking all at once, the energy with which M. Tomès and M. Desfonandrès defend the application of a particular remedy, each assuring the bewildered father by turns that Lucinde will infallibly die if the treatment prescribed by the other is adopted,—all this was irresistible. Much of the force of the satire lies in the character of the indis- pensable soubrette, who in her lively Molièrean manner condoles with the doctors on the wrong done to them when a man runs an antagonist through the body

instead of allowing them to prescribe for him, and who
declares that a man should be said to die, not of a
fever, but of four doctors and two apothecaries. "Man's
greatest weakness," says another of the faculty, "is
love of life, which we turn to our own profit by our
pompous galimatias. Let us work in concert in treating
our patients, so that while getting the credit of the
cures we effect we may be able to blame Nature for the
failures of our art." Altogether, the piece gave rise to
a world of merriment, both at Court and in town.
Everybody, Guy Patin tells us, went to the theatre
to "laugh at the Court doctors." The indignation
of the faculty at this "outrage upon science" was
necessarily very great, but they had at least some
comfort in the fact that the dramatist had selected the
most prosperous members of the profession as the chief
objects of his attack.

The Greek names given to the four physicians
were probably decided upon at one of the literary
dinners which Boileau now gave every week at his
house in the Rue du Vieux Colombier. His most
intimate friends, such as Molière, Lafontaine, Racine,
Chapelle, and Peter Mignard, assembled there once a
week to share his genial hospitality, to discuss matters
in which all were interested, to place ideas at each
other's disposal, and generally to spend an afternoon
and evening in a manner both pleasant and edifying.

Bearing in mind what these peruked and ribboned men accomplished, we must describe the party as one of the most brilliant the world had yet seen. The Augustan age of French literature had begun, and in four of the men here brought together the most prominent representatives of that age are to be found. The great Corneille, it is true, was not amongst them, but the work on which his fame may be said to rest— the series of plays beginning with the *Cid* and ending with *Polyeucte*—belonged to the preceding reign. It has been remarked that when literary men are few in number—when the area of competition is narrow— they have more hate than love for each other. In the meetings under Boileau's roof we have at least one grateful instance to the contrary. " Envy and malignity," as one of the guests tells us in the *Amours de Psyché et de Cupidon,* "had no existence in that little band. They reverenced the ancients, did justice to the moderns, spoke of their own achievements in a modest spirit, interchanged sincere advice," and also, it might have been added, enlivened each other by much wit and pleasantry. Even at this distance of time we seem to hear the roar of laughter which greeted the host when he made his appearance amongst his friends for the first time after one memorable incident. Meeting Chapelle in the street, Boileau took occasion to rate him soundly as to his over-devotion to the bottle. The inebriate listened with the utmost attention, seemed to take the homily to heart, and then, remarking that they might as well be seated as stand, led him into a tavern and called for wine. In the warmth of his denunciations of the pernicious habit in question, Boileau frequently emptied his glass, which was as frequently refilled by the cunning rogue—he must certainly have kept his face very well—on the other side of the table. In the result, the advocate of temperance, whom a few potations sufficed to overcome, had to be removed to his house in a coach, and Chapelle went on his way rejoicing. This, no doubt, was only one of many anecdotes related at the dinner parties in the Rue du Vieux Colombier, the fame of which soon spread all over Paris. In years to come it was remarked that the honour of belonging to the Turk's Head Club was not inferior to that of sitting in Parliament for Westminster. No less esteemed in the days of Louis Quatorze was the honour of being admitted to the circle in the Rue du Vieux Colombier.

Nicolas Boileau, now on the threshold of his splendid reputation, exercised so direct an influence upon the literary quality of the French drama that we may take this opportunity of improving our acquaintance with him, the more readily because it was only at such times that his character could be fully understood. In his case, it is clear, the child had not been father to the

man. He was so dull in early life that his family
regarded him as a born fool. In this dulness, it would
appear, M. Boileau père, who officiated as clerk to the
Parlement, saw much cause for satisfaction. " I have
great hopes of Nicolas," he used to say ; " he has no
esprit, and will never speak ill of anybody." Perhaps
the career of an elder son, the graceless Gilles Boileau,
had not been of a nature to justify much faith in wit
and satire as a means of making way in the world.
The hopes centred in Nicolas were not to be realized.
High intelligence came to him as he grew up, together
with a turn for sarcasm which a playless boyhood may
have done something to develope. Nor was he to be
deterred from using the weapon thus placed in his
hands. He made war in verse upon the poetasters and
romance writers of the age. He pitilessly exposed and
ridiculed their puerilities, their inaptitudes, their
prolixity, their abuse of words, their romanesque jargon,
the literary tricks they had borrowed from Spain and
Italy. Excellent in point of workmanship, but still
more remarkable as examples of satirical power, his
broadsides created an immense effect. The Chapelains
and the Scudéris immediately lost their hold of the
public at large, and a new and invigorating atmosphere
stole over almost every walk of literature. In possession of an independent income, the triumphant critic,
although urged by his friends to devote himself to

theology or law, became a man of letters by profession. He felt that " son astre en naissant l'avait formé poëte." In saying this, it must be confessed, he overrated his gifts. He was not so much a poet as a writer of verse which is not poetry. He had no warmth of imagination, no acute sensibility, no enthusiasm for nature. He was even dead to the pantheism of universal life revealed in the mythology of Greece. His poetry, if by courtesy we may call it poetry, is that of severe reason and good sense, with truth as its paramount object. In the end, shrewdly perceiving the limits of his muse, he aspired to become only the literary Mentor of his contemporaries, a position which he attained in right of his fine taste, wide reading, and a singularly nervous and polished style. To his victims he showed no mercy, but it is obvious that in dealing with them according to their deserts he had some difficulty in steeling himself to the task. He was certainly no stranger to humane and generous feelings, as his guests in the Rue du Vieux Colombier must have frequently perceived.

The most considerable of these guests, it need hardly be said, was the man who had achieved unbounded popularity as a dramatist, who assailed the vices and follies of his time with equal courage and force, who was unrivalled in the representation of characters of a broadly humorous type, and who had come to be

regarded by the king as something more than a servant.
For Molière, it is clear, Boileau cherished something
like an affectionate veneration. He seems to have lost
no opportunity of doing him honour in both writing
and conversation. In truth, Molière's verse and prose
all but came up to Boileau's standard of literary excellence, and it is easy to understand that a keen sympathy
should have subsisted between the author of the *Satires*
and the author of *Les Précieuses Ridicules* and *Don
Juan.* If hilarity had been the chief object of the
reunions under the shadow of Saint Sulpice, Molière
would have been poor company. He could never
entirely shake off the depression caused by his wife's
misconduct. He often fell into a wordless reverie. He
would rather listen than speak. He was ever on the
watch for an amusing or instructive trait of character.
Boileau used to call him " the contemplator." By
this time, indeed, the habits of observation which he
acquired in early life had become a second nature. On
one occasion, it is said, "without uttering a single word,
he watched three or four persons of quality who were
bargaining over some lace ; he appeared attentive to
what they were saying, and it seemed by the movement
of his eyes as though he were looking into the very
depths of their souls for their unspoken thoughts."
Boon companion he was not; but it may readily be
believed that when he did plunge into conversation—

and a little good-tempered raillery probably sufficed to draw him out—he was again a wit, a scholar, a polished man of the world.   In felicity of expression, perhaps, he was equalled by none of those around him. One evening, as he entered his coach, a mendicant to whom he had given a louis under the impression that it was a silver coin apprised him of the mistake.   "Keep the money, my friend, for thine honesty," he replied; " ma foi, où la vertu va-t-elle se nicher ! "

Lafontaine was nothing less than an enigma to his friends.   His perpetual smile, his sleepy look, his child-like simplicity, his absent-mindedness, his indolence, his indifference to fame and fortune, his inability at times to remember what a few minutes previously had occupied his thoughts,—all this was not easily to be reconciled with the intellectual vivacity he not unfrequently displayed.   If, we are told, a controversy arose at table upon a point which interested him, he flung himself into the thickest of the fray with the power to hold his own, an expression of keen intelligence temporarily lighting up his finely-cut features.   In his too-licentious *Contes*, recently finished, and especially in the immortal *Fables*, now in preparation, he rose equal to himself for the first and last time.   We look in vain among these compositions, all thrown off *currente calamo*, for one which is not impregnated to a large extent with the most graceful fancy, the most delicate humour, the most tender appreciation of the beauties of inanimate nature. In the last of these qualities he presented a marked contrast to other poets of his time, who sought their inspiration in the region of morals. The child of his age, he yet brought to bear upon his work an active sympathy with three widely differing periods of the world's history, classical antiquity, mediævalism, and the Renascence. Even when these rare gifts became fully manifest, however, his very existence was ignored by the Court, for the simple reason that in an *Elégie aux Nymphes de Vaux* he had had the courage to deplore the fall of his earliest patron, Fouquet. The licentiousness of his *Contes* was matched by that of his private conduct, but his geniality and benevolence caused all those who enjoyed his friendship to regard him with something like affection. He came to be spoken of on all hands as the " *bonhomme* "—a title which Molière conferred upon him in referring to a little pleasantry indulged in on one occasion by Boileau and others on the score of his mysterious abstractions.

Racine, we may be sure, was not the least attentive listener of the group, however much he may have been led by a turn for sarcasm to deride the follies of others, or by a morbid vanity to demonstrate his scholarship, his wealth of ideas, and his knowledge of the world. Unlike Molière, he had much to learn in the way of verse-making, and his education on this point must have been materially advanced by the discourse of his companions in the Rue du Vieux Colombier. Even here we find an illustration of a grave defect in his character. Boileau had a copy of Chapelain's *Pucelle* kept open on the table, and if any of those present chanced to violate a law of French grammar they were condemned to read aloud, for the amusement of the others, a page or less of this sadly unpoetical poem. Indebted to Chapelain for the first recognition of his talents, if not for the pension he was now living upon, Racine yet took part in this singular pleasantry, although he must have known that by the laughter it excited out of doors it tended to embitter the declining years of his benefactor. The task which should have been his was undertaken by one whose acquaintance with the derided poet was of the slightest. "Are you well advised," said Molière to Boileau, " in displaying so much asperity towards Chapelain? He is a man of influence in the world, and is greatly esteemed by Colbert. By condemning the *Pucelle* you may get yourself into bad odour with the Minister, perhaps with the King himself." " The King and M. Colbert," was the somewhat tart reply, " will do as they please ; but unless his majesty expressly commands me to pronounce Chapelain's verses worthy of respect I shall always maintain that the man who has written *La Pucelle* ought to be hanged." Molière, as we shall soon see, did not fail to make dramatic capital of this sally, which appears to have elicited no word of deprecation from Racine.

The manager of the Théâtre du Palais Royal had still greater reason than Chapelain to complain of ingratitude on the part of his *protégé*. Racine had just sent to him another tragedy, *Alexandre le Grand*. Opinion was much divided as to its merits. St. Evremond waxed eloquent in its praise. "No longer," he said, "does the decadence of Corneille fill me with alarm as to the immediate future of tragedy." On the other hand, Corneille himself, to whom the manuscript was submitted, thought that M. Racine did not unite with his rare gifts as a poet a turn for the drama. In this he was deceived; but it is also true that if Racine had written nothing after *Alexandre* we should be constrained to adopt the same opinion. Notwithstanding the vigour with which the conqueror is occasionally brought before us, the general effect of the play is inferior to that of *La Thébaïde*, and the prominence given to the character of Porus argues an imperfect sense of dramatic proportion. Moreover, the author was still under the influence of the author of *Cinna*, though in some of the scenes we meet with gleams of tenderness all but new to the stage. In the middle of December, however, *Alexandre*, with a few alterations suggested by Boileau, was played at the Palais Royal, the hero being impersonated by Lagrange,

Axiane by Mdlle. Duparc, Porus by Lathorillière, and Cléophile by Mdlle. Molière. The last-named, we are told, was "ablaze with the precious stones in which India abounds." Contrary to an oft-repeated statement, the piece met with good success. Molière had had some superb scenery painted for it, and the acting was meritorious enough to elicit special praise from Robinet. Nevertheless, Racine was not satisfied with what had been done for him. He made no secret of his belief that the tragedy had not created the effect of which it was susceptible. The sycophants who hover about a rising man soon found a means of consoling him. Had *Alexandre* been played by the Troupe Royale, always superior to the Comédiens du Roi in tragedy, the result, they maintained, would have been very different. Racine eagerly caught at the suggestion wrapped up in this remark. He secretly sent a copy of the play to Floridor, at the same time extracting a promise from Mdlle. Duparc, in whose talents he had a lively faith, that she would transfer her services from her old manager to his rivals. Hastily but efficiently rehearsed, *Alexandre* was brought out at the Hôtel de Bourgogne on the occasion of its sixth performance at the Palais Royal, and the novel incident of a play being represented in two theatres at the same time naturally gave rise to some excitement in Paris. It need hardly be said that the unavoidable comparison between the two troupes was to the disadvantage of Molière's, as the cast included Floridor (Alexandre), Montfleuri (Porus), and Mdlle. Desœillets (Axiane). Molière may well have felt profoundly hurt by what had occurred. He had behaved with the greatest kindness to Racine, receiving him constantly as a guest, lending him much-needed money, keeping *La Thébaïde* in the bills at a loss to himself rather than allow it to be supposed that the piece had not had a fairly long run, and producing *Alexandre* with a splendour which the chances of its success certainly did not justify. In return for these and other favours the young poet had publicly affronted the troupe, had exposed it to damaging comparisons, and had robbed it of an actress whose place could not easily be supplied. It was in no half-hearted manner that Molière resented the black ingratitude with which he had been treated. He never spoke to Racine again.

Alexandre was not the only play which gave rise to opposition between the two theatres this year. The Troupe Royale appeared in a new comedy by Quinault, *La Mère Coquette, ou les Amants Brouillés.* Raimond Poisson played the best character, a marquis, and acquitted himself so well that the Duc de Créqui presented him with a superb coat. Curiously enough, a piece bearing the same titles, and somewhat similar in plot, appeared a few days later at the Palais Royal, the author being Devisé. In all probability the writer of

Nouvelles Nouvelles had deemed it politic to be on good terms with so prosperous and influential a manager as Molière, who, having too keen a sense of self-respect to betray any annoyance at the attacks made upon him in that delectable work, did not repel his advances. No sooner had the second *Mère Coquette* come out than Paris was enlivened by a sharp controversy between the two dramatists. Each accused the other of deliberate and wholesale plagiarism. Devisé declared that he had communicated the idea of the piece to Quinault at a social gathering; his antagonist averred that the story had been derived from a Spanish source. The resemblance between the comedies is not so marked as to exclude the idea that the authors worked independently of each other, but if either of the statements they made be true we may assume that the culprit was Quinault, inasmuch as he neither denied Devisé's statement nor named the Spanish play referred to, and as on more than one occasion his sense of the difference between *meum* and *tuum* in dramatic matters had not been conspicuously keen. In whatever way he may have come by his materials, they were certainly treated with excellent effect. His *Mère Coquette*, unlike Devisé's, became a popular play.

Molière had now finished another great comedy, but the death of Anne of Austria, in whom he had found an excellent friend, induced him to shelve it for a longer

period than even etiquette required.   Meanwhile, however, the players of the Hôtel de Bourgogne ventured
to try the effect of two novelties—*Agésilas*, by Pierre
Corneille, and *Antiochus*, a tragi-comedy, by his brother.
Yet another proof of the continuous decadence of the
author of the *Cid* was found in the former of these
pieces.   Even Fontenelle has but little to urge in its
favour.   "It must be admitted," he says, "that *Agésilas*
is by M. Corneille, seeing that his name is on the title-
page, and that a scene in it between the hero and
Lysandre could not easily have been written by any
other hand."   But, unfortunately for Corneille, now a
sexagenarian, one fine scene will no more make an
acting play than one swallow a summer, as the prompt
withdrawal of the tragedy from the boards proved.
Fontenelle hints that the failure was accelerated by the
derision of a sect who had been led by a too ardent
admiration for Racine to decry Corneille.   In this, I
think, he was entirely mistaken, as Racine had not as
yet produced anything which could justify his being
regarded either as a rival to the older dramatist or the
founder of a new school of dramatic art.   Fontenelle's
supposition was probably based upon the fact that an
epigram of the day—

> J'ai vu l'Agésilas,
> Hélas !

emanated from Boileau, who continued to evince a warm

interest in the fortunes of the young dramatist without seeking for a moment to palliate his conduct towards Molière, and who, as became a critic, spoke of Corneille's writings as he found them.

Molière's new comedy, *Le Misanthrope*, a striking picture of contemporary Parisian life, but pregnant with universal truth, was at length produced (June 4). For many reasons it must have taken the audience by surprise. The misanthrope, Alceste, impersonated by the author himself, was a character wholly new to the stage, and, unlike the central figures in other plays from the same pen, is intended to enjoy at least our respect, and even a certain measure of sympathy. He is no vulgar hater of mankind, no churlish or brutal cynic. High and noble in nature, he is alienated from the world by its want of heart, its insincerities, its more or less veiled falsehood, its hypocrisies of complaisance, its thousand petty foibles. He regards it as nothing less than a crime that men should exchange civilities simply as a matter of form, should breathe a syllable against those whom they call their friends, or should gloss over their opinion of execrable verses when the author asks for it. His practice is at least equal to his theory ; and at the end of the second act, when he is taken off to the Maréchaux to account for his denunciation of the last sonnet by Oronte (Ducroisy) he uses

the words with which Boileau had replied to the question
as to Chapelain—

Hors qu'un commandement exprès du roi me vienne
De trouver bons les vers dont on se met en peine,
Je soutiendrai toujours, morbleu ! qu'ils sont mauvais,
Et qu'un homme est pendable après les avoir faits.

His contempt for the harmless hypocrisies of every-day
life, however, does not prevent him from becoming
the slave of a woman in whom they are fully represented, the sprightly, accomplished, heartless coquette
Célimène (Mdlle. Molière).   He is conscious of his folly
even as he gives way to it the most, and it is upon the
conflict in his case between head and heart, terminating
in the predominance of the former, that the interest
of the play chiefly depends.   " The skill with which
Célimène alternately plays with his patience, evades his
reproaches, preserves her own independence while
lessening his, elicits fresh proofs of his affection while
only affording such glimpses of her own as shall serve to
keep him from breaking his chains, and eventually
making him more angrily in love than ever, is altogether," as one writer well remarks, "a triumph of
delineation such as has rarely, if ever, been equalled."
The figure of Alceste gains much by contrast with that
of Philinte (Lathorillière), the perfection of *savoir vivre*.
He genially yields to the habits and customs of society,
not because he wholly approves them, but on the

principle that it is wise to make the best of circumstances, to take the world very much as one finds it.
In this character, it seems to me, the moral of the play
may be discerned. Molière enforces the necessity of
social toleration, though in doing so he casts no ridicule
upon Alceste, whose misanthropy is simply the out-
come of virtue in excess. Some of the other *dramatis
personae* call for at least passing mention—the gentle
Eliante (Mdlle. Debrie), the poetaster Oronte (Ducroisy),
Acaste (Lagrange), and the prude Arsinoë (Mdlle.
Duparc). From a strictly dramatic point of view *Le
Misanthrope* is not without defects, but it occupies a
place by the side of *Don Juan* and *Tartuffe* in right of
its beauty of style, its felicitous delineations, and
its refined pungency as a satire against more than one
fashionable false pretence. Its purely literary merit was
so high that Boileau hailed it as his friend's masterpiece ;
but Molière was not of the same opinion. "Vous verrez
bien autre chose," he replied.

The fate of the *Misanthrope* at the Palais Royal has
been a subject of much needless controversy. That
it was coldly received at the outset there can be no
reasonable doubt. "Molière's piece has failed," somebody said to Racine on the following day ; "nothing
I have seen is tamer. You may take my word for
it, as I was there." "In that case," replied Racine,
probably glad to have an opportunity of saying a

word in favour of a man to whom he had behaved so badly, "you have the advantage of me ; nevertheless, I cánnot believe that Molière can have written a poor piece. See it again." In truth, the significance and beauty of the *Misanthrope* were not sufficiently appreciated at the first representation to atone for the comparative weakness of the plot, and the audience were put into an ill-humour by the fact that the thoughts and diction of Oronte's sonnet, which they had thoughtlessly applauded, were shown in the sequel to be

> De ces colifichets dont le bon sens murmure.

In a short time, however, the play met with the success it deserved, both at Court and in Paris. In his short-lived *Muse Dauphine*, a rhymed gazette in the style of that of Robinet, Subligny, an Advocate to the Parlement, writes—

> Une chose de fort grand cours
> Et de beauté très-singulière
> Est une pièce de Molière.
> Toute la cour en dit du bien ;
> Après son *Misanthrope* il ne faut plus voir vien :
> C'est un chef d'œuvre inimitable.

The interest taken in the play on its own account appears to have been augmented by a rumour that most of the characters were drawn from life. The Duc de Montausier, who affected misanthropy, was held to be the original of Alceste ; and it is not unlikely

that the quidnuncs of Paris, anticipating the com-
mentators, recognized in Oronte the Duc de Saint-
Aignan, an incorrigible poetaster, and in Célimène the
once coquettish but now austerely pious Duchesse de
Longueville, who for divers reasons had provoked and
been a concealed spectator of a duel in the Place
Royale between her lover and the affianced husband
of Madame de Montbazon.   Saint-Simon, writing many
years afterwards, says that the Duc de Montausier,
indignant at being identified with a stage-figure, went
to the theatre to chastise the author, but after seeing
the piece invited him to his box, embraced him again
and again, and overwhelmed him with thanks. "If,"
he said, "you have taken me for the model of your
Alceste, the most perfect of men, you have done me
an honour I shall never forget."   I more than suspect
that the whole story is apocryphal, as the rebuke
administered by the King to the Duc de la Feuillade
was not calculated to encourage another attack upon
the dramatist.   But to return to the fortunes of the
Misanthrope. Instead of being a dire failure, as Grimarest asserts, and as scores of unsuccessful dramatic
authors have found it convenient to maintain, it was
played to good houses for the then considerable number
of twenty-one nights—a fact which has given rise to
the impression, hardly less erroneous, that the comedy
was a triumph from the first performance inclusive.

The quidnuncs were not exactly correct in their conjectures as to the origin of the chief characters in the *Misanthrope*, for the sufficient reason that the originals are to be found in the players who represented them on the stage. Indeed, I am tempted to describe the work as a pathetic autobiography in the third person, of course under assumed names. Molière himself was no misanthrope, but in what the life and beauty of the character of Alceste mainly consist—the struggle of a high-minded man against a passion for one on whom it is thrown away—we have a clear and vivid reproduction in verse of the touching narrative to Chapelle in the garden at Auteuil. Many passages in point might be quoted : here is one. " The love I bear for her," says Alceste,

> Ne ferme point mes yeux aux défauts qu'on lui trouve ;
> Et je suis, quelque ardeur qu'elle m'ait pu donner,
> Le premier à les voir, comme à les condamner.
> Mais avec tout cela, quoi que je puisse faire,
> Je confesse mon foible ; ella a l'art de me plaire :
> J'ai beau voir ses défauts, et j'ai beau l'en blâmer,
> En dépit qu'on en ait, elle se fait aimer ;
> Sa grace est la plus forte ; et sans doute ma flamme
> De ces vices du temps pourra purger son âme.

In Célimène, too, we have the bewitching Armande herself, though in one or two respects the portrait must have been consciously softened. In the meeting of the husband and wife on the stage in a position so akin to their own as that of Alceste and Célimène

the play ceased to belong to the domain of fiction.
However little the audience may have suspected it, each
scene between them was a terrible reality, especially
when the lover says—

> je fais tout mon possible
> A rompre de ce cœur l'attachement terrible ;
> Mais mes plus grands efforts n'ont rien fait jusqu'ici,
> Et c'est pour mes péchés que je vous aime ainsi.

Molière, indeed, could never have played *Alceste* without
keen anguish—so keen, in fact, that we ask ourselves
in wonder what fascination had led him to lay such
a burden upon himself. Then, as though to complete
the identity of the picture, Eliante was no other than
her representative, Mdlle. Debrie. "For myself,"
Philinte says to Alceste,—

> si je n'avais qu' à former des désirs
> Sa cousine Eliante aurait tous mes soupirs ;
> Son cœur, qui vous estime, est solide et sincère,
> Et ce choix plus conforme était mieux votre affaire.

The infatuated lover replies,—

> Il est vrai ; ma raison me le dit chaque jour ;
> Mais la raison n'est pas ce qui règle l'amour.

Here we find a divergence between the real and
the unreal. Eliante was lost to Alceste, but Mdlle.
Debrie was not to be lost to Molière. Her graces of
character began to regain their power over his mind
now that his wife had dishonoured him, and in the

end the voice of "reason" did not appeal to him in vain. Before the summer passed away the house at Auteuil had a mistress,—and her name was not Armande.

The *Misanthrope* did not need the aid of a good afterpiece, but on the 6th of August, when the great comedy was played for the twelfth time, *Le Médecin Malgré Lui* was added to the bill. In this piece, which is erroneously supposed to have gained a hearing for its predecessor, Molière utilized the popular fabliau of *Le Vilain Mire*, together with some fragments of his *Fagotier* and *Médecin Volant*, and again provoked a general laugh at the expense of the medical fraternity. Martine, the wife of an intelligent woodcutter, Sganarelle (Molière), meets two men in search of a doctor for Lucinde, who, in order to get rid of a lover favoured by her father, the stupid Géronte, but not by herself, has feigned dumbness. In revenge for a little corporal chastisement to which she has been subjected by her husband, Martine at once recommends him to their notice. He is, she says, a skilful doctor, but will not reveal the nature of his calling unless cudgelled into doing so. Her hint is acted upon; and Sganarelle, informed of the reason of the assault made upon him, avows himself what they suppose him to be. He is then carried off in triumph to Géronte's house. It must be admitted that he plays his part very well.

He takes kindly to the conical hat and long gown peculiar to the faculty. He amasses a large variety of medical phrases. He adorns his discourse with a sufficient quantity of incoherent Latin to impress those about him with a conviction that he is a very clever man. Nay, it is a question with him whether he shall not remain a doctor all his life. "It is the best trade out," he tells us; "payment comes whether we kill or cure. No responsibility rests upon us; we may hack about as we please the stuff given us to work upon. If a patient dies it is his own fault, never ours. Lastly, dead men, of all people the most discreet, tell no tales of the doctor who has sent them to their long account." His self-possession, too, seldom deserts him. Géronte having gently reminded him that, contrary to what he had said, the heart was on the left and the liver on the right side of the body, "yes," is the reply, "that was so formerly; but nous avons changé tout cela" (this was how the phrase originated), "and we now adopt an entirely new method."

Both the populace and the Court were hugely diverted by the new pleasantry discharged at the faculty. It became the rage of the hour, a subject of general conversation. Molière appears to have been a little surprised at its success. He could see in it nothing but a "farce sans conséquence." For this

undue modesty he was good-temperedly taken to task
in the *Muse Dauphine* :—

> Molière, dit-on, ne l'appelle
> Qu'une petite bagatelle ;
> Mais cette bagatelle est d'un esprit si fin,
> Que, s'il faut que je vous le die,
> L'estime qu'on en fait est une maladie
> Qui fait que, dans Paris, tout court au *Médecin.*

Boileau, too, deprecated the self-disparagement of the
dramatist. "In all Molière's farces," he said, "there
are excellences which the finest comedies by other men
do not exhibit." *Le Médecin Malgré Lui* justified this
eulogium by profound humour, telling sarcasm, and
last, but not least, a singularly rapid, nervous, and
airy dialogue. In one respect, perhaps, it was weaker
than *L'Amour Médecin.* It brought no well-known
doctor before the audience *in propria persona.* If
Sganarelle resembled anybody at all it was the gigantic
perruquier of the Cour de Saint Chapelle, Didier
l'Amour, who thrashed a sharp-tongued wife without
effect, and to whom Boileau refers in the second chant
of *Le Lutrin.* Indignant at Molière's continued disrespect for science, the faculty again lodged a complaint
against him at Court, but to as little purpose as
before. "The doctors," said Louis, "bring so many
tears to our eyes that they may well enable us now
and then to laugh."

In connexion with *Le Médecin Malgré Lui* a curious

anecdote has been related. Molière, it may be remembered, causes Sganarelle to sing :—

> Qu'ils sont doux,
> Bouteille jolie,
> Qu'ils sont doux
> Vos petits glougloux !
> Mais mon sort ferait bien des jaloux,
> Si vous étiez toujours remplie.
> Ah ! bouteille, ma mie,
> Pourquoi vous videz-vous ?

Meeting Molière at the Duc de Montausier's one evening, Roze, secretary to the King, accused him of having
appropriated a Latin epigram imitated from the Antho-
logy. Molière warmly maintained its originality, and
challenged Roze to produce the epigram he spoke of.
" Here," said the secretary, " is a copy of it : "—

> Quam dulcis,
> Amphora amoena,
> Quam dulcis
> Sunt tuae voces !
> Dum fundis merum in calices,
> Utinam semper esses plena !
> Ah ! cara mea lagena
> Vacua cur jaces ?

Molière stood confounded ; but after the lapse of a few
minutes Roze confessed that the lines were simply a
translation by himself of Sganarelle's song into Latin.
His majesty's secretary, it is clear, was an adept at
writing doggerel in that tongue.

Early in December, before the laughter evoked by
the *Médecin Malgré Lui* had died away, the dramatic

troupes of Paris, foreign as well as native, assembled
at St. Germain's to take part in a *fête* in that historic
château, where the Court was then staying. Each of
the entertainments they gave was made a portion of
one long ballet, arranged for the purpose by the ever
active Benserade. The Muses, charmed by the encouragement extended by the King to the arts and
sciences throughout his realms, came one after another
to St. Germain's, and each entry was followed by a
play, a dance, or a piece of music. On the appearance of Thalia there was represented a *pastorale-comique*
by Molière, who in this branch of composition, it was
officially stated, "peut le plus justement se comparer
aux anciens." Only a few fragments of this piece
have been preserved, but we find that it was inter-
spersed with music and dances, and that Molière himself,
aided by Mdlle. Debrie and Lagrange, was one of the
players. Next came a *pastorale-héroïque* by the same
hand, *Myrtil et Mélicerte*. Molière had not been able
to finish more than two of the three acts in which
the story was to have been treated, but an incomplete
piece from his pen was more acceptable than a complete
piece from any other, and the incidents, derived as they
had been from an episode in Madeleine de Scudéri's
Cyrus, were so well known that the audience had
merely to appeal to their memory for the sequel. In
all probability, however, the absence of the third act

occasioned more than a passing regret, for Molière, though unable to do justice to themes of this kind, had imparted no inconsiderable tenderness and grace to the speeches of the lovers, and the representative of Myrtil, one Michel Baron, not yet fourteen years of age, but lately made a Comédien du Roi, was charming to both the eye and the ear. Most of his comrades found employment in the piece, Molière himself appearing as Lycarsis. The crown of the *fête* was a masquerade, in which the King and Queen, with a large section of their suite, including Madame de Montespan and the retiring Louise de la Valliere, and accompanied by some of the players brought from Madrid six years previously, danced in picturesque Spanish costume to Spanish music. Seldom had so brilliant a scene been witnessed at the Court of Louis XIV.

The youthful player who appeared in *Myrtil* and *Mélicerte* calls for more than passing mention. Not long previously, it appears, an organist of Troyes, Jean Raisin, came to Paris with four children, and, establishing himself in the Foire St. Germain, announced that on a particular day he would exhibit what might be justly regarded as the eighth wonder of the world. It was only a spinnet of three keys, but the marvellous thing about it was that after two of the keys had been played upon the third repeated the music without

being touched. Nothing like this had yet been seen
or heard of; and some of the spectators, satisfied that
the Devil was no stranger to the business, beat a
precipitate retreat. Before long everybody was talking
of the wonderful spinnet, the consequence being that
Raisin received orders to exhibit it at Court. The
performance over, the King requested him to explain
the mystery. He accordingly opened the instrument
when a pretty boy of five, dressed and equipped as
Cupid, sprang lightly out, assumed a studied attitude,
and drew his bow with infinite grace. Their majesties
successively took the little fellow on their knees, and
Raisin, in recompense for the exposure of at best a
poor deception, received permission to form a troupe
of juvenile players under the title of "Comédiens du
Monsieur le Dauphin." Michel Baron, the only son
of the two players of that name at the Hôtel de
Bourgogne, was one of the first children engaged for
this purpose. Born in 1653, he became an orphan in
his tenth year, and until fate brought him into contact
with Raisin was supported by friends of the family.
The organist dying, Madame Raisin took her little
company into the country, where, falling into the
clutches of a needy adventurer, she lost all the
money which her husband had made by his spinnet.
Molière good-naturedly placed his theatre at her disposal for three days, and, chancing to look in during

one of the performances she gave, was so pleased with
Baron's acting that he literally purchased him from
her there and then. The boy must have found it
difficult to realize his good fortune. Molière gave him
a home, educated him for the stage, introduced him
to Boileau and other friends, and generally treated
him as a son. Handsome, symmetrical in figure,
graceful of bearing, and endowed from childhood with
the power of expressing various passions, he never
failed to increase the interest of the performances in
which he had a share. Robinet, in his chronicle of the
22nd February 1666, says :

> Le fils de la Baronne,
> Actrice si belle et si bonne,
> Dont la Parque a fait son butin,
> A, comme elle, le beau destin
> De charmer chacun sur le scène,
> Quoiqu'il n'ait que douze ans à peine ;
> Et certe il sera quelque jour
> Fort propre aux rôles de l'Amour.

His performance of Myrtil went far to justify this
friendly prediction.

No sooner had the *féte* at St. Germain's concluded
than the King gave orders that it should be repeated
in the following month. But Molière ventured to make
one important alteration in the programme. Dissatisfied with *Myrtil et Mélicerte*, he put in its place
a comedy-ballet in one act, *Le Sicilien, ou l'Amour
Peintre*. The story of the piece is half told in the

title. Enamoured of Isidore, a Greek slave (Mdlle. Debrie), who is about to marry her master, Don Pedre, a Sicilian gentleman (Molière), Adraste, a young Frenchman (Lagrange) obtains access to her in the guise of a portrait-painter,—much to the discomfiture in the end of her elderly admirer, aggravated by the fact that by an ingenious arrangement he has been made to bring it in a great measure upon himself. If Molière relied upon the excellent appearance and talents of Baron to give effect to the part of Adraste he was to be grievously disappointed. Hating her husband's friends as much as she seemed to like his enemies, Armande naturally conceived an antipathy to Baron, and on one occasion went so far as to slap his face in the presence of the whole company. High-spirited and impulsive, the boy resolved to forego all the advantages of his association with Molière rather than run the risk of being again subjected to such an indignity. He abruptly left Paris, to be heard of soon afterwards as one of a band of strolling players. Accordingly, early in January, when the *fête* at St. Germain's was given, with *Le Sicilien*, to which Lulli had set music, as the chief dramatic feature in the arrangements, the Court missed the well-favoured young actor who had charmed it as Myrtil, and to whose reappearance, we may presume, more than one lady was looking forward with some

interest.   Molière's little play was delightfully brisk
and pointed, and additional importance was conferred
upon it by the fact that in the concluding ballet,
danced in Moorish costume, the King and Queen
themselves appeared.

Soon after Molière returned to Paris, the great
Corneille, estranged for some unknown reason from
the Hôtel de Bourgogne, brought him an *Attila*, which
he bought for 2000 livres, and which appeared at
the Palais Royal at the end of February.   However
weak the tragedy may be in other respects, the
portraiture of the King of the Huns is not without
breadth and force, and Lathorillière appears to have
impersonated the character with considerable spirit.
In the result, *Attila* met with "rather good success"—
nay, was elevated to the dignity of ə stock play.
Boileau could not have overlooked its merits, but he
was unable to resist the temptation to supplement the
epigram already quoted—

> J'ai vu Agésilas,
> Hélas !

by another sarcastic couplet

> Mais après Attila,
> Holà !

These decidedly unflattering lines, which elicited
high praise from Chapelain until he came to know
who wrote them, were pleasantly turned by Corneille

to his own advantage. " Do you not see," he said,
with well-affected seriousness, " that M. Despréaux "
(this name, derived from a meadow situated at the end
of the garden attached to old M. Boileau's house at
Croises, had been given to the satirist in early life
to distinguish him from his brothers) " wishes it to
be understood that *Agésilas* has attained the chief
aim of tragedy, since it excites pity, and that *Attila*
is the *non plus ultra* of tragic art ? " Molière himself,
as became a manager, was not blind to the inequalities
in the verse of the new tragedy. " Corneille," he
said, " has a familiar who from time to time puts
noble lines into his head, but immediately afterwards
leaves him to get on by himself ; he then fares very
badly, and the aforesaid familiar waxes merry."

Hitherto the two dramatists had met only by
chance ; they now became close friends. With the
admiration he felt for the man who had created French
tragedy and comedy, and who, brusque as he might
seem, was not less generous than high-minded, Molière
blended a feeling of deep personal gratitude. " When
Le Menteur came out," he said on one occasion to
Boileau, " I was longing to write a play, but did not
know how. My ideas were confused. Corneille's
comedy served to fix them. The dialogue taught
me how educated people talked. In Dorante I saw the
necessity of character, the true nature of refined

pleasantry, and the value of a moral in comedy. Had *Le Menteur* never been written, in fact, I might have produced some pieces of intrigue, such as *L'Etourdi* and *Le Dépit Amoureux*, but not, I fear, *Le Misanthrope*." Boileau, as may be supposed, was deeply moved by this unexpected avowal. "Embrace me," he exclaimed ; "what you have just said does you more honour than the finest of your plays." Molière, I think, overrated his obligations to *Le Menteur ;* he left it at an immeasurable distance, and the lessons it taught him must soon have come to him by intuition. But the spirit which prompted his avowal to Boileau derives higher lustre from this fact : it was as though the author of *Macbeth* and *Lear* had declared that but for Peele and Marlowe he would not have been possible. In tragedy, of course, the comparison between the illustrious Frenchmen now brought together told the other way. Molière could no more have equalled the splendid inspirations of the Corneille of old, especially in such passages as the "Qu'il mourût" and the "Je crois," than Corneille could have imparted to a comedy the rich humour of *L'Amour Médecin*, the satirical trenchancy of *Les Précieuses Ridicules*, the refinement of *Le Misanthrope*, or the insight into character revealed in *Don Juan*. Each, however, could appreciate the other ; and a warm friendship, cemented by the high-mindedness they had

in common, quickly sprang up between them. The
gaunt figure of the author of the *Cid*, now bending
under the light weight of sixty years, was often to be
seen at the door of Molière's house in Paris, although
a sense of his awkwardness in company, joined to a
mistaken dread of Boileau, induced him to hold aloof
from all the pleasant parties at Auteuil.

At one of these parties, it must be confessed, he
would have been quite out of his element. Boileau,
Chapelle, Lulli, De Jonsac, and Nantouillet arrived at
Auteuil one evening, all in a convivial mood. Molière,
being too ill to join them, requested Chapelle to do the
honours of the house. The "French Anacreon" bore
much practical testimony to the excellence of the wines
on the table ; his companions, the wise Boileau not
excepted, were easily led to follow his example, and
before midnight came the whole of the party were
drunk. Instead, however, of going to bed they engaged
in a discussion of a somewhat gloomy nature. They
began to deplore the evils of life, to contemplate the
pomps and vanities of the world in a fine philosophical
spirit. Had not a writer of antiquity declared that the
greatest happiness was not to be born, the next to die
promptly ? "Messieurs," said Chapelle, after an interval of deep silence, "are we not cowards ? It is
a noble maxim that we have just quoted ; let us act
upon it. The river is hard by ; let us drown ourselves.

It is stupid to murmur when we can escape from what we murmur against." The motion having been carried unanimously, the drunkards rose from their seats, embraced each other "for the last time," and were actually on the point of departure when Molière, alarmed by the total cessation of noise in the house, came down-stairs. His 'guests at once informed him of the resolution they had come to. "How," he asked in a reproachful tone, seeing that remonstrance or argument would be useless, "how could you propose to carry out so noble a project without allowing me to share in it? I believed you had more affection for me." "You are right," said Chapelle thickly; "we have done you an injustice; come along, then, with us." "Gently," replied Molière, "regard must be had to the time when such a sacrifice as this is made. If we drowned ourselves at this hour it would be said that we were either drunk or driven to despair. It will be the last action of our lives, and its heroic nature must be made patent to the world. No; let it be when the sun is high in the heavens, when people are astir, when it will be seen that we are in full possession of our faculties." "Right," cried Chapelle; "yes, gentlemen, we will throw ourselves into the Seine after breakfast; meanwhile let us finish the wine on the table and snatch a few hours' sleep." And sleep they all did, with what result we need not say.

Molière s illness proved grave enough to keep him off the stage for the long period of four or five months. Never very strong, he was now in a rapid consumption, and it was only by restricting himself to a milk diet that he could hope to retard the progress of the disease. The doctors could do little or nothing for him—a fact which, compared with their extravagant pretensions, may well have prompted him to follow up the attack begun in *L'Amour Médecin.* Nevertheless, he seems to have at least received visits from one member of the faculty, M. de Marvilain, for whom he conceived a high esteem, and for whose son he procured from the King a canonry in the Chapel Royal at Vincennes. "But how comes it that *you* have a doctor?" Louis XIV. exclaimed in his surprise one day to Molière; "how do you get on together?" "Sire," replied the dramatist, "we agree well enough, though only to differ. He writes prescriptions for me, I take no heed of them, and my health improves." Elsewhere he spoke of M. de Marvilain as a very respectable doctor, whose patient he had the honour to be. Having regained strength as the summer approached, he reappeared at the Palais Royal on the 10th June, when *Le Sicilien* was played there for the first time. Here is Robinet's chronicle of the event:—

> Depuis hier pareillement
> On a pour divertissement

> Le *Sicilien,* que Molière,
> Avec sa charmante manière,
> Mêla dans le Ballet du Roi
> Et qu'on admire, sur ma foi.

Molière himself, we learn,

> S'y remontre enfin à nos yeux
> Plus que jamais facécieux ;

so much so, in fact, as to make the chronicler " laugh with all his heart."

But it was not merely to produce *Le Sicilien* that Molière had so carefully nursed himself. He had good reason to hope that before long his *Tartuffe* would see the light. The Queen mother, who had allowed herself to be made an instrument in the hands of his opponents, had gone to her rest. Both true and false *dévots* continued to attack him with a vigour and pertinacity which justified him in asking for the abrogation of the decree of 1664 as a matter of sheer justice to himself. Finally, as a result of the readings already adverted to, a desire to see the comedy acted became manifest in nearly all quarters. Molière was not slow to profit by this concatenation of circumstances in his favour. He addressed to the King —then on the eve of his departure for the army of Flanders—the undated letter which is usually printed with the play. Bearing in mind, he said, that comedy should " corriger les hommes en les divertissant," he had thought that, as chief Comédien du Roi, he

could not do better than assail the vices of his time
with the weapon of ridicule. Of all these vices hypocrisy was the most prevalent and the most dangerous, and to expose its wiles he had written *Tartuffe*.
He had acquitted himself of this task, as he believed,
with due regard to the delicacy of the subject, doing
all he could to distinguish true from false piety, and
erasing every passage which might confound good with
evil. But all his precautions had been useless. The
Tartuffes had profited by the King's sensitiveness in
matters of religion to put the piece before him in a
wrong light. They had succeeded in inducing him to
suppress it. Moreover, in contempt of the approbation
extended to it by his majesty, the legate, and the
majority of the prelacy, a certain curé, without having
read it, had spoken of its author as one who ought
to receive no mercy from God. Calumnies like these,
Molière remarked in conclusion, necessarily did him
great harm, and it would at once be seen how great an
interest he had in proving to the world that they were
wholly without foundation. Free to obey the dictates
of his own common sense in this matter, mindful of the
wide-spread interest taken in the fate of the comedy,
and anxious, perhaps, to spare his favourite player un-
deserved pain, Louis XIV. did not turn a deaf ear to
the petition. He verbally withdrew the prohibition,
stipulating, however, that the name of *Tartuffe*, which

for some unexplained reason was disliked at Court,
should not be employed, and that the hypocrite should
appear, not in the semi-clerical and sombre costume he
had worn at Versailles, but as a well-dressed man of
the world.

The King joined the army; and on the 5th August,
during the siege of Lille, *Tartuffe* was produced at the
Palais Royal under the title of *L'Imposteur*. Never had
a new piece brought together so large and excited an
audience as this. Every nook and corner of the house
was occupied; each spectator seemed to have a direct
interest in the result. The first two acts, which are
designed simply to prepare us for the character of the
impostor, were probably listened to with a suspicion
of impatience, although strengthened by the acting of
Molière as Orgon, Béjart as Madame Pernelle, Mdlle.
Molière as Elmire, Hubert as Damis, Mdlle. Debrie as
Mariane, Lagrange as Valère, Lathorillière as Cléante,
and Madeleine Béjart as the irresistible Dorine. Dressed
as the King had suggested—in the superbly laced coat
and other bravery affected by the exquisites—Tartuffe,
now called Panulphe, at length came on in the person
of Ducroisy, who realized the author's intention with a
thoroughness possible only to a fine artist. His costume
was not in keeping with the character, but any sense of
this inconsistency among the audience was merged in
admiration of the depth and force of the conception, the

dramatic power displayed in the delineation of the
hypocrite, and the withering yet dignified satire which
pervaded the whole.   It was to no purpose that the
hypocrites sought to raise a hostile demonstration
against the piece, however little convinced some of the
vrais dévots may have been, even after hearing the
speech of Cléante that the object of the author was
not to sneer at religion itself.   Every sign of hostility
was promptly drowned in applause, and in the enthusiasm manifested on the fall of the curtain Molière saw
substantial compensation for the annoyance he had
suffered in connexion with what he regarded as his
best essay.   " When you described the *Misanthrope* as
my masterpiece," I imagine him saying to Boileau, " I
told you that you would see something very different ;
—it is now before you."

No play had ever been launched under fairer auspices
than *Tartuffe ;* yet, to the intense astonishment of the
Parisians in general, it was abruptly taken out of the
bills.   If Molière's enemies were powerless in the theatre
they were not powerless in the world.   Induced to
believe that the comedy was as irreligious as it had
been declared to be, and that in sanctioning its production the King had been deceived as to its real
tendency, the Parlement of Paris, by the hand of its
First President, the excellent Lamoignon, issued an
order forbidding its repetition.   If an oft-related story

be true, this order did not reach the theatre until the players were on the point of commencing the second performance (August 7), when Molière informed the assembled audience that as " M. le Premier Président ne voulait qu'on le jouât" the piece could not be represented. Now, "ne veut pas qu'on le joue," it need hardly be said, may mean either " objects to the piece being played" or " objects to be caricatured on the stage." More than one writer has gone into raptures over this peculiar equivocation, but it may well be doubted whether Molière could have publicly hurled such an insult at a man with whom he is known to have been on terms of friendship, who had lent a new grace to the French magistracy, and who in this matter was bound to give effect to the decision of the Chamber. Fortunately for the poet's reputation, the whole story is a pure fabrication. The order from the Parlement, as we learn from Lagrange's *Register*, was delivered at the Palais Royal by an usher on the day after the first performance, or twenty-four hours before the time fixed for the second. Many years previously an alcalde in Madrid had been made the victim of a pleasantry similar to that in question ; and it is not improbable that some enemy—perhaps one of those stung by the satire in *Tartuffe*—profited by a knowledge of the incident to put into Molière's mouth a speech which might serve to embroil him with the authorities.

The dramatist, of course, found it difficult to reconcile himself to a decision which deprived him of the chance of adding to his fame, of vindicating himself from unjust aspersions, and of attracting to his theatre a long succession of good audiences. He despatched Lagrange and Lathorillière post-haste to Lille with an appeal to the King against the decision of the Parlement. Beginning with a well-turned apology for importuning a monarch in the midst of his conquests, he stated that *Tartuffe*, although produced in the manner suggested by the King, had not been permitted to profit by the royal favour bestowed upon it, had been suppressed at the instance of " the cabal " by a power which commanded respect. " I respectfully await," he went on to say, " the reply your majesty shall deign to make on this subject ; but it is very certain, sire, that I must give up writing comedies if the Tartuffes are to be able to suppress them." Louis was in his tent under the walls of Lille when the two players arrived. He received them very graciously, carefully read the letter they had brought to him, and, to judge from the time he kept his unexpected visitors, found it difficult to make up his mind. He was predisposed to accede to any request from Molière, but was not blind to the impolicy of quashing a decree of the Parlement without at least feigning to inquire into its cause. In the result he determined to maintain the suspension, at the same time promising that on his return to Paris he would re-examine the comedy and have it performed. And with this answer, of course, the dramatist had to be content. But his enemies did not succeed in entirely suppressing the obnoxious piece. Probably under his own auspices, an anonymous *Lettre sur la comédie de l'Imposteur*, an analysis by a playgoer of the plot, with some striking passages set out at length, was published towards the close of the month.

Molière stood greatly in need of *Tartuffe* to bear him up against an attraction held out at the rival theatre in the autumn. Corneille's popularity had fallen to a low ebb, partly on account of the decay of his genius, but chiefly because he was being tried by standards which he never attempted to reach. His neglect of orderly and symmetrical arrangement was repugnant to the now dominant taste for formalism in both literature and art. His inequalities and incorrectness as a writer could not but give offence at a time when the critical principles of Boileau were unreservedly accepted. Above all, the Parisian world at large, without forgetting that the author of the *Cid* and *Cinna* had added to the lustre of the French name, had begun to find his plays wanting in variety of interest—had grown a little weary of these direct appeals to their admiration, these spotless heroes and heroines, these elaborate solutions in dialogue of political problems, these perpetual representations of love as a means of exalting the personage it possessed. Might not the drama be employed to represent humanity on a more comprehensive scale? it was asked. Quinault and Molière successively answered this question in the affirmative, the former in his *Astrate*, a pathetic story of the affections, and the other by disregarding the example of Corneille so far as to treat the passion of Alceste for Célimène as the "faiblesse d'un grand cœur," as a source of weakness instead of strength. Racine now saw that he could not too soon discard the model he had hitherto adopted. Reversing the policy of Corneille, he would appeal to the head through the heart, not to the heart through the head. He would make it his business to move his audience to pity rather than admiration, to tears rather than enthusiasm. He would occupy himself with delineations of the tenderer passions, reduce heroic characters to something like natural dimensions by making them neither absolutely good nor absolutely bad, and invariably aim at a combination of faultless dramatic architecture with sustained beauty of diction. Full of these ideas, the Prior of Epinay invoked the muses in favour of an *Andromaque*, which appeared at the Hôtel de Bourgogne on the 26th November.

No ordinary surprise awaited the audience assembled

there on that occasion. *Andromaque*, in addition to
being a tragedy of the order so long desired in vain,
was to them what the *Cid* had been to their progenitors
in the days of Richelieu, the sudden revelation of a
genius previously unsuspected.   In framing his plot,
it will be observed, Racine deviated very widely from
the legend of the captivity of Hector's widow and
son at the palace of Pyrrhus, King of Epirus, at
Buthrotum.   No fewer than three distinct and con-
flicting interests are brought into play.   Andromaque
(Mdlle. Duparc) is loved by Pyrrhus (Floridor),
Pyrrhus by Hermione (Mdlle. Descœillets), and Hermione by Oreste (Montfleuri).   It is only by becoming
the wife of her tyrant that Andromaque can save her
son from being delivered up to the vindictive Greeks ;
a deep-seated reverence for the memory of Hector
struggles with the impulses of maternal affection, and
at length, with a determination not to survive the
marriage ceremony by an hour, she consents to the
sacrifice required at her hands.   Betrothed to Pyrrhus,
whom she has left Greece to wed, the daughter of
Helen, stung to madness by her humiliation, causes
him to be assassinated on the altar-steps just after the
safety of Astyanax is assured, the chosen instrument
of her vengeance being Orestes.   But a fierce revulsion
of feeling sweeps through her mind as the latter tells
her of the crime she has urged him to perpetrate.   Far

from giving him the expected reward of his devotion,
she assails him with bitter invective, goes away in an
agony of remorse, and finally destroys herself on the
bier of her victim. For the rest, the new queen of
Epirus,

> Andromaque elle-même, à Pyrrhus si rebelle,
> Lui rend tous les devoirs d'une veuve fidèle,
> Commande qu'on le venge;

and Oreste, stunned by the discovery that he has
lost his honour to no purpose, is hurried by Pylades
and other friends beyond reach of the punishment with
which he is threatened. In elaborating this impressive
story, so different from that related in the Greek play,
Racine manifested much of the power required to do
it justice. Blemishes in the work there unquestionably
were; yet, viewed as a whole, it left no doubt that
in the field opened to him by Quinault and Molière
he would reign supreme unless another Euripides
should arise.

The fate of *Andromaque* may be inferred from the
nature of a controversy which now began to divide
Paris into two camps. By a large majority of the
playgoers, it is certain, the author was hailed as a
successful rival of Corneille—that is to say, was
awarded what they thought to be the highest distinction a dramatist could hope to win. Nor was
that judgment entirely erroneous. In some respects,
it is true, the elder poet gained by the comparison to

which he found himself exposed. He remained unequalled in fitful splendour of inspiration, in depth of
thought, in unforeseen dramatic effects, in condensed
energy of expression, and in the representation of
humanity in its sterner and more commanding aspects.
He must also be credited with a higher regard for
historic truth and the dignity of tragedy than Racine,
who, notwithstanding his wide knowledge of antiquity
—a knowledge so wide that he could impart to the
leading personages in *Andromaque* the peculiarities of
the different nationalities they represented—thought
fit, in compliance with the romanesque spirit of his
time, to introduce the gallantry of Versailles, the
"commerce rampant de soupirs et de flammes," of
feux and *beaux-yeux*, into his most idealized pictures
of the past. Pushed a little further, however, the comparison is distinctly in favour of the younger poet.
His work is rich in qualities to which Corneille could
lay no claim—pathos, tenderness, delicacy of sentiment, unalterable grace of style, refinement of taste,
the dramatic skill needed to develope an intricate
plot with clearness and force, and an all-pervading
harmony akin to that attained by Raphael and Mozart
in other walks of art. Moreover, he drew near his
great predecessor at his best, whether as regards
vividness of imagination, subtlety of reasoning, the
portraiture of energetic manliness, or sentences designed

to carry away an audience. Had Corneille penned the
burst of anguish with which Hermione turns upon Oreste
after he has assassinated Pyrrhus at her own behest—

> Mais parle : de son sort qui t'a rendu l'arbitre ?
> Pourquoi l'assassiner ? qu'a-t'il fait ? à quel titre ?
> Qui cela te l'a dit ?—

his enthusiastic biographers, no doubt, would have
deemed it worthy of a place by the side of the " Qu'il
mourût " itself. In a word, Racine, though unequal to
Corneille as a poet, surpassed him in variety of natural
and acquired power as a dramatist; and the public,
enchanted with the psychological interest and literary
beauty of his work, were disposed to overrate rather
than detract from his greatness. He was even regarded
as the founder of an entirely new school of tragedy, but
it would be more correct to say that he simply enlarged
the scope of and gave a statelier form to that which
had been established in France before he was born.
Corneille, who seems to have made no attempt to
disparage the achievements of the new luminary, was
not without some compensation for the loss of the
absolute pre-eminence he had so long enjoyed in
tragedy. By a small but energetic minority, with
Madame de Sévigné as one of its chiefs, his right to
that pre-eminence was resolutely upheld; and if the
controversy they provoked did not lead to a reversal of
the general verdict, as was certainly the case, it at least
served to deepen the admiration and respect in which

the author of the *Cid* and *Polyeucte* was held by most of
the Racinians themselves.

The young writer whose name now stood so high and
bright before the world, would scarcely be cited in
support of an idea that the personal character of a
dramatist is indicated by the sympathies he displays
in his pages. Judged exclusively in that way, Jean
Racine might be deemed one of the most loveable of
men. *Andromaque*, like the rest of his works, seems to
have sprung from a mind amenable to every ennobling
influence—earnest, full of tender sensibility, and tremblingly responsive to all that is gracious and winning in
life. But in private life, as a few incidents I have already had to record would suggest, he created a very
different impression, some anecdotes to his honour
notwithstanding. He was insincere, vain, arrogant,
envious, and cold-hearted. Invariably professing the
deepest enthusiasm for religion, he almost daily con-
sorted with irreverent wits, gave himself up to low
amours, and sought to promote his mundane interests
by winning favour in the eyes of women in a more than
doubtful position at Court. He resented anything in
the shape of criticism or raillery upon his tragedies as a
personal affront. His manner was marked by a hauteur
which raised up a legion of enemies against him. He
persistently disparaged the achievements of contemporary tragic dramatists, now by word of mouth, anon

in most caustic epigrams. Finally, but above all, he
was incapable of gratitude, even to the point of consciously injuring those who had put him under lasting
obligations. His ill-requital of the kindness shown to
him by Molière and Chapelain affords sufficient evidence
of this, though it is less conclusive than a little history
contemporaneous with that of the sudden development
of his genius. Desmarets, now devout enough to lament
that he had ever contributed to stage literature, albeit
at the instance of a Cardinal, got up a pamphlet against
the Jansenists, whom he execrated as soul poisoners
of the deepest conceivable dye. Nicole took up the
cudgels in behalf of his co-religionists, and, remembering
how the Sieur Desmarets had occupied his leisure in
bygone days, austerely classed concocters of plays
and stories with " public malefactors." Never blind
to his own importance in the world of letters, Racine
imagined that these words were aimed chiefly at himself, especially as one of his relatives at Port Royal,
a certain Agnès Racine, was almost daily imploring him
to abandon the theatre. He launched a ₊bitter *Lettre*
against the recluses who had sheltered him in his
friendless youth, had given him the best of his education, and had habitually treated him with something
like parental affection. He brought to his sorry task
an aptitude for sarcasm which few have surpassed ;
the Jesuits hung in raptures over the book, and the

Port Royalists perceptibly writhed under the obloquy it heaped upon them.   This, however, was not enough for Racine.   He proceeded to follow up the attack.   Boileau then interposed.   " These letters," he tersely said, " may be very clever, but they do no credit to your heart."   In the end, by the advice of the sensible poet, whose continued association with him was due simply to the pride felt by a tutor in a brilliant and successful pupil, Racine consented to suppress the second broadside, at the same time endeavouring to stop the circulation of the first.   Neither spontaneous nor adequate, this reparation cannot be accepted as a set-off against the readiness with which he allowed himself to be provoked by one of the friends of his boyhood into assailing them all, and which, joined to his conduct towards other benefactors, forces us to hold him guilty of ingratitude in its worst form.   It may be thought strange that a man of such a nature should have been a master of pathos and tenderness, but a glance at the character of Bacon, whose lofty and far-reaching thought could not save him from becoming the "meanest of mankind," will lessen the surprise we naturally feel at so marked a contradiction.   Racine the poet and Racine the man may be described as separate and distinct individualitie may be described as separate and distinct individualities. Genius sometimes raised him to the skies; his moral defects often chained him to the earth.

NOTES.

A, page 18.—Such, at least, is the usually received account of the arrangement of the stage at the Hôtel de la Trinité. In *Les Mystères,* however, Petit de Julleville, following M. Paulin Paris, endeavours to prove that the divisions were on the same level, side by side. His argument is not without plausibility, but the older account is certainly the more probable of the two.

B, page 33.—It might have been expected that the profane Mysteries would lead to the introduction of a " history-play," but these are about the only works of the kind to be met with.

C, page 44.—Thirty-two years afterwards, in 1611, Larivey published three more pieces, which, however, do not seem to have been represented. Their names will be found in the chronological table appended.

D, page 154.—Scarron was certainly a cripple when he wrote *Jodelet,* but the story of his smearing himself with honey is contradicted. See *Le Roman Comique,* edition Jouaust, preface, pages 12 and 13.

E, page 209.—Most authorities agree that Duparc joined Molière's company at the outset; others, however, say that he did not do so until, in 1653, it visited Lyons. It is probable that the two pieces evidently written by Molière for this player—*Gros-René Écolier* and *La Jalousie de Gros-René*—were produced in the interim.

F, page 211.—Henri Chardon, in his *Troupe du Roman Comique devoilée,* has shown good reason for supposing that the company referred to in Scarron's book was Filandre's. But this, of course, may not have prevented Scarron from making Destin like Molière.

G, page 299.—The case against the credibility of the legend of the *en cas de nuit* is ably set forth in *Le Théâtre Français sous Louis XIV.,* by Eugène Despoi pp. 311—21. In addition to employing the argument mentioned,   points out that the incident in question, though of a nature to be mu   talked of at Court, is not referred to by Saint-Simon, and was not recorded in print until Madame Campan's *Mémoires* appeared.